T0400546

Our Infinite Fates

Our Infinite Fates

a novel

Laura Steven

WEDNESDAY BOOKS
NEW YORK

This is a work of fiction. All of the characters, organizations, and events portrayed in this novel are either products of the author's imagination or are used fictitiously.

First published in the United States by Wednesday Books, an imprint of St. Martin's Publishing Group

OUR INFINITE FATES. Copyright © 2025 by Laura Steven. All rights reserved. Printed in China. For information, address St. Martin's Publishing Group, 120 Broadway, New York, NY 10271.

www.wednesdaybooks.com

Designed by Devan Norman

Case stamp border © Media Guru/Shutterstock

The Library of Congress Cataloging-in-Publication Data is available upon request.

ISBN 978-1-250-33388-9 (hardcover)
ISBN 978-1-250-33389-6 (ebook)

Our books may be purchased in bulk for promotional, educational, or business use. Please contact your local bookseller or the Macmillan Corporate and Premium Sales Department at 1-800-221-7945, extension 5442, or by email at MacmillanSpecialMarkets@macmillan.com.

Originally published in the United Kingdom by Pan Macmillan
First published in the United States by Wednesday Books
First U.S. Edition 2025

10 9 8 7 6 5 4 3 2 1

For Blair,
the light of my life

Our
Infinite
Fates

Prologue

Several hundred years ago

The ribbon binding their wrists together was red as a wound.

It was late Sólmánuður and a fine day for a wedding. Scant clouds wisped across the pale sky. The sea lapped at the pebble beach, afternoon sun splicing its surface with fractal shards of gold. Rounded rocks rose through the shallow foam, sprayed with salt and the vague echo of siren song—if one believed in such a thing, which the bride did not.

But she believed in love, and in the man who stood before her.

The groom's long chestnut hair was threaded with copper. His beard—impressively thick for a man not yet eighteen—was braided with metal rings and porcelain beads, scented with the pine resin and sage of his best oil. He wore a neat dark tunic and trousers, a gold arm ring, and a leather belt fastened at his waist. From the belt hung a glorious longsword, its hilt studded with rubies. A family heirloom.

A smile pulled the groom's crooked mouth wide, his eyes glistening with joy. He had known the bride since the day he was born, and had dreamed of this day for over a decade. She was the golden strand running through his life, tying his past and future together in a harmonious bow.

The bride, however, was coiled like a spring. Dressed in a long linen dress of palest cream and beaded silver, she cut a tall, lithe figure.

Every taut line of her body lay in wait.

Half huntress, half hunted.

The groom barely noticed. He was too caught up in the moment, in the caw of seagulls and the felted words of the elder officiating the ceremony.

As formalities were exchanged, their hands remained fastened. The red ribbon had been woven from the tunic of the groom's late mother so that she might still play a part in the ceremony. Indeed, the groom felt his mother's presence there, as both a spectral smudge in the middle distance and a reassuring solidity around his wrist. His heart swelled, pressing painfully against the cage of his ribs.

At the bride's curious insistence, they exchanged weapons instead of rings. Knives, forged by her brother, the curved silver blades each engraved with the Valknut. Odin was the groom's favorite god; he found himself inexplicably drawn to the interweaving of past, present, and future, to the perpetual knot of life and death and rebirth.

The wizened elder nodded for the groom to utter his vows.

"By the light of the sun and the power of the gods," the groom said, a marble of emotion rolling in his throat, "I pledge to love and honor you always."

He drew his sword and touched the jeweled hilt to his bride's shoulder.

The elder nodded once more, solemn, almost funereal. "I believe the bride has penned her own vows."

Something strange darted over the elder's aged face.

Scorn?

The bride shivered. She had been cold since sweating out her

Our Infinite Fates

maidenhood in the hot springs the day prior, and the elder's dispassion was unsettling.

A breeze picked up, and the sea whipped itself into sharp peaks.

The bride's voice was low, crystalline, as she spoke to her betrothed. "Like the sway of the sea and the tug of the tides, love is a moving, eternal thing. Let us not be afraid of the wax and the wane, the rise and the fall, the eternal undertow. Each time our souls meet, let us submerge our bodies in the bright blue cold, and let the waves make us anew." A tear slid down the apple of her cheek. "I love you, and I have loved you, and I will love you."

The groom pressed his warm forehead to hers. "I love you, and I have loved you, and I will love you."

They waited for a few moments, sure they would soon hear the elder's blessing of the union. A wave tumbled and fizzed, and a plume of smoke rose from the fresh-lit fire where the meat would be roasted for the feast.

The silence unfolded an inch too far, and a murmur traveled through the crowd.

Confusion registered on the groom's ruddy face, but the bride's body understood something dreadful before her mind caught up, a warning bell tolling deep in her chest.

And then came the crisp, cutting words, like the bite of a shovel into frosted earth.

"Did you truly think I would not find you?"

The bride and groom looked up in horrified unison to find the elder's eyes glowing like crucibles. Her lined face was washing itself smooth, and her nails lengthened, thickened, blackened.

The groom stumbled backward. Without pause, the bride swiped her marital blade across his throat, opening a mouthlike slit from which blood choked and gurgled.

He grabbed for breath, but none came.

Shock flashed briefly across his face before he crumpled to the pebbled shore.

The bride fell a second later, gasping, though her own throat remained unmarred. The bloodied blade fell from her hand, the Valknut still glinting in the oblivious daylight.

The last thing they saw before the world blinked out was the red ribbon of fate still binding their wrists.

El Salvador

2004

The dining table was set for a feast, but all the carving knives had been hidden. The last thing we needed was the stabbing of an oligarch over carne asada.

Twelve of us sat around the banquet: Familia Sola on one side, Quiñónez on the other. Servants bustled around us, laying down blue plates piled high with pupusas and yuca frita. Firelight flickered in silver candelabras, and footsteps echoed below the vaulted ceiling. The air smelled of charred meat and cilantro.

"How is the Pacamara production?" Papá asked, trying to disguise the tension in his voice. Our guests owned a large coffee plantation in Chalatenango. "A poor year for growth, no? Almost no wet season at all."

Señor Quiñónez shifted in his wooden chair. "Rafael has been experimenting with new processing techniques, and the quality is exceptional." He fixed my father with a defiant stare. "We are meeting with a major European buyer next week."

"Glad to hear it," said Papá through pursed lips. He had clearly never been less glad to hear anything in his life.

He was famous for his irascibility, for his endless cursing and hot temper, but I knew there was tenderness at the very heart of him. A fondness for rock music, a love of architecture, a wicked

6 ✳ **Laura Steven** ✳

sense of humor. Genuine adoration for his children, evident not in mawkish compliments or bedtime stories but in the way he worked himself to the bone to give us a good life.

I missed him before I was even gone, a kind of preemptive grief I'd grown accustomed to over the last several centuries. In a futile attempt at self-preservation, my mind rehearsed loss before death closed its fingers, as though practicing it would lessen the blow. It never did.

My eighteenth birthday was only a few days away.

Which meant that soon, I would be dead.

And in the next life, Papá would be but a stranger.

Without conscious thought, I studied our guests with a careful sweep of the gaze, then the servants milling around the table, searching for that *spark,* that *pull,* that . . . *something.*

But my attention didn't snag on anything—anyone—suspicious.

Scanning faces was a paranoid tic that came as naturally to me as breathing. Hypervigilance had never saved me before, and yet the behavior was too deeply ingrained to excavate.

"Buen provecho," Mamá announced, gesturing for our guests to tuck into the food. She looked the perfect hostess in her puff-sleeved white dress and stark red lipstick, but there was fraughtness etched around her eyes.

"It'll be all right, Mamá," I'd whispered to her in the kitchen before their arrival. "You all want what's best for your kids. That's all that matters."

She'd squeezed my hand, sighing. "You always think the best of people. Of situations. I don't know where you came from, mi rayo de sol, but I hope you never change."

La familia Sola and la familia Quiñónez were old friends turned bitter enemies. Our interests had mostly aligned throughout the twentieth century—our plantations kissed at the borders—until both farms were razed by a rogue arsonist at the outbreak of the

Our Infinite Fates

Civil War. The families blamed each other, claiming that an attempt to sabotage their competitor had backfired on their own land.

Now a temporary truce had been called, because my fool-hearted sister, Silvia, had fallen in love with the eldest Quiñónez son, and our fathers preferred any related bloodshed to occur *before* the wedding.

"So," said Señor Quiñónez, signaling that the small talk was over. He stabbed a piece of black-edged beef with his fork, pausing halfway to his mouth.

Papá grimaced. "So."

Señor Quiñónez narrowed his eyes, and neither man said any more.

"We could just skip the Montague–Capulet performance, no?" I asked cheerfully, stuffing yuca frita into my mouth. "For the children?"

A little reckless, perhaps, but in my defense I was an immortal being due to die any day now.

This always happened as my death date drew near—a loosening of the tongue, a spilling of secrets, an airing of the things that needed to be said but never were.

Mamá shot me a look of betrayal, while Rafael Quiñónez, the other family's middle son, stifled a laugh across the table. Dark brown hair fell around his face in waves, and his lips quirked playfully.

"No seas tan dunda," my usually silent grandmother hissed— she was forever urging me not to be so *stupid*.

I shrugged. "We should be celebrating. Love is in the air, after all. *Love is in the aaair.*"

I sang this last part with toneless gusto, and Rafael could not suppress his snort of laughter.

Papá glared at me warningly. "Adella, you need to—"

8 ✳ Laura Steven

"Get some air?" I smiled sweetly, climbing to my feet as my sister's mouth fell open. "I agree."

Without a backward glance, I shoved through the mahogany double doors to the courtyard in the middle of the house. The last thing I heard was my father apologizing for his clown of a daughter— only for Señor Quiñónez to gruffly retort that I'd inherited Papá's singing voice.

Ice broken.

You're welcome, Silvia.

I did not fear the aftermath; my father's ire would not kill me.

Only one thing—one person—*could.*

Outside, the evening air was warm and stagnant. The maquili-shuat trees were in brilliant bloom, pink trumpet flowers fluttering seductively like dancers in bell skirts. All the cobalt-blue shutters were flung open.

I walked over the baked terra-cotta tiles to the small kidney-shaped pool in the far corner. It lay in the partial shade of an orange tree, green algae gathering at its murky edges. Slipping off my espadrilles and hitching up my flowing skirt—cerulean blue embroidered with red and gold roses—I perched on the side and dangled my feet into the cool water. Through a barred window of the house, I heard a servant drop something with a muttered curse of "¡Puchica!"

The double doors banged open and shut again, letting loose an eruption of heated voices in the gap, and for a moment I thought my mother had come to lecture me on running my mouth.

But it wasn't Mamá.

It was Rafael.

The middle-born Quiñónez and I went to the same private school and frequented the same smoke-filled clubs. Still, we rolled in different circles. There was a kind of performed loathing between

Our Infinite Fates

us, though it often lacked the depth our fathers might have hoped for. In reality, I didn't care much about him either way.

Yet at the sight of him approaching, my breath hitched.

Could it be . . . ?

No. I'd never felt the slightest flicker of suspicion in his presence.

"¿Qué onda?" he asked, his footsteps soft on the tiles.

I said nothing, only narrowed my eyes.

"You were funny back there." There was a smirk in his voice, almost flirtatious. "Like you don't care what happens to you."

I shrugged, trying to bridle the uneven canter of my heart. "It's all so—"

Before I could finish my sentence, there was a knife at my throat.

A sharp bolt of adrenaline; a hollow pit in my stomach. The blade was warm from where it had been tucked into his pocket.

I sighed a long-suffering sigh, letting my eyes flutter close. "For fuck's sake, Arden."

My tone dripped with sardonic boredom, but my chest thumped wildly. No matter how many times I was murdered, it never got any less painful.

And, in truth, I hadn't suspected Rafael for a moment.

Arden was getting better at this.

How had I not known? How had I not felt that wrenching soul tether, that intimate magnetism? How could I ever hope to protect myself, to survive, if I didn't see the threat coming?

"It's a shame, Evelyn," he murmured, his breath brushing my ear like a silk scarf. He was bent down on one knee, as though proposing. "Adella Sola suited you."

I swallowed hard, the knife pinching my skin. "Usually you make me fall in love with you first."

"Thought I'd mix things up."

"Bullshit."

I slammed my head back as hard as I could into his face, crunching his nose with a bloody spurt. He grunted and fell backward, the knife slipping away from my throat.

"Siberia hurt you as much as it hurt me." Swinging my legs out of the pool, I rolled away from him, wincing as my knees grazed the rough tiles. "Is that why you kept your distance this time?"

"Believe what you want."

He lunged forward, arm outstretched with the pocketknife angled at my chest.

I dodged at the last second. Using his toppling momentum against him, I grabbed a fistful of hair at the nape of his neck and slammed his head into the ground. The impact reverberated up my arm, the way jumping from a too-high tree branch jars your knees.

The knife skittered across the tiles as he went limp—not unconscious but definitely starry-eyed.

Blood roaring in my ears, I grabbed the wooden handle of the knife, then rolled Arden's body supine. He groaned blearily as I straddled him, knees planted on either side of his waist, and some traitorous part of me throbbed at the feel of his body beneath mine.

Focus.

This time I wanted to look him in the eye as I killed him.

Unlike in Nauru.

I pressed the tip of the knife under his chin. "And still you won't tell me why you hunt me through every life."

"It's insulting that you don't remember."

His hips jerked sharply to the side as he tried to shove me off him, and he gave it enough sudden force that it worked.

The blade slit his throat right as we both tumbled into the pool.

Body thrashing, he choked on the water and his own gurgling blood. The water was warm and thick, and the blade slipped from

Our Infinite Fates ✳ 11

my already-weakening hand. My mouth and nose filled with chlorine as I gasped for air, hands pushing away from him or maybe toward him, a confusion of turquoise tiles and metallic scarlet swirling into water.

Then, as though our lifestrings were woven fatally together, my own pulse waned.

A sun falling below the horizon, a slow orchestra fading out.

Old blood ebbing to a temporary trickle.

This brief life flashed before my eyes. My father's awful singing, my sister's knotted frown as she painted her watercolors, my grandmother's knitting needles clacking together, scorching afternoons with my mother in the dusty city, the scents of clay and coffee and heat, all of it doomed from the start.

Grief twisted through me, thick and sharp, the loss never getting any easier, the unmooring from history never any less disorientating.

Moments after Rafael's final gargled breath, the darkness creeping at the edges of my vision finally swallowed me whole. Floating in a pool of crimson, our hearts stopped beating as one.

Every *fucking* time.

Wales

2022

Tragedy struck the Blythe family often and hard, like a river flooding the same sorry houses year after year. And it didn't matter what defences we tried to build; there was no outsmarting this act of nature, or god, or the devil himself. It was human folly, or hubris, to think we could wrong-foot forces like seasons and time, to think we could build a dam against life and death. But that didn't stop us from trying.

When I was eight, my father was killed by a drunk driver on Christmas Eve as he walked home from the pub. Pinned against a stone wall, crushed until blood wept from his eyes, until everything in him ruptured and burst. A tragedy, though not the first, and certainly not the last.

A few months later we buried his parents—our beloved Granny and Gramps. They died one after the other, a heart attack and a stroke, two dominoes too devastated to stay upright any longer.

To make matters worse, eight was usually around the age I began to remember my ultimate fate. The realisation would come to me slowly, at first, the sense of a storm looming on the horizon, or maybe an atomic bomb, but not truly understanding the *who* or *why* or *what*. And then an image would break through—a knife to the chest, a garrotte round my neck, poison in my heart—

Our Infinite Fates

13

and I would *remember*. I would spend the next six or eight or ten years wondering how and when Arden would strike again.

How and when I would die by their hand.

Grappling with my own impending demise was one thing, but doing it at the same time as losing half my family was quite another. Life after life, cruelty after cruelty, and the unbearable weight of being human was beginning to wear me down. The constant cycle of love and loss, as inevitable and natural as the rolling seasons.

But I would always try to build the dam anyway.

Two weeks before my eighteenth birthday, I sat in the hospital where my grandparents had died and watched my bald sister play the violin.

The last note rang out smooth as velvet. The polished maple was tucked beneath her pale pixie chin, the concentration on her face relaxing as she looked up expectantly.

"Excuse me." Mum sniffed, dabbing at her eyes with a tissue. She stood up swiftly and left the room, paisley scarf fluttering behind her. Without her lavender perfume, the room smelled hospital-stale.

Gracie rolled her hazel eyes, resting the violin in her lap. "Maybe I should have chosen a less melancholic instrument. The drums, perhaps. Or a ukulele. Do we think the nurses might decapitate me if I took up the banjo?" I recognised my own resolute sarcasm in her voice—a little kid copying her older sister's bravado.

"Mum's just scared," I said. "You're her baby."

"I'm fourteen," Gracie retorted, as though this settled matters.

Gracie had been diagnosed with leukaemia about a year ago, when she'd finally got her endless bruising checked out. She'd been stoic, for the most part, though I had the distinct feeling it was to combat Mum's cloying sadness. I understood it, of course, but I sometimes found myself annoyed that Mum couldn't muster a brave face for Gracie's sake.

In truth, the thought of anything bad happening to my sister was deeply painful for me too, even if I likely wouldn't be around to see it. I'd loved a lot of siblings in a lot of lives, but Gracie was a firm favourite. Sharp, weird, bright in an entirely unique way. So *alive*. The image of her body lying empty in a cold, damp grave was so incongruous that my body folded in on itself whenever I thought about it.

And the idea of my mum up in that big farmhouse all alone—a farmhouse once filled with a family she adored—cleaved me in two. But it wouldn't come to that. I wouldn't *let* it.

Gracie nodded to the beige plaster on my upper arm. "How'd today's injection go?"

The doctors were prepping my body to donate stem cells. "Nothing compared to chemo."

"In your infinite experience of chemo."

I twirled my hair up into a bun. "It is quite famously horrible."

And yet still a miracle. I had lived long enough to remember hacksaws grinding through bone, teeth gnawing desperately on sodden rags, all of it so brutal and so futile. Modern medicine was a wonder.

Gracie eyed my hair enviously. She used to have the same smooth copper sheets. "I am a bit bald, it has to be said. Though I've always been eccentric, so perhaps the protruding skull fits my persona. I might start carrying a scythe to really freak people out."

A sudden sharp image came to me: a sickle propped against a dark stone wall.

It felt deeply, viscerally important, and yet there was no context attached.

These flashes of past lives felt like tiny splintered fragments of a gigantic mosaic, the full picture always beyond my reach. Like

Our Infinite Fates

the twist of a kaleidoscope, rearranging the pattern every time I tried too hard to study it.

I remembered the last five or six lives in Technicolor detail— the sights and smells and emotions, the casts of loved ones I'd left behind, every line of Arden's new faces. But the lives before that became less and less distinct the further back they went, until everything was smudged with fog.

Occasionally a new detail would come to me, stark and unmistakable, but I couldn't recall how it fitted into the big picture of my curious existence. I knew there was a row of grim pyres by a bobbing harbour, an olive grove in sun-dappled Andalusia, a trader ship in the buffeting wilds of the Indian Ocean, but the specifics had been lost to time—or to my own woeful memory.

And beneath it all, shrouded under several layers of love and fear and confusion and hurt and grief and anger . . . there was a *why*.

A *why* that had eluded me for centuries.

Over the course of a hundred lifetimes, I had considered this *why* from every possible angle, from the human and the mundane (a grudge, a rivalry, a bet) to the supernatural and the arcane (an ancient curse, a deal with the devil, a particularly malevolent bridge troll). There were glimmers of reason, of truth—such as when Arden had let slip, in darkest Siberia, that it was a deal made long ago that had sealed our fate—but nothing solid enough to build that *why* into a robust structure.

And for whatever godforsaken reason, Arden would never willingly share our origin story.

I was so lost in my thoughts—absorbed in the blade-sharp image of a sickle propped against a dark stone wall—that I didn't realise Gracie was talking.

Or, rather, performing.

"'. . . and I thought of how it feels to hold you, each season of you,'" she proclaimed, holding a leather-bound poetry book in her pale hands. "'Our love blossoming afresh, year after year, century after century, new flowers from old roots, an eternal seed from which life will always bloom.'"

Something in me prickled with recognition I couldn't quite place. "What is that?"

Love blossoming afresh, century after century?

A strange turn of phrase for the average poet.

Gracie shrugged dismissively, tossing it onto the bed beside her blanketed legs. "Some poetry book? Becca brought it for me on her last visit." Becca was Gracie's equally macabre best friend, who wore exclusively black and talked in an exaggeratedly low voice to disguise her natural chirpiness. "She did this whole care-package thing. It was a bit tragic."

"Yes, but what's the book?" I angled myself to get a better look at the cover.

Ten Hundred Years of You.

My heart went unnaturally still in my chest.

"It's a viral sensation," Gracie said scathingly. She eschewed popular culture out of principle. "Honestly, what was Becca thinking? I have cancer, not bad taste. Speaking of which, I'm honoured that you're still wearing the necklace."

Gracie pointed toward the black ribbon around my neck.

My hand went to the ugly "jewellery" she'd made me a few weeks ago. The pendant was a discarded chicken wishbone, and it still smelled vaguely of roast thyme. It was completely disgusting, but I could tell by the triumphant look on her face as she handed it to me that it was a challenge. I had to pretend to love it and wear it all the time, even though it was a literal carcass. And if I took it off, she'd guilt-trip me for months.

I bit my lip, trying to forget about the strangely apt poetry book. "Yes. It's beautiful."

Our Infinite Fates

She pressed her lips together, trying desperately not to laugh.

A sudden metallic clatter echoed from the corridor, as though a supply trolley had overturned, and I jerked in my seat. My nerves had never been quite the same since the front lines of the Great War—as if being hunted like an animal through every existence wasn't fraying enough.

I watched the doorway for a few moments, half expecting Arden to appear amid the commotion, but no murderous silhouette materialised.

"What's the first thing you're going to do when you get out of here?" I asked my sister, voice rattling slightly, like the brittle bars of a cage come loose. "Because you *are* getting out of here, Gracie. I promise."

The absurd thing was that I genuinely believed it.

"Why the obsession with things we might do in the future?" Gracie smirked. "You're such a daydreamer."

"You say that like it's some fatal disease."

She gave me a pointed look. "I found your extremely tragic list. The things you're going to do when you're an adult, as though adulthood is some mythical state."

My cheeks warmed. I'd kept such a list in every life I could remember, filled with things I'd do once I broke the curse and finally *lived*. Because if you can imagine a future, then surely, surely, it must be real, must be possible.

"I'm an optimist, all right? So what *are* you going to do when you're free of this?"

Gracie considered the question, fiddling absently with her violin strings. "Go to the cemetery."

"Why?"

I expected her to say something profound, like visiting our family graves or paying respects to her ward friends who hadn't made it.

She stroked her chin. "One of my old teachers died. He once called me 'unsettling.' I'd quite like to deface his tombstone."

Once my shocked peals of laughter had subsided, I checked my narrow gold wristwatch and jolted at the time. "Shit, I'm going to be late for work."

I grabbed my backpack from the faded linoleum floor and stood reluctantly. My vision pitched and blurred. Needles made me woozy, but it seemed a pathetic thing to complain about given what Gracie was going through. It also made very little sense. I'd once had my torso blown open by a grenade, but god forbid a trained medical professional perform a blood test.

Flipping the sheet music on the stand beside her bed, she adjusted her thin blue blanket, picked up her violin, and said, "Bye, Bran Flakes."

Even though I was Evelyn right down to my marrow, her pet name for me was one of many reasons I felt so at home as Branwen Blythe.

Tossing my backpack over my shoulder, I gave Gracie a kiss on the forehead. "Love you too, Porridge Face."

"You can't take the piss out of a leukaemia patient's complexion!" she yelled after me. "You insensitive motherfucker!"

I looked back at her briefly before I went, love inflating in my lungs like a balloon.

Gracie was the only thing that had kept Mum and me sane after Dad died. She was too young to understand the gravity of it, and so spent the ensuing few months telling awful made-up jokes and performing dramatic soliloquies in a Venetian mask, foxtrotting around the living room in my mother's highest heels as we wept by the fireside. She was simultaneously human sunshine and darkly gothic. One of her first full sentences was "The shadows are very quiet today."

There was a whole six-month period when she dressed in stripes

Our Infinite Fates

and performed as a mime morning, noon, and night. Her teachers wanted so sincerely to be angry, but her cartoonish facial expressions and carefully choreographed routines were impossible not to laugh at.

A born performer. A pristine strangeness.

It seemed so unfair that someone so full of life could be sucked clean of it by a brutal disease. Yet while I had lost a lot of people in a lot of lives, I could *save* her.

A rare power. A gift in a lifetime of curses.

I just had to survive long enough to do so.

I would turn eighteen in exactly two weeks. The stem cell procedure was slated for four days' time, after my final cell-boosting injection. I was the only relative whose tissue matched Gracie's—without me, she'd have to go on a national register with a waiting list as long as the River Wye.

If Arden found me before the procedure, there was every chance my sister would die too.

Wales

2022

Strolling around in public made me feel jittery and exposed, as though I'd got up from the operating table in the middle of a heart transplant with my chest hanging open.

As I'd so rigorously trained myself to do, I walked down the corridor on high alert, scanning every face, familiar or otherwise, for that lurch of recognition, that yank of the tether, that crackle of innate fear.

Not that it had saved me in El Salvador; my gaze had slid right over Rafael Quiñónez.

Arden could be anywhere. Could be anyone. All it would take was a momentary lapse in concentration and they could pounce. A knife in my back, a bullet in my head. It wouldn't matter how brazen. They didn't need to get away with it, because it would kill them too. Our lifestrings woven fatally together.

Four more days. I just had to stay unmurdered for four more days.

My every instinct told me to spend those four days deep in hiding, but I was needed at the hospital for the daily injections. And I'd learned from bitter experience that making myself a sitting duck was rarely a good thing. Far better a moving target, if I had to be a target at all.

Our Infinite Fates
21

I passed Mum exiting the ground-floor cafeteria with a take-away coffee cup in each hand and a pack of almonds tucked under her arm. She held out a coffee cup, her nose pink from the constant stream of tissues, then nodded to the pack of nuts.

"The doctor said Gracie needs to eat healthily, and god knows she'd rather flay herself alive than eat a vegetable."

I snorted. "I don't think cancer can tell almonds and fizzy laces apart."

She shook her head with a tight smile. "God. The two of you are so . . . You make the whole thing seem funny. All the joking and sarcasm. Maybe it's a generational thing."

If only I could tell her that my original generation was born more than a thousand years before hers. Most adults and authority figures acted like they'd been around longer than me and thus had some greater understanding of life, but while I'd never lived past eighteen, and my frontal lobe had never fully formed, I'd still seen some *stuff*.

"For what it's worth . . ." I said, "I think Gracie would appreciate it if you tried to do the same. Joke around a little. Remember how she cheered us up after Dad died? We owe it to her to try and do the same. So maybe crack a smile every now and again. Take the piss out of her head. Call her a hard-boiled egg, or, at the very least, learn to foxtrot."

Mum smiled, but it didn't reach her eyes. "I'll try."

As I left the hospital, I passed Dylan, the farmhand who'd been helping Mum out for the last couple of years. We waved at each other from opposite sides of the rotating doors. The pockets of his plaid lumberjack coat were stuffed with sweets and a film magazine—the perfect antidote to almonds and sincerity. He was in his early twenties and loved Gracie like a little sister. Our whole family was a patchwork blanket of relationships that shouldn't quite work but did. Housekeepers turned godmothers, postmen turned babysitters, every Sunday roast an eclectic mix of people who made us smile.

The sky over Abergavenny was a pale, romantic blue; winter had lost its teeth. It was warm for mid-March, and honey-sweet blossoms drifted on the breeze. The main street was lined with low pastel buildings, the dramatic hills towering behind them in great arches of forest and grassland. There was an old-fashioned café with wicker chairs on the pavement, a bakery that smelled of strawberry tarts, and a barber's shop buzzing with the sound of clippers.

I kept my gaze broad but focused, sharp, eyes homing in on any sudden movements, anything that looked slightly different to how it had yesterday, anything that made my attention *snag*. It was exhausting, living in this state of heightened awareness, the constant need for vigilance, but if it kept me alive long enough to save Gracie, it was worth every second.

Outside the florist's, there was an unfamiliar face, and my heart skipped several beats.

A boy stood by the silver buckets of flowers, examining the bouquets. Tall and blond, with close-together eyes and a slender frame. His slow gaze met mine with a sudden prickle of fire.

I quickened my pace. I knew pretty much every person my age in this town, and that blond stranger was not one of them.

But he'd already looked away again, checking the price tag on a bunch of red dahlias. I exhaled long and slow, trying to steady my heartbeat.

I made it to the bookshop four minutes after my shift was supposed to start. I worked at Beacon Books, a small indie in the middle of town, having dropped out of school the minute it was acceptable to do so. After centuries of education in varying forms, I had entirely lost interest. Syllabi were becoming less and less imaginative as the decades wore on: commutative algebra and

Our Infinite Fates   23

subjunctive clauses, plant-cell structure and periodic tables, the Technicolor brilliance of life reduced to nuts and bolts and quadratic equations.

The same could not be said for Arden. Arden loved words, and ideas, and poetry, and plays. Arden loved to learn, to express, to weave long and meandering thoughts about the human condition. They always carried a little notebook in every life, jotting down these thoughts and ideas and poems, and while I'd never been allowed to read them, I found it hopelessly endearing. It was utterly incongruous with the relentless killer I knew them to be, but perhaps that was why I found them so compelling—those little quirks and foibles that made them the same person, no matter who or where we were.

Whatever a soul was, it could be carried in a notebook.

It was why I'd badgered Mr. Oyinlola, the owner of the bookshop, for months until he'd finally hired me to work alongside his daughter.

In every life, Arden was drawn to literature like a bee to nectar.

So if I was going to find them anywhere, where better than here?

Because this time, I wanted to find them first. I wanted the upper hand, not to be caught off guard like I had been in El Salvador, nor to beg for my life as I had in Siberia. It didn't really matter either way, since mutually assured destruction would always be the end state, but it had become a matter of pride.

In the great game of our existence, I didn't want to lose.

After a half-hearted lecture from Mr. Oyinlola about my tardiness, I got to work restocking the nonfiction section. I always kept a close eye on the jacket copy to see if any new titles might deep-dive into the strange phenomenon of conscious reincarnation, but other than a book about near-death experiences, nothing was potentially useful. I'd been trying to make sense of this cruel curse for as long as I could remember, but not even the darkest corners of the internet had anything insightful to say.

Every time the little bell over the entrance tinkled, my gaze shot up, expecting to see a sharp-eyed stranger of exactly my age walking through the door. My assassin. But today most of the clientele consisted of pensioners searching for wildlife annuals, harried parents towing unruly children toward the picture books.

As the sun cracked over the horizon like a brilliant orange yolk, I helped Nia cash up the till. Nia was a timid, serious girl with dark skin and owlish glasses, black hair shorn almost to her scalp. She had the most impeccable collection of chunky-knit cardigans I'd ever seen, and she never looked anyone in the eye.

Nia was highly knowledgeable about a few disparate interests, such as chess, birdwatching, and nuclear warfare, and treated almost every other topic of conversation as though nothing had ever been so dull. I liked her very much, and had brushed up on my Oppenheimer knowledge to try to talk to her, but she kept me steadfastly at arm's length. I didn't take it personally, since she flinched away from even her father's affectionate shoulder squeezes.

Today, though, she initiated conversation as I was counting the ten-pound notes.

"We finally got stock of this," she said, voice gentle and sweet as a flute, with a subtle tremor running through it. She reached under the counter and pulled out a familiar book with a plain black cover and gold-foil text. "I set aside a copy for you."

As she handed it to me, I ran a finger over the title.

Ten Hundred Years of You.

Author unknown.

The same book of poetry Gracie had performed in the hospital.

Something sickly and fearful lurched in my ribs, though I couldn't quite say why. A prickle of danger on the periphery of my mind.

Our Infinite Fates 25

"Have you heard the hype?"

I shook my head numbly. "I'm not on social media."

Not just out of some vague sense of self-preservation but out of principle. Over the past lifetime I had seen the way it eroded democracy and gamified conflict, the way it splintered attention spans and polarised opinions to dangerous extremes, the way it devalued art and fed the leeches of artificial intelligence, the way it jacked adrenaline and manipulated dopamine and narrowed human awe to a singular flickering point.

"Oh." Nia blinked four or five times in rapid succession, her deep brown eyes fixed on a spot just over my shoulder. "Well, a travel journalist found this handwritten book of poetry about re-incarnation in the Siberian wilderness. It's apparently decades old, and they have no idea who wrote it, but they published the original in Russian and now it's become a sensation. Translated all over the world. The best they could anyway. The poetry is lovely and sad and strange, and then there's the mystery of who wrote it in the first place—I read one theory that it was sent to Earth by some kind of celestial being."

I nodded a wordless thanks, hardly able to believe what she was telling me.

Siberian wilderness.

For centuries I'd begged to read their writing, to no avail.

And now the twin forces of fate and synchronicity had handed it to me on a platter.

This was Arden's poetry. It had to be.

Russia

1986

Mikha had been digging the grave for several hours, and still the snow held firm.

He worked methodically, heating coals on a fire and then spreading them over the permafrost. Once it had melted slightly, he raked off the coals, dug as deeply as he could, then repeated the process. The steam of his breath swirled around his fur hat like cigar smoke.

We lived in one of the coldest inhabited places on Earth, colder even than Mars. Every gulp of pristine air was liquid silver in the lungs.

Under the starry Siberian sky sprawled miles of rugged taiga, black conifer forests muffled with blankets of white. The aurora borealis glowed science-fiction green above us. We were finally coming out of the obsidian winter—when daylight disappeared for two straight months—but the cold was still enough to make my bones ache.

"How long do you think she has left?" I asked, sipping homemade cherry liqueur from Mikha's hip flask. The sweet burn licked down my throat. Beside me the bonfire crackled and spat, warming the exposed skin on my face enough to thaw my eyelashes.

"A few days, at most." He finished laying a fresh batch of coals on the snow and crossed back to sit with me on a felled tree trunk.

Our Infinite Fates

Our enormous fur coats pressed together, and even through the layers of thick mink, my blood fizzed at the touch.

I scraped at the permafrost with the sole of my reindeer-skin mukluk boot. "Do you want to talk about it?"

"Nyet."

I supposed he'd lost countless mothers. He just couldn't admit that.

Instead, I cupped his jaw with a gloved hand, mouth quirking with an unspoken question. He turned his face toward me with a slow smile, then lifted a suede glove to my jaw. I loved his face in this life: narrow black eyes and dark, fluffy brows, with a wide, flat nose and smooth ochre skin.

We angled our bodies together, and as his lips brushed mine, I flinched.

They were freezing.

Even though everything in me wanted to keep kissing him, to let this moment roll on and on like a tundra, the overwhelming desire to protect him made me pull away. "You're too cold. We should go home. Finish this tomorrow."

A subtle test.

Tomorrow was my eighteenth birthday, and I had my suspicions about this grave.

Yet neither of us had admitted knowing each other's true identities.

Here, we weren't Arden and Evelyn. We were Mikha and Nadezhda, two simple Siberians who'd fallen in love at fourteen when our fathers took us ice fishing. I still remembered the bolt of adrenaline when I'd first seen Mikha, the visceral knowledge that we had met before. The raw magnetism pulling us together, like I was a planet he would always orbit.

"I'm fine." There was an anger to the words I didn't quite understand.

"Mikha." I laid my hand over his on the rough tree trunk. "After what happened to your fingers, I—"

"I said I'm fine, all right?" He pulled his hand out from underneath mine, the hand that had succumbed to last winter's frostbite. He'd been rescuing my dad, who had been injured while out hunting, and lost track of the cold ache in his body. The nearest hospital was two days away, so his brother had cut off Mikha's pinkie and the better part of his ring finger with nothing but a bottle of vodka for anesthesia.

I took another sip of the cherry liqueur, relishing the fiery sweetness. "Come on. I know you better than that. Is it about your mamushka?" I'd always liked the Russian word for *mother,* the way it bounced over my tongue like a folk dance.

"Eh. We never really got along."

I offered him the hip flask, and he shook his head. Probably the first time in this life he'd said no to a drink.

Shrugging, I screwed the cap back on. "She's still your mamushka. The village shop won't be the same without her."

"Ah, yes. Who'll scowl at people as they buy reindeer milk now?" He laughed bitterly. "I've never quite gotten used to the way smiles here are earned, not given."

We both froze; a minor slip.

If he'd only ever known Siberia, there would have been nothing to get used to.

My chest started to pound. An inevitable climax was building, and I wasn't ready. I never really was, but I'd grown fond of this life. Of milking the reindeer with my mama as the peach-pink sun rose over the taiga. Of visiting my toothless grandfather and hearing his stories of the railway construction. Of curling up in bed next to Mikha, my head heavy on his chest, listening to his heartbeat, no words spoken but some invisible current pulsing between us.

Our Infinite Fates   29

The cherry liqueur made everything a little blurry, but one thing was crystal clear: it all came down to tonight.

"You know it's for us, right?" Mikha said grimly, staring into the ash-white coals on the bonfire. "The grave. You know who I really am."

Heart lurching like a sled, I gulped back a wave of desperate emotion. "I've always known. I just thought maybe this time I could change your mind."

He scoffed, half his face in shadow from the orange glow of the flames. "So you never really loved me. It was all a ploy to save your skin."

"You don't believe that for a second."

The thermal spring—our village's lifeblood—babbled mournfully nearby.

"I just want to know why," I whispered, trying to keep the pleading note out of my voice. "Can't you give me that, at least?"

He peered up at the sky, as though searching for solace in the glowing green light. "It'll hurt you more to know."

"Did I . . . do something to you? In one of those long-ago lives that I can't remember but you can? Is this about revenge?"

"It'll hurt you more to know," he repeated rigidly.

My vision swam, from the liqueur and from fear.

Surely he wasn't going to do this. Not this time.

"I wish I could remember, Arden. You don't think I spend every day of every life mentally combing through the last thousand years? It's just . . . with the earlier lives, it's like trying to recall memories from when I was a baby. Sometimes I catch a sound or a sight or a feeling, but it's gone before I can pull it out of the periphery. I don't know where my soul began. Where *we* began."

Silence settled around us, pulling the air taut. When digging into the permafrost to make a grave, you had to be careful not to hit a pocket of methane or it'd cause an explosion severe enough to crater the ground. This conversation felt like that: the quiet devastation of digging a grave, made infinitely worse by the threat of detonation.

He reached into the inner pocket of his coat, pulling out the brown leather notebook he spent long nights writing feverishly inside. He clutched it to his chest, as though its contents could warm him through.

"I don't want to do this, Evelyn." His voice cracked on my name, and my heart fissured with it.

I grabbed him by both shoulders, forcing him to look at me. His eyes were like the mouths of volcanoes: deep and dark, with something eternal and deadly churning below.

"So don't. What happens if you just . . . don't?" I shook my head ferociously, locks of snow-crisp hair wisping free of my fur hat. "What happens if you don't kill me, and I don't kill you, and we can be together?"

I could see it so clearly, the life we might lead. A small, simple wedding by the frozen lake. Teaching our wildling children to milk the reindeer, to feed minnows and wax worms onto fishing rods. A house of our own, front door painted red, only a few yards from everyone we held dear. I wanted it so badly.

My fingernails would've dug crescents into the ridges of his shoulders had there not been several inches of fur and suede between us. "Why can't we just . . . be?"

Regret played out like a silent movie across his beautiful face. Could he see it too? The future unfurling before us, if only he made a different choice? Or was he so hell-bent on this course of action that he wouldn't allow himself even to *imagine*?

With a pained grimace, he gestured to the hip flask. "It's too late."

All the stubborn hope in me withered.

The cherry liqueur, spiked with sleepy poison.

"I knew my willpower would falter at the last minute," he whis-

Our Infinite Fates

pered, every word a puncture wound. "We're eighteen tomorrow. It had to be now."

"Why?" The question floated out on a plume of breath. "Not the big *why*. But why eighteen?"

"We can't live to . . . We can't. It would ruin us."

I let go of him, my limbs growing sleepy. "Have I lived to eighteen before?"

A terse nod. "Twice."

"And? What happened?"

Yet more silence. I slid off the tree trunk onto the icy ground, leaning my head back against the wood. The lovesick teenager in me wanted to throw my arms around his calves, to spend my last few minutes in this life pressed against his body before we were wrenched apart once more.

Instead I said, "You piss me off, you know that?"

He chuckled bitterly. "I love you too."

It wasn't the first time he'd said it in this life, but it might have been the last.

"Even after the crossbow at Mount Fuji?"

"Even after the crossbow at Mount Fuji. Right through the eye. Couldn't do it again if you tried."

"Do you have a crossbow handy?"

It was a joke, but his face folded into a pained grimace. He leaped to his feet like a snow leopard, hands clasped over his head. "Fuck, I don't want to do this. I love you. I *love* you. What am I doing?"

"Damned if I know." I laughed, but nothing had ever felt less funny. It was just *sad*. Sadder than anything else.

He started pacing back and forth in front of me, kicking up ice scrapings with his boots. "No. No, no, no. I need to undo this. No. I won't let you die this time. We'll . . . we'll just have to figure the rest out."

My heart bucked wildly. We'd been in love in countless lives,

32 ✳ Laura Steven ✳

but this was the first time he'd ever changed his mind about killing me. The first time he'd ever changed his mind, period. A stubborn mule of a human, so doggedly determined in all matters, so unwilling to alter a course once it was set.

And yet it was too late. The knowledge was a bear claw closing around my ribs.

"There's no antidote?" My insides churned, dread and poison melting together.

He stopped pacing and turned to face me, wild with despair. "Can you make yourself vomit? I'll hold your hair back."

"What a gentleman." The night swam before me, my vision swooping and diving, his edges blurring. Nausea crept up my throat. "But I think it's too late. Everything's going . . . Everything's going."

He choked back a sob. "I'm sorry. I'm so sorry."

"Why this time? Why is this the time you changed your mind?"

Maybe if I knew why, I could stop him in the next life.

"Last night, when we were in bed . . . I can't explain. No language I've ever encountered can express what we have to go through over and over again." He knelt before me, resting his forehead on my knee. "All I know is that I'd do anything to lie in that bed with you just once without thinking about how I'm going to have to kill you soon. That's all I want. You. Alive. With me." He looked up at the sky as though pleading with some sadistic deity. "The thought of waiting another sixteen or seventeen years to see you again is too much to bear." His voice was soft and hoarse. "And I'm just so tired of this. I'm so *tired*, Evelyn."

Anger throbbed at my temples.

How could he act like a victim when this was his choice to make over and over again?

"I'm tired too, on account of the fact you poisoned me," I

snapped, instead of what I really wanted to say, which was that I loved him too, despite it all. Then, quietly, softly: "Lie with me?"

As I climbed to my feet, all the blood rushed to my head, my pulse thin and watery. He held me steady, thick arms around my waist as we climbed into the grave.

Because he was about to die too. Whatever unnatural cord bound our souls together wouldn't allow one to survive without the other.

Mikha lowered me to the frozen earth, the stars and the aurora swirling above. I turned to him as he lay beside me, existential pain etched in every contour of his face. I slid off his glove on the frostbitten hand, pulled off my own, and laced my fingers through his. My skin screamed at the excruciatingly cold air, but he squeezed me tight.

"I love you, and I have loved you, and I will love you," he whispered, hoarse, tortured.

My throat ached. "I love you, and I have loved you, and I will love you."

Then, very seriously, he added, "I hope we don't have to eat frozen reindeer in the next life."

The sky seemed simultaneously very far away and right in front of me. I wanted to sink into the sounds of the babbling hot spring, to swallow down big gulps of liquid silver while I still could.

"Normal souls don't remember where they were last," I murmured, watching our whorls of breath float up into the night. I looked over at him, drinking in his outline one final time. "They don't have hopes for where they go next. Why are we like this?"

He pressed his eyes shut and tears slid down his face, freezing like beads of glass just below his cheekbones. "Because of a deal made long ago."

"What did you . . . ?"

Say, what did you say?

I begged my mouth to finish the question, to stay awake long enough to hear this new answer, but I was slipping,

slipping,

slipping,

and there,

in a grave colder than Mars,

next to the soul I'd loved for a hundred lives and lost in every one,

we took our final breath beneath the indifferent stars.

as I gazed upon the first bramble,
I thought of how the world reinvents itself
year after year,
century after century,
summer deepening always into autumn,
winter brightening always into spring,
growing new flowers from old roots,
and I thought of how it feels to hold you,
each season of you,
our love blossoming afresh,
year after year,
century after century,
new flowers from old roots,
an eternal seed from which life will always
bloom

—AUTHOR UNKNOWN

Wales

2022

I was carrying Arden's soul in my hands. Of that much I was certain.

As I lay on my bed drinking sweet, milky coffee, I read *Ten Hundred Years of You* from cover to cover, every line, every stanza etching grooves into my chest. It was as though Mikha were back from the dead, that version of Arden I so often missed. A different person entirely from the cold-hearted executioner in El Salvador.

One poem described Arden's heart as a haunted house surrounded by a moat of their own digging. It cast their stoicism in a new light, made me think that perhaps they hated the way they had become, so closed off and unfeeling, but that it was less painful than the alternative: letting themselves love, with the knowledge it could only end one way.

I thought of my own preemptive grief, the way I doggedly rehearsed loss as though it somehow protected me from the inevitable pain, and I thought maybe Arden had a point. Almost everyone I had ever loved was dead, and the hurt never went away; I just learned to exist alongside it.

Yet, for better or worse, I always let myself love anyway.

Call it courage, call it insanity; both would be correct.

In truth, a part of me believed that everyone I'd ever loved would come back to me again in another life, in another form.

Our Infinite Fates   37

They wouldn't necessarily *know* we had met before, and nor would I, but that energy would still thrum between us, that recycled love, that historic bond.

A few years before the Great War, a travelling psychic medium called Anais Lamunière had visited our small French border village, and I'd snuck out to see her against the will of my parents, who believed spiritualists defied biblical teachings. In a tiny café with fogged-up windows, Anais had adjusted her floral headscarf and told me, in a hushed, conspiratorial voice, that lost souls were drawn to the love still felt for them by the living. This meant that parents were often reborn as their children's own children, and siblings who died together were reborn as twins, and various other dynamics that I'd found troubling and yet strangely resonant.

I wasn't sure if I entirely bought into Anais's theories, but something about her belief system rang true. Whenever I thought of the patchwork blanket of love surrounding the Blythe family, I had to wonder whether those seemingly disparate people—postmen and farmhands, nurses and teachers and classmates—were drawn to us by some ancient, enduring force. They had once been more to me, to my mother, to my sister, to my late father.

And so, in the absence of any abiding religious convictions, this was the one blind faith I had: that love was a physical force, and it was never wasted. Once it was called out into the universe, it would echo back to us forever.

When I'd told Arden as much, back in the rat-infested trenches, and asked if he believed the same, his eyes had fluttered closed, head tilted back against the dugout wall, and he'd said, "No, I don't think I do."

"You believe love dies with the body?" I'd muttered incredulously. "Then how do you explain what happens to *us*?"

He didn't have a good answer.

As I read Arden's final poem, a new suspicion came to me, half-formed, cloaked in shadow.

Could Nia be my longtime assassin?

She'd been so awkward, so shy, as she handed me the book.

No eye contact. Bashful, almost.

She'd *always* been closed-off around me. Hell, around everyone.

It didn't make much sense by the numbers. She'd been the year below me at school, though it was possible she'd been held back. And I'd worked alongside her all year without suspecting a thing. There was no electric current when our fingers brushed while counting copper coins, no knowing glances.

Then again, there had been no electric current in El Salvador.

Nia was obsessed with chess, with birds, with nuclear warfare.

Did that tally with Arden? I had a fleeting vision of a chessboard in the desert, decades ago, or maybe centuries, the image sharp and bright, then murky and indecipherable. This was how memories of early lives came to me—tiny vibrant bursts, like butterflies I could never quite pin down. The ever-changing kaleidoscope, twisted by some great hand.

So Arden and I had played chess before, and the love of nature had always been there, which would explain the birds. Had they taken much interest in nuclear warfare during the Cold War? I couldn't remember. So many details of Arden had been washed away like seashells on an ebbing tide, leaving behind only a blank plain of sand and foam.

In any case, if Nia was Arden, why hadn't she killed me before now? Had she been waiting for the book's publication? Did she want me to finally read a thousand years' worth of love poems about myself before my inevitable demise?

Yet Arden had guarded their writing for centuries. Why offer it to me on a platter? In this life, where we'd barely exchanged

Our Infinite Fates

39

words? Was it to make up for the cold brutality of El Salvador? To remind me that, despite it all, they still loved me?

Everything in me bristled at the thought that Nia could be Arden.

It would mean another round of this twisted game lost to my hunter.

The next day, I saw the blond stranger again on my way in to work.

He was sitting outside the café next to the bookstore, sipping a black coffee and reading a newspaper. This struck me as an oddity—a modern-day teen reading a physical broadsheet—but I couldn't put my finger on exactly *why* my attention kept snagging on him.

Was it his unfamiliarity? The way he lurked on the periphery of my life?

He glanced up at me as I passed, and a flicker of *something* darted across his pointed features.

My instincts twitched like spider legs beneath a magnifying glass.

Who was he? Where had he come from? Should I be more worried about him?

Perhaps. First, I had to rule out Nia.

As I passed the café, my gaze went to the vacant retail space next door. It had been many things in the last few years—a greeting card shop, a delicatessen, a hardware store—and sometimes I liked to fantasise about opening a vintage boutique there.

Few things brought me more pleasure than beautiful clothes. I often coveted the idea of gathering old, rare pieces from around the world. It would be like reliving my past lives, in a small way, to collect flapper dresses and tailcoats, baroque breeches and airy culottes, then adapt them for the modern wardrobe. New buttons, fresh embroidery, sharper cuts, and clever window dressing.

Yet the sewing machine in my bedroom had been gathering dust for nearly a year.

It wasn't that I'd stopped believing such a dream could be possible. Even after all this time, there was still a chance, especially because Arden had changed his mind in Siberia. It was more that all my energy had been absorbed by my sick sister, and the need to keep her, and by extension myself, alive. But once I'd accomplished that—and I *would* accomplish it—nothing would feel better than the first glide of dressmaking scissors through a bolt of clean fabric, the way the Singer would judder beneath my palms, milky coffee growing cool beside me.

The first item on my list of things I'd do upon survival: make and sell beautiful clothes.

I wanted it so badly I could taste it, and I still believed I could reach it.

So much power in those three simple words.

I still believe.

Beacon Books smelled like ink and paper and stale shortbread, sawdust from the stockroom and old coffee from the little back office. The space was small and neat, only a few thousand books on the shelves, but all lovingly curated by Mr. Oyinlola and his daughter. Antique oddities were dotted around the tables—sepia globes on squeaky hinges, quills and inkwells, broad-winged moths preserved in amber.

It was surprisingly busy that morning, and Nia determinedly did not make eye contact with me while she was serving customers on the till. I wandered the shop floor, offering recommendations to anyone who needed them, checking the stockroom for a title I knew perfectly well we didn't carry. As the hours trundled on, I didn't think I'd ever get the chance to speak to her, but eventually the crowds parted like clouds and it was just the two of us. I hovered near the till, aimlessly rearranging the selection of locally printed calendars.

Our Infinite Fates

"I read the book," I started, keeping my tone as neutral as possible.

"Oh." Her hand, heavy with an eclectic mix of gold, silver, and jade rings, stilled. "What did you think?"

Her nervous edge made *me* nervous.

"Beautiful," I answered carefully. "If a little overwrought in places."

A subtle test, to lightly criticise the work, but she didn't take the bait.

"Who do you think wrote it?" I prodded. Drawing on centuries of maintaining my composure when deep down I wanted to *run,* I kept my tone lightly curious rather than outright accusatory.

She tapped a pile of loyalty cards into a neat little stack. "Someone who'd found their soulmate, and who also believed they'd met before. And that it would end in unspeakable tragedy."

She delivered her theory plainly, but I didn't miss the bob of her throat as she swallowed.

There was emotion there.

"It means something to you. This book."

She nodded but said nothing more.

"Why?"

She shrugged. "I just . . ."

The sentence trailed off to nothing. She was deeply uncomfortable, and I worried I'd pushed too far. But I had to know. There had to be something that would ease the truth loose.

"Do you think you've met *me* before?" I asked finally.

"No," she replied, then gave a curious little yelp of laughter. "I think I'm brand new."

And then she disappeared back into the stockroom, her chin tucked to her chest, her eyes not quite meeting mine.

I left the conversation feeling more confused than before. She was right; she *did* seem brand new. Uncertain, of the world and of herself. Nia did not have the jaded air of a centuries-old killer. And I'd never felt any sort of tug or pull toward her, any kind of fateful undercurrent towing me in her direction.

Yet Rafael . . . We'd circled each other for years without me ever guessing he was Arden.

How much better at hiding had they become?

I spent the rest of the afternoon in a state of jittery unease, studying Nia for glimmers of Arden. But we didn't say anything else to each other, and there was nothing suspect in the wooden way she restocked shelves or rearranged tote bags.

About an hour before the end of my shift, I worked on refreshing the window display with some new middle-grade fantasy releases. Just as I was perching a papier-mâché dragon on an overturned cardboard box, I glanced out at the street and saw the blond stranger.

The blond stranger, standing once again outside the flower shop.

The blond stranger, hand cupping a peach-pink rose, lifting it to his face like a perfumer.

The blond stranger, staring straight at me.

Watching.

And then he smiled, slow and cocky, and I knew.

He had appeared in town as if from nowhere, then never left my orbit.

It wasn't Nia. It was *him.*

Fear and desperation mired together.

I knew I shouldn't confront him—not yet anyway. My hand went to the hideous wishbone around my neck. I had to save my little sister first. She needed my stem cells. She was an integral part of the patchwork blanket that would keep my mother warm when I died.

Our Infinite Fates

43

Yet pride would not allow me to hide.

I could not lose this game again.

Flooded with star-bright adrenaline, I clambered inelegantly out of the shop window and stormed onto the street, barely looking for cars as I crossed the narrow road. My blood roared in my ears, the pastel shopfronts blurring around me, a horn blaring, clusters of clucking pedestrians hardly registering. The hills towered beyond it all, as vast and indifferent as sleeping gods.

Thrusting my hand into the pocket of my handmade tea dress—red, my favourite colour—my fingers closed around the Swiss army knife I'd picked up a few months ago. It was cheaply made, and the parts had been stiff and reluctant. I'd spent hours each night opening and closing the blade, wearing down the hinge until it flicked out with ease.

I didn't withdraw it yet, but it steadied me to know it was there.

The blond stranger watched me approach with a lazy confidence, and my blood pulsed with loathing. He was playing not just with my life, or his life, but with my little sister's. And that I would not abide.

His mouth opened as I got within a few feet of him, but before he could speak I planted a palm on each of his shoulders and shoved with all my might.

Sheer surprise sent him careening off balance, tripping backwards into a bucket of orange and yellow carnations and sending the whole lot clattering into the street.

Gasps rippled down the sleepy pavement. The bucket rolled into the road, and car brakes screeched.

"Not this time, Arden," I growled, pulling myself up to my full height as I stood over him, blocking the sun from his face.

He blinked up at me and then down at his bleeding hand. He must've gripped the thorny rose stem as he fell. Its neck lay broken in his palm. "What the hell?"

"Leave me alone, all right?" Blood roared in my ears, an animalistic desperation filling my limbs. "My little sister is sick. She needs me. So *please,* Arden, just leave me alone for a few more days until—"

"Who's Arden?" He scuttled backwards like a beetle, knocking over a brushed-steel watering can, then held up his hands like he was under arrest. Blood slicked down one white wrist in a dark red rivulet. "Look, I'm sorry for smiling at you—it was probably a bit creepy, but I'm not good at flirting, and this . . . this is a bit much, all right?"

A flicker of doubt crossed my mind. He seemed genuinely confused—and a little afraid.

But it wouldn't be the first time Arden had tricked me into lowering my guard. And though the blond stranger didn't seem to be armed, he could have been concealing a weapon until he had a clean shot. It would be no good merely to injure me, especially if he ended up in a jail cell unable to finish the job.

Better safe than sorry.

I swallowed hard. "Show me some ID."

The name would give me nothing, but his date of birth would tell me everything I needed to know. If we'd been spawned on the same day in late March, he was my immortal enemy.

Eyeing me like I was a rabid mountain wolf, he reached into his back pocket and pulled out a black leather wallet, handing me the turquoise provisional driving licence tucked between a crumple of receipts and bus tickets. I squinted at it against the stark daylight.

Ceri Hughes, born on the sixth of October.

He'd turned eighteen several months ago.

Blood rushed to my cheeks with a shameful heat, but I didn't have time to fumble for an explanation because the florist appeared in the doorway with a miniature watering can in one hand and a pair of secateurs in the other.

Our Infinite Fates

Angharad Morgan. My mum's friend from Welsh class.

"Bran?" Angharad's voice shook as she peered at me. Her frizzy brown hair was pulled back from her middle-aged face with a daffodil-printed headband. "What's going on?" Then she threw a scathing look at Ceri. "Are you giving her bother?"

"Just a misunderstanding," I replied quickly, shooting Ceri a look that hopefully said *Play along or I'll decapitate you here and now.*

He nodded vaguely, never tearing his eyes away from mine.

"Just a misunderstanding," he echoed, the words shot through with a kind of jest, as though this were just some whimsical private joke we were sharing.

The pale blue depths of his eyes sparked with something I couldn't name.

Intrigue? Entertainment? Or just plain and simple confusion?

Why would he willingly lie for me, if he was not Arden?

"Well, if you're sure . . ." Angharad's features twisted with dismay as she surveyed the wreckage we'd caused. "But you'll pay me back for the ruined flowers, won't you, Bran?"

"Of course," I mumbled, guilty heat rising to my cheeks. "Sorry."

She smiled warmly. "S'all right. Now clear off, won't you? All the fuss is bad for business."

As I strode shamefaced back to the bookshop, I didn't look back at Ceri, but my heart skittered like a snare drum.

Had I just laid my palms on Arden's chest?

Had I just spoken my first words to them in nearly eighteen years?

Or had I just made a royal fool of myself?

The blond stranger had seemed genuinely bemused by my ambush, and his date of birth would suggest he wasn't my perpetual hunter. And yet confusion could be feigned, and driving licences could be forged, and after being caught so off guard in El Salvador, I felt more uncertain in my own instincts than ever.

How could I figure out whether this stranger was telling the truth?

And if he was Arden, how could I survive the next three days when he was right here in Abergavenny?

Nauru

1968

On the deck of a tiny trawler off the coast of Nauru, Elenoa's body thrashed like a fish on a line.

She *never* let me see her sleep. Now I knew why.

The sun was sinking below the horizon, staining the sky the color of blood-orange flesh. I lay flat on my back, staring at a fixed point on the outrigger, the wood of the deck warm and salt-rough under my bare legs.

We'd both been born girls in this life, and I adored the softness of it, all sweet tongues and gentle edges.

Loving someone of the same sex wasn't without its challenges, of course—throughout history we'd faced the constant threat of flogging and branding, castration and execution—but in the last few lives I'd had a sense that the overall arc of the world was curving in the right direction. Some cultures were broadening their arms to all kinds of love, the different colors and textures it could be woven from. Girls loving girls was still illegal on this small, conservative island, but it didn't stop us from stealing kisses beneath the stars, from lacing our fingers together like ribbons in plain sight.

It had been a good week on the boat—a small red trawler passed down from Elenoa's uncle. We'd caught coral trout and groupers, lobsters and giant clams. We'd sat on the bow with our legs dangling over the edge, eating mangoes and pawpaws with juice running down our chins. We'd watched every sunset, taking turns to swig at the bottle of sour toddy made from fermented coconut flowers.

Propping myself up on my elbows, I looked back at the island, now washed in warm red light. It was beautiful, in an apocalyptic sort of way. Almost a third of it had been strip-mined for phosphate, leaving behind a jagged plateau of limestone pillars and pinnacle-dotted white coral. It was even more dystopian from the land, abandoned tram tracks and rusted kerosene tins littering the once-lush landscape.

Humans were a blight.

We'd gained independence from the British earlier that year, and the more optimistic Nauruans thought this heralded a glittering new era. But I'd lived through enough postcolonial periods to know things were rarely that simple—especially when your fortunes were quite literally built on bird shit.

The island was ringed by shards of coral, making a port impossible but keeping us largely safe from pirates. It was just beyond the jutting reef that Elenoa and I lay on the deck of the fishing boat—our hold full to bursting with freshly caught tuna—watching the sun set.

Or at least that's what we would've been doing if she hadn't fallen asleep.

"No, please . . . no . . . arghhhh," she moaned, head thudding repeatedly on the hollow wooden boards. Her soft, tanned limbs jerked violently, and she started to roar as though being tortured.

A nightmare.

This had happened before, I recalled, in the asylum in Vermont, and even before that, though those earlier memories were hazier, like the washed-out background of a watercolor landscape.

I ran a thumb over the dagger-shaped chunk of coral in my

Our Infinite Fates   49

palm. I could do it now. I could kill her now, in her sleep, and save us both the heartache of saying goodbye yet again.

Or I could try, yet again, to push for answers.

To convince her to let us *stay*.

My ridiculous optimist's heart, always believing that this time it could be different.

Tucking the coral into a folded pile of netting, I laid my hand over hers. My callouses—forged from years of working the tag lines—notched between her knuckles, like our hands were puzzle pieces always meant to slot together.

An image came to me, raw as a wound and deep as a well: our hands fastened together with a ribbon of red. But the picture vanished as soon as it came, leaving behind an empty grave. Fallow earth.

Elenoa's curved body twisted away from me in another vicious judder, anguished shouts echoing around the bottom of the boat. I pressed myself against her back, burying my face in the thick dark hair at her neck, wrapping an arm around her gentle waist.

Warmth spread through me, halfway between pleasure and ache. We'd never had sex in any of our lives—a matter of principle, for Arden, on account of the inevitable and often imminent murder—but the gentle tug in my lower belly was becoming harder to ignore.

"Elenoa." I nuzzled into her shoulder blade. "Elenoa, shhh. It's okay. You're dreaming."

As I felt her wake up, the writhing slowed and the groans stopped but her body remained stiff as a plank. Even without seeing her face, I knew she was embarrassed.

"What were you dreaming about?"

"Just nightmares," she said gruffly.

"What about?" I'd never been one to let her off the hook easily.

"Doesn't matter, Heilani."

50   Laura Steven

"Sounded like you were being tortured."

"Leave it, all right?"

Shaking my head, I sighed into her back. "You're the most stubborn person I've ever met. Stubborn, and proud, and infuriating."

Her hand found mine and squeezed. "You're still here, aren't you?"

"Sometimes I feel like I have no choice," I admitted. "Not in a bad way. In an our-souls-are-destined-to-meet kind of way."

The boat bobbed softly below us, and my eyes stung from a day of searing South Pacific sun. I could understand the appeal of falling asleep, and yet there were too many questions and not enough time.

There was never enough time.

"How do you always find me?" I whispered, my forehead pressed against her shoulder blade, my arms tightening around her waist like she was a buoy at sea.

After several moments of contemplation, she murmured, "There's, like . . . a tether, or something. It thrums between us. Draws me to you, like a magnet. And until it finds you . . . it's like always being hungry. It gnaws at me." Her chest rose and fell as she swallowed. "You don't feel it too?"

I chewed the inside of my cheek. "I do, but it doesn't point me to you like a compass. It's more like a deep yearning. Only it doesn't ease when we're together. It intensifies."

Was that how all humans experienced love? I'd never know for sure.

"Saudade," whispered Elenoa, and the word lit a spark of recognition from a past life.

Before I could translate it, though, Elenoa unfolded herself and turned to face me. The warm light of the sunset made her skin look like liquid copper. White salt crusted around her temples from the heat of the day.

Our Infinite Fates

51

Her eyes bored into mine, dark and fierce. "Do you actually want to be with me?"

"*Yes.*" It was the truth. "And that . . . that stretches back as far as my memories do. Further, if that's possible. Can you remember our beginning?"

"Yes," she whispered softly, as though the word itself were a knife to the heart.

"I'm not ready to let go again." Familiar desperation began to claw up my throat. "I want to be with you long after we turn eighteen. I want us to be little old people who sit and play chess together. Who bicker about whether or not it's going to rain." Tears stung at my waterline. "And I'll never understand why that can't happen."

But her answers had finally dried up, and she just gazed at me in pained silence.

I cupped her jaw in my rough palm. "Look, if I didn't want to be with you, I'd bunker myself up in a mountain cave and wait it out alone. Until I came of age and you got off my back."

The corner of her mouth quirked upward. "Because that worked out so well for you in Portugal."

Portugal. That was where I'd heard the word *saudade* before. It wasn't easily translatable. A kind of longing, a nostalgia, a sense of incompleteness, not just romantic but existential, rooted in the very fabric of our people. It had suited Arden. Portuguese was the tongue of melancholic dreamers, of lonely poets.

"You know how we're bound together, somehow?" I mused. "If you couldn't find me in one life, for whatever reason . . . do you think that if you killed yourself, I'd die too?"

Something flashed across her face, but it was gone before I could parse it. "Maybe. Maybe not. It's never seemed worth the risk."

Frustration crested in me so suddenly that I almost lost my breath. "But what are you *risking*?"

The question inflated in the silence, then withered as it remained unanswered.

Clambering to her feet, Elenoa crossed over to starboard and gazed out to the horizon. The sun had almost set, its final rays glowing red as a phoenix. "My love for you could fill an ocean, Evelyn." There was an awful resignation to her tone. "But it can't stop the tide of time."

I knew in that moment that she was going to do it, and so I resolved to do it first.

The boat bobbed right in front of a particularly treacherous barb of reef, rising from the water like a sword.

Taking in one last breath of salt tang and fresh fish, I steeled myself against the wave of guilt and pushed Elenoa forward with all my might. The shudder ripped through me as her chest was impaled on the coral.

We died right as the sun fell below the edge of the world.

Wales

2022

The next day, the blond stranger I'd assaulted outside the flower shop came into Beacon Books while Nia was on her lunch break.

The floor was deserted, and I was perched on an old stool behind the counter, flipping through one of the last remaining copies of *Ten Hundred Years of You* for any clues I might have missed. Not that it would help me now—the poems had been penned decades ago. But still I yearned for a *why,* a *how.* Why was this happening to us? How could I break free? Maybe the simple act of putting ink to paper had dislodged something my searing questions could not.

At the sight of Ceri, I shoved the book beside the till, climbing to my feet for no discernible reason. Some vague sense of being battle-ready, perhaps.

His blond hair was fine and neat, and he wore a green sweatshirt, frayed at the neckline, and black jeans hanging loose on his angular frame. There was a subtle left hook to his nose, like it had been broken on a rugby pitch and never quite reset, and a smattering of freckles on his white skin.

As he approached the counter, his lips curled upwards in a coy smile, as though the whole fiasco had only made me more intriguing. "Well, you certainly made my second day in Abergavenny interesting."

Nausea rose in me as I remembered the tang of chlorine in the Solas' pool, the metallic swirls of blood in the turquoise water.

Was I about to meet my death once more?

How much was it going to hurt?

And yet . . . I didn't feel that profound pull, that raw magnetism. I didn't feel the rich undercurrent of love.

Could this really be the soul who had held me in the trenches of the Great War?

Paranoia uncurled like a beast from hibernation, and I tried to focus on the facts. He had appeared in Abergavenny as if from nowhere, and immediately fixated on me not two weeks before my eighteenth birthday. He had stood outside the flower shop two days in a row without buying anything—just *staring*.

Surely that meant something.

"What was that about anyway?" He hoisted the strap of his backpack farther up his shoulder. There was a keenness to his close-knit eyes, and he didn't seem to care about the fact it was awkward to stare so unapologetically. "Did you mistake me for someone else?"

I shrugged nonchalantly, but I felt fraught as an arrow nocked in a bow. "Guess so."

He laughed, even though it wasn't especially funny. "Hopefully we'll get better acquainted, then."

Was he . . . flirting?

Or just toying with me?

Surely he wouldn't still be interested in me if he *wasn't* Arden. Nobody in their right mind would pursue a girl who'd randomly attacked them outside a florist's.

It's Arden, it's Arden, it has to be Arden.

"What's your story anyway?" My throat was dry as sandstone, and my hands shook. I gripped the counter for support. "You said it was only your second day in Abergavenny."

Let something slip. Go on. So I can be sure.

Our Infinite Fates 55

"Just moved here from the sticks." Sure enough, his voice was rural-rough round the edges. "Escaping an alcoholic father and controlling nightmare of a mother. Eventually realised I'm better off alone." He scoffed in a self-deprecating sort of way. "Sorry, that's probably an overshare."

"It's fine."

Except it didn't feel fine at all.

I'm better off alone.

His heart a haunted house surrounded by a moat of his own digging.

Suspicion curdled inside me. Everything was pointing in one direction, and that direction led to my imminent death.

And yet I couldn't bring myself to ask him outright. I didn't want to provoke a confrontation before I could save Gracie. I thought of her parading around the living room like a ballroom dancer, small and funny and innocent, and protectiveness swelled in my chest. There had been so many people in my lives that I could not save— neither from famine nor drought, plagues nor crossbows—but I could save *her*.

"I really need to get a job." Ceri sighed, but there was an air of performance to it, a subtle exaggeration. "I'm renting the flat above the petrol station at the moment"—he gestured to the garage down the street—"and cash is already running low. I don't suppose they're hiring here, are they?"

I made a mental note of where he lived. Just in case.

I shook my head. "Sorry. It took me six months of badgering the owner until he finally relented and took me on. I don't think I'm actually necessary to the operation."

"Fair enough." He smiled almost apologetically. "Hey, sorry to be ridiculously forward, but I don't suppose you'd want to go out for a coffee with me sometime?"

Surely nobody but Arden would ask me out in such a situation.

56   ✳ **Laura Steven** ✳

Surely.

It had been nearly eighteen years since we'd last spoken, and as much as I dreaded the sharp agony of death, a tiny, ridiculous part of me was exhilarated that I might be in Arden's presence once again.

We had loved each other for so long, through the darkest times in history, through impossible circumstances, through terrible fates and insurmountable grief. The joy and pain we shared had knotted the very fabric of us together.

Nobody knew me better. Nobody else *understood* what this was like. There was a kinship between us, our shared secret a fortress that could never be breached from the outside. Without Arden, I felt utterly alone in the world.

I thought of sweet, stubbled kisses in a rank trench. Of our bodies folded around each other on a salt-licked fishing trawler. Of thick fur bedding in darkest Siberia, of my head on a broad chest, of forehead kisses and laced fingers and how it felt to be slowly, fatally poisoned.

The love, then the death. Until El Salvador.

A change so sudden, so stark, that I still had not made sense of it.

I studied Ceri carefully, realising I felt nothing for this stranger.

But after the Solas' swimming pool, that did not mean it was not Arden.

My mind unreeled, a fishing hook catching on nothing.

"Why would you *want* to go out with me?" I asked steadily, my mind smeared with conflicting emotions. "I attacked you."

He shrugged carelessly. "I like interesting girls."

Such an un-Arden answer. It wasn't poetic or deep. It didn't pulse with unspoken meaning.

"No rush. Just think about it." He held out a hand, fingers long and pale and slender. "Have you got a pen? I'll give you my number."

Our Infinite Fates 57

As I handed him a Biro, a sudden whim took me. I passed the pen over on top of the copy of *Ten Hundred Years of You,* studying Ceri closely for a reaction.

His gaze snagged on the title, but his expression betrayed little. "Is that what you were reading when I came in?"

"It was." My pulse pattered like mice through the walls of our farmhouse.

"'Author unknown.'" He shifted from one foot to the other, and I couldn't read him, and I hated that I couldn't. "What is it?"

My hands were shaking so hard I clasped them together, left fist balled up in the palm of my right. "A book of poetry they found in the Siberian wilderness. It's about love and reincarnation and soulmates."

A flicker of something darted across his face, but it was fleeting, like the vivid snapshot memories I struggled so hard to pin down. "What do you think of it?"

Was he asking like an awkward teenage boy making conversation? Or like a writer with an immortal soul who had finally, unwittingly, shared his work with the world?

"It's beautiful," I admitted, feeling a low heat spread over my cheeks. It was about me, after all. And if Ceri really was Arden, I wanted him to know how much it meant to read it. "I'm glad it was finally published."

He paused for a moment, staring fixedly at the cover, then nodded as though suddenly deciding something. "I want to buy it."

My blood fizzed as I rang it through the till and passed it to him. Was he buying something back from a past version of himself? Or was I imagining the wistful texture to the conversation?

On the receipt, he wrote his phone number and handed it back.

When Ceri left the shop, I couldn't relax, couldn't let loose the breath I'd been holding since the second he'd walked in.

Because even though I was safe for now, I was not safe for long.

I thought about our interaction for the rest of my shift, replaying it over and over in my mind, searching for unimpeachable evidence, turning over each and every word like I was checking precious pearls for imperfections. I found none.

And yet that feeling of unease calcified into certainty as the hours wore on. The sudden appearance, the immediate gravitation toward me, the interest in the poetry book . . .

Checking my phone at the end of my shift, I saw that Gracie had messaged me:

> mum called me a hard-boiled egg last night
>
> she looked like she wanted to die from discomfort
>
> why do I feel like this was your doing

As I fired off a reply, my stomach still clenched with anxiety.

There were only two more booster injections to go before the transplant.

Two more days I had to stay alive.

Wales

2022

When I knocked at the door of the flat above the petrol station, nobody answered.

The plan was just to go and talk to Ceri. To figure out if he really was Arden. And, if so, to tell him all about Gracie and my predicament in the hope he'd agree to postpone the slaughter until after my stem cells were safely in her body. Surely he still held enough love for me to allow me two more days.

Patting the knife in my pocket to make sure it hadn't dropped out, I rang the doorbell twice, waiting for the sound of footsteps plodding down the stairs to the small white door. And then I waited some more, unsure what to do next.

I could have just texted him. Assumed he was Arden and told him about the transplant, begged for his mercy in the hope that our time in Siberia had meant as much to him as the poetry book suggested. But I wanted to gauge his reaction, search him for pressure points, press down on them like bruises. I didn't want him to be able to dodge the conversation. I needed him to understand how important this was to me.

And maybe, just maybe, I *wanted* to see him again.

Darkness had fallen, the doorway lit neon from the garish signs above the fuel station, and I found myself missing the subtle glow of gas lamps. The twenty-first century was so *gauche*. Sometimes

60 ⁘ Laura Steven ⁘

I marvelled at how far forward the world had moved—the beauty of modern medicine, and how it gave my sister a fighting chance—but other times I thought of smartphones and steel buildings and plastic-filled oceans and longed for a time long gone. Witnessing the changing trends of the last few centuries had been like experiencing the gradual pixellation of the Sistine Chapel, or Michelangelo's raw genius flattened into sixteen bits, or grand orchestras stripped back to a single synthetic keyboard. Though modern sewage systems were pretty great. I didn't miss the tide of eternal shit running down the streets of Rome.

I yanked my wandering mind back to Abergavenny.

There was only one car at the petrol pumps, and I could see its elderly owner inside buying cigarettes at the counter. The entrance to the flat was on the other side of the building to the road, so I was perfectly concealed on the doorstep.

When my third knock went unanswered, another idea came to me.

I'd learned to pick locks during my time stealing diamonds from the royals in imperial Kenya, and even if I couldn't remember many details of that life, my hands still remembered what to do. Muscle memory, or something similar. It was a pretty useful skill, no matter who or where you were, so I made sure always to own a rudimentary toolkit with at least a skeleton key, a diamond pick, and a tiny tension wrench. They were currently tucked in the back compartment of a red snakeskin purse Gracie had got me for Christmas.

If I could get inside and search Ceri's flat, maybe I'd find the ironclad proof I was looking for. In fact, I was sure I would. Because that's the thing about humans—we leave traces of our souls everywhere, as unique and identifying as fingerprints.

Before I could talk myself out of it, I withdrew my lock-picking kit, scanned the petrol station one final time, and got to work.

The door to the flat had an old brass lock, scratched to within

Our Infinite Fates   61

an inch of its life by an endless stream of tenants. At first my fingers fumbled, rusty and uncertain, the picks and wrenches jostling each other awkwardly, inexpertly.

But eventually I felt the gratifying click, the sighing give, and allowed myself a small smile of satisfaction.

I didn't risk flicking a light switch inside, as I didn't want Ceri to arrive home and spot the glow through the windows. Instead, I flipped on my phone's stark white torch and climbed the carpeted staircase. It was littered with junk mail and takeaway menus, which struck me as odd. If he'd only moved in two days ago, how could this much unread post have accumulated? As shady as landlords were, I doubted they'd leave the place in a state like that for a new tenant.

Had I just caught him in his first lie? Had he actually been in Abergavenny for a while, biding his time until the right murderous opportunity arose?

Inside, the flat itself was almost entirely devoid of personal belongings. On the walls hung generic landscape art—which could have belonged to Arden, I supposed, but it seemed more likely to have been chosen by an estate agent to make the place look more homey. There was a grubby cream carpet, a cheap-looking grey sofa and yellow throw cushions, a low coffee table with a few tea-stained mugs scattered over it, and a single pair of off-white trainers discarded by the black television stand.

The kitchenette was tiled a grimy mustard yellow, the grout stained a dull brown-grey. A glance inside the fridge and cupboards gave me no insights. There was just a tin of instant coffee, a bag of sugar, and an unopened packet of custard creams. I didn't know whether this pointed to Arden. He drank his coffee black, and there was no milk in the fridge, but the bag of sugar was incongruous. Unless, of course, it had been there when he'd moved in. Whenever that was.

62   * Laura Steven *

After checking the bathroom, which had only hand soap, a toothbrush and paste, shampoo, and a single black bath towel hanging on a rail, I slipped into the bedroom.

The double bed was neatly made with a blue-checked duvet set, and there were more generic landscape paintings hanging above it. The top drawer of his dresser was open, revealing several pairs of identical black socks with different-coloured heels. The other drawers contained jeans and sweatshirts, for the most part, and only two wrinkled shirts hung in the loose-hinged wardrobe.

The poetry book was sitting on a pine bedside table, a bus ticket sticking out of the top as a bookmark. He was less than ten pages in. That didn't seem like the frenzied reading of an author who'd discovered a past life's work.

I was about to give up and label the mission inconclusive when my gaze snagged on a large black object on the windowsill.

When I realised what it was, my heart lurched.

A typewriter.

Old—very old—and not very recently used, by the looks of things. There was no stack of paper next to it, no ink spools inside. The keys were a little dusty, as though it had recently been taken out of storage.

This was it. The sign I'd been looking for.

Why else would someone like Ceri have this? Why, when he had so few other belongings, would he bother to bring this typewriter from his family home? Or buy it from a junk shop, when he had so little money he was worried about rent?

The sole furnishing he had chosen for his lonely haunted house. The written word, his eternal companion, his only confidant. The image of him sitting outside the café with a black coffee and a newspaper . . . I should have known then.

An old soul.

Our Infinite Fates   63

New flowers from old roots, an eternal seed from which life will always bloom.

My hand trembled as I reached out to touch it—to close the emotional gap between us, as though this typewriter held the part of his soul he kept so hidden—but I snatched my fingers back just in time. The keys were dusty. He'd notice if they'd been touched.

Stepping back, trying to silence my roaring heart, I racked my brain for the right course of action.

Should I get out now, before he caught me, and try to stay out of his way until after the transplant? Or should I wait it out and confront him when he returned home? Even though it had been my original plan, the latter now struck me as too risky. A fight could so easily go wrong, and I didn't want to give him reason to kill me before I could save Gracie.

I should cut my losses. Get out. Regroup.

But as I slipped back out the front door, a run-down old car pulled up and parked off to the side of the petrol station. A male figure climbed out, drawing a hood up over his blond head.

Ceri.

No.

Arden.

Chest pounding painfully, I snuck around the edge of the building in the pooled shadows. Behind the petrol station was a small copse of trees, and I crept over to them as silently as I could, hiding behind a narrow trunk to watch him enter the flat.

I hadn't relocked the door. Would he notice?

Sure enough, as he slotted his key into the lock, he paused. Frowned. Jimmied the handle.

And then he looked around, as if he knew an intruder was somewhere nearby.

Right at the spot where I was hiding.

I stayed perfectly still, hoping the darkness obscured me. My pulse was a thundering drumroll.

After several agonising beats, he looked away again, then slipped inside.

All the fight left my limbs, and I slid to the wood-chipped ground, the bark of the tree rough against my coat.

My muscles were watery, my guts loose, and I let out an involuntary whimper.

Arden was here.

He had found me. And very soon, he was going to kill me.

So why had I wanted so badly to run into his arms?

Algeria

1932

Two days after my father was shot on the beach, I had to work.

I'd been a waiter at Chez Anouilh since I'd left school the previous summer, bringing squat glasses of black coffee to the French expats who'd taken over the town. The cold Parisian owner insisted I come straight to my shift from my dad's funeral, cheeks dry and salty, the scent of geraniums and wet earth following me around like a ghost.

The café was a few streets back from the beach, notched between a tobacconist's and a bakery. It was a pretty boulevard, lined with fig trees and cars, the smell of fresh bread mingling with the tang of gasoline. When the locals sought shade inside during the peak of the afternoon, the pavements crawled with cats. Today, the tobacconist sat outside his shop in a folding deckchair, smoking and watching the world go by.

The sky overhead was black with clouds, and the humid air threatened rain.

I set an espresso down in front of Farid, a tall, scrawny gentleman who spent all day every day at the same outdoor table, reading newspapers from cover to cover while chain-smoking. We'd grown close over the last few months—a kind of uncle–nephew feel to the relationship—making jokes and exchanging stories. As I gave him his final coffee before he switched to a carafe of wine,

66 ✴ Laura Steven ✴

my hands trembled so much that the sachet of brown sugar fell to the ground. I went to pick it up, but Farid beat me to it.

Straightening up and tearing the top of the sachet, he said, "I was so sorry to hear about your loss, habibi. Your father was a good man."

"Thank you." Tears stung fiercely at my eyes, and shame rose in me like a flame. Boys shouldn't cry—at least not in public. I looked up at the charcoal sky to force the emotion back down.

"Such a senseless tragedy." Farid shook his head as he stirred the sugar into the espresso. The whole table wobbled as he did, despite the ashtray wedged under its wonky leg. Dark brown liquid sloshed onto the red oilcloth.

"Yes." It was all I felt able to say.

"He lives on in you. Remember that."

I nodded, blinked, looked away.

A white French family with crisp accents arrived, twin boys in matching sailor suits—clearly Pieds-Noirs, though I didn't harbor the same intrinsic loathing for them as other natives did. Arden and I had been French in our previous lives, dying for our country in the blood-soaked trenches of the Western Front. And now here I was on a shore that—justifiably—loathed the land I had sacrificed myself in the name of. Whatever divine hand was responsible for our reincarnations clearly had a sense of humor.

Just as I was about to take the French family's order, a short, handsome, and well-dressed boy around my age stopped outside the café.

He looked into my eyes with a familiar, heavy nod.

For the second time in as many lives, I felt not fear but relief.

A truck bumped along the uneven cobbles behind him, kicking up a cloud of dust. I offered him a weak smile, nodding toward the deserted interior of the café. He followed me wordlessly inside.

"You found me, then." I laid down my tray and notepad on

Our Infinite Fates

67

the counter and busied myself changing the coffee filter. Nerves jumped in my chest as I looked around the café, painted a muted, peeling red. "A better fate than the trenches, I'm sure you'll agree."

He surveyed some of the framed pictures on the walls. There were several illustrated proverbs that the owners had translated from Arabic to French. Badly.

Arden gestured to the watercolor brushwork of the phrase that should've been "Inda al botoun da'at al 'okoul." *In the stomach, the mind is lost.* Only, they'd mistranslated *mind* as *ears*.

"That's wrong," Arden muttered, visibly aghast. "It should be something like, 'Dans les ventres, l'esprit est perdu.' Or maybe a different tense? Perhaps—"

"Such a pedant."

"Translation in a colonized state is an act of violence, and . . ." He trailed off as his gaze finally pinned itself to me. "*Hi.*"

Strange, how much emotion could be carried in a single syllable.

I took in his new appearance. He had golden skin and a long nose with a boxer's crook. His dark hair was slicked back and he wore a button-down shirt, a tight-fitting jacket, and a red tie. Clearly he came from wealth. I felt grubby with my patchy facial hair and faded, stained apron, my burn-scarred hands fumbling with the tie at the back. Tugging at the knot, I only tightened it further, and the frustration finally let loose the grief in my chest.

Dropping my elbows onto the counter, I pressed the heels of my hands into my eye sockets and succumbed to the racking sobs.

"Evelyn," said Arden roughly. "What's wrong?" He didn't reach out to touch me this time, and my traitorous heart wished he would.

"My dad d-died. He was killed, actually." Starbursts danced behind my eyes as I pressed harder against my palms. "A random act of evil. No motive, no nothing. I can't make sense of it. And I don't want to live without him. So just do it. Now. Please."

I reached under the counter where dishes were drying on a rack and handed him the knife I used to slice baguettes. Its edge was serrated. It would hurt like hell, but no worse than the feeling of losing my father. His big soft belly and his warm hugs, his love for birdwatching, his sage advice on becoming a man as we took evening strolls along the docks.

Never again.

How could anyone bear the weight of *never*?

I supposed most *never*s were not as long as mine.

Arden looked down at the knife and then back up at me. "Evelyn . . ."

"I know it's still a year until I'm eighteen, but this is too much to bear." The tears had stopped flowing, and my tone had taken on a coarse, gravelly quality. "You'll be doing me a favor."

He shook his head slowly. "That's not who you are. You don't hide from this."

I wiped my sodden cheeks with the bottom of the floury apron. "What?"

"The Evelyn I know . . . they love over and over and over again, even though it can only ever end in tragedy. Even though they've lost everyone they've ever loved, and they miss them in the next life, and the next, and the next. Never have they developed hard edges like I have. Never have they tried to protect themselves from that pain. They love softly, and fiercely, and openly, and it's the bravest thing I know. The most human thing I know."

He'd expressed a similar sentiment on the Western Front, but it felt different hearing it seventeen years later, between the quiet red walls of the café.

My father had felt like the final straw, his death scrubbing my heart raw. Trying to keep the people I loved alive was like trying

Our Infinite Fates

to cup the rain in my palms, every drop so precious and fragile and important, only to watch them seep, inevitably, back into the earth. I clung to what Anais Lamunière had told me twenty years ago, tried to imagine what my father had been to me in my past, tried to imagine what I would be to him in the future, tried to imagine the new love that would bloom from our ashes.

"We're all born that way." Arden gripped my hand so tightly it almost hurt. "All little children are like that. They're not afraid to feel, to love. Life hardens most of them, but you . . . You've lived for nearly a thousand years and still—"

"Please," I whispered. "I'm begging you. Kill me."

"I've never met anyone as ruthful as you," Arden went on, as though he hadn't heard me.

I frowned. "Do you mean *ruthless?*"

He shook his head vehemently. "*Ruthful,* the original. From the thirteenth century, or around then. How can you have forgotten? It means endless compassion, a deep empathy for others." His jaw was taut and his gaze was urgent. "I hope you never lose that bottomless capacity for love. I hope you hold on to what makes you human."

I met his intense stare, feeling, like I had a thousand times before, that those eyes could swallow me whole.

Voice a mere whisper, I said, "This time it hurts too much."

I craved the cotton-wool baby years of my next life, before my mind developed enough to remember everything that had happened to me. Everything—and everyone—I'd lost.

Shifting on aching feet, my elbow jostled a half-empty carafe from the edge of the counter, and it went careening to the tiled floor, shattering into smithereens.

"Aaaaaaaaarghhh!" I yelled, so loudly and suddenly that Arden recoiled.

Something hideous and agonizing shaken loose in me, I grabbed another carafe and hurled it at the back wall. It crashed into a framed newspaper clipping of a famous visitor, sending both to the tiles with a smash.

I threw another, and another, and another, panting with the exertion, my eyes blurred with tears, until finally I slumped raggedly to the counter, sobbing into my forearm.

For a moment, there was silence—then a voice so soft and tender it threatened to unravel me all over again.

"Come here, habibi," Arden whispered.

I looked up. Several faces were peering into the window of the café, but none had come inside to check on the furor.

Arden walked around the side of the counter, bumping his hip on the sharp corner without a wince, and lifted my chin with a gentle thumb. Once I was upright, he wrapped his arms around me. The sensation of his body against mine after seventeen long years brought a familiar yearning, an insistent tug behind my ribs and below my belly. I sniffed into the hollow of his shoulder, letting the warmth of his chest and the steady thump of his heart moor me once more.

this is how bees make honey:
they suck careful nectar from open flowers
and bring their bounty back to the hive,
where they kiss it from mouth to mouth
until it runs thick and sweet.
every parent we have ever loved walked this glorious earth
gathering nectar from the flowers of their lives,
kissing it into the mouths of their children,
and now the honey is ours.

—AUTHOR UNKNOWN

Wales

2022

After breaking into Ceri's apartment, I didn't see him again for a couple of days. Not outside the flower shop, not in the café reading a newspaper, not in the bookshop's poetry section.

My insides felt like a beehive, writhing and buzzing with anticipation, though I couldn't quite ascertain whether I wanted to see him. True, a confrontation could be disastrous, but it was *Arden.*

Arden, less than a mile away, after decades apart. A sweet nectar I had never been able to resist.

Whenever I heard my teenage peers explain that they liked someone because they were *funny* or *smart* or *kind,* it all seemed so reductive, so one-dimensional. Sure, I could ascribe such bland descriptors to Arden—they were poetic, and creative, and stubborn, and reserved, and wise. Gentle with wildlife, tapped into the natural world in some fundamental way. Philosophical, deep, if often melancholic. The embodiment of saudade.

But what I felt for Arden transcended most people's understanding of love. Their personhood was not as simple as a list of definitive attributes and traits, and they had no fixed body to marvel over. What fascinated me, what compelled me so profoundly, was that theirs was a *soul* in the truest sense. A way of thinking, a way of feeling, their emotional contours shifting with culture and history and experience but never yielding entirely.

Our Infinite Fates

Arden was a vast tapestry that grew more detailed with every incarnation. Perhaps the raw material began as a simple expanse of goodness, of loyalty, of creativity and imagination, but with every life they lived—and every life they took—another section of elaborate beadwork was stitched through the silk. Each piece of knowledge gained was a jewel in the border; each new person they encountered was an intricate patch of embroidery. All this texture made them so endlessly interesting, made me want to run my fingers over every inch so that I could explore it, understand it. Unravel it.

How could anyone who'd only lived one life compare?

But while we had loved each other for centuries, we hadn't *talked* in nearly four decades. El Salvador had been so brutal, so breviloquent. I needed more, like an addict craved the poppy. I craved their presence, their conversation, their embrace—even if it would ultimately result in our death.

It was a yearning so complex that it defied all reason.

As I lay in bed each night, I cupped my phone to my chest, trembling with the possibility of it.

Never before in history had I been able to send Arden an instantaneous message. Never before had I been able to tell them I loved them on a careless whim, a flight of fancy, the kind of recklessness a thousand years of living gave you. There was much to condemn about the internet, but there was no denying how flint-fast it made the art of connection. How easy modernity had made it to declare love—a funny video shared with a friend, real money sent to virtual coffee funds, a snap of the flowers your grandmother picked from her garden. The everyday tenderness of "I saw this and thought of you."

Arden and I would never have that kind of casual relationship. Another small alienation from the world around me. Another tiny untethering from humanity.

Instead, we had blades to the throat. Poetry books found frozen in the taiga. Arrows through the heart. Great monuments burned to the ground. A sense of both permanence and impermanence. Transient, ephemeral, but also somehow enduring.

An antique typewriter sitting proudly on a windowsill, waiting.

I typed out and deleted several messages to Ceri about Gracie's illness, and about how I so badly wanted him to leave me alone until I could donate my stem cells.

He would understand, I was certain of it.

I remembered Algeria, after my father was shot on the beach, how he'd comforted me in the café, glass carafes shattered at our feet, my head pressed to his chest, the contours of our bodies lined up so neatly. He knew what family meant to me. He knew how much it destroyed me to lose the people I loved. There was no way he would kill me gratuitously before I could save my innocent sister.

Yet part of me didn't want to cheapen our love with a collection of pixels on an ambivalent screen. I didn't want to reduce our symphony to a singular note.

And I certainly didn't want to beg.

If he confronted me tomorrow, I would deal with it then.

I would roll the dice on his love for me, and trust that he would not let me die.

At least not yet.

I tucked my phone away and instead pulled out *Ten Hundred Years of You*. I ran a fingertip over the page where Arden described grief as clay—clay that could be used to sculpt something beautiful—and began to sob.

The transplant appointment arrived, and Arden did not, and I could barely believe my good fortune.

Usually I walked the mile from the bookshop to the hospital, but

Our Infinite Fates 75

since rain was falling in sheets and the charcoal sky was threatening thunder, Dylan—the farmhand who helped my mum out—offered to give me a lift in the Jeep pickup. He was waiting in the nearest car park in grubby overalls, windows down despite the weather, rapping his fingers on the steering wheel to some indie folk music.

Dylan was a hippie through and through. I'd caught him talking to trees on more than one occasion. Despite his quirks—or maybe because of them—I'd lusted after him since the moment he'd turned up on my mum's doorstep and asked if she had any work going on the farm. He'd just finished sixth form and wanted to save up some money to go travelling. I was fifteen or sixteen at the time, studying at the kitchen table for my final exams, and the attraction had fluttered pleasantly through me.

He had a kind of natural cheer to him that struck me as so antithetical to Arden. After centuries of running from the dark, his presence was a sudden blinding light. Cheesy jokes and whistled tunes, laughter so rich and raucous that it spread through every room. Bear hugs and buoyant folk music, rugby balls spinning on a fingertip, fresh-baked bread and a window propped open to let in some air. A golden retriever in human form.

Our paths hadn't really crossed in school, since he was a couple of years older than me, but I'd always admired him from afar. Yet despite the occasional flirtatious glance in the early days, he treated me with a kind of respectful distance.

It was probably for the best. My attraction had always been wrapped in a suffocating layer of guilt, as though I was betraying Arden in some way. I couldn't imagine them turning up in my life to discover me in love with someone else. The way that would forever alter the dynamic between us.

In any case, Dylan had truly become a part of the family—a warm patchwork square in our emotional support blanket. And although he had worked on the farm for two years now, he still showed no sign of travelling any further than Bwlch. Judging by the soft, almost narcotic glow he got after a day tending to the land, I suspected the Welsh wilds had burrowed under his skin.

"How are you feeling?" he asked as I climbed into the front passenger seat. His dark shoulder-length hair was pulled back in a low knot, accentuating the sharp lines of his square jaw.

"Fine," I said, tucking the seat belt around me. It had been chewed by a goat and was frayed to a worrying degree. "Excited to finally get this done."

"I really admire you. You know that?" Dylan said, spinning the steering wheel and exiting the car park. His forearms were rippled with sinewy muscle, and he had several strands of twine and string knotted around his wrists. "You've taken all this in your stride."

"It's Gracie you should be admiring. She's the one who has somehow become more herself through a life-threatening illness."

I pictured my bald sister defacing a grave with a can of spray paint and stifled a laugh.

I adored that girl.

"I can admire you both, can't I?" Dylan looked at me affection- ately, like he might want to reach out and ruffle my hair but had decided against it.

For the thousandth time, I felt beyond grateful that even if the worst should happen to me, he would still be here to pick up the pieces. That he could make my mum pot of tea after pot of tea, ensure she was eating, resting, healing.

"Thank you," I said simply.

"For what?" he asked, smiling that broad, infectious smile, but I didn't need to answer. He knew.

There had been a time when I'd suspected Dylan of being Ar- den, if only a little. He'd been two years above me in school, so we couldn't have shared a birthday, yet the tingle in my fingertips, the

Our Infinite Fates

flutter in my lower belly, the love he had for the earth . . . they were hard to dismiss as adolescent lust and simple coincidence.

So I'd set tiny traps in every conversation we had, sprinkling them with historical details from times I knew we'd lived through together, searching his face for the faintest glimmer of recognition. Misquoting lines from Arden's favourite poets—Keats, Byron, Coleridge—to see if he could resist correcting me. Using obscure words from extinct languages, expecting him to pick up on them.

I'd even once *called* him Arden, to see if his head would snap up from the kitchen sink in surprise, but he'd barely registered the slip of the tongue.

Gradually, the paranoia had faded and something like kinship had knotted in its place.

As we drove to the hospital, I stared out at the arcing hills, their peaks disappearing into an ominous mist. Foreboding traced its gnarled finger down my spine. I couldn't fight the feeling that something awful was about to happen. That Ceri was about to leap out from behind a tree and stab me before I could explain Gracie's predicament.

Arriving at the hospital felt like floating on a cloud of disbelief, but that sense of disquiet followed me through the corridors like a shadow.

Too good to be true, purred a silky voice in the back of my head, but I tried to ignore it. I'd lived so many lives, and I'd been a blind optimist in almost every single one. Why change now?

The final hurdle was a blood test to make sure my blood contained enough stem cells to make the transplant viable. A matronly nurse with close-cropped grey hair took the vials in stilted silence, with just a "sharp scratch" warning right before the stinging needle pierced my skin.

While they took my sample away to be examined, I hung out in Gracie's room with Dylan, eating fizzy sweets and watching episodes of the lesbian vampire show she was obsessed with. Mum dozed off in a high-backed armchair, the back of her head periodically sliding sideways down the padded fabric before jolting back up again. She'd been sleeping here a lot. The whole thing had aged her exponentially. There were pronounced bags under her eyes and a fresh spray of silver-grey hair around the coppery crown of her head.

"Has she made any more jokes?" I whispered to Gracie, gesturing toward Mum.

Gracie nodded gravely. "She handed me a baseball cap and called it my 'egg cup.' It was embarrassing for everyone involved."

"At least she's trying." I felt a pang of affection for our sad, lovely mum.

"She's a good egg," said Dylan, deadpan.

Gracie groaned.

"What?" Dylan looked fake-affronted. "I really thought that would crack you up."

"I hate you," Gracie said, which was her way of insinuating the exact opposite.

"On that note, I brought you something," he said, scooping his backpack off the floor. Unzipping it carefully, he pulled out something wrapped in brown parcel paper, tied with a frayed length of twine in a clumsy bow. There was a mud print on the front that looked suspiciously like a pig's hoof.

Frowning as though he'd presented her with her own obituary, Gracie tore open the paper and stared at the contents. I could make out the back of a large photo frame, but not what was inside.

"Erm, thanks," she said slowly, unconvincingly. "What—erm—what is it?"

Dylan's cheeks flushed red, and he suddenly became very interested in the label at the corner of her blanket. "Well, you're not allowed to bring flowers into hospital these days, so every time

Our Infinite Fates   79

I saw one on the farm that reminded me of you, I took it home. Dried it and pressed it. And, erm, there you go."

Curious, I peered over Gracie's shoulder at the pressed flowers. Dylan had arranged the petals—pink and blue and violet and yellow—into the shape of a violin. Except he was not a particularly gifted artist, and the shape was clumsy, the bow too small, the body too wide.

And yet it was perhaps the loveliest thing I'd ever seen.

"That is unbelievably tragic," said Gracie, stuffing it under her pillow, but she had to clear her throat shortly afterwards. I didn't miss the way she looked up at the harsh ceiling light, blinking furiously. "Now, if we can all stop acting like I'm already dead, that would be fantastic."

"Far from it," replied Dylan with an earnest beam. "I don't know anyone more alive." He reached out a hand, then withdrew it again. "I was going to ruffle your hair, but you don't have any."

"Twat," snapped Gracie, but she was laughing once more.

Eventually two doctors entered the room. One was Dr. Onwuemezi, the oncology consultant overseeing Gracie's treatment, and the other was a medical student with floppy blond hair and the general aura of the very hungover. As he fumbled with his stethoscope behind Dr. Onwuemezi, the doctor's impatience wafted off her in such severe waves that I was genuinely quite fearful for the student's safety.

They stood at the end of Gracie's bed, holding clipboards and looking generally grim. Anxiety gripped my stomach like a noose. There was still a strip of gauze taped to the crook of my elbow, the adhesive pinching my skin.

"I'll get right into it." Dr. Onwuemezi pushed thick-framed glasses up the bridge of her nose. "Despite our best efforts with the booster injections, Branwen's blood doesn't contain enough circulating stem cells to make a transplant successful." Despair plummeted in my stomach like a stone. "This doesn't mean it can't work, but it means we'll have to extract bone marrow from the hip instead, if that's something she's willing to consent to."

"Of course," I replied quickly, pulse pounding. It wasn't over yet. "Anything. Let's do it right now."

Another grimace from Dr. Onwuemezi. "Unfortunately—"

"Let me guess. I've got an infection," Gracie said, her tone flat, her brow clammy in a way I hadn't noticed until now. "Again."

"Yes. Thankfully, it is minor and under control, but it does mean that we won't be able to go ahead with the transplant while the infection is still active. So our plan is to treat the infection first, go through another round of chemotherapy conditioning, and then proceed with the harvest and transplant in two weeks' time."

My heart fell through the floor.

I turned eighteen in ten days.

Which meant I'd likely be dead in two weeks.

"More chemo." Mum's voice was pained, tense. "Is that really necessary? It makes her so sick."

"It's needed to destroy her existing bone marrow cells and make room for the new ones, as well as to destroy any existing cancer cells and to suppress the immune system."

Dylan chewed his lip worriedly. "Why do we want to suppress it? You just said she's getting infections as it is."

"Because if we don't," said the med student, looking up at his mentor for approval, "there's a much higher chance her body will reject the transplant?" Dr. Onwuemezi nodded reluctantly.

After answering a few more medical questions from my mum, the doctors left the room.

Gracie, who had been sitting cross-legged in the centre of her bed, threw herself back against the stack of pillows. "Remember when we were little, and Mum used to put Sudocrem on literally everything? Whatever insect bite or rash or scratch or bruise we

✳ Our Infinite Fates ✳ 81

had? And she said it was magic cream and it could fix anything?" She puffed the air out through her nose in a half scoff, but I could see the pain behind it. "What a load of shit."

"I'm sorry." Mum sniffed. "I shouldn't've made you believe——"

"Oh, for fuck's sake, Mum, it's not an apology thing." Gracie yanked the zip of her hoodie all the way up to her chin. "Just something I remembered."

"Don't swear at me, Gracie." Mum dabbed at her eyes with her cardigan sleeve.

Gracie laughed bitterly. Her maple violin lay on the bedside table next to a bunch of red grapes and the poetry book. "What are you going to do about it? What could you do to punish me when things couldn't possibly get any worse?"

But they could. Arden could kill me any moment now, and my sweet, foul-mouthed sister would never get the transplant.

No. I wouldn't let that happen.

I had to take matters into my own hands.

I had to live past the age of eighteen, no matter what.

Pulling out my phone, I finally typed a message to Ceri:

let's have that date x

France

1915

Over the congealing trenches of the Western Front, there was a sunset of peach and pink and purple smudged across a canvas of gold. It never failed to amaze me, even after all these centuries, that the elements cared not for human pain. That the sky and its stars paid no heed to the obliterated corpses below. That the birds still sang each morning, no matter how many men had fallen the night before.

Sometimes that sense of insignificance was a comfort. But here, languishing in a rotten maze carved into the ruined earth, I felt nothing but despair.

How simple and beautiful life could have been. How far from that humanity had strayed.

Existence had become barbed wire and stacked sandbags and stepping over the lifeless corpses of your friends. It was reeking mud and unwashed bodies, the metallic tang of gunpowder and blood, the scratch of lice and the perpetual dampness, the echoing patter of bloated rats between ground-shattering drops of random shells. And, when the weather was bad, the sensation that we were at war with the world itself—with rain and wind and sliding earth, with the booming sky and the crimson ground.

I had never known fear—nor boredom—like it.

Much to my parents' horror, and despite my own inclinations

Our Infinite Fates 83

toward pacifism, I'd lied about my age in order to enlist. My reasoning had been twofold. First, I could not die by enemy bullet, and so I owed it to my country to donate that unique quirk of nature to the greater good. And second, some part of me hoped Arden would not find me in the trenches. Even if they were born in a male body, there was a chance they'd been spawned just over the German border from the tiny village I called home, and if that were the case, we'd be fighting on opposite sides. Reaching an enemy front alone would be nigh on impossible.

No such luck; Arden was male, and French, and he'd followed me here.

Henri had found me on the front line a few months before we turned eighteen, having searched every communication and reserve trench behind me. Despite knowing immediately that it was Arden, that he was here to kill me, I simply didn't *care*. I needed him. I needed him in a way that frankly terrified me.

His arrival had felt like all those letters I'd sent home had been replied to at once. What should have been a threat had felt like a comfort, like sugary tea from a warm flask, like my mother brushing a kiss on my forehead as a child.

He had rounded the corner, and I had run to him, following that undeniable tether, pressing my rough face into the crook of his neck. It had taken all the willpower in my arsenal to prevent the tears spilling onto his starched collar.

"Do you want to go now?" he had whispered softly.

Do you want it to be over? Will death be a relief?

Though it was tempting, I had shaken my head. "No. I just want you. At least for a while."

And so, between the bouts of fighting, we talked, and we held each other, and it was awful and terrible but less so for his presence. He told me of the life he had left behind in Lille, his father's woodworking shop, his mother's atrocious cooking, his twin brother's untimely death. And I told him of my life, of my farmer parents and of Anais Lamunière, of my three sisters and of the ramshackle cottage we called home. I knew I would never return there, but the talking helped anyway.

A few weeks later, beneath the oblivious sunset, Henri and I sat side by side in our horizon blue uniforms, booted feet kicked out over the duckboards, pinkie fingers entwined. We'd sustained several days of harsh enemy fire. Big losses and bigger grief. We'd been due to rotate back to the support trenches earlier that morning but had been held on the front for strategic reasons we were not privy to. The soldiers around us were subdued with exhaustion, and mourning, and a maelstrom of other darknesses.

"Can you find anything poetic to say about any of this?" I muttered, stomach cramping with hunger, skin shriveled with cold and wet. I couldn't stop staring at a clumsy sculpture of a rose made from spent shells, which had been the pet project of Capitaine Dupont. He'd died a few days after its completion, on a fruitless reconnaissance mission with four of my closest comrades.

Henri, or Arden, rested his head against the wooden base of the fire step, gazing up at the watercolor sky. "A few things."

"Do share."

"The metaphors are half-baked right now. Pencil sketches at best."

I scoffed. "We'll be dead before they become oil paintings."

His eyes fluttered shut, dark lashes pressing into crescents. "This is fucking awful. That's all I can really say."

There was a single gunshot somewhere in the middle distance, and I flinched instinctively. Arden unraveled his pinkie from mine and laid his palm over my hand, squeezing tight.

I studied the length of my filthy, too-short trousers, wishing I could prise them off. As someone who had always taken great pleasure in fine clothing—in the creativity and self-expression fash-

Our Infinite Fates

85

ion afforded—there was something uniquely dehumanizing about wearing a military uniform.

Like I was one of many. Like I was entirely expendable.

"Your words have always brought me solace, you know," I whispered, so that the others wouldn't hear. "It's one of the things I love most about you. You have the soul of a poet."

Suffering broke over his face like a storm, and I couldn't quite make sense of why that hurt him to hear.

"What else?" he muttered, hoarse.

"Hmm?"

"What else do you love? It's never quite made sense to me."

"Nor me," I admitted, and it was the truth. There was an existential pull between us, yes, but I also just *loved* Arden. Painfully, normally, humanly. "I guess . . . it's not just the surface-level stuff. You're darkly funny and fiercely bright. You believe yourself a villain, but still create pockets of goodness inside your life. And . . . I can't explain it. It's like you have a depth that other people lack. Maybe it's who you are, or maybe it's how long we've lived. There's a . . . texture? A richness? To your heart. It fascinates me. I want to peel back the layers until I find your center."

I swallowed hard but found I couldn't stop now that I'd started. "You see me to my very core. I know that to be true. Nobody has ever known me, or will ever know me, like you do. That's such an intimate thing. You can't help but be drawn to someone who understands your every word, your every step, your every heartbeat. And I love the connection you have to nature. Your roots are buried so deep in the earth. When I see a gnarled tree branch or a beautiful lake, I think of you. It makes it feel like you're all around me, in every twig and leaf, in every butterfly and every bramble."

Something on his face relaxed, as though my words had coaxed free a knot in his muscles. "'The Poetry of earth is never dead.'"

"See? A poet's soul."

He frowned disparagingly. "That's Keats, you heathen."

I rested my head on his shoulder, resisting the urge to sink into him entirely. "Sometimes I fantasize about growing old together in a little cottage by the sea. You could spend your days tending the garden, and I could embroider elaborate patchwork blankets and knit cardigans for our children, or tailor expensive suits for the upper echelons of high society, and then we could come together over bowls of soup, and you could share your poignant observations about the ocean."

Arden's body stilled beneath my cheek. "You think about that stuff?"

"You don't?"

"No. It hurts too much, because it can never be." His voice was coarse, quiet, though nobody was really listening to us anyway. "But for what it's worth, that's what I love about you. It's not just how kind you are, or how deeply, stupidly brave. It's how you still allow your heart to be tender. How you never lose faith in humanity." He wrapped his arm around my shoulders. "Do you know how powerful that is? Do you know how rare you are, in a world where the sky rains fire?"

"I don't know about that." I grimaced as a rat scuttled through the trench, blood on its whiskers from whatever corpse it had gorged on. "Right now my faith in humanity is stretched a little too far."

"What's your secret, Evelyn? How does the candle of hope in your chest never burn down to the wick?"

Gazing up at the phoenix sky, I searched myself for the answer, like running my fingers over an ancient map. "I think I understood a long time ago that big joy and small joy are the same. It sounds trite, but it's true. Last year I won a major tennis tournament and brought home a huge cash prize for my family. I would've been on my way to the Championnat de France, if it weren't for the war. Big joy. Really, really big joy.

Our Infinite Fates   87

"But that victory felt no different from curling up in an old armchair with a faded blanket and reading my little sister a bedtime story. It felt no different from a perfect pot of coffee, or a warm croissant fresh from the bakery. And so even when there's no big joy—even when it feels like we'll never leave this trench alive—there's still the small joy. A sunset, a flask of tea. Your hand in mine."

Arden let this idea wash over him. "I thought I was supposed to be the poet." A sigh, long and low. "Though, without you, there would *be* no poetry. I would have only the harsh lens of my own worldview. I wouldn't be able to see the beauty of life, because I only see it through your eyes. *Muse* is too simple a word for what you are to me."

My mouth twisted into a rueful smile. "And yet, life after life, you take away the possibility of the cottage by the sea."

Silence swelled between us at the mention of our inevitable fate. "Please know that what I do, it is for us, for this." He spoke gently, as though his proclamations might break me. "If I didn't, the hell we'd go through . . . Please trust me. Do you trust me?"

A complicated question. "No, but also yes. I don't know, Arden."

His arms tightened around me. "You have faith in all of humanity. You have faith in love. Please, have faith in *me*. I do this to protect you. Do you understand that? That I would lay my body over yours, war after war after war, life after life after life?"

I nodded numbly, stunned by his sudden outpouring. He pressed his lips to the top of my head, not caring who saw. It was a less uncommon sight than one might have thought, in trenches like these. Play-wrestles that went on a few moments too long. Hands on shoulders and hands on hands. Words of comfort turned words of affection. The pent-up emotions, the pent-up *drive,* the despair and the kinship and the vulnerability. It was a wild furnace in which romantic love was often forged and, as the war raged on, many were becoming more brazen about it.

When he spoke again, it was so softly into my ear that I shivered. "I love you, and I have loved you, and I will love you."

The words sent a ripple of familiarity through me, a ghost of a memory. The sensation that our love was a palimpsest, written over and over again so that I could no longer read the original.

I lifted a dirt-smeared hand to his jaw, pulling his mouth toward mine. Our lips brushed together, light as a breeze. "I love you." Another kiss, so tender I thought I might unravel. "And I have loved you." The third kiss was deeper, richer, shaking loose a sigh from Arden. "And I will love you."

Then artillery blew the watercolor sky apart.

Fear detonated through the trenches as bodies scrambled to their feet. At the crack of enemy fire, there was always an initial jolt of confusion, of disorientation, of remembering where you were and what you had to do. Of willing your weakened body into horrible action. Preparing yourself to kill or be killed.

Arden's eyes met mine in a wordless question: *Is it time to go yet?*

I shook my head, gesturing around at the men who had become my brothers. Pierre and his woeful shanty-singing, Antoine and his vicious nightmares. Yannick, the way he comforted Antoine in the damp dugouts we called our bedrooms. I couldn't desert them now, couldn't take the coward's death when it would leave them without support.

Boots stomped up the fire steps beside us. Grim-faced men— boys, really—swarmed the trench mortars, haphazardly stuffing them with projectiles, everything off-kilter, uncoordinated, out of sync.

None of us were made for this.

I grabbed my rifle and climbed to my feet, but as I turned I saw a female figure striding toward us.

Our Infinite Fates

89

Sheets of white hair fell around her cool face, black nails curling away from her fingers like withered fossils. She was dressed in the same horizon-blue uniform, a bloodied bayonet notched in the hollow of her shoulder.

At first I thought she was a mirage. There were no women on the front line, and certainly none so casual and unaffected as this figure.

Was she a ghost? An angel come to save us?

"This has gone on long enough," she rasped in our direction, eyes flitting between Arden and me.

A scintilla of understanding flared in my mind, but it was darting, elusive. I only knew that it had something to do with our twisted fates. I knew it in my very marrow.

And I also . . . I knew *her*.

She meant something to me, something deep and awful and complex.

Every inch of my skin speckled with goose bumps.

"What do you mean?" I asked distantly, ears roaring, suddenly frantic with the need to *understand,* to finally understand this thing that had evaded me for so many centuries. "Who are you?"

And why do I want to run to you?

But Arden had pulled the pin on a grenade, striking the percussion cap on its base before lobbing it at the white-haired woman.

"No," I breathed, running toward the woman, toward the grenade, unwilling to lose this opportunity to *know* at last.

"*Evelyn,*" Arden bellowed, and his hands grabbed at my waist, trying to haul me back from the impending blast.

Determination cracked through my mind as though lit by gunpowder. I shook him free and reached the cruel-faced woman, dropping my rifle and shaking her by the sharp shoulders. "Who are you?"

Her lips tugged wide into a deranged grin.

The grenade detonated, and I was torn apart.

For a moment, there was only blinding, deafening pain.

The kind of pain that untethered me from the world, that separated me from all my other senses until I existed only inside of it.

It was all-consuming, unrelenting. It should not have been possible, pain like that.

It was larger than me, than the war, than the world.

Death found me not a moment too soon.

Wales

2022

I dreamed of the trenches again. I often did.

The sour tang of blood and sweat. The scratchy coarseness of my damp uniform. The deafening sound of the sky being cracked down the middle like a rib cage. Ice-cold adrenaline peeling the marrow from my bones.

And then, her.

White hair, black nails, bayonet notched in the hollow of her shoulder.

This has gone on long enough.

What has? I would wake up screaming. *What has gone on long enough?*

The meaning was clear.

Evelyn and Arden, the perpetual cycle, the snake eating its own tail.

She knew the *why*. But the loose grenade had robbed me of the chance to finally glean answers. I had spent decades trying to parse who—or what—she was. A forest witch, a bog demon, some ancient god we had angered long ago. Someone with whom we had made a dreadful bargain.

In the fresh-dug grave in frozen Siberia, I had once again asked Arden why. Not for the first time, and certainly not for the last.

And Arden had pressed his eyes shut, tears frozen like beads of glass just below his cheekbones. "Because of a deal made long ago."

The white-haired, black-nailed woman was surely the being with whom we had made the deal.

But what were the terms? What had ever driven us to such a terrible fate?

And when would she find us again?

A week before my eighteenth birthday, Ceri agreed to come and pick me up at the house before we headed out for a coffee.

Despite it not being a real date, I spent almost an hour picking out what to wear, purely for the pleasure of it. Because, depending on how the date went, these could be my final hours as Branwen Blythe, and I was determined to squeeze all the possible joy out of them.

I had two huge antique armoires in my bedroom, handed down from my great-aunt when she'd packed up her life to travel the world. Mum and I had spent a whole weekend painting them a creamy duck-egg blue, replacing the worn brass handles with floral ceramic knobs in white and turquoise and pink. Both wardrobes were packed with thrifted clothes, that unmistakable dust-mote smell still lingering on every oversized lapel and age-stained petticoat.

Tucked beneath the bursting fabrics was the old vintage sewing machine that had once belonged to my grandmother. An original Singer, it was the bright, glossy red of a postbox, with the waxy sheen of a candy apple. I'd been obsessed with it, at the age of ten or eleven, painstakingly following simple patterns with bolts of wacky fabrics, imagining the high-end fashion line I'd have one day, the initials *B.B.* hand-stitched on labels and sewn into the necklines of glorious gowns.

My first pieces had been *bad,* all clumsy hems and awkward tailoring, but I'd slowly and steadily improved until my creations became actually wearable. Tea dresses and waistcoats and pleated skirts, paired with my mum's own knitted cardigans.

Then Gracie got sick. Then I couldn't afford to waste my time on such trivialities when I had to devote every ounce of energy to the art of survival.

I touched a hand to the list of dreams in my pocket, a sheet of lined letter paper folded into a neat square.

Eventually I chose a poppy-red shift dress I'd found vintage shopping with Gracie, some white cowboy boots, a fur coat I'd raided from my great-aunt's dusty attic boxes, and some chunky plastic sunglasses from a Claire's bargain bin. An eccentric meshing of eras and styles, of all the different Evelyns I had been. And, always, red. My favourite colour, though I'd long ago forgotten why.

I went downstairs to find it was one of the rare days Mum was home instead of at the hospital. While it was nice seeing her perched at the kitchen island with a cup of tea, like in the before times, it was highly inconvenient for my twisted plan.

"I don't understand your clothes, Bran," said Mum at the sight of me, and I felt a traitorous pang of longing for my costumier mother in nineteenth-century Vienna. The chaotic warmth of the opera house, the scent of old fabric and perfumed pomades.

One would think having so many mothers in so many lives would have a diminishing effect, but my love for them never felt spread thin. Rather, it felt like a muscle, strengthened from centuries of purposeful use. Or maybe it felt easy because each new mother was born from a recycled soul I had loved before.

"That's all right," I replied cheerily. "You don't have to. I dress for me."

"And I admire it. Back when I was your age, I cared so much what people thought of me. I let it stop me from wearing and saying and doing what I really wanted to. But you're not like that. You're so . . . *assured.*"

That's what a thousand years of existence will gift you, I thought, but I answered only with a warm, genuine smile. A glance down at my bonkers outfit.

A momentary thrill before I remembered I might die in these clothes.

"Listen, Bran, before I forget . . . I think you should start seeing Dr. Chiang again."

At the mention of my old therapist, I paused in the doorway. "Why?"

She stared at me as though the question was the most absurd thing she'd ever heard. "Because your father died a tragic death, and your sister has a life-threatening illness, and in order to save her you're going to have to go through a tremendous amount of physical pain?"

She had a point, but my inner animal bucked against the idea. I'd cut my previous sessions with Dr. Chiang short when I'd found myself almost spilling the details of my curious curse. It was incredibly difficult to talk about the trauma in my life without addressing the root of it all.

And yet grief was tucked into every corner of my world. The kitchen, for example, would never stop reminding me of my father. Though it had been ten years since he'd died, I could still picture him whistling as he peeled vegetables in the Belfast sink, his apron stained and floury.

Even now, a blade of longing carved through my chest, the acute sense of being robbed of something wonderful and warm and safe. The mental image of blood seeping out of his eyes, the crush of his organs and bones. My mother's feral wails when she'd heard, Christmas music still playing in the background. The absolute unfairness of what had been taken, combined with the shuddering violence of the way it had happened.

I had lost a lot of people in a lot of lives, but that was one of the worst.

Our Infinite Fates 95

Until we meet again, I thought, resting a palm over my heart.

Maybe Mum was right. Therapy wasn't such a bad idea.

"I'll think about it."

"So, this Ceri boy." Mum sipped at her steaming mug of Earl Grey. She wore a hand-knitted navy cardigan over a flowery blouse, and her shoulder-length ginger hair was pulled back in a tortoiseshell clasp. So *mumsy.* So unlike the Viennese tour de force of a parent who had shared my love of raiment. "Is he from a nice family?"

"I don't think he talks to them," I said vaguely.

I wondered if, by the same logic as my strengthened muscle, Arden's familial bonds had become weak, atrophied, irritating spasms to be quelled whenever possible.

Mum frowned. "Why? That makes me suspicious."

"Something about his dad being an alcoholic and his mum being a controlling nightmare."

Mum took another sip of tea, her small lips pursed like a field mouse's. "Your dad always liked a drink, so he did. But I like to think I'm not too controlling."

I laughed, crossing over to the biscuit jar by the kettle. "Are you joking? You're the opposite. When I asked to go to a nightclub at the age of fifteen, you just laughed and told me to crack on."

A smile spread across Mum's face. "Well, I knew you wouldn't get in. Better to let the bouncer be the bad guy than me."

"You came and picked us up, remember?" I said, spraying biscuit crumbs all over the rough slate tiles. "And you brought a flask of tomato soup in case we were cold or hungry."

There was a wistfulness to her expression. "How do you remember that?"

I smiled at her warmly. "I always remember the little things you do for us."

Tears pricked at her eyes, and for once I didn't feel the need to tell her off for it. "Love you, Bran."

A lump bobbed in my throat. "Love you too."

My phone buzzed with a text from Gracie.

> can't believe you're out shagging while I'm dying in the hospital, how dare you honestly

As I chuckled and fired off a reply, Mum drained her tea, popped the mug in the sink, and grabbed her handbag from the counter. "I'm going to nip to Waitrose and pick up a lasagne. Do you want anything?"

Thank god for that. She wouldn't be here when Ceri arrived. A small mercy.

I shook my head.

"All right. Well, good luck on your date, then. Don't put out straight away. Or, if you do, wear protection." Her lips quirked mischievously, and it felt good to see her being playful for once.

I took in her familiar outline, the laughter lines framing her mouth, the gentle rounds of her hips, the scent of lavender, and the sound of her humming the *Frozen* song long after Gracie and I had outgrown it.

The second item on my list of dreams: take her and Gracie to Lapland at Christmastime.

The lights would twinkle and the snow would flurry and we would sip at hot chocolate in clumsy mittens, and we would recapture the festive magic of our childhood, before Dad had died on Christmas Eve, before Gracie had got sick, before we'd stopped believing in flying reindeer and boots down the chimney.

The image steeled me as I prepared myself for what I was about to do.

What I *had* to do.

Wales

2022

Fifteen minutes later, the doorbell rang.

Ceri stood on the porch in a red crew neck sweatshirt and those loose-hanging black jeans. His short hair had wax slicked through it, and I realised he must have bought it especially for tonight. It hadn't been in his bathroom when I'd rooted around.

After all these years, decades, centuries, Arden still wanted to make an effort for me. His beautiful, aching poetry echoed in the chambers of my heart.

He's going to kill you, I reminded myself, *and, in turn, your sister.*

He cleared his throat and gestured around the porch. "This is nice."

Our family farmhouse was a rugged, handsome thing. Old grey stone and sage-green window frames, pretty planters full of magnolias and carnations that Dylan kept neat and watered. Dotted around the main house was a hotchpotch collection of barns and outbuildings, and there was always the smell of manure and tractor fuel lingering on the forecourt.

I liked living on a farm, the way it made me feel connected to something greater than myself. The circle of life, the cycles of sowing and reaping, every birth and death so purposeful.

"Thanks," I replied with a forced smile. *Arden, Arden, this is*

Arden. I could barely think over the roar of blood in my ears. "Do you want a tour?"

"Sure." He smiled at me, pressing the lock button on his car key with a slight tremble of the hand. The old Corsa's headlights flashed.

As we headed to the barn where the machinery was kept, my chest convulsed with fear. There were so many ways in which this could go wrong. But it was too late to back out now, and I was running out of options.

"Do you like living out here in the country?" he asked, eyeing my outfit with a trace of amusement. "I mean, don't get me wrong, you look amazing." A slight flush to his cheeks. "But most farmers' daughters wear Hunter wellies and Barbour jackets."

"Mmmm," I said vaguely, too distracted to think of anything even close to charming.

"Living in the sticks drove me mad, personally. I need noise. People."

Was he trying to throw me off the scent?

The Arden I knew could live in solitude for years without craving conversation.

I studied him for any sudden motions, any subtle movements that looked like he might be reaching for a weapon, but despite the light sheen of sweat on his face and the flickered glances he kept throwing my way, he didn't seem to be contemplating my demise just yet.

Doubt darted across my mind, but it was soon cut short.

We came to an ancient magnolia tree, its boughs dense with white-pink flowers. Ceri stood beneath it and looked up through the snarled branches.

And then he said, "As I gazed upon the first blossom, I thought of how the world reinvents itself year after year, century after century."

Our Infinite Fates   99

My heart stopped.

The poem.

From *Ten Hundred Years of You.*

Cited perfectly.

It was him.

It *was.*

I was talking to Arden. Walking beside him, peering across at him.

"A beautiful poem," my throat scratched out.

He just smiled wistfully and kept walking.

There was so much more I wanted to ask, to say. I wanted to explain how it felt reading those words after so long wondering what he was writing about me. I wanted to sit down with him over a pot of tea and discuss every detail, every syllable, tracing the Easter eggs all the way back to our origins.

But I couldn't. Not yet. He couldn't know that I *knew* until the last possible second.

"If you could live anywhere in the world, where would you live?" I asked, heart skittering unevenly like a stone skimmed over a lake. I didn't know why the question had come to me, but it seemed a fitting gateway into the inevitable, terrible conversation.

"Hmmm," he replied, without a trace of suspicion. "I think . . . Tokyo, maybe? It seems so alive."

Another bright, sharp image: a red pagoda surrounded by candy-pink cherry blossoms, the peak of Mount Fuji arcing behind it. The sky a wan pastel lilac, streaked with indigo whorls.

As we approached the outbuildings, my whole body felt alight with foreboding. I'd once witnessed a minor tsunami in the Philippines—watched with slow horror as the sea suddenly fell away from the shore—and right now my whole existence felt suspended in that terrifying moment before the crushing impact of the wave.

"How about you?" he asked. "If you could live anywhere."

"Right here," I said at once, defiant. "I never want to leave this life."

And it was true. I had lived in a lot of amazing places, experienced a lot of Golden Ages, but something about this life had *stuck*. It was the people, of course—my sensitive, playful mum, my sharply hilarious sister, cheerful Dylan and quietly intelligent Nia and the enduring memory of my adoring father—but also the place itself. The bright smiles and tight-knit community, the pastel buildings and the kitschy tearooms, the way Beacon Books smelled first thing in the morning—of old pages and fresh ink and nutty coffee grounds.

It felt so soft, so easy. And after a lifetime of sharp edges and terrible ends, I needed all the softness I could get.

Truthfully, I could see a future for Arden and me here, if the situation were different. This . . . It was the kind of life I had dreamed about, back in the trenches.

He would be so alive on the crags and moors, the wild grassland and rugged mountains. He would return home each night flushed and happy from a day tilling the earth, dirt beneath his fingernails, a flower tucked behind his ear. And I could have my vintage boutique in town, keeping whatever erratic hours I wanted. I would travel all over the world sourcing the most unique thrifted pieces, and I would tailor and tinker with them until they were perfect. I would meet up with Nia on our lunch breaks to moan about difficult customers, and when Arden and I came back together over a glass of wine by our roaring cottage fire, we would just . . . enjoy each other. In every meaning of the word.

Such a simple thing, it would be, to bicker over what to eat for dinner. Such an ordinary pleasure so many took for granted.

All I wanted was a life with him.

All I wanted was a *life*.

Our Infinite Fates 101

And yet here I was, viciously plotting against him.

The smell of fuel was stronger in the barn, and there was the subtle bite of something metallic. Pigeons cooed in the high rafters. Though Dylan tried to keep everything tidy, the concrete floor was scattered with mice droppings, tiny white feathers, and straggles of hay.

The shovel was exactly where I'd left it, propped against the corrugated wall.

Ceri was looking around at the various tractors and combine harvesters as my hands closed around the smooth wooden handle.

While he was facing the other way, I swung at his head. Not so hard that the blunt force trauma would kill him, but enough that the flat side of the shovel would knock him clean out before he realised what was happening.

Thunk.

He fell straight to the ground.

I thought of fallen soldiers and blood-soaked trenches, discarded helmets and blank stares, and, for a moment, I felt like I might throw up.

Guilt throbbing at my temples, I dropped the shovel and grabbed him by the ankles. I had to work quickly and quietly. Dylan was still somewhere on the farm and could be back at any minute.

Putting all my worldly strength into it, I dragged Ceri's limp body back out through the open side of the barn and across a narrow walkway, nudging open the door of another outbuilding with my hip.

As I worked, something hitched in my mind. Something from the recent conversation that jutted out like a frayed piece of driftwood. But I couldn't put my finger on what, exactly, had given me pause, so I tried to shake away the disquiet.

The former stables hadn't held horses for a long time, so Dylan never went into them. Which made them the perfect place to hold Ceri until I could turn eighteen and save Gracie.

It was a chaotic and slightly ill-conceived plan, but it was the best one I had. Ceri lived alone in a serial killer's flat, and he was estranged from his family, so hopefully nobody would report him missing any time soon.

Dragging Ceri into a stall right in the middle of the building—I didn't want him to be able to pound on the corrugated metal wall and raise attention—I bound his ankles together using some rope I'd gathered earlier. Sweat slicked down my spine, and I regretted the fur coat.

I propped him against a post that held up the rafters, wrapping his arms behind it and tightly securing his wrists with another rope.

Then, for a few brief moments, I sat back on my heels and stared in horror at what I'd done. His head slumped forward, chin pressed to chest, and only the light rise and fall of his shoulders let me know he was still breathing. Blood bloomed like a rose in his light blond hair.

Despair racked me, like an old witch shaking me by the bones.

Had a hundred lifetimes of love really led us here?

Would we ever break free? Or were we just doomed to repeat this terrible cycle for the rest of time?

I wanted more. I wanted so much more.

Pain-stricken, I thought of the poem he'd quoted at me, of the final lines: *our love blossoming afresh, year after year, century after century, new flowers from old roots, an eternal seed from which life will always bloom.*

How had he made such an awful thing sound so beautiful?

Then it finally hit me, the imprecise detail I had snagged on.

Ceri had said: *As I gazed upon the first blossom.*

But that wasn't how the poem began.

It was *bramble.*

Not *blossom.*

Our Infinite Fates

The doubt rose in me afresh, but I tried to quash it as best I could. It had been decades since he'd written that line. Perhaps he'd simply misremembered.

Just as I was climbing to my feet, there was a shuffling sound behind me.

Then a throat-clearing that made every hair on my body stand on end.

I turned around.

Dylan.

Leaning against the stable door in his mucky overalls, watching my every move.

"This is a bit much, Evelyn. Even for you."

Wales

2022

Back in Siberia, snowstorms flurried in horizontal sheets. When I stood with my back to them, it felt like hurtling backwards through a tunnel—except I was standing completely still. That was how I felt now, disorientated and confused, standing still but moving so unbearably fast.

"It's you," I whispered, hoarse and suddenly weak.

Dylan bowed his head, a loose lock of dark hair dangling free of its knot, his squared-off jaw clenching fiercely. "I'm sorry."

My vision starred. "You can't be you. You're twenty. You were always two years above me in school."

He shrugged, but it was far from nonchalant. It was stiff, apologetic, self-loathing. "I skipped a few years in primary. Something about my advanced grasp of the English language, and the fact I remembered how to do long division at the age of six."

"I set so many traps," I murmured, voice distant even to my own ears. I leaned back against the wall for support, the stone cold and rough through my dress. A pigeon cooed somewhere in the rafters. "The poetry, the references to past lives. I even *called* you Arden."

His face twisted in a half smile. "Every conversation felt like Russian roulette. I haven't relaxed in two years."

"But you're . . . you're . . . Dylan is *cheerful*." My shocked brain was creating curious detachments between Arden and Dylan, as

Our Infinite Fates   105

though they were entirely different people. "He whistles along to the radio. He tells *jokes*."

Arden just smiled tightly, the upbeat facade dropped like a mask.

Dylan.

Arden was *Dylan.*

My mind scrambled to process it.

There had always been a charge between us. Childish infatuation on my part, a familiar warmth on his. The careful distance he kept was not because I was his employer's younger daughter, but because I was his fated lover—and fated prey.

It scared me how good Arden was getting at hiding beneath new identities. How able he was to slip into my life without me realising, how he had created a new persona to throw me off the scent. I hadn't figured it out in El Salvador either, yet this time . . . he had woven himself so seamlessly into my family. Flower petals pressed into the shape of a clumsy violin, wrapped in brown paper, and handed to my sister with a brotherly smile.

"I didn't plan to get so close," Arden said, staring up at the echoing rafters as though reading my thoughts. "I wanted to keep a careful distance, like I had in El Salvador. Keep you in my periphery, but not under my skin. But Gracie . . ." He trailed off, voice thick with an emotion I couldn't name. "She drew me in with her ridiculous humour. Made me perform in her cabaret shows. And before I knew it, I *cared*."

He sighed the last word like it was a terminal disease.

I ran my hands through my hair, feeling at once frantic and weak. "You do genuinely care about her?"

"Yes." The answer was quick as a whip.

"Why? I know you guard your heart against the inconvenience of loving people."

"Gracie's different." His face was etched with a pain I hadn't seen on him since Siberia. "I was hoping you'd be able to save her before . . ."

Before you die.

Before I kill you.

Suddenly, my legs couldn't bear the weight of me any longer, and I folded to the ground like a puppet cut loose of its strings. He sat down too, back against the opposite wall, several feet away from me. It should have put me at ease, but his broad physique blocked the only exit, and I knew I could never overpower him.

I was going to die.

I would never leave these stables again.

Never suck in great lungfuls of the ripe country air, never watch the sun rise over the Beacons.

Mum is buying a lasagne, the child at the heart of me wanted to scream. A tiny detail on to which my brain so willingly latched. *She's buying a lasagne for our dinner.*

You can't kill me. You can't.

The lasagne.

Strange, the things that torture you in your final moments.

I should have hated him. I should have hated the person in front of me. I should have wanted to cross the room and punch him in the face. I should have wanted to hang him from the rafters with the very rope I'd used to restrain Ceri. I should have wanted to devour the world with my rage.

But I didn't. I *ached* for him. I ached to go to him, to feel his heart beat against mine, to press my face into his neck and just sob and sob and sob.

Memories came to me as visceral images: a head on my shoulder as we lay beneath a goat-hide tent in the desert; two ravenous bodies pressed together in a steaming hammam; my jaw cupped in rough hands as I wept beside a pod of dancing whales. Battle-

Our Infinite Fates

fields and asylums, olive groves and caravels, the whole world a backdrop for our doomed love, for our infinite fates.

Sometimes it felt like I spent the first sixteen or seventeen years of every life holding Arden's existence in my chest like a precious stone, hard and heavy and glittering, only for it to burst suddenly outwards when we met again. An utter evisceration. The sun exploding, devouring the entire galaxy.

It was *Arden*. Arden was here, with me.

He had been here for years.

Watching, caring.

It made me feel vulnerable, but also comforted. I had not suffered alone.

"Are you going to kill me now?" I asked, my voice thick with emotion, dread making it impossible to swallow.

"I think I have to," he replied, a little tremulously. He rolled the bracelets up and down his wrists, his hands shaking. "There's only a week left."

"But Gracie . . . The transplant." The anger finally threatened to spill over in me, the way it had in the Viennese opera house, but I knew I had to keep him talking if I were to have any hope of walking out of these stables alive. I softened my pitch. "If you kill me now—"

"I know." His eyes fluttered shut, long lashes brushing his skin. "Fuck, I know, all right? But at least we won't be around to watch her go."

The sheer heartlessness of his statement stole the air from my lungs, and the rage became impossible to temper.

"That's possibly the worst thing you've ever said," I snapped, shaking my head in disgust.

I thought he might meet my heat with his own, but instead he looked appalled at himself. "I didn't mean—"

"My mum, Arden." I kicked at a strand of hay, wishing it were one of his ribs. "Jesus. Think of my mum." Tears sprang to my eyes unbidden. I wished I could cling to the righteous fury, but it was already ebbing into deep despair. "How will she cope with losing all of us at once?"

Arden's body had stilled, as though moving a single muscle might have betrayed some secret emotion he was trying desperately to keep buried. Somewhere in my chest I understood that he had not always been like this—that the mile-high walls round his heart were a relatively recent construct—but I couldn't think back to when he'd first started laying the foundations.

He leaned forward, resting his elbows on his bent knees. "Gracie might find another donor."

"She might not," I insisted. "She's just an innocent kid. How can you sentence her to die? Just so you can fulfil some twisted vendetta you have against me? God, I hate you."

He raised a fist and glared at the floor, as though about to punch a hole through it. "It's not just— Arghhhhh." The groan was deep enough to rumble the earth. "I would give anything in the world not to have to do this. You *know* that, Evelyn. You've seen me grapple with it life after life, death after death. Back in the trenches, you told me you trusted me. Trusted that I did this for the right reasons. Nothing has changed."

I shook my head sadly. "No. *You've* changed. Ever since Siberia. The cold killer in El Salvador . . . That wasn't you." Forcibly reining in my breathing, I added in a rush, "Look, just give me a few more days. There's still a week until we turn eighteen. Maybe I can find a way to do my part of the transplant before then. They can store the marrow until Gracie's well enough to take it."

His fist unfurled the slightest bit, and he looked up at me. The grief in his daylight-blue eyes threatened to unravel me, and sud-

Our Infinite Fates

denly I could not remember how that handsome face looked when it smiled. "How are you going to do that?"

"I don't know," I admitted. "But I have to try."

Maybe it was impossible. The health service worked in mysterious and rigid ways. Where would I even begin? How could I justify my burning need to have my marrow extracted this week? Perhaps I could find a way to have it done privately, but again, what excuse would a medical professional accept for the absurd rush?

Once I got out of these stables, I could think of a plan.

First I had to get Arden to agree. He'd spent two whole years weaving himself into my family, braiding himself into our traditions and rituals, stitching laughter and bear hugs into our most intimate moments. That had to count for something.

The chink in his armour was there. I just had to drive the spear in.

"Arden, you've seen me grieve a hundred family members. You've seen how it destroys me. You've held me as I sobbed like a child over fathers and mothers and brothers and sisters. You've seen me hollowed out and weak from loss after loss after loss." I swallowed down the lump in my throat. "I know you don't let yourself get so close to people any more—self-preservation, and I get it—but I'm not like that. I can't do it. I would walk to the ends of the earth to save Gracie. So help me do that. For all the past versions of us. For all the times you stroked my hair and told me you *understood*."

For a second he looked like he was about to concede: a subtle nod, a slight easing of the tension across his shoulders. Then he shook his head almost frantically, as though trying to usher away an intrusive thought.

"Why not?" I urged, desperation clawing at me like a rabid animal. "You said yourself, you adore the bones of Gracie. Why wouldn't you let me try and save her?"

A heavy moment, followed by a pained whisper. "Because you might run."

I crossed my arms. "I won't run."

"It wouldn't be the first time."

He had a point. I thought of the mountain cave in Portugal, of how sure I had been that Arden wouldn't find me. Of how the tether had led them to me anyway.

"You have my word that I won't run." My pulse was high and thin in my temples. "I'll let you kill me when the time comes."

He laughed bitterly. "With absolutely no due respect, I do not believe you."

"So don't leave my side. Ever." I slid over to him on hands and knees, shuffling over hay and concrete, resisting the urge to grab his ankles and beg. "Stay in the bookshop while I work. I'll spend my days off on the farm with you. Apart from when I have to go to the hospital, but you can come with me. I'll never leave your side. There won't be a chance for me to run."

He laid his head back against the wall, the muscles in his jaw flickering, clenching. "What about at night?"

"We'll tell my mum we're seeing each other. She's pretty lax, so she'll probably let me stay in the cottage with you. Tie me to the bed before you go to sleep, if you have to."

Running wilderness-rough hands over his exhausted face, he finally said, "Okay."

"Okay?" I repeated, disbelieving.

His hands dropped, and he fixed his gaze on me. "Six days."

"And on the seventh, we die." I swallowed hard. It never got any easier, the knowledge of impending demise. "Whether I save Gracie or not."

Nodding, he whispered, "It's the way it has to be."

It was a terrible deal, but it was the only one I had.

Austria-Hungary

1898

The opera was reaching a crescendo, and I couldn't hear a single note.

Still, it was enough just to be there, the opera house packed to the rafters, the rich current of electricity in the air, the warm bodies in their best gowns, the noiseless thrum of it all.

Mutter nudged at my shoulder, and when I turned to face her, she mouthed, *Excuse me, Tobias, can you let me out? I need the bathroom. Danke.*

Leaving the show during such a climactic moment would've been a criminal act for anyone else, but we'd been here every night for a month—my father was the star of the show.

No sooner had Mutter left the back row than an unfamiliar body slid into the seat beside me. There was a subtle ripple in the atmosphere, a shift in the heat of the air, as I turned to face him.

His eyes were a murky hazel, his features narrow and pointed, and ash-blond curls fell around his face in waves. He wore a navy sack coat with a matching waistcoat, a high-collared white shirt, and a tall top hat. Resting beside him on the velvet seat was an ornate wooden cane topped with gold. His right foot bent inward at a harsh angle, the muscles on the leg severely atrophied.

112   ✳ **Laura Steven** ✳

"Are you enjoying the music?" he asked inanely. As I read his lips, I picked up that the German was accented; he was Hungarian, perhaps, or Bohemian. I'd become proficient at lipreading over the roar of the machinery in the cotton mills of Girangaon, and it served me well now.

"No," I said flatly, watching his face. "I'm profoundly deaf. The shapes made by their mouths look lovely, though."

A flash of awkwardness slid across his face. "Ah."

"It's fine." I gestured down to my own sharply cut tuxedo; the winged shirt collar and neatly pressed red pocket square, the careful embroidery of a silver dove I'd stitched around the breast pocket. "I'm here for the fashion."

In all my lives, I'd been poor more often than I'd been wealthy. Needless to say, I far preferred the latter, not just because I loathed being cold or hungry or vulnerable, but also because money could buy *clothes*. Fin de siècle Vienna was particularly perfect for me, because my mother was an esteemed costumier on the operatic scene, having trained at the Académie de l'Opéra National de Paris before moving to Austria-Hungary with my father. She was now a revered pioneer of the women's fashion revolution, eschewing wasp-waisted dresses in lieu of more comfortable—but still beautiful—cuts.

Even though fashion was considered a peculiar fascination for a young boy, I'd been following my mother around since I was twelve, pins pressed between my teeth and sweat on my brow as I lifted heavy underskirts backstage, loving every moment of my apprenticeship. Mutter always said the atmosphere was pure chaos, but since my own world was entirely quiet I could disappear into the beads and boning, the luxurious fabrics and intricate embroidery, the glittering jewels and dramatic waistcoats, the sharp tailoring and silky bolts of crêpe de Chine.

"How did you get tickets?" I asked the boy I assumed to be

Our Infinite Fates 113

Arden. The production of *Der Ring des Nibelungen* had been sold out for months.

He grimaced. "My father. He's a decorated hussar in the Honvéd. And by *decorated,* I mean he committed horrific atrocities in Bosnia and Herzegovina and they love him for it."

A kind of pacifistic despair bolted through my chest. "The bloodlust never stops being celebrated, does it?"

"Stimmt. He wanted me to follow in his footsteps and has spent my whole life bitter that I'm . . ." He gestured to his cane, and the atrophied leg beside it. "Part of me is glad I won't live past eighteen. I can't take his resentment much longer."

"How lovely that you're so well-adjusted to death and murder," I snapped, and a heavy-browed woman in a pink blancmange dress glared at me from along the row. Lowering my pitch, I added, "I, for one, will miss this life. The future I could've had in it."

"It does suit you." He looked me up and down, from the Maison Spitzer topcoat to my deeply polished shoes.

"Vielen Dank," I muttered, the words dripping with sarcasm.

"What's your name? Your here name, I mean."

"Tobias. You?"

"Ferenc." Studying me intently, he quirked his thin, purplish lips. "Which you feels the most like you?"

The question caught me off guard. "What do you mean?"

"Girl? Boy?" There was something hawklike in the search of his eyes. "There's a German activist, Ulrichs, who talks of a third gender, though he seems to use the notion purely to explain men who love men."

I leaned back in my seat. It was something I'd given great thought to over the centuries, while navigating ever-shifting and perpetually confusing gender norms, but I didn't quite know how to articulate it.

"I don't feel like any of them," I said slowly. "I don't feel, in my heart, that I'm a boy. But neither do I feel like I am inherently a girl. My soul isn't rooted to any of them. I'm just me. No particular body feels more 'right' than the other, nor more wrong. They're just vessels. And with you . . . it doesn't matter to me how you look, what form you take." I tapped the top of his cane. "You're just you."

It was true. Even though he was here to kill me, my heart burned for him. I wanted to nestle my face into his neck, to breathe in the papery-soft skin there. I wanted to talk, to touch, to share. To revel in the only soul on earth that truly understood me. I wanted time—which, for an immortal soul, was a curious thing to be lacking.

We had been so in love, in our previous life. We'd worked in the cotton mills of Bombay, whispering sweet nothings in earthen Marathi as we walked back to our chawls each night. We had grown up side by side, Arden a long-haired girl with a fiery temper, me a scrawny-limbed boy with bad lungs. We had shared every meaningful moment of our lives, from early childhood to adolescent rebellion.

On the night she'd killed me, rage against the abominable British had simmered in every cracked pavement, in every muttered conversation held beneath the roar of machinery. Fat chimneys jutted into the lilac sky, chuffing out a thick smoke that smudged the dusty night around us. The whole of Girangaon's factory district was fragrant with the scent of pav bhaji. The day before our eighteenth birthday, the streets were being set up for Sharad Navratri, and a gaggle of traveling dancers had practiced their tamasha beside us.

As Arden withdrew the inevitable knife, her final words had been: "Until we meet again, my love."

But here in the Viennese opera house, Arden's reappearance

Our Infinite Fates

didn't feel like love. It felt like a cruelty, a farce, a writhing pit of frustration from which I longed to clamber free.

Arden visibly mulled over the idea that I felt no connection to a physical vessel. "You really don't have a preference?"

"No," I said, clipped. "Do you?"

He removed his hat and peered into the bottom as though about to pull out a white rabbit. "I think I prefer being a boy, but I couldn't say why, exactly. It almost defies language, the way it's impossible to describe the exact taste of a strawberry." Then he said something else, but his face was tilted too far around for me to lip-read.

Glancing up, I noticed my mother returning from the bathroom, her pearl-beaded periwinkle gown sliding along the parquet floor. A cord of grief yanked through me, letting loose a furious geyser of anger. Anger at the situation, at Arden, at what was soon to happen. What *always* happened, no matter what I did, no matter how far and fast I ran.

"You're procrastinating," I muttered, with a sudden leap of panic. I didn't want my mother to see this.

He shrugged, replacing his hat atop perfect pale curls. "There's no particular urgency to proceedings. We don't turn eighteen for another three months."

"So would you like to spend that time falling in love, only to destroy me anyway?" I asked, heat rising in my belly. "Or shall we get it over with now?"

"Evelyn—"

"Nein. Do you even care what you take from me over and over and over again?" My mother was almost at the end of the row. I shot her a final look of love: a goodbye, and a thank-you, and an apology. The air in the opera house was pulled taut by my father's denouement. "I've always believed our souls find each other, somehow, but that was wrong. You don't have a soul."

Emotion twitched at his jaw. "You don't know what you're say—"

"Oh, verpiss dich."

I pulled out the gold pistol tucked in my breast pocket and shot Ferenc neatly in the head.

Wales

2022

In the stables where Arden and I had made our deal, there was a muffled groan a few feet away, and my attention snapped to the body slumped in the corner.

The body starting to shift sluggishly.

The innocent body I had knocked unconscious and hauled here like an animal.

"Shit," I muttered, dropping my head into my hands. "It wasn't Ceri. What have I done?"

Arden climbed to his feet, dusting off his trousers. "Not your finest hour."

"What am I going to do?" I raked my fingers through my hair.

"What had you planned to do?"

I bit my lip. "Leave him tied here until I could save Gracie."

Arden nodded sagely, leaning casually against the doorframe, as though we had not just been discussing the finer details of mutually assured destruction. "A very sane course of action. It's a real shame that lobotomy in Vermont didn't take."

Ceri groaned again, blond eyelashes fluttering against his cheeks.

"So leave him tied here regardless," Arden said. "We can free him before we . . . you know."

"Perish. Yes." I stood up and began pacing the hay-strewn floor. "Not exactly ethical, though, is it?"

"I think perhaps that line has already been crossed. Danced over, even. A veritable foxtrot over the boundaries of morality."

This was an utter disaster. "I suppose I can't let him go. He'll tell the police and we'll get arrested."

"We?" Arden looked affronted. "I haven't touched the chap."

Chap. In an instant, I was back in horse-drawn London, begging the baker to employ me—for the heat, and for the bread, and so that my family would not starve. I loved it when slivers of bygone eras slipped into Arden's speech. He collected words and slang expressions like shells on a beach, cockles and conches and cantharus, and brought them out to admire when I least expected it. Back in the trenches, he'd told me he'd have given anything to *snerdle*—to curl up beneath a cosy blanket and while away the day.

Arden frowned, chewing at a hardened straggle of skin beside his thumbnail. His hands had stopped shaking now that he knew he had a little more time before death. "Could you blackmail Ceri into not going to the police?"

I ran this idea over in my mind, but it was like trying to feed yarn onto a wheel spinning far too quickly. "I don't know enough about him to do that. Only that his parents don't know where he is . . . But threatening to tell them might not be enough to keep him silent. Or they might find him anyway, and our leverage is gone."

"Trust me, my parents don't care enough to find me."

The voice came from the floor.

Ceri was awake.

Cautiously I turned to face him. "Ceri. Ceri, I'm so sorry. I'm so sorry about this."

His head bobbed heavily on his neck. "Not sorry enough to *not* blackmail me. Did that sentence make sense? God, I'm dizzy."

Our Infinite Fates   119

"Are you hurt?"

"You cracked me around the head with a shovel. Of course I'm hurt." A weak, lopsided smile. "But I promise not to tell anyone if you let me go. Please. I don't want any part of this."

A kind of erratic laughter bolted up my throat. I felt like a hit-man who'd taken hostages, like a pantomime criminal. "There's no way you're not going to tell the police about this." I bowed my head in apology. "Case of mistaken identity, by the way."

Ceri nodded, but it was more of a loll. "I heard enough of your conversation to deduce as much, but I can't say it made any sense." Adjusting himself on the floor with a badly disguised grimace, he added, "Honestly, I wouldn't go to the police. You have my word. But I am in quite a lot of pain, and I can't see too well. I think I need medical attention."

My will faltered.

Arden spotted the subtle guilty twist of my face and shook his head. "Evelyn—"

"Evelyn?" Ceri asked in confusion.

"Branwen," Arden corrected. "It's not worth the risk. You have to keep him here."

Ceri looked from me to Arden, then back to me. I couldn't parse his expression at all; it was oddly vacant and dreamy. "Someone will find me. I can shout pretty loudly."

"You're just asking to be gagged at this point," said Arden.

Ceri winced as his shoulders strained against his bonds. He looked up at me intently. "Please. I just want to forget this ever happened." Another groan. "God, my *head*."

I tried to weigh my options, but my mind was a helter-skelter, a beehive, a pit of snakes. The confrontation with Arden had left me wrung out and freshly devastated, not to mention anxious about how exactly I was going to save Gracie. There was no brain space left to deal with accidental captives.

120 ✳ Laura Steven ✳

Leaving Ceri here did seem like the easiest solution, but shame pulsed through me at the thought.

And yet Arden was right. If Ceri went to the police, I wouldn't be able to save Gracie. I couldn't organise an earlier bone marrow transplant from a cell.

But maybe I wouldn't need to. If we were taken into custody, Arden and I would be separated. Then he wouldn't be able to kill me in the next seven days. I would live past my birthday, and surely I could have the bone marrow transplant performed in jail. Surely there were allowances that could be made.

Had what I'd done been bad enough to justify imprisonment? Possibly not. Even if I was charged, I'd almost certainly be granted bail. My safety from Arden was not guaranteed in the least.

In any case, letting Ceri go felt like the best course of action. After so many lives on the wrong side of the law, the police didn't scare me. Cell or no cell, bail or no bail, there would still be a chance of saving my sister's life—without leaving an innocent boy bound and gagged in a crypt-cold stable.

I stepped forward, eyes fixed on Ceri's bonds, but Arden stepped forward too.

"You can't let him go." His voice was soft but firm. "I'm sorry. If we end up arrested and separated, I won't be able to get to you before we turn eighteen. And we can't turn eighteen. We *can't*."

Ceri's gaze flicked once again between me and the farmhand he'd never met before. "Very weird energy in here."

I crouched to the ground, about to untie him. "It's just cruel to leave him here when he's innocent."

Arden laid an insistent palm on my shoulder, tugging me ever so slightly back. I knew he could do it harder if he needed to. If he needed to physically stop me, he could.

It was times like this I hated having been spawned as a girl. I missed the casual bulk of myself in France, the way I could protect

Our Infinite Fates

myself and my sisters, even if it had led me to the trenches. There was a certain ease to a male body, an innate safety I never took for granted.

"You were willing to leave Ceri here in order to save Gracie before," Arden said. "The stakes haven't changed."

I rolled back onto my heels. "So you're saying you'll kill me now if I let him go."

Self-loathing snapped across Arden's weary face. "I'm sorry. It's the way it has to be."

Coldness spread through my chest like a wave. "Do you even have a weapon?"

He patted a knife-shaped bulge in his front jeans pocket.

Ceri's eyes widened. "So you're threatening to *murder* her now?"

Arden's gaze snapped to Ceri. "Oh, it's not a threat. I am going to murder her."

I knew the forceful thrust of his voice was intended to scare Ceri, not me, but it still had that effect anyway.

It wasn't the killing itself that frightened me. Pain in and of itself was not the root of the deep, lurching fear in my stomach. It was the astonishing weight of *never,* so devastatingly absolute, so impenetrably permanent. I would never laugh with Gracie again, never have a cup of tea with my sweet mum. Sure, I could come back for them in a future life, but that had worked out so horribly in Vardø. I would not be who I once was to them.

That *never* was hurtling toward me like a train.

Ceri looked at me in astonishment, but his dim gaze was unfocused. "And you're fine with this. It's like . . . just a fun little . . . deal you've made." His words were effortful, breathless.

"I've murdered him plenty in return," I said, pulse hammering against my temples. "It evens out."

Letting his chin drop to his chest, Ceri grunted. "I . . . definitely have a concussion. I . . . do not feel good."

Speech slurring drowsily, his head swung like a pendulum. The blood in his blond hair had dried into a brown crust, but I wondered how much damage I'd done internally.

Was his brain swelling against his skull as we spoke?

Despite his estrangement from his family, Ceri had people who cared about him. He was a son, a grandson, a brother, a friend. Sure, he was also a person in his own right, but a thousand years in this world had taught me that we only truly exist in relation to the ones we love.

If I kept him from medical attention and the worst happened, there were people who would mourn him long after Arden and I were gone.

"I'm letting him go." The decision struck me sharp and sudden as a stab wound.

Arden took two steps toward me. "Don't, Evelyn. Don't let it end like this. I'll kill you before you can save your sister. It's more important to save Gracie than this guy."

"I'd quite like to save both, actually." My voice was a hot snap, my stomach clenched into a fist.

I untied Ceri's ropes.

Would calling Arden's bluff work? Or was I about to feel a knife in my back?

I'm sorry, I murmured inwardly to Gracie. *I'm so sorry if this doesn't work.*

The skin on Ceri's wrists was pale and soft beneath my fingers, his green veins leaping against my touch.

I could practically hear Arden's mental indecision behind me. A shifting of his weight, a heaviness to his breathing.

But no knife.

No death.

The ropes fell to the ground, but Ceri didn't move immediately. Fear spiked through my heart—was he already beyond help? After

Our Infinite Fates 123

several agonising beats, he finally brought his hands to his lap, the movements slow and clumsy.

"Thank you," he murmured, eyes fluttering open, then closed, as though the tide of sleep was pulling him under.

"Listen, Ceri." I cupped his face and pulled it up to look at me. "Can you listen to me?" He nodded, stubbled jaw grazing my palm, but his eyes did not reopen. "We can take you to the hospital, but you can't go to the police. Because Dylan will kill me if you do. The second we hear sirens, there will be a knife in my chest. Do you understand? I will get my comeuppance soon enough. I really will." I swallowed hard, the brief image of my mum and Gracie at my wake so devastating it stole the breath from my lungs. "Do you promise me?"

He nodded again, a lolling swoop like a kestrel diving toward prey.

I looked up at Arden. His face was etched with anger, a kind of anguished self-loathing that he hadn't been able to do what he'd threatened to. "Let's get him to the hospital."

As we piled Ceri into the back of the pickup truck, my blood thrummed with the small victory. I had called Arden's bluff, and I had won. He hadn't killed me the second I'd loosened Ceri's ropes. Which meant there had to be hope that he would let me live past eighteen.

He'd changed his mind once before, in the silver-cold of darkest Siberia.

I could get him to change it again.

My hand went to the folded square paper in my pocket.

I still believe.

United States of America

1862

Through the small, high window on the asylum wall, Vermont was a single square.

It was an insult, the beauty of it—the bonfire of autumn leaves in red and orange and brown, the yellow-bellied goldfinches bright against the clean blue sky. A postage stamp of exaggerated color against the peeling wallpaper, once a calming pale green but long since faded to gray. The pipes snaking along the bottom rusted raw, dripping a metallic grunge onto the tiled floor.

And still the birds sang.

As with so many such institutions, Allum had started off admirably enough. A place to heal, to repose, to make new. Burgeoning philosophies and morally sound treatments. Reading, painting, writing, walking, prayer. A grand turreted building surrounded by landscaped gardens and sprawling woods, with a close central core and long annexed wings, giving patients privacy and comfort, sunlight and fresh air.

Like houseplants in straitjackets. Insanity, domesticated.

Things had taken a sharp downturn when the pharmaceutical company had opened its lab in the northern wing. They trotted

Our Infinite Fates

out experimental drugs like a baker tossing half-proved buns in the oven, as though failure would mean nothing more than wasted flour. Patients' lives were worth even less than that.

Once Allum's founders realized the money that could be made on their cattle, the asylum quickly became an abattoir. It hired less and less qualified staff, who employed brute force in lieu of true medical expertise. It fell victim to chronic overcrowding—naked, unwashed patients stuffed into every corner of every room, the corridors lined with cages when the wards could take no more frantic bodies.

It was in two of these cages that Arden and I lay, side by side yet separated by bars, in the hallway with a single postage-stamp window.

Here we were both girls of seventeen—she Augusta and I Harriet—pale and bony from malnourishment and various other maladies.

I'd been admitted for mania a year prior, after an off-duty "physician" had heard me confronting Augusta on the street. Apparently, wailing about a supernatural curse and immortal murders and the semi-conviction that you are a ghost does not a sane person make. Augusta, realizing that I was shut away out of her reach, had had herself committed a month later for melancholia—a common affliction of poets.

Mania and Melancholia fast became our morbid pet names for each other.

Yet it did not take long for Augusta to regret her choice to follow me here.

At first it wasn't so bad. We were in cages, yes, but in our own clothes, no matter how crusted with filth. A small retention of our personhood. Our fingers could lace together through the bars, and we could talk freely into the night, for everyone already thought us insane. We were fed twice a day, offered counseling from a young, wiry-haired doctor who was vastly out of his depth.

But then the alternative therapies began.

The ice baths from which we never truly warmed up. The rotational therapy, in which we were strapped to a chair suspended from the ceiling and spun around over a hundred times in a single minute. The starvation, not necessarily through barbarism but through negligence and disorganization. A cold hunger that burrowed into the bones of us.

No reading, painting, writing, walking. No privacy or comfort. A reality that felt beyond even prayer.

It was no wonder Augusta decided to put us out of our misery early.

She'd been led away for her ice bath one day when, several minutes later, her nude figure came sprinting back down the corridor toward my cage. Dark hair in a knotted braid that bounced against her hollow chest, ribs visible between the smallest of peaks. A thick snare of pubic hair, her legs bowed and angular. Eyes lupine, feral.

A sharp medical instrument in her outstretched hand.

When the orderlies caught up with her, she was only inches away from plunging it into my throat.

I was sorry she had failed.

She was packed into a starched white straitjacket, then chained upright to one of the cage's vertical bars so that her spine was flush against it. She slammed her head back against the steel until she lost consciousness—just so she wouldn't have to look me in the eye.

A few days later, the researcher from the pharmaceutical lab called her name. I watched an orderly take her away, thrashing

Our Infinite Fates

127

like she was being led to the gallows, all the way to the northern wing.

She came back a few hours later, but she never *truly* came back.

I didn't know what was worse: watching her struggle, or the moment she stopped. Her ferocious eyes glazed and vacant from whatever experimental drug they'd pumped into her.

Was she still in there? If so, for how much longer?

As gut-wrenchingly terrible as it was to see her like that, the hopeful heart of me began to see the situation for what it was.

If I could escape, I would not just be free of Allum. I would be free of Arden.

The thought was a yellow-bellied goldfinch against a clean blue sky.

And so I studied every single doctor, nurse, and orderly for weeks, drawing spirographs in my mind of their movements. Who does what, when and where and why? How might I slip through the blank spaces of that pattern?

Stealing the key to my cage was not too difficult. Pickpocketing on the streets of Shanghai had been only two lives ago, and my fingers remembered the deft sleight of hand, the feather touch, the art of distraction. The fact that seduction was the most powerful weapon in my arsenal.

One of the orderlies had a reputation for romancing the patients—something about the power dynamic was innately appealing to him. He was a slippery man, with too-light footsteps and a sharp gaze, a high forehead and a narrow chin. But he also had keys, and he patrolled the corridors around midnight every night. The first curve of the spirograph.

"Howard," I whispered through the bars as he passed my cage one night, when half the asylum was asleep and the other half howled like a pack of werewolves.

His pale eyes snapped toward me. "Yes?"

"I heard what you did with Minnie." I smiled coyly, so dripping with syrup I thought he was bound to see through it. "Made me jealous."

Something lit up on his face, but it only made him look more sinister, somehow. Like a candle held to a chin, casting strange shadows on the peaks and valleys of his features.

His polished black heels swiveled on the tiles, and he slipped softly over to my cage. I was sitting on the floor with my legs tucked to my chest, looking up at him through my eyelashes. He stooped to one knee, his joints clicking as he did so, and murmured, "And why is that?"

I ran my tongue around the inside of my cheek. There was a hole in my upper right gum where the doctors had recently pulled a rotten tooth—without morphine, without any numbing at all. I'd tried to climb up from the chair halfway through, and one of the orderlies had given me a black eye.

"I think you know why." My voice was a purr, thick and feline, intoxicating as incense smoke. I tried to ignore the sour reek of my own breath.

I crawled on hands and knees toward the place where he knelt, playing up the helpless prisoner angle. Sure enough, the very tip of his tongue brushed the corner of his lips, and I knew I had him.

My stomach turned as I reached out a filthy hand and stroked his cheek, tracing a fingertip down the dull ridge of his jaw. He'd been trying to grow a beard, but there were large patches with no hair at all. There was a brownish hot-pot stain on his chin.

At the same time as the sickening caress, my other hand was at his waist, working free the loop of keys from his belt. He did not notice the latter.

"Do you want me?" he asked, reaching a hand through the cage

Our Infinite Fates 129

and cupping my breast. At his touch, my insides lurched with disgust, and I forced myself to imagine how it would feel to run gaily through those burnished bonfire woods.

The loop finally slipped from his waistband, tucking itself silently into my palm.

An oozing pipe dripped rusted orange onto the floor behind me.

"Tomorrow," I whispered, grabbing at his crotch just hard enough to hurt. He recoiled, but only slightly. The rest of his body pressed right up against the bars. "After my bath. Come and find me then. I want to be clean for you."

"What if I like you dirty?"

God, I hoped Arden was too comatose to witness this.

"Tomorrow," I said again, and then I pulled myself back to the corner of my cage.

After a long, lecherous stare, Howard got to his feet, adjusted the rigid bulge in his pants, and resumed his patrol.

The keys were warm in my palm.

The danger of assuming someone is insane is that you also assume they cannot outsmart you.

The next spirograph curve bent at around six in the morning, when Howard was doing the shift changeover with Bessie, who was sufficiently hard of hearing not to hear the rattling of a key in a locked cage. She was a lumbering woman, not too bright, but with a casual cruelty that cracked like a whip whenever she was in a bad mood—which was often.

I hoped she and Howard would be punished for allowing me to escape.

As the patients' werewolf howls dimmed at dawn, I made my move. It took a few tries to find the right key on the densely packed loop, but when the padlock finally sighed open, a sharp thrill bolted through me. I slipped out of the cage barefoot, scarcely able to believe my fortune.

130   ✳ Laura Steven ✳

Clarence watched me blankly from the cage on my other side. He'd been dosed with a different drug than Augusta, but the effect was largely the same. Less drool, but nothing behind the eyes. Guilt cramped in me.

Was I a monster for leaving them here?

I would make it right, I vowed to myself. If I lived the full life I'd always dreamed of, I would dedicate it to eradicating these vile places altogether. I didn't have Arden's gift for the written word, but I would bang down the door of every journalist who would listen until one agreed to expose this horror for what it was.

In a last-minute fit of shame, I tossed the loop of keys to Clarence's feet. He eyed them with vague interest but didn't move to pick them up. Despair mounted in my chest, but what could I do? I couldn't force the will to escape into someone.

Footsteps clacked near the end of the hallway. I had to move.

I could not look back at Augusta's limp frame. The patch of drool on her redundant straitjacket. The vomit tangled in the dark mass of her hair.

With a final apologetic glance at Clarence, I turned in the opposite direction and tiptoed as silently as I could past the ward, past the nurse's office, past some of the optimistic private bedrooms that had been first built into Allum's sunny outlook.

The northern wing was almost deserted. The laboratory technicians went home every night, to warm beds and home-cooked dinners and families who loved them despite their cruel experiments. I tucked myself into a small alcove between doorways and waited.

The final spirograph curve: the groundskeeper's predictable movements.

From being led to and from my "treatments," I knew there was a door leading to the landscaped gardens in the seam between the

Our Infinite Fates

northern and western wings. Every morning the groundskeeper would unlock it, prop it open with two plant pots to breathe fresh air through the staleness, then head to the staffroom to make a cup of coffee before beginning his duties. Once he started work, the gap in the pattern disappeared. Medical staff, gardeners, pharmaceutical bigwigs, and cleaners roamed the wings—and thus blocked off the open door. But as the kettle boiled, there was the smallest of windows in which escape was possible.

Sure enough, the groundskeeper arrived around seven, whistling in his grubby overalls. He was a jolly-faced man, ruddy and bright-eyed, with grassy hair on his forearms like molasses. He never met anyone's stare when he was inside the building, as though avoiding a gaze meant avoiding complicity. *If I can't see the atrocity, the atrocity can't see me, and I don't have to do anything about it.*

The door was propped open. The kettle began to whistle on a distant stove.

And I ran.

The dewy grass was a gasping shock on the filthy soles of my feet.

The air was almost too pure, too rich, and my lungs choked on it.

As I sprinted on weak, wobbly legs, I expected a chorus of yells from behind me, a slew of orderlies ready to tackle me to the ground.

None came.

I reached the woods, panting, and sank to my knees. Exhaustion, disbelief.

I grabbed big fistfuls of crimson leaves, traced fingertips over their ridged veins, held them up to my face, and breathed in the earthy tang of them, as though they would cleanse me of Howard's touch. I looked up to the canopy, to the abstract curls of sky between the towering branches, hoping to spot a yellow-bellied goldfinch.

I was free.

Not just from the asylum, but from Arden. From our twisted fate.

I had lost track of time in recent months, maybe years, but I was certain our eighteenth birthdays would soon be upon us. Yet there was no way Augusta would be able to escape that straitjacket, that cage, that medicated stupor, that grotesque abattoir.

Her ferocious eyes, glazed and vacant.

Freedom sprawled out in front of me like a prairie, and I kept waiting for the euphoria to sink in, for the crisp air and the sharp light to breathe life into me, yet everything about it felt wrong.

I have to go back for her.

The thought came to me diamond-bright, but I shook it away.

No. I had waited countless lives for an opportunity like this. I *would* go back for Arden, but after I turned eighteen, after the curse had been broken. I would go back with police and journalists and politicians, kicking down the gates of this cruel world.

But what if Augusta didn't survive that long?

What if I was too late to save her?

Worse, what if she survived, but was forever changed? Empty? What if she was reduced to a patch of drool on a sad shirt collar, to soiled underwear and empty stares?

Would I ever find another love like Arden's again? Or would I spend the rest of my days with a gaping hole in my chest?

How would the rest of my days even *look*? I had no family in this life save for the grim-faced uncle who'd taken me in when my parents died of influenza. My vague smattering of friends had disowned me when I was admitted to Allum. I had no money, no

Our Infinite Fates 133

education, no prospects. And without Arden, the promise of life felt hollow.

It wasn't just that I wanted a future. It was that I wanted a future with *them*. I wanted——

A vision came to me, so stark and raw that it hit me high in the stomach.

A world of white bone and falling ash, of pleading and begging so animalistic I couldn't tell where it came from. Pain so large it took on a form of its own. Pain so absolute it was like the darkest pitch of night, like a black hole in the universe.

Arden, weeping—only, they were not Arden; they were a spectral smudge, a vague outline.

"I told you," they whispered, voice hollow and ringing like the inside of a church bell. "I told you it would ruin us."

Understanding briefly arranged itself in my chest, dust motes gathering into an approximate shape, but as a bird sang in the trees above me, the vision dissipated, leaving only a directionless dread in its shadow.

Come back, come back, I begged the vision, because, as horrifying as it was, it was the first real insight I'd had for decades, centuries. A crucial puzzle piece in the *why* of my existence had sputtered out, leaving only the lingering scent of smoke in its stead. I dug my hands into the forest floor, feeling the cold, wet dirt wedge itself under the ragged crescents of my nails.

What does it mean, what does it mean, what——

Sunlight dappled through the canopy, and my heart scudded and flipped.

As soon as the bone-white world had evaporated, that sense of almost-understanding had vanished too. But some part of me knew that even if I left Arden in Allum, there would be no future. There would be only . . .

Ruination. That was how the vision had felt. Like utter ruination.

Arden was doing this for a reason. And that reason was to protect us.

My bones knew it. My blood, my guts, my soul. It was written in the very fabric of myself.

With a final shuddering breath, I turned and ran back in the direction of the asylum.

my heart is a haunted house
surrounded by a moat of my own digging,
kept empty of warmth so that I will not miss it come
    winter.

skin hunger; the feeling that if you do not touch
another human soon you will lose your mind.
it hurts, the absence of it, but less so when you have only
    ever been cold.

and then, in you come.
throwing open the windows, sweeping ash from the hearth
so that you might light a new fire.

and my skin sings for you, my bones ache for you,
but the ghosts stalking the hallways tell me
that we will not leave this place alive.

—AUTHOR UNKNOWN

Wales

2022

Ceri played along when we told doctors he'd fallen badly onto some farm equipment—though perhaps only because staying conscious required all his energy. After he was discharged with some sturdy painkillers and strict instructions to rest, Arden and I drove back to the farm in stilted silence.

I was driving next to Arden.

To anyone else, a moment of astounding normality. The dark hum of the road, paper coffee cups between us, some nameless pop song on the radio. His coat blanketing my shoulders, since the hospital waiting room had been far too cold. A low thrum between us, vibrating in the places our skin could've touched and didn't. The blare of headlights, the sprinkle of stars, the bump of cat's eyes beneath tyres.

Astounding normality—but with *Arden*.

We were together again.

The things I could say. The things I could do. I could reach out and touch his body, fingertips tracing over the rugged bridge of his knuckles. I could tell him that he was, in all meaningful ways, my home. I could reminisce about lives and experiences I'd had to keep buried until now: the salt-and-smoke scent of the Algerian streets, the dystopian beauty of coral-sharded Nauru, the existential despair of the Western Front. All the things we had shared,

Our Infinite Fates   137

survived. The great tapestry of our love, and the new beadwork it had gained.

But I didn't, because something had changed. Here he was not the snow-softened boy from the frozen taiga. He was still the cold-faced killer from El Salvador.

And I had no idea how to bring Arden back. Bring *us* back, quickly and deeply enough to make him want to keep me alive.

For now, it had to be enough just to exist together, suspended in amber, a brief but interminable peace.

Six days. No matter what, we had these six days. Hardly an infinity, and yet infinite nonetheless—in possibility and in raw potential.

Mum was heating the oven for the lasagne when I walked back into the kitchen, leaving Arden standing in the hallway.

"Hi, love," she said. "How was your date?"

"Oh, it was all right. But, erm . . . I actually have something to tell you." I leaned on the island with my elbows, clasping my hands together to stop them from shaking.

She stilled a little, clutching a bag of salad leaves. "Oh?"

"I really hope you won't be upset."

I was still wearing Dylan's fleece-lined lumberjack coat—a vial of sugar water tucked in the top pocket, in case he needed to save any wounded bumblebees—but she didn't seem to notice the red plaid.

"Great start, Bran." Her shoulders slumped in frustration. "Go on, then. What did you pierce? I do hope it's not your nipples, because honestly, if and when you get pregnant, they'll—"

"It's Dylan," I interrupted, before I could talk myself out of it. "We've been seeing each other. In secret. And, erm, we've been in love for a while now." An understatement. "We're actually the same age, since he skipped a few years in school, and—"

"Bran!" She swivelled on her heel, a beam spreading across her face. She brandished a garlic baguette like a cutlass. "I think that's bloody brilliant."

I blinked in disbelief. "Really?"

"Of course!" She tossed the baguette and the salad bag onto the counter. "I trust Dylan, and I trust you." She cupped her hands to her suddenly rosy cheeks. "Oh, it's so lovely. You and Dylan!"

"I'm so glad you think so." Guilt cut through me. I hadn't been expecting so much unbridled joy on the back of a lie—although I supposed the foundations of it were true enough. Love didn't even begin to encapsulate what I felt for Arden. I just wished it were as straightforward as she believed it to be.

"I've needed some good news this week." She sighed happily, leaning back against the white edge of the sink. "This has really brightened my spirits. Where is he? I want to give him a big old hug, I do."

"Just outside." I jerked my head toward the double doors. "With his ear pressed against the keyhole, no doubt."

"Dylan, you big idiot!" Mum called, her accent broad and swooping. "Come in here."

Dylan—Arden—peeled open the door, and from the bashful look on his face, he'd heard everything. Judging by the way he couldn't meet my eye, he felt as terrible as I did for the mistruth we'd told my mother.

Mum crossed over to him and threw her arms around his neck, despite the fact he was a good ten inches taller than her. He rested his chin on her head in a way that was so subtly affectionate it made my chest ache.

"Don't break her heart, all right?" Mum said, voice muffled in his woollen jumper.

"Wouldn't dream of it," he replied roughly, a thousand emotions pulsing beneath the words.

Everything in me hurt.

Our Infinite Fates   139

If only this were real.

How many times over the centuries had I wished our love for each other were as simple as this? As simple as a mother's soft approval, as firelight on our faces as we kissed by a hearth, as a thousand tiny pleasures and kindnesses adding up to an entirely ordinary love story?

But our love story was not like that. It was blood and pain and death, an awful cycle doomed always to repeat.

Desperate to quell the grief tugging below my ribs, I pressed on. "While you're all overjoyed and such . . . can I stay in the cottage with him tonight?"

Pulling away from Dylan again, Mum turned to me and raised an eyebrow, but there was a hint of amusement to it. Then she shrugged. "I suppose there's no point in saying no. I was having sex in car parks at your age."

"Mum! Jesus!" I pleaded, but couldn't help a bark of surprised laughter. After seeing her so cowed and frightened for so long, the unexpected banter was a balm—the flush to her cheeks, the dimples bracketing her smile, the twinkle in her eyes. It was a flash of the mother I'd known before Gracie's diagnosis, and it warmed me through like a cup of hot tea. And I would do anything to make it last.

Resolve steeled inside me like a freshly forged blade.

I had to win Arden round.

The farm cottage was warm and clean but haphazardly messy. There was a pokey living room with two tweed armchairs and six overflowing bookcases, discarded jumpers and loose sheets of paper strewn over the furniture. The galley kitchen's walls were hung with frames filled with rare flower pressings and pencil sketches of botanicals and herbs. Houseplants on every available surface, fronds and ferns spilling onto the floor from hanging

140 ✳ **Laura Steven** ✳

baskets. Leather-bound volumes of poetry pressed between vases and terracotta pots, pens and notebooks stacked on top of the microwave, every inch of the space filled with carefully curated life.

Now I understood why he'd never invited me inside. The space was so stuffed full of his love for the natural world and the written word that I would've known instantly it was Arden.

It wasn't late by the time we arrived at the cottage—only just after nine—but the day had been long and fraught, so we headed straight up to his bedroom. My heart pounded with every step on the staircase, the beat so heavy and fast I was sure he would hear. But he said nothing as I traipsed behind him, watching the muscles ripple in his back as he moved. If he was cold without his coat, he didn't show it.

The bedroom had a double bed pressed against the far wall, a scuffed writing desk set up in the bay window, an oak wardrobe with two matching bedside tables, and a Persian rug over the faded cream carpet. On the walls were more framed flowers and botanical sketches, plus several sepia-stained letters from famous poets.

The room was nothing spectacular, but it just *felt* like Arden. Like stepping inside his very soul and curling up next to the fire. Intimate and familiar.

"This is nice," I said, the statement so laughably mundane, and yet it was all I could think to say into the silence. I laid down my overnight bag next to a tall potted fiddle-leaf.

He flipped on a bedside lamp, washing the room in a soft golden light. "Thanks."

There was a copy of *Ten Hundred Years of You* on the bedside table. "When did you hear about it?" I asked, gesturing to the well-thumbed volume.

"Heard a news segment on the radio," he said, the words like a too-tight belt round his chest. "I don't know how it's allowed.

Our Infinite Fates ☀ 141

How can they profit from something a dead boy wrote, without permission?"

"I suppose the colonizers have been looting and pillaging to fill their museums for centuries. Why stop now?" I laughed bitterly. "I guess they're just gambling that nobody's still alive to sue them."

He nodded, then averted his gaze. "Have you . . . Have you read it? I saw the display in the bookshop." He looked all of a sudden boyish, insecure, a kid showing a painting to a friend for the first time.

I nodded and swallowed hard, feeling at once as though I'd betrayed him, like I'd breached his privacy in some fundamental way. "It was beautiful."

He pressed his hand to his chest, took a steadying breath, but said nothing. I remembered Mikha, the brown leather notebook clutched to a snow-tipped fur coat. The tears frozen to his cheekbones as we died. My heart felt like an ice pick had been thrust through it.

"Do you write new poetry in every life?" I asked, not wanting to pry but at the same time desperate to know more about this facet of him he'd always guarded so closely. "Or do you transcribe all your old work from memory every time you're respawned?"

"It's all new," he mumbled, gruff and suddenly embarrassed.

The thought was rich with promise. Littered all over the world—scattered through history like confetti—were notebooks full of Arden's love for me. How many more had been discovered? Discarded, published, tucked away in dimly lit museums? Our love preserved behind glass, taken out and polished by a neatly gloved hand, positioned between the Gutenberg Bible and the Diamond Sūtra. The idea made me feel immortal in a whole new way, like I existed outside myself.

"No photos of your family," I noted, pointing at the frames on the wall.

"Easier that way."

He'd been like this since at least the turn of the twentieth century—with the possible exception of Siberia—but I knew it hadn't always been so. He used to live and breathe for his family. I just couldn't say for certain when it had changed—whether there even was a fixed point, a clear axis, or whether the walls had been constructed slowly over time, brick after brick, stone after stone, until one day he'd looked up and they were impenetrable.

Impenetrable but for Gracie. And that meant something.

"You didn't kill me," I said slowly. "Back in the stables, when I freed Ceri. You said you would, but you didn't. Or couldn't."

His whole body stiffened, but he said nothing.

"Why?" I prodded.

Quiet seconds rolled out before us like the golden rise and fall of the desert, the silence wholly alive.

Then he whispered, "Because I'm . . ."

He trailed off and never picked the sentence back up.

"Because you're what?" I urged.

He shook his head. "Never mind." Before I could ask him anything else, he gestured jerkily toward the landing. "Bathroom's that way."

I recoiled at the dismissal. "Aren't you afraid I'll climb out the window?"

"There's no window," he replied humourlessly. He looked entirely wrung out.

In the tiny, clean bathroom I shrugged off his coat, brushed my teeth, ran a tortoiseshell comb through my hair, and scrubbed my face until the skin was pink and raw. I changed into a pair of red flannel pyjamas, then headed back into the bedroom. The curtains had been drawn since I'd left.

Arden was sitting on the edge of the bed, stony-faced. Beside him on the patchwork blanket was a pair of steel handcuffs.

Our Infinite Fates 143

I stared at him in disbelief. "You're actually going to cuff me to the bed?"

Elbows on his knees, he sank his head into his hands, his silence a terrible confirmation.

"That seems wildly unnecessary."

"I have to sleep sometime," he said into his palms. "And when I do, it'll be too easy for you to flee. Or knock me out and tie me up like you did Ceri."

"Why do you even have those?"

"Same reason you carry a knife. Just in case."

I sat next to him on the bed, mind and pulse both racing. The tension between our two bodies was palpable, an electric crackle. I held out my wrist, and he closed the first cuff around it. Then he reached over my lap and fixed the other round a slat of the wooden headboard, turning the tiny key in the lock with a metallic click.

Panic bolted up my spine, the feeling of being trapped, helpless, small.

Finally, he crossed to the writing desk and shut the key in the top drawer.

Trying to make myself comfortable, I climbed under the covers and rested my head on the pillow, grunting as the cuff pulled awkwardly at my wrist. A shudder racked me from head to toe. In a second I was back in that awful asylum, restrained like a feral beast, prodded and dehumanised and humiliated, frozen and starved and drugged. Arms strapped to waists in starched white straitjackets, patches of drool on the collars.

In my darkest moments, I regretted going back to save Arden. Would I have lived a full, normal life if I hadn't? Would I have broken this curse forever?

That stark and terrible vision might have been just that: a vision. A work of imagination.

But from the white-haired, black-nailed woman's appearance in the trenches, I knew it had rung true.

If we turned eighteen, it would ruin us.

And so maybe it was too much to hope for, that Arden might keep me alive this time. Maybe I'd be better off searching for the *why,* at long last. Not just a vague outline, but every dimension of the truth, every nook and cranny of our fate. The full, unabridged story.

But god, I *wanted.* I wanted so much.

"I'm so sorry," Arden said, finally turning to look at me. His eyes were rimmed with tired pink.

"Are you?" I snapped, if only to give the desperate emotions in my throat somewhere to go.

He looked pained by the question, no matter how rhetorical. "Do you really need to ask that?"

When I didn't respond, he knelt down and pulled out a thick beige blanket from beneath the bed. Rolling it out on the floor, he grabbed a cable-knit jumper from the wardrobe and bundled it up as a pillow. Finally, he flipped off the lamp on the bedside table, and the room was plunged into darkness.

I heard the unbuttoning of his jeans, and the clink of his belt buckle as both fell to the floor. Another brush of fabric as he pulled his soft marl jumper over his head.

After a few seconds, my eyes started to adjust. I made out the silhouette of his body, the way his shoulders swept wide, the way he narrowed at the hips, the way his muscles corded in his back. A similar build to Henri, back in the trenches. My breath caught in my throat. He curled up on top of the blanket, tucking his knees to his chest.

"Aren't you cold?" I asked, my voice somehow louder in the dark.

"If you're uncomfortable, I should be too."

Our Infinite Fates

My cuff scraped against the headboard as I adjusted my position. "And I'm the martyr."

He said nothing.

The silence was taut and fragile. I could almost hear the frantic whir of his brain, almost feel the tensed muscles in his body. A gust of wind rattled the window in its frame, shaking it by the bones.

"Let me in, Arden," I whispered. "Two heads are better than one. Maybe we can find a way out of this together."

I knew he would resist, but I had to try. I thought back to Siberia.

No. No, no, no. I need to undo this. No. I won't let you die this time. We'll . . . We'll just have to figure the rest out.

There was the white-haired woman, the diamond-clear vision of ruination, but if he'd relented back in Russia, maybe there *was* something we could do.

For the briefest of moments, he'd let himself believe as much.

But now, in this chilly farm cottage at the foot of the Brecon Beacons, he simply said, "There's no way out. Good night, Evelyn."

Wales

2022

After tossing and turning for what felt like hours, I eventually slept in fits and starts until I was awoken by a yell of agony. I sat bolt upright, forgetting that my wrist was cuffed to the headboard—I winced as it yanked at an awkward angle. My eyes strained against the darkness.

Arden was roaring raggedly, almost feral, as though some invisible hand was peeling the very skin from his chest. The sound grabbed me by the ribs, a lit match held to every nerve ending.

"Arden," I said urgently. "Hey. *Arden.*"

Still he screamed.

"ARDEN!" I yelled, tugging futilely at my bonds, so intense was the urge to go to him.

He awoke, the sound dying suddenly in his throat, his body jerking and starting.

Breathing heavily, he stayed perfectly in place.

"What was that?" I asked, flopping back onto the pillow, my own heart thudding.

A brief pause, and then quietly: "Just a nightmare."

I'd seen this before, on a fishing trawler off the coast of sunset-drenched Nauru, right before I killed Elenoa on a jutting reef. Mangoes and pawpaws and sour toddy, red light washing over her soft, tanned body, my eyes stinging from sun and salt. Limbs

Our Infinite Fates

147

juddering against the wooden deck. My body pressed to her back, hushing.

I rolled over the revelation in my mind, unsure how to broach it. If I went in too hard, Arden would clam up. And yet it felt important, somehow. As though it might have something to do with us.

"You have them a lot," I whispered into the night.

"Yes."

Still his body lay unmoving, just the soft rise and fall of his chest. Now that my eyes had cleared of sleep, I saw from his outline that he was facing me. A shard of silvery moonlight sliced through a gap in the curtains, illuminating the hard ridge of his jaw. A tangle of dark hair on a cream jumper pillow.

The screams still echoed in the caverns of my mind.

"Is it the same thing every time?" I asked, trepidatious.

A single nod.

"The asylum? The trenches?" I fought back a shudder. "They haunt me too."

Another beat, then the shutters went down.

He rolled over to face the window.

We both lay awake—albeit in fraught silence—until the sun rose orange over the valley. The peach light washed through the curtains, pouring over Arden's tensed body. He was covered in goose bumps. Sharp shoulder blades protruded from the tanned skin on his back, which I noticed was cross-hatched with pink-red scratches. They were fresh and bright.

Had he been clawing at himself during the nightmare?

"Do you want some coffee?" he asked gruffly, as though he felt my eyes on him.

"Yeah. Thanks."

He sat up and riffled through his drawers, pulling out a plain white T-shirt. He tugged it over his head, then grabbed his jeans from the crumple on the floor and started working them over his ankles.

I rattled the handcuffs pointedly. "Take your sweet time, by all means."

"Shit. Sorry." He clambered to his feet and shuffled awkwardly to the bed, trousers still around his knees.

Don't look at his boxers don't look at his—

"Remember the coffee in the Ottoman Empire?" I asked, in a bid to distract myself.

For some reason, this was also the wrong thing to say. Fresh tension built in his arms, and something untraceable flickered behind his eyes.

"We probably shouldn't talk about Constantinople," he said, every syllable measured carefully.

"Why—?"

But before I could finish the thought, I remembered something suddenly and vividly—our naked perfumed bodies, both of us male, a rough hand at my waist in the sweet steam of the hammam, a desperate tongue flickering over mine, the desire so raw and intense that my entire body was flooded with heat. I tried to clutch at the memory so it wouldn't disappear, but in a moment it was gone, leaving only my blushed cheeks in its wake.

The cuff loosened around my wrist, his fingers delicately brushing my palm, and I was agonisingly aware of how close he was to me. How I could rest my hand on the narrowest point of his waist, how I could bring the other to that clenched jaw and tug him down toward me.

But he turned away, leaving the air around me cold.

Arden remembered it all, and I did not. For a fleeting moment, I understood the walls Arden had built up. How much must it hurt, that I had forgotten so many intimate details of our lives together?

And more importantly: Why did I forget and he did not?

Our Infinite Fates 149

Why did the past come to me in fractal shards, while he held the vast and complex landscape of our existence in his memory? I remembered the broad strokes for the past hundred or so years. From the asylum onwards, my memories were dull but distinct, yet before that was murky, patchy, blurred with old age. Entire lifetimes swallowed by fog.

Was that a natural effect of living for so long? Or had the brutal experiments in the Vermont asylum wrecked my head more than I'd ever realised? Were my suppressed memories a trauma response?

So many questions, and never any answers.

For now, I just had to focus on the only thing that mattered: saving Gracie's life.

Dr. Onwuemezi peered over her glasses. "You want to do the bone marrow extraction this week?"

So many fates depended on what happened next.

Mum, Arden, and I were sitting by Gracie's bed. My sister was dressed, inexplicably, in a three-piece suit, a monocle notched on the breast pocket. There was no discernible reason for her dress other than keeping things lively, and for that I loved her even more. Even as she'd gone on a long diatribe about how if anyone should be sick it was me, because I'd spent far too much time in the sun as a child, when she had sensibly spent her youth playing video games with the curtains drawn.

"You have a unique worldview, kid." Arden had chuckled at the sight of her. "You know that?" His tone had been a curious blend of wistful and admiring.

It was strange watching him interact with Gracie, knowing who he really was. It should have made me feel anxious, on edge, afraid for her safety. But instead, it was oddly touching.

As we spoke to the consultant, we sipped cappuccinos from

the hospital cafeteria. I could feel the heat of mine on my tongue, but it tasted of nothing. Not like the rich, dark coffee in Constantinople, bitter and potent and delicious. I tried to root myself back there, tried to access the memories my mind held in a locked vault, but I couldn't grasp them in full, couldn't peel them back, like the skin of a ripe fruit, to expose the core.

I nodded in response to Dr. Onwuemezi's bemused question. "I'm nervous about the giant needle of it all."

"I see," said the doctor, betraying no emotion, and I hauled myself back into the room. Her hapless med student wasn't with her today. She laid down Gracie's chart on top of a medicine cabinet and leaned back against the wall, folding her arms over her neat white lab coat. "Your mother informs me you're allergic to anaesthesia, and so we'd likely be performing the procedure while you're awake."

Gracie took an enormous crunch of apple. "First time in my life I've ever respected my sister."

I laughed, but it was a brittle, unconvincing thing.

The doctor kept her eyes on me. "Is that a source of worry?"

In truth, it was. I'd found out I was allergic to general anaesthetic the hard way. At the age of six, I'd gone to have a ruptured appendix removed and ended up in anaphylactic shock. The doctors had almost missed it, and I'd been a hair's breadth from death. I had made it through, thanks to a vigilant nurse and a curious ability to stay alive when others would not, but my parents had been thoroughly traumatised.

We weren't sure whether the condition extended to local anaesthesia, but on our way to hospital that morning, Mum had talked me into doing the procedure without any pain relief, because she couldn't risk losing us both. I had nodded in quiet devastation, knowing there was a decent chance that would happen anyway.

Our Infinite Fates

151

"Yes," I mumbled, embarrassed at the admission.

"Well, I can't lie to you." Dr. Onwuemezi's mouth pressed into a flat grimace. "There will certainly be some pain involved."

Arden's hand went protectively to mine, squeezing it almost imperceptibly, and I hated how good it felt. Both Mum and Gracie watched the gesture with small smiles on their faces.

"You're a brave girl," said the doctor. "It's clear you love your sister very much."

Gracie rolled her eyes, but her cheeks pinkened and she stared down at her lap.

I chewed the inside of my mouth. "I do, but I'm still worried. Struggling to sleep too. I'd rather do it sooner, so that I can relax and just be here for Gracie and Mum."

Please say yes. Please say yes. Please say yes.

"Well, I certainly understand that instinct." Dr. Onwuemezi rubbed at her temple with the tip of her forefinger. "The storage of the marrow is not an issue, in itself—we can easily preserve it until required. And in an ideal world, the health service would be able to accommodate such things. But we're understaffed, and I don't think there's going to be another surgical slot available until at least the week after next." She grimaced apologetically. "Would you like me to try and pull it forward to the Monday or Tuesday?"

Better than the two weeks originally planned, but still not fast enough.

I would turn eighteen on Saturday.

Swallowing roughly, I pulled my hand away from Arden's. It was his fault I was in this awful situation to begin with. I had to remember that. Let the resentment calcify inside me, so that I might have the strength to see all this through.

"Is there a chance someone might cancel their appointment before then?" Arden asked the doctor, his voice oddly gruff.

She gave a semi-nod. "Of course, although it's uncommon. I'll make sure you're the first person we contact if that happens, but I'm afraid that's the best I can do."

As the doctor left the room, I looked across at Arden. His tanned face had taken on an ashen pallor, and he was staring at Gracie as though willpower alone could cure the cancer roiling in her innocent blood.

Arden wanted to save her almost as badly as I did, but unless I found a way to give my marrow before Saturday, he would have no choice but to kill me anyway.

Dutch
East Indies

1770

The docks of Batavia clanged with trade as our boat came in to moor. I watched the land arrive from the forecastle deck, my pulse high and thin in my ears.

I would turn eighteen in mere minutes.

There had been many times in this life in which I'd believed I wouldn't make it this far.

The first had been when I'd contracted a deep, penetrative fever as a boy, shortly after setting sail for Amsterdam in 1764. I'd just turned twelve years old, and the reality of my fateful entwinement had only just sharpened. I could not remember the how or the why, only that I would die at Arden's hand within half a dozen years. It always took a decade or so for this terrible truth to fully register: that it was not a childish nightmare or an irrational fear but instead a very real impending doom.

As I lay tangled in sweat-soaked sheets, hallucinating pirates in my cabin and sharks in my belly, I remember dimly wondering whether my own death would consequently kill Arden, wherever they were. But to my memory, neither of us had ever died prematurely, which did seem unlikely—bordering on miraculous—given the wars, plagues, and famines we'd lived through.

Sure enough, despite the doctor's sincere assurances I would not recover, my fever broke.

The second time was only a few months later, when a rollicking storm almost overturned our galleon somewhere near the Cape of Good Hope. The Brouwer Route was notoriously fraught with danger—storms, ills, pirates—and the crew believed we were finally falling victim. Towers of water thrashed down on us from above, until, as though by some divine command, the clouds parted and the vessel righted itself at the last possible moment.

Many died.

Sure enough, I did not.

Around then, I came to wonder whether it was a curious condition of the tether that bound me to Arden; maybe the only thing that could kill us was each other.

The third time was two years after that, when the skin on my forearm began to turn black. It started as a brownish mole, but its borders soon spread like a greedy empire claiming stolen land. It grew pink notches and ragged edges, pushed upward in a bleak dome. Unmistakable cancer. The fatal roots soon burrowed down into my bones until I awoke screaming with the pain of it. If it ended how it had for my mother, I'd soon be clutching at my torso as though trying to dig the organs from my body.

My father and the doctor arrived at my cabin with a scalpel and a bone saw, determined to remove the arm. But by then, I was curious about my own immortality. Would the cancer spread? Or would I somehow live through this too? Convincing my father that I would take my own life if he took my limb, I survived the encounter with the arm intact.

Sure enough, the cancer kept spreading over my skin's surface, but never to my liver, my kidneys, my heart.

Our Infinite Fates

The fourth time was that morning, when I awoke to a garrotte at my throat.

Arden had found me at last.

This time she was a girl half my size, with a shaved head and feral eyes.

I'd fallen asleep propped up against the wall behind my bunk, reading a tome on modern pathology by Giovanni Battista Morgagni—medicine had become a keen interest of mine since my arm had declared civil war on itself. I woke to find that Arden had a palm planted on the wall on either side of my neck, the garrotte pinching sharply into my skin.

"Ouch," I said plainly.

Perhaps I wouldn't have been so casual, but Sander Schoonhoven, the seven-foot-tall first mate, had also entered my room and was mere inches from hauling her off.

Now she was tied up with thick ropes in the cargo hold, and I was about to turn eighteen. It had been my birthday for several hours, but since I'd been born around midday, I was a few moments shy of that elusive number.

Four minutes, to be exact.

The boat bobbed against the side of the dock, the gated harbor a maze of stacked crates and coiled ropes. Four servants stood by a gilded palanquin, ready to escort the governor general into the city—he was the most important dignitary we'd transported in over a decade. Word had traveled about my father's inhuman ability to weather any storm, and soon enough he was a captain coveted by the most powerful people in the empire.

Several sailors hopped down to secure the galleon to the harbor, nodding hello to the row of musketeers in knee-length breeches. The air smelled of pepper and cloves, nutmeg and cinnamon, vanilla and salt and fish.

156 ⁎ Laura Steven ⁎

Sander Schoonhoven stood beside me on the forecastle deck, muttering to the purser about how much profit would be made from the next eight-month voyage if the spices and silks were not spoiled over the course of the journey.

Three minutes.

My father appeared at Sander's side, cheer-faced and weather-beaten. We had survived another trip. He just had no idea his good fortune was owed to his lucky talisman: a semi-immortal son. Would the ship capsize the moment I died? If I died.

Two minutes.

I could barely register what my father was saying over the sound of my blood roaring. This was the closest I'd ever come to surviving past childhood. And with Arden bound and gagged several decks below, it would take nothing short of a miracle for her to kill me now.

One minute.

Anticipation beat in my chest like wings.

Would I feel some kind of tether snapping when I became a man? That existential tug loosened at last. The hold Arden had over me, snipped by the hand of time. A centuries-old curse finally broken. Freedom rolling out before me like the open sea, with nary a storm cloud to be seen.

A bell chimed somewhere deep in the city.

For a split second, nothing happened.

And then I buckled.

The tether was not snipped.

Instead it grew a thousand times stronger.

All the breath was sucked from my lungs. An invisible lasso tightened around my middle. There was a ferocious burning at the back of my neck, as though a puppeteer had hooked me on a string and hauled me backward.

Then a roar from behind me, a body slamming into mine, a

Our Infinite Fates ✳ 157

flash of bald head and feral eyes, a gust of eternal wind, a shattering of barriers,
    and we fell
    fell
    fell
    before the brutal harbor edge came to meet our fragile skulls.

Wales

2022

I awoke to the sound of Arden muttering softly to himself. As my bleary eyes sharpened into focus, I saw him hunched at the writing desk, fully clothed and poring over *Ten Hundred Years of You.*

"What are you doing?" I asked, stretching my loose arm above my head with a stiff, twisted wrench.

"There wasn't supposed to be a line break there." He made a furious mark on the page with a fountain pen. "It was just where I ran out of space in the journal. It totally alters the cadence of the piece. They've absolutely bastardised it. And look, here. They've added a comma. The original didn't have one, I'm sure of it."

I snorted. "Heathens."

Such a small thing, but his pedantic grouching made me laugh. We were about to die because of some fatal curse that had dogged us for a thousand years, and yet he still had the capacity to be irritated by comma placement.

Only Arden.

But his irritation mounted as he flipped through the pages, raking his hands through his dark, messy hair. "And this translation—it's just woeful. Here I used *toska,* and they've translated it into *boredom,* but it's more than that, isn't it? It's . . . melancholy, longing. Spiritual anguish. Nabokov described it as 'a dull

Our Infinite Fates * 159

ache of the soul, a sick pining, a vague restlessness, mental throes, yearning.' And, in particular cases, 'the desire for somebody or something specific, nostalgia, love-sickness.' I've never found a word like that before, that so perfectly sums up how I feel about us."

"Why——?"

"Actually, that's not true. There's *yuánfèn,* from Mandarin——a tragic fate between two people. Oh, if only I could find the poems from Algeria. *Ya'aburnee* was a favourite. It means 'may you bury me.' It's the idea that one person in a pairing longs to die before the other, because living without them would be too excruciating. I wrote about how we'll never have to worry about that." A bitter bark of laughter. "Silver linings, I suppose. Maybe I should rewrite it. How good is my Arabic these days?"

His words took on a muttered, frantic quality, as though he were talking to some goblin in the back of his brain instead of me.

I left him to it, after that.

Later that day, I sat on the front seat of the bobbing tractor beside Arden, rubbing at my exhausted eyes. The sky was an apathetic grey over the rolling land, and the fields were a muted patchwork of brown and gold and green. In the middle distance, a stream burbled.

"What am I going to do?" I sighed. "I can't just spend the next few days hoping someone decides not to go through with their donation."

Arden steered the tractor over a ditch with a thump. Now that we'd fed the livestock and sprayed the crops, I wasn't entirely sure what we were doing other than driving aimlessly around the wheat fields. "First of all, it's *we*. I'm going to help you as much as I can."

"My hero." The words dripped with sarcasm.

I'd spent the morning calling all the private practices within a hundred miles of Abergavenny, trying desperately to arrange a new marrow harvest, but the very few who were accepting new patients wouldn't do so without preexisting medical insurance—which took weeks to apply for and process. And with that door closed, I was firmly out of options.

The tractor slammed to a sudden stop. Arden picked a small, rumpled notebook out of the front pocket of his half-zip red fleece and jotted down a few farm-related numbers with a blue Biro. "I don't suppose we could find a list of the patients with earlier surgical procedures than you and tie them up like you did Ceri? Then you'll get their slot."

I stared at him as he tucked the notebook away again. "I can't tell if you're joking."

"Why not?" He shrugged. "You've already crossed that moral line. What's once more?"

"We can't," I insisted, trying to persuade myself as much as I was him. "It's not right. What if someone else on a transplant waiting list dies because we've abducted their donor?"

"I'm sure they'll be able to take your slot when you . . ."

"Are brutally murdered, yes." I folded my arms across my chest, angling my body away from him. "But what if that's too long for their recipient? I can't let anyone else die, Arden."

He made a *pfft* noise, as though my moral concerns were trifling and inconvenient. "Bribery?"

"Of another donor?" I shivered at the bitter breeze drifting through the tractor's open window. "Same issue. Another innocent person might die."

He leaned back in the driver's seat and kicked his feet up onto the dashboard. Dried mud flaked off his boots and into the footwell. "What about bribing Dr. Onwuemezi? Or the receptionist, or whoever's in charge of appointments?"

Our Infinite Fates

I shook my head. "It's all the same problem. The slot has to come from somewhere."

He picked up his sky-blue coffee flask from the cup holder and took a swig. "So, in summary, we're fucked. Gracie is fucked. And you're just going to let that happen."

This insinuation that the whole situation was my fault made me finally crack.

"I would dearly love some other suggestions that don't involve kidnap and possible manslaughter," I retorted, anger rising in my voice. "And I would also love it if you could stop treating me like a complete moron for having a heart."

Despite the hot snap of my tone, he handed me the coffee. "Honestly, I would kidnap quite literally anyone to save that kid. But I respect that you won't."

I took the flask, letting the warmth seep into my frigid hands. "Do you actually?"

"What?"

"Respect me." There was an insistent thrust to the words, underpinned by rage but also deep insecurity.

He pursed his lips. "Don't be ridiculous."

"No, I'm serious." I took a sip from the flask. The coffee was sweet and milky, warming down my gullet. Arden usually took it black but had made it how I liked it. I was once again wearing his plaid lumberjack coat with the vial of sugar water tucked into the pocket. "Do my rigid morals seem absurd to you?"

He drummed his fingers on the gearstick. "Mine are just as rigid. They're just different."

"In what way?"

He considered this for a moment, as though it were a mathematical equation to balance. "If a hero is someone who will give up love to save the world, then a villain is the reverse. Someone who will give up the world to save love."

"So you're a villain. You admit it."

He shrugged. "There's no line I wouldn't cross to keep a loved one safe."

I laughed, albeit bitterly. "By design, you don't have any loved ones."

There was a heavy pause, in which I feared I may have wounded him too deeply, but then he muttered, "I have you."

He was under there, somewhere. The Arden I had loved again and again and again. The frostbitten boy in deepest Siberia. The one who'd changed his mind, the one who'd decided to let me live, only too late. And as long as that Arden was still in there, I had hope. Stupid, defiant, illogical, furious hope.

The wind through the valley intensified, carrying the scent of hay and manure, of fresh leaves and crystalline rivers. A few spots of rain dotted the windscreen before deciding against it, as though a cloud had sprung a leak, then promptly patched it back up. The conversation felt charged and ripe and urgent, like the sky just before a thunderstorm.

I turned to face him. His hair was pulled back in a low bun. He hadn't shaved for a couple of mornings, and his sharp jaw was shadowed with dark stubble. There was a practised stillness to his posture. I'd known him long enough to know that he wanted to say something—or ask something.

Resisting the urge to rest a palm on his knee, I asked, "What is it?"

"Why did you come back for me?" he said stiffly, staring straight ahead at the corrugated iron siding of the goat barn. "In the asylum."

"You were aware of what was going on?" I'd thought Augusta was pumped so full of crude drugs that she had no idea what was happening. The vacant stare, the rod-straight back, the patch of drool on her collar.

Our Infinite Fates

"Barely. But enough. You escaped, and then you came back."

I leaned my temple against the headrest. "I did."

"Why? You had me beat."

"In that moment, it didn't feel like a game." I drained the last of the sweet coffee and stuffed the flask in the glove box.

"It doesn't make sense." His grip tightened on the steering wheel, and I tried not to think about how beautiful his hands were in this life: broad palms, short nails, sun-golden skin stretched over the peaks of his knuckles. Those twines and ribbons tied around his wrists. My gaze hitched on a piece of narrow red, though I couldn't say for certain why. Only that it yanked a cord somewhere deep in my chest.

"Love rarely does." I smiled ruefully. "And you'd have done the same for me."

"That was one of the worst deaths." His eyes fluttered closed, the dark crescents of his lashes stark against tired skin. "Killing you after what you'd done for me . . ."

"Still a better alternative than those *therapies*." The ice baths and the starvation, the endless spinning and the cold steel bars, the crackling electrodes, the sterile brutality, every day bleached white and cruel.

Then, through the heavy black clouds of the conversation, a fork of lightning. A realisation so obvious it felt like a physical blow.

"That's it!" I said, thumping a palm on the seat.

Finally his eyes snapped to me, a look of absolute bewilderment on his face. "What?"

"Therapy."

An eye-roll. "Oh yes, now everything makes sense."

I shook my head passionately. "When Gracie was first diagnosed, Mum found me a therapist. I had a lot of shit to work through, what with that and my dad being crushed to death. I haven't seen Dr. Chiang for months—it was tiring having to skirt round the truth of what was going on in my head, since I could hardly tell her I was being hunted by a supernatural killer."

He gritted his teeth. "That's how you think of me?"

I waved my hand impatiently. "It's just a pithy way of describing the situation, isn't it? Anyway, she's married to a surgeon at a private practice." I felt jittery with the realisation, with the sliver of hope. "I wonder if I could convince her to give me an emergency referral."

He frowned. "How on earth are you going to do that?"

"I'll think of something."

A smile spread across my face—always the optimist, even when it was downright absurd to be so. Even when another life was reaching its crescendo.

Wales

2022

Dr. Chiang agreed to see me the next evening, out of hours.

Arden drove me into Abergavenny and sat in the deserted waiting room while I talked to my therapist. The appointment was the longest we'd spent apart since he'd agreed to let me live, but if he was worried about me sharing our darkest secrets with a third party, he didn't show it—just gave me a tight smile as I entered the office without him.

The space was large and neat, lined with mahogany bookcases and painted a soothing cream colour. Dr. Chiang was a short, round woman in her forties who had a particular fondness for model trains—her desk was lined with miniatures. She wore floral dresses and woolly tights, and had big gold-rimmed glasses that made her look like an owl. She was badly allergic to dust and sneezed almost constantly. At the familiar, warming sight of her, I couldn't remember why on earth I'd stopped coming in the first place. She rushed around the desk toward me.

"Oh, Branwen," she said, in her soft Bangor accent, and I all but collapsed into her.

I was never quite sure whether it was all right to hug your therapist, but while Dr. Chiang never initiated, she always reciprocated. She rubbed my shoulder soothingly with her palm, and

I fought the urge to sob into the shoulder of her chunky-knit cardigan.

I was so tired. And I was so sad. And I was so afraid.

But then, as all the words withered and died in my throat, I remembered exactly why I'd stopped coming: because the thing that caused me the most distress was the fact I'd likely die before I ever saw Gracie recover. Dancing around that core truth had become too exhausting.

A small part of me wondered what might happen if I told Dr. Chiang that truth tonight. All of it, every word, every single thing I knew about my entire existence. The idea filled me with relief— a burden not only shared but also unpacked. In reality, though, I knew she'd probably think grief had made me lose my marbles— and I was fairly sure they wouldn't let a psych inpatient consent to something like a bone marrow harvest.

Then again . . . maybe I could ask for her help. I could tell her that the boy sitting in her empty waiting room right now was an abuser, that he'd threatened my life if I left his sight. Would she believe me? She had no reason not to. Maybe she would call the police, and he'd be taken in for questioning. He'd never be charged with anything, since I had zero proof, but I could use that time to escape.

And yet where would I go, knowing the tether would lead him right to me anyway?

I needed to focus. Arden was likely going to kill me, no matter what I did, so the priority needed to be Gracie. I needed to use Dr. Chiang's good favour to convince her wife to do pro bono work in the next few days. That in itself was no small ask.

So I decided to walk the tightrope between truth and omission, sharing with her just enough that it would convince her to refer me for minor surgery.

Pulling apart from the hug, Dr. Chiang gestured for me to take

Our Infinite Fates 167

a seat on the navy velvet chaise longue arranged in front of the desk. I sank into its familiar comfort, grateful for the existence of offices like this. One of the things I loved most about modernity was how suffering was no longer simply accepted as a necessary part of the human experience. It was impossible to escape entirely, yet great lengths were gone to in an attempt to thwart it, to dismantle it, to interrogate it.

"Thank you for agreeing to see me so last-minute," I said, unsure where to start. I was surprised how steady my voice sounded, although it seemed very far away, like I was at the end of a distant tunnel.

"It's not a problem." She smiled. I felt like I was sitting with a beloved aunt; maybe she had been, in a past life. "I've been wondering how you are for months. So—how are you, Branwen?"

Where to begin?

"Scared," I said, thinking it as good a place to start as any.

"That's understandable. What do you think is causing you this fear?"

I bit my lip. "It's not just my sister's potential death, although that . . . I can barely think about that, to be honest. It's too painful."

"I understand. And you know, sometimes it's good not to preemptively agonise over loss too much. Practising grief is of no real benefit to anyone. Losing a loved one is not something you can rehearse—at least, not in a healthy way. It's better to enjoy the time you have with her."

Her words tolled in my chest. It was something I had always done—tried to prepare myself for loss, as though it would lessen the blow when it finally came.

"I know, and I really want to be able to just be there for her, to make her laugh, to play dumb games we used to enjoy as kids. But I'm struggling to even do that. This bone marrow harvest—I'd do anything for Gracie; you know I would. It wasn't even a question. But having to do it without general anaesthetic . . ."

God, I didn't know how to do this. How to bridge the conversation toward needing Dr. Chiang's wife's help.

When I didn't say anything else, the doctor simply said, "You're very brave. I hope you know that."

"I'm not brave. I'm terrified."

"It's impossible to have bravery without fear. Bravery is picking up the fear and carrying it alongside you, rather than allowing it to block the path."

One of the things I loved about Dr. Chiang was her ability to come up with proverbs on the spot—wisdom that sounded ancient but was actually just how she thought.

"To be honest . . . it's not just the pain. That's not the only reason I'm here."

Her expression remained wholly neutral. "Oh?"

Softly, softly, I told myself. *Don't make her think you're using her.*

"It's the fact that the procedure is still so far away. I keep worrying that if something bad happens to me in that time, it won't just be me who suffers or dies. It'll be Gracie too."

Dr Chiang pushed her glasses up the bridge of her nose. "The chances of something bad happening to you in that time are vanishingly small. But I understand that anxiety can make you fixate on the worst-case scenario."

"You have to admit that the worst-case scenario is pretty terrible."

She laughed sincerely, a warm chuckle that felt like a cup of tea and a hug. "That's what makes it so compelling to our brains. And I want you to know that while your thoughts feel desperately emotional, they're also very logical. Our brains naturally want to preempt and solve problems before they occur. You are not broken for feeling this way."

Our Infinite Fates

169

She left the conversation open for me to continue. She always did this—gave me space to fill should I want it—then, if I didn't, she would steer us down another conversational road. Today, though, I couldn't give her the wheel. I needed to double down on this particular topic.

"I'm scared to leave the house," I said, letting a light wobble into my voice. It was a genuine bubbling of emotion, not just for my therapist's benefit but a real overspilling of fear. "Even driving here, my heart was in my mouth the whole time. I can't sleep, for fear I won't wake up again. I don't even want to eat, because what if I choke?"

"It sounds like you're in a difficult place."

I nodded, staring at the hands folded in my lap. "I just keep thinking that if there was some way to do my part of the procedure earlier, I could let go of all this fear and actually enjoy my time with Gracie, you know?"

Dr. Chiang said nothing, simply waited for me to go on. I knew she was highly unlikely to offer up her wife in the first instance, but a desperate part of me hoped that might happen anyway.

"She's had an infection," I whispered. "Gracie. I'm not sure how bad it's been, because the doctor didn't go into detail, but it was enough to force her into more chemo and to push back the transplant. I'm so unbelievably terrified that the infection might get worse overnight, and these days with her might be the last, but whenever I'm with her I'm just so racked with worry that I can't . . . I can't really be with her. Does that makes sense?"

"Perfect sense."

Deep inhale, deep exhale. "I started calling private practices, hoping one of them might be able to do the procedure sooner. But I don't have insurance, so they wouldn't even let me register as a patient."

170 ⁎ Laura Steven ⁎

"These things can be very complicated."

Her immaculate composure made me want to drop to my knees, throw my arms round her ankles and beg and beg and beg. Instead I just mumbled, "I don't know what to do."

She considered this for a moment. "I think the only thing you can do is sit with your difficult feelings and process them as best you can. And that's why I'm here. I'm glad you've come back, Branwen. I think this is a good place for you to be at a time like this."

Chewing the inside of my cheek, I pushed on. "Do you know if surgeons ever do pro bono work?"

"It's highly unusual. There's no real need, thanks to the NHS. But I suppose it's not impossible."

"In what circumstances might one consider it?"

"I'm not too familiar with the intricacies." I could hear the beginnings of a frown in her voice. "You look very tired, Branwen."

"Like I said, I can't sleep." Tears sprang to my eyes, and I let them fall. Not just because I needed the catharsis, but because they might work in my favour in convincing Dr. Chiang. "And it's a vicious cycle, because the less I sleep for fear of dying, the higher the chances of dying from sleep deprivation."

I looked up to see her face etched with concern.

"If it helps, I don't think it's possible to die from sleep deprivation in such a narrow time frame." She rubbed her temple with her forefinger, and the sapphire of her engagement ring glinted in the light. "It would take months and months. You might hallucinate, yes, but your body will take over eventually. It'll force you to sleep."

Time to take it up a notch. I'd never been a great actress, but I just had to hope she was in a receptive, uncynical mood.

"What if I do something dangerous while hallucinating?" I wailed, dropping my head into my hands. "Oh god. Oh god. Oh god."

Our Infinite Fates   171

"I'm sorry," said Dr. Chiang hurriedly. "It wasn't my intention to put another troubling thought in your head."

"I know." I sniffed, wiping at my cheeks with my jumper sleeve. "I'm just so tired. And so scared." Both were true enough.

"Oh, Branwen. You're going through such a difficult thing."

"Do you know anyone who might be able to help me?" I said desperately, aware of how manic my wide, pink-rimmed eyes must look. "Does your wife know anyone who'd be willing to take on a pro bono patient?"

For a moment Dr. Chiang didn't speak, but this time it was not an invitation for me to continue. It was a clear weighing of her words. She shifted slightly in her chair.

"Is that why you came back to me?" she asked evenly. "To ask about this?"

I had nothing left to lose. I nodded. "I'm sorry. I just . . . I would do anything to save Gracie."

"I see." She pulled her cardigan tighter around herself, folding her arms over her chest. It was a closed posture she seldom adopted. Usually she was warm, open. "I don't think that would be appropriate, Branwen. It's not technically crossing any lines that I'm aware of, but it would be sort of . . . validating your anxieties. Not that they're *invalid*. That's not what I mean. It's entirely understandable, how you're feeling. But I don't want to affirm this belief that you're about to die in a freak incident. Does that make sense?" She looked out the window on the west side of the room. The sky was darkening into indigo. A wry smile; an attempt to soften the blow. "Besides, my wife is so busy that I myself barely see her."

The rest of the session passed in a haze of disappointment.

It hadn't worked, and I could barely believe it. That was the great peril of living in perpetual hope, of letting unbridled optimism inform your every move. When things didn't work out the way you hoped, the way you believed they would, there was also the genuine shock to contend with. A subtle rearranging of your worldview. Unwanted evidence against the faith you held so dear.

It hadn't *worked*.

That ever-burning candle of hope in my chest—the one Arden had remarked upon in the blood-soaked trenches of the Great War—sputtered, but it did not extinguish.

Not yet.

Norway

1652

For the first time, I was reborn near enough to a previous life that I could return to visit my old loved ones. Unfortunately, those loved ones were altogether spooked when a tall, pale girl with waist-length blond hair darkened their doorstep, claiming to be their daughter who'd died seventeen years ago. Especially when said daughter had been short and slight, with hair the color of a roasted walnut.

The journey from Kuopio to Finnmark had been an arduous one atop a stubborn horse's back. I had stolen her from a neighboring farm, and she'd resisted my command for the first hundred miles. The map I'd copied down was also woefully out-of-date, and, despite pilfering the finest compass I could find, I'd taken several accidental detours into western Russia. It had been a long, hungry few months, but there had been nothing left for me in Kuopio. I was an only child to two parents who had died of smallpox within days of each other, and my heart was tugging me toward the last place my soul had felt at home.

Little did I know that Vardø would be in the middle of quite a serious witch trial by the time I returned. Paranoia had tucked itself into all the dark nooks and crannies of my old hometown, panic lapping at the island's shores.

Despite sitting on top of the world, the port was ice-immune

174 ✳ **Laura Steven** ✳

thanks to a warm and steady North Atlantic drift. By the time I finally arrived, the midnight sun was a dusty pink behind the village kirke, washing the treeless tundra and sprawling fortress in a soft lilac light.

My chest ached with the familiarity of it, but one thing was new: the row of grim pyres by the port. I tried not to look at them as I wound along my path home, passing countless houses with fearful crosses nailed above the threshold.

At my knock on the door—oh, the door, the same old door, how was it possible to miss a *door*?—Mamma's head appeared in the curtainless window. She frowned before opening the door just a sliver, afraid of a vague evil force that wore many masks.

Her face was more lined than before, her hair now the white-silver of winter frost. She wore her summer dress, a pale heather-purple with thick white stitching around the squared neck. It hadn't aged well, with its ragged seams and dark stains around the pits. I'd always been the best at darning. Who had taken up the mending after I'd died? Certainly not fire-hearted Hedda, who hadn't the patience for such things, nor Branka, who hadn't the head.

"Can I help you?" Mamma asked, her voice so cold and clipped it stole the breath from me. I couldn't remember her ever talking like that when I was alive, though the isolated island saw few strangers.

"I'm sorry it's so late." Despite not having spoken in this tongue for nearly two decades, it flowed from me clear as water. "Only, I know you do not sleep well."

Her eyes narrowed to slits. "And how would you know how I sleep?"

I didn't know how to begin. "Where is Pappa? I mean—Anders. Anders Nilsson."

Suspicion twisted my mother's expression. "My husband died last year. What business is it of yours?"

Something inside me crumpled. My wise, gentle father. A

Our Infinite Fates

voice like powdered snow. Knowledge of the sea so intimate it was almost arcane. His rough hands deboning fish in seconds. His endless patience with Branka when my mother's had long since worn thin.

Dead in the ground.

Time was such a cruel thing. Hard enough for most mortals to bear, but uniquely ravaging for me, the relentless forward rush of it, a ship that never anchored, the flotsam of everyone I'd ever loved bobbing in its wake.

I wanted to drop to the floor and wail, but it would not help my cause.

Wringing my trembling hands, I mumbled, "I do not know how to explain this, and so I am asking you to just . . . believe me, for a moment. I can prove it."

"Prove what?" Mamma's words were smooth and hard as pebbles.

"In my last life, I was your daughter. I remember everything. And I miss you very much."

Mamma's searing stare could have cauterized a wound, but she said nothing.

"My name was Urszula. You named me that because it means 'small bear,' and you always called me your cub. I had two sisters. Hedda and Branka." My throat choked with tears unshed. "Hedda is strong-willed and stubborn and hates the smell of fish. Branka was fifteen when I last saw her, and she had never spoken a single word in her life. Pappa . . . he always went very quiet whenever we sisters fought. Like he was studying us. In the summer we picked white reinrose for—"

A wall of black went down behind my mother's eyes. "Speak another word, witch, and I'll have you burned."

"No, Mamma! I'm not—"

"I am not your mamma," she snarled, low and monstrous. "And I am not afraid of you."

176 ⁕ **Laura Steven** ⁕

And then she started shrieking.

"Heks! Heks! Heks!"

Witch.

Witch.

Witch.

Desperation clawed at me. "Please, let me come inside. I have traveled so far. How can I prove to you who I really am? Bring Hedda out. She'll know it's me. Please."

Shrill as a church bell, she continued to scream. "Heks! Heks! Heks!"

"Mamma, don't do this," I begged, the little girl at the heart of me splintered by the rejection. "I did not mean to frighten you."

"Heks! Heks! Heks!"

"Jeg elsker deg," I whispered. *I love you.*

A long, low hiss slipped through my mother's teeth, as though I'd cursed heinously.

"Hedda!" I yelled into the narrow house behind my mother's body. "Hedda, are you in there? Branka, vær så snill," I begged.

Hulking bodies spilled out of neighboring houses. A man I didn't recognize wielded a pair of leg irons, and he set off toward me with a hungry lurch to his gait. Next to him was Eyjolf, the noaidi—a shaman from a long line of shamans, but not so kind as his predecessors.

I looked around wildly. I had left my horse tied up on the mainland before borrowing a small boat to sail over to the island, but that left my situation precarious. A quick getaway with travel-leaden legs would be impossible. Why had I not anticipated this hostility? Whispers of the witch trials had grown louder the farther north I'd traveled. I'd ignored them at my own peril.

How long would it take an immortal soul to burn on the pyre? How long would the flames lick pain up my skin before it melted?

I was doomed.

✳ Our Infinite Fates ✳ 177

But then a cloaked figure appeared at the end of the street, running toward me in a fearless sprint, and I knew before I knew. Arden.

In the body of a Norse god, tall and sculpted and golden.

The man wielding the leg irons was knocked out with a single blow to the back of the head. Arden bellowed at the others to back off, his voice a low rumble of thunder—and despite his coarse Finnish accent, they did.

Thick arms scooped me up and, with a grunt of effort, Arden tossed me over a broad shoulder. The last thing I heard before we rounded the corner was my mother's hysterical wails, the word *heks* indelibly etched on my eardrums.

Hastily, Arden set me back on my feet and we sprinted down to the port, clambering back into the peeling red boat I had stolen to cross from the mainland. Another tiny vessel bobbed next to my own, which hadn't been there when I'd arrived.

Breathless, we pushed away from the shore, and Arden rowed with long, rotting oars. The harbor stank of smoke and salt and burning whale fat.

"How did you find me?" I gasped, winded from the confrontation, winded from being tossed over a shoulder, winded from running, winded from Arden, here, *now.*

"You stole my horse." He snorted, brushing a long lock of blond hair from his piercing blue eyes. "I have followed you ever since. You are . . . not good at reading maps. I thought we might end up in Novgorod."

I buried my face in my hands, breath ragged against my palms. "You couldn't have put me out of my misery a little sooner?" I wasn't sure whether I meant by showing me the right direction or by killing me. Not a distinction most people had to consider.

Voice gruff over the soft lapping of seawater, he said, "This journey seemed important to you."

I laughed bitterly. "It was a mistake."

"Perhaps." He did not look back at me, his gaze on the icy horizon to the north, where a pod of whales danced as though human hysteria was of no consequence to them. "But I understand why you did it."

The harsh reception from Mamma had left me aching in places I hadn't known it was possible to hurt. I was so tired of sailing through history like a hunk of driftwood that could never grow roots.

Once my breath fell back into a steady metronome, I raised my head and studied every line and curve of Arden's body. The penny dent in his chin, the bulge of muscles in his arms, sealskin coat taut across his shoulders. I tried not to think of our naked bodies pressed together in an Ottoman hammam, hot and breathless and desperate.

No matter how many lives I lost, no matter how many families moved on without me, I would always be known by Arden. Perhaps he was my true homeland; our existence a language only we could speak.

"You're here," I half whispered, half moaned, and then I threw myself forward, the boat pitching dangerously beneath my shifting weight, and hugged him tight. My face pressed into the warm, soft skin at the crook of his neck, his fast pulse fluttering against my cheek.

He rearranged himself so that I pressed more comfortably into his arms, my body nestled between his broad legs, and we sat like that for a few moments, both relishing the feeling of not being alone.

I brushed my lips just below his ear, savoring the sound of his breath hitching in his throat.

One of his palms came to the back of my head, thumb stroking my tangled hair.

"I missed you," he whispered, so quietly I almost didn't hear it.

My voice choked. "I missed you too."

There was always Arden.

Our Infinite Fates   179

There would always be Arden.

Even when our families grieved and moved on, even when our ancestors lay in the dirt, even when we slipped through the cracks of time like ghosts, there would always be us. No matter how twisted and broken, we were the one true constant, our love like a river wending its way through the earth year after year, century after century, growing deeper and wider with every twist and bend. A certain peace came with knowing the water would always flow a particular way.

"Sometimes it feels like my heart breaks when yours does," he murmured in my ear. "I *knew* the moment your mother rejected you, even before I rounded the corner and saw it for myself." A sigh, as his hand went from my head to the small of my back, warmth spreading through me. "You deserved better. You have always deserved better."

Before I could convince myself it was a mistake, I pulled my head back from his neck, cupped his rough, stubbled face in my hands, and kissed him as though I had spent six months battling through the frozen wilderness just for this very moment.

And perhaps I had.

He reciprocated, soft and uncertain at first, then harder as he gave way to the longing I knew he felt too. He tasted of sea salt and windswept skin and the cold itself, of hope and salvation and loss.

My heart clenched in a fist as I released our lips, pressing my forehead against his, gazing into those furnace-like eyes. There was always so much behind them; emotion churning and writhing, so rarely given a way out. I often felt like I could spend another thousand lifetimes trying to coax it free, and it wouldn't be long enough.

After a strange, loaded beat, he leaned back ever so slightly, raking a hand through his golden hair, broad chest rising and falling unevenly.

His hand was tanned and knotted with stark veins, and the sight of it loosed a memory: our hands fastened together with red ribbon, both speaking a language not unlike this one. The sea whipping itself into peaks, the scents of pine resin and sage oil, a voice so crisp and cutting it chilled me to the bone.

But then the image was gone, taking the moment of raw passion with it.

I hugged my knees to my chest on the narrow bench, palms pressed against the thick woolen stockings covering my shinbones. "You know, the ancient Greeks believed that a soul is something human beings risk in battle and lose in death. But we do not lose ours in death. So what does that make us? More than human? Or less than?"

Arden did not answer, instead becoming fixated on the small puddle of rank water at the bottom of the boat. A shoal of red fish darted below us.

"Maybe I am a witch," I muttered, to weigh his reaction more than anything. "Maybe we both are."

His grip on the oars tightened, knuckles stretched white. "Why do you say that?"

"It would offer some sort of explanation, at least. Folklore says witches are just women who made a pact with the devil. They offered something valuable in exchange for magic powers. To cure infertility, to smite a former lover, to save their own skins." I leaned forward on the bench once more, resting my hands on his knees. He jolted at the touch, and delicious fire kissed my palms. "Is that what happened to us, Arden? Did we make a deal with the devil? And is the valuable thing we sacrificed . . . adulthood? Our futures?"

Finally, he lifted his rough jaw and met my searching stare. "Something like that."

But from the way his eyes darted from mine a second later, I knew he was lying.

life gives us grief like mounds of wet clay,
ripe and heavy beneath our reluctant hands,
     and with it we can do one of three things.

we can carry it with us wherever we go,
stooped beneath its awful weight,
we can shove it to the back of a wardrobe,
buried beneath an old waxed coat,
or we can make something beautiful,
and let it live on beyond us.

—AUTHOR UNKNOWN

Wales

2022

The next morning—after another nightmare-ridden night—Arden and I had breakfast in the farmhouse with my mum. I hadn't told her about my therapy session with Dr. Chiang, and the omission made me uneasy, trepidatious. A gnarled root in the soft ground between us, one I had to be careful not to trip over.

With an almighty sigh, I slumped into my usual seat at the worn oak dining table. Arden slid into the chair next to me. The kitchen smelled of creamy porridge and strawberry jam—the same breakfast my mum had eaten ever since I was little.

"Morning, you two." Mum seemed chipper, buoyed by the sight of us entering the kitchen side by side. "Coffee?"

"Please," we both said at once. I pulled my sleeve down to disguise the reddened area around my wrist where I'd yanked against the cuff in the night.

"Lovely. I'll do a pot." She started clattering around with a steel stovetop kettle. "Did you sleep well?"

"No," I groaned, rubbing my eyes furiously, woozy from sleep deprivation. "Dylan snores."

He bristled next to me. "And Bran sleep-talks."

Mum chuckled. "You both look rotten, right enough. The things you put up with for young love. Toast all round? Or shall I do some croissants?"

Our Infinite Fates 183

"I don't mind," said Arden, at the same time as I replied, "The more pastry, the better."

Mum turned on the oven with the toe of her slipper boot. Once the kettle was on the stove, she busied herself arranging croissants on a baking tray. "What are you two going to do today? Are you working, Bran? Or are you out on the farm again?"

"Working."

Arden finally spoke as he poured our coffees. Mine first, always. "Actually, I was wondering if I could have the day off? I'll go out and spray the crops right after breakfast, but after that—"

"Of course." Mum waved her hand. "You know, I don't think I've heard you ask for a day off in the entire time you've been here." Her eyes twinkled, and she looked at me with a knowing grin. "Was there someone you wanted to stick around for, hmm?"

Arden gave a tight smile. "Something like that."

If Mum noticed the subtle change in her beloved farmhand—the unceremonious dropping of the golden retriever act—she didn't mention it. Maybe she wrote it off as simple exhaustion.

We ate our croissants, slathered in sweet jam and salty butter, and chatted for a while about Gracie, who messaged me throughout. Overnight she'd been assigned a new nurse and had fallen swiftly and irrevocably in love with her, as fourteen-year-old lesbians were wont to do.

> she's an absolute ten Bran, even though she's ancient.
> like twenty two at LEAST. a veritable hag
>
> but I have caught feelings for real, mary on a cross
>
> and I can't tell if it's that I like being taken care of???
>
> it's the mummy issues for me

jokes our mum is okay really

as long as she's not trying to, you know, make jokes

Though it was a light conversation, it made me ache.

The third item on my dream list: watch my sister grow up.

I could see it so clearly, how our relationship would shift and mature without ever really *changing*. We would visit each other's houses and chat about our jobs over a bottle of wine (or mead, in her eccentric case), walk our dogs in the park on a Sunday morning (hers a Great Dane called Tiny), and when she fell in Big Love, I would make her wedding dress—or wedding tuxedo—myself, stitching my pride into every seam (though she would punish me severely if it wasn't sufficiently ugly).

I supposed that even if I didn't survive this encounter with Arden, she might still find another donor, and I could keep tabs on her from a distance in my next life. Technology had made it much easier to watch someone lovingly from afar. No more fraught journeys through snow-bleached Scandinavia only to be marched to a pyre—I could simply follow her on social media.

The thought was both laughably mundane and profoundly comforting. The absolute absurdity of modern connections: a spider's web with so many strands you couldn't quite see the real world through them. The internet was a Russian doll, gifts tucked inside curses tucked inside gifts, no way of knowing which formed its core.

Swallowing hard, I stood abruptly and grabbed one of the croissants left on the plate. "One for the road, if that's all right?"

Mum smiled. "Of course. I've got to run a few errands in town." There was a rosiness to her cheeks as she watched Arden and me, and I couldn't bear it. "Love you, Bran. And you know where I am if you need me, okay?"

Our Infinite Fates * 185

Arden sensed my melancholy as we left the house into the brisk March morning. The sun of the previous week had succumbed once more to a bitter windchill, and a low mist had drifted up from the valley. Glittering frost speckled the rosebushes, and the flowerbeds wrapped round the foot of the farmhouse. Arden pulled his checked lumberjack coat tighter around himself, kicking at a jagged stone on the forecourt.

As we walked past the stables, he shot the low building a furtive glance. "I wonder how Ceri's doing."

My breath plumed in front of me. "The doctor seemed confident he'd make a full recovery. God, I feel awful about it. I know I was just trying to save my sister, but . . ."

"Love can make a villain of anyone," he muttered, looking out to the mountains, low as an incantation, deep as a litany.

With his profile outlined in the ethereal mist, he was almost infuriatingly handsome. Then again, I was yet to meet a version of Arden I wasn't attracted to.

"So you're coming to hold down the fort at the bookshop with me?"

He nodded. "Remember when you actually held down the fort during the siege of Tenochtitlan? Took the Spanish days to break through."

"To be honest, no. I don't remember." My stomach cramped painfully. I always felt horribly exposed when Arden could remember something I did not. As though my past were being studied from behind a one-sided police mirror, and all I could see in return was my own reflection.

When we got to Beacon Books, Mr. Oyinlola was away at an independent booksellers' conference in London, so it was just Nia and me on the shop floor.

"You don't mind if my boyfriend hangs around, do you?" I asked her, gesturing to Arden, who stood awkwardly by the nonfiction. "We hardly get any time together."

She shrugged and adjusted the shoulder of her rust-coloured cardigan, which she'd draped over a corduroy pinafore dress. Her nose was firmly notched inside a book on modern chess openings, and it made me think of my brief suspicion that she was Arden. It still could have fitted—quiet, bookish, a little odd but in an endearing way.

"In fact, why don't you go and read your book in the back?" I suggested, warm and casual. "I'm happier out here, talking to customers, and you're happier back there, ignoring the world. If anyone asks, I'll say you're doing a stock check."

For a split second, I thought this might be a mistake—it was her father's shop, after all, and I was encouraging her to bunk off—but a grin tore across her face, revealing a row of pearly white teeth I rarely saw. "Amazing. Thanks, Bran. You're a real one."

She hopped off the stool behind the counter and traipsed through to the back, face still so buried in the book that she stubbed her toe on the doorframe and didn't seem to notice.

Arden and I continued the talk of sieges and wars throughout the rest of the day. He spent most of it loitering by the historical fiction section, fact-checking every blurb he read.

"What's the worst battle you've ever been in?" I asked him, in a gap between customers. I had taken Nia's spot at the counter, flipping through a catalogue we'd been sent by a publisher detailing their upcoming releases.

His eyes scanning the back cover of a book about the Napoleonic Wars, he puffed the air through his lips. "Siege of Jerusalem." Something dark and grief-shaped flashed over his face. "I was so young, but I remember so much. We poisoned the wells and cut down the trees surrounding the city, but nothing we did could hold back the tide of Crusaders. Seeing so many

Our Infinite Fates ✳ 187

of my people slaughtered—so many of the children I played with . . ."

Given the haunted expression on his face, I felt grateful, for once, that I had no memory of the time. He had lived with those gruelling mental images for a millennium. The thought made me want to hug him tight, but I didn't want to be the first to instigate any intimacy in this life. Another matter of pride. He couldn't bind me to a bed like an animal and expect me to want to embrace him, to kiss him, to cup his jaw in my hand and gaze into his eyes, to press my soft body against his hard planes, to . . .

"Have you ever killed anyone?" I asked him, keen to quell the heat pooling low in my belly. "Besides me, of course."

"Several times." He clenched his jaw. "To save loved ones, mostly, but in battle too. When I had to. History was a brutal place. You?"

I shook my head, thinking of what he'd said out in the fields a few days ago: *If a hero is someone who will give up love to save the world, then a villain is the reverse. Someone who will give up the world to save love.*

"Never?" He gaped at me now, the flap of a dust jacket pressed between his thumb and forefinger. "Not even on the Western Front?"

"Not that I can remember anyway."

There was a reverent silence, like there always was when one of us brought up the trenches. I looked around now at the quiet, orderly bookshop and felt a distinct pang of gratitude for my life as Branwen Blythe. Jam-slathered croissants and warm baths. The flip of soft, new pages. Clean bedsheets and a snoozing dog. A big, brilliant sky over pristine hills. If I were an artist, I would consider it an exercise in contrast, the way the darkness made the light seem so much brighter.

Just as I was pondering the meaning of existence, the door

chimed for the first time in nearly an hour. At the sight of the customer's livid face, the brief peace evaporated.

Ceri.

With a face like thunder.

Wales

2022

The crusted blood had been cleaned out of Ceri's hair, and his skin's ashen pallor had warmed up. His eyes were no longer dazed; rather, they were utterly incandescent. The bleary concussion had made way for blazing anger.

At first he didn't spot Arden tucked behind a bookshelf. "What the fuck, Bran? Do you know how much it hurts to be smacked around the head with a shovel?"

"No worse than a musket," Arden muttered, making a curmudgeonly tutting noise.

At the sound of the second voice, Ceri swivelled on his heel, then narrowed his eyes at the sight of my accomplice.

"You," he growled.

Arden made a little mock salute.

"I'm so sorry, Ceri." There was a note of pleading to my voice, but it didn't stop me from glaring pointedly at Arden. "We both are. I don't know what else to say."

Pausing as though debating whether to lunge at Arden, Ceri slowly turned back around. "Look, can we talk alone?"

"I think you must understand by now that I can't allow her out of my sight." Arden's tone was bored, his finger running over the narrow spines in the poetry section, but his ambivalence didn't fool me. I saw the way he stood up a little too straight, shoulders squared and senses heightened, the angles of him too sharp, as though waiting for an attack.

Ceri shook his head ferociously. "A lot of the aftermath was hazy, but I distinctly remember this guy threatening to kill you if you freed me. Then, when you freed me, he didn't kill you, but he said he would if I went to the police?"

My stomach flipped. "And he will. You have to know that."

"I won't. Provided you tell me what the hell is going on."

A kind of exhaustion spread over me, and all at once I couldn't fathom why I shouldn't just confess to everything. "You want the truth? Fine. Here it is."

Arden turned to me, grim warning on his face. "Don't."

And I *hated* that he was warning me. That he felt he had the right to order me around, after everything he had done to me.

"Or what?" My frustration was rapidly swelling into anger. "I've called your bluff once before. Or are you going to hurl all-new threats at me? Are you going to find all-new agonising ways to take my life?"

The fury rose hot and biting in my chest, as though my body had suddenly remembered all the brutal and humiliating ends I'd been subjected to. How could I have been content to just stand here in a bookshop, idly chatting about old battles, with the being whose sole purpose was to destroy me?

Arden's chest rose and fell in ragged peaks, meeting my rage with his own, but he tempered it. His blue eyes burned like the heart of a flame. "Him knowing the truth won't undo what you did."

I ignored him. "Ceri, you have a right to know."

An idea struck me then, sudden and breathless. A plan far more concrete than the abstract desire to make Arden want to save me this time.

Our Infinite Fates

191

A real, solid course of action that might actually lead to my survival.

My phone lay on the counter beside the till. It would have been too obvious to go through the rigmarole of opening the voice note app, but I subtly pressed the camera button on the home screen and swiped it to video.

I hit Record, making sure my voice was loud and clear.

"I can remember all of my past lives—or the last half-dozen, at least, though they go back much further. In each and every one, I've been murdered before my eighteenth birthday by the same killer who hunts me through every life. I still don't know why, or how. But I've never made it to eighteen."

Some of the tentative colour washed out of Ceri's face once again. "Oookay."

"You don't have to believe me." I folded my arms, feeling defensive, remembering the doctors examining me curiously in Vermont. The diagnosis of *mania* slapped to my chest like a scarlet letter. A patch of drool on a bleak collar. "The outcome will be the same, regardless."

"I think you must know how insane that sounds." Yet Ceri's gaze darted between Arden and me, as though remembering the fraught negotiations in the stables.

I took a steadying breath. "The reason I shoved you outside the flower shop, and the reason I tried to restrain you in the stables, is because I thought you were that killer. That you'd finally arrived in Abergavenny to end it all again. And I needed to stay alive as Branwen Blythe a while longer to save my little sister."

"But I'm not a killer." Realisation slowly dawned on Ceri's face, turned it from fury to disbelief. "You think he is?" He didn't have to point to Arden for me to know who he meant.

"Yes." The betrayal stung afresh. I still couldn't process the fact that Dylan, my almost-brother, was the person destined to slaughter me. "We've known each other for a long time, so I should have seen it coming, but I didn't." I took a deep breath, then said in a rush, "Do you believe me?"

Clenching his jaw, Ceri replied, "No. But I believe that *you* believe it. That you both do. And that's what scares me." He turned to face Arden, a taut apprehension to his movements. The furious bluster of his entrance had evaporated. "So you really are planning to kill her?"

Please say yes. Please say yes, so I have proof.

After what seemed like an eternity, Arden said flatly, "It has to be done."

Bingo.

"But why?" Ceri asked, mouth agape. He took a subtle but unmistakable step back, as though Arden might lunge at any moment.

"Good luck with that line of questioning," I snorted. "It's never got me very far. How are you going to kill me this time, Dylan?" I made sure to use the name he was known by locally. "Have you made up your mind yet? Poison served you well last time. Though being hung, drawn, and quartered looks like a wild ride."

"Don't push me, Bran." His voice was a low, coarse rumble.

"Or what?" I goaded. "What could you possibly threaten that's worse than death?"

"I can certainly bring that death forward," he said, with the cadence of a quip—but, given the situation, it landed rather south of funny.

Ceri shook his head vehemently, as though trying to wake himself from a strange dream. "This is nuts. This is all entirely nuts."

"I know. So go," I urged. "Walk away. Forget you ever got involved. Please."

He fixed his eyes on me imploringly. "You can't just . . . let this happen."

"I don't have much choice."

Our Infinite Fates ✳ 193

"We can restrain him." His voice rose with desperation now, and I was a little touched at the fact he wanted to save me despite what I'd done to him in the stables. "Here and now. I have to help you, somehow." He eyed Arden nervously, as though my killer would turn on him at any moment.

"Why?" I asked, utterly aghast. "After what I did . . ."

He shrugged, but it was tense, urgent. "None of this quite makes sense, but I think you're a victim of something bad. Psychological manipulation, emotional abuse, whatever. And for all her faults, my mother raised me right. You see someone in trouble, you help them. No matter what they've done to you in the past."

"Thank you, Ceri," I said, and I meant it. Humanity was full of goodness, as long as you wanted to see it. "But there's nothing you can do."

Silence settled in the store, yet it was anything but peaceful. It was taut, charged, like an electric cable slowly lowered into still water.

"I can't just walk out," Ceri said eventually, rubbing his face roughly. "You've just told me you're about to be murdered by . . . by this sick bastard."

A ridiculous defensiveness bucked in my chest. I knew with absolute certainty that Arden had never derived any pleasure or satisfaction from hurting me. He had a moral code, no matter how different from my own. He was no simple psychopath, no cold killer.

He did this because he had to.

I thought of the vision I'd had after escaping the asylum: a bone-white world, ash falling like snow. Pain larger than anything. Arden pleading at my feet. And that woman in the trenches, with her pale sheets of hair and her gnarled black fingernails.

This has gone on long enough.

Arden was just trying to protect me, even if I didn't fully understand what from.

Yet I acknowledged, even as I thought it, how twisted that logic was. How any modern psychologist would have said I was trapped in an abuse cycle, suffering from Stockholm syndrome, romanticising violence—none of it particularly flattering, nor particularly accurate.

"Please, Ceri." The fight was deserting me once more, that righteous anger making way for existential exhaustion. A sense of utter futility. "Go."

Another long, tense pause. "Fine." He turned to Arden, who was staring out the window, lost in his thoughts. "But you're not going to get away with what you're doing to her. I'll go to the police right now."

"The next time you *or* the police come near," Arden said, cold and slow and quiet, "I'll kill her before you can even say hello. Do you understand? You trying to stop me will be the death of her."

Ceri stared loathingly at Arden's knit-clad back for a few more moments before storming out of the bookshop, the cheerful tinkle of the bell almost an insult.

I stopped the video recording on my phone, heart hammering against my brittle ribs.

"So you're just going full villain now?" I asked, trying to inject a bit of levity into the atmosphere, but it landed dead at my feet.

Arden hunched to his knees, sank his head into his palms, and let out a pained roar. I couldn't tell what emotions were spilling over—frustration, hatred, terror—only that they were.

"Arden . . ." I whispered, half soothing, half fearful.

"Don't," he snapped, but the anger didn't seem to be directed at me. "Just don't, all right?"

We stayed in terse silence for the rest of the shift. Eventually he climbed to his feet and sat with his back to the wall, flipping

Our Infinite Fates   195

through a copy of *Ten Hundred Years of You* even though he had one at home. His expression was impenetrable as he read. Were the flowery declarations of love from decades ago difficult to bear? Did he remember the emotions all too well, or were they like the musings of a stranger? And why was he reading them now? To remind himself of what we once were? What we could be still?

A few customers came and went, and as they asked for recommendations—an espionage thriller for an uncle, something funny for a bereaved friend, a literary masterpiece for a discerning daughter—Arden visibly bit his tongue. It was as though the child at the heart of him desperately wanted to talk about books, but he felt he couldn't, because of the situation. How much of ourselves we had lost to this cruel fate, interests and passions gradually taking back seats to the driving force of our existence—imminent death. We were ruled by the twin pillars of pursuit and escape, our souls reduced to Tom and Jerry, the Road Runner and Wile E. Coyote, the crude concepts of hero and villain, chaser and chased.

The phone recording burned in my pocket like a hot coal, and as I thought about what I was going to do with it, my blood filled with fire.

Furious, hopeful, righteous fire.

When I finished locking up the shop at the end of the day, my phone flashed with a missed call and a voicemail from a local number.

Something like dread flickered in my chest. Had Ceri ignored Arden's threats and gone to the police anyway? Were they calling to check up on me? What would Arden do if so? He'd reneged on his threats back in the stables, but I doubted he'd do so again.

Hand trembling, I hit Play, holding the phone up to my ear.

A familiar calm voice sounded through the speaker.

"Branwen, hi, it's Dr. Chiang. Listen, I couldn't stop thinking about what you asked of me. Playing it over in my head again and again, unsure whether I'd done the right thing. You seemed in such a dark place, and, truthfully, I'd never forgive myself if something bad did happen. So I explained the situation to my wife, and she's willing to perform the procedure pro bono. Can you be in Newport this Friday afternoon? Give me a call back when you can."

All the breath was sucked from my lungs.

Friday was the day before I turned eighteen.

It had *worked.* My blind optimism had not been unfounded after all. Validation surged through me, rich and potent and golden.

If I stayed alive for two more days, Gracie would get my marrow.

And after that, I was going to live.

Ottoman Empire

1472

After several long hours in the sultan's library, I went to soak in the hammam.

I was painstakingly translating Ptolemy into Turkish at the behest of Mehmed himself, who had summoned me from Athens upon hearing of my linguistic capabilities—so advanced for a boy of seventeen. My head was a wrung-out dishrag after a day of slow writing, and I longed to steam away the intellectual rigor of the task.

It was late afternoon, and the külliye thrummed with activity. I strolled past the domed central prayer hall—arched with bands of colored stone and mosaic tiles—and the pretty arcaded courtyards with babbling fountains, then past the cluster of madaris, where my new friend Raziye was teaching a class on the Islamic sciences.

Beyond the campus lay the whole of Constantinople.

The sultan's mosque was built upon the high spine of the city, and everything within the city walls unfurled below—neat gardens and small farms, domes and colonnades and great monuments, towering marble columns topped with bronze statues and

198 ❋ Laura Steven ❋

gilded crosses, and the jewel in the sultan's crown: Hagia Sophia herself.

When I'd first arrived by sea, Constantinople was a fairy tale. A glorious marble palace was built into the seawall, dotted with countless balconies and grand statues of sea beasts, and it felt like I had entered a storybook. Now I understood the depths of the poverty in the place, the way the poor lived in the narrow cracks between the rich like ants in the grout between tiles, the way disease spread like a flash flood and hunger gnawed at the bones of children.

All great empires were the same, at the heart of them.

Still, I sucked in lungfuls of cypress-tinged air, the scent laced with lemon and jasmine and Mehmed's favorite honey-pistachio baklava, and smiled inwardly. I had only been here for a few months, but the seven-hilled city was starting to feel like home.

The changing room in the hammam was cool and quiet. At the center was a marble fountain, ringed with wooden galleries in which several members of the sultan's Porte relaxed with tea, coffee, and sherbet beneath the vaulted mosaic ceiling. The air was a mingling of heady perfumes: bergamot and patchouli, cedarwood and citronella, lavender and neroli. The pegs were hung with some of the finest garments I had ever seen—jewel-toned kaftans of brocade and velvet, taffeta and cashmere, embroidered with metallic thread in motifs of flowers and branches and endless knots, suns and moons and stars. I was at once painfully aware of my good fortune and profoundly grateful that I had not spent another life begging for scraps on the streets of Yerevan.

The men's hammam was fogged with steam, and the main bath was empty but for a cluster of the sultan's advisers talking in low voices, so I slipped into one of the smaller domed chambers notched between the īwān corners. Sparks of pain shot up and

Our Infinite Fates

199

down my wrist and into my thumb—the perils of too long spent writing—and I shook them away with a grudging wince.

After steeping in the sensual heat of the water for a few moments, another young man of around my age climbed into the private bath with me.

Immediately I sat more upright, averting my gaze to the small woven basket he had set down. It contained a key purse, perfumes, and a comb studded with mother-of-pearl. A richly embroidered towel was laid over the top, along with an extraordinarily thick-lensed pair of fogged eyeglasses.

"Merhaba," he greeted me, running his hands along the tiles as he submerged his torso in the water. "Apologies if I bump into you. I am almost entirely blind."

I nodded a subtle acknowledgment before realizing that was useless to him. "Merhaba."

"I hope you do not mind the company," he went on. "Only, I have not spoken to another soul all day long."

"Not at all," I replied, my Turkish smooth and natural. I would always favor good company over solitude.

There was something familiar about the boy—his deep brown eyes, his close-cropped hair, his beaked nose, and his high cheekbones flecked with beauty spots. Had I seen him at an ulamā chamber, perhaps? He seemed too young.

He rested his head against the edge of the bath and sighed into the warmth. "Have you ever thought about how many trees are felled just to power the hammam's furnace? Sooner or later, we will be using wood faster than the earth can grow it. Although we have recently begun to use olive pits and sawdust as fuel, and they seem to work adequately enough."

Leaning my head back until it was submerged in the water, I ran my fingers through my hair and sat back up. "You work in the hammam?"

"No, but I have a deep compassion for the world around me." He rested his arms along the ridge of the bath, making no effort to wash himself with the soaps and scrapers he had brought with him. "The cycle of nature, of flora and fauna, of growth and death. Our earth is the most precious thing we have. We do not think enough about protecting it."

Perhaps due to the heat in the bathhouse, the softness of his tone, or the very nakedness of our bodies, the moment seemed oddly intimate, as though he had confessed something expressly vulnerable.

My eyes went once again to the toiletry basket; something about it had snagged my attention. A brown leather-bound notebook tied with a slender red ribbon, the whole thing no larger than a pocket square. Next to it lay a narrow pen made of intricately patterned reed.

That was when I knew.

In every life in which it was possible, Arden carried a notebook. In all his centuries, he had likely written more words than he had spoken aloud. He'd once told me, on a canal boat in Venezia, that a thought did not become real to him until written in ink.

"Arden," I whispered.

His shoulders tensed almost imperceptibly, ripples of muscle twitching on the boned ridges. "Quite. Although here I am Emir." A light snort. "You are beginning to know me rather well, even though most of our encounters have been as short as they were fraught."

Nerves flooded my body, and our familiar banter slid from my tongue unbidden. "I admit I am glad to see the back of the Wars of the Roses."

He tilted his head in my direction. "Mmmm. Though I do wonder how it all worked out."

Arden, here, naked, beside me.

Our Infinite Fates

201

Our bodies, mere feet apart, bare for each other's eyes to roam, more vulnerable and exposed than we had ever been before each other. I wondered just how much of me he could truly see. Had the tether led him so easily to me despite his dim vision?

Tucking my feet up on the seating ledge—legs covering my chest and heels covering elsewhere—I asked, "Do you really serve the sultan, then? Or are you only here to kill me?"

He gave me a wry smile. "The sultan commissioned me to illuminate a muraqqa of the stories of the devil Iblīs."

My brow furrowed in confusion as I thought of how detailed the miniature paintings were, how intricate and precise the calligraphy. "But you have poor eyesight."

"Indeed. It was a shock to me when I was summoned. I think the sultan really wants me for his seraglio."

The royal harem.

Arden's expression betrayed no emotion; he was getting better at concealing his feelings.

Still, I caught the flicker of dread as he added, "The High Porte has been grooming me rather heavy-handedly."

A barb of jealousy spiked my heart. Mehmed famously had a taste for young noblemen. Trying to disguise how protective I felt of him, I asked casually, "Will you go?"

His jaw was tight as he answered, "I might not have much choice."

The revelation sat between us for a few moments, as potent and tangible as the perfumed steam. Questions rattled through my mind, chaotic and unclear. Was he only staying here because of me? Would he kill me sooner, to free himself from the situation? And, most ridiculously of all—

"Have you ever . . ." I started, but trailed off, throat dry.

He quirked an eyebrow at me, as though he knew exactly what I was trying to glean from him. "Ever what?"

"Made love." The words sounded simultaneously crass and childish, and my cheeks pinkened. "To anyone, in any life."

"For coin, yes," he said flatly. "You?"

I shook my head, feeling like an almighty fool. Of course Arden was no virgin. Still, the thought of him being so intimate with another person . . . It should not have felt like a betrayal, but it did.

Plucking a bar of lilac soap from his basket, I began scrubbing at my chest in an attempt to dispel the awkwardness that had descended. "How did you convince Mehmed to summon me from Athens? How did you know I was there, let alone of my skills?"

"I did not."

I blinked, the soap suspended above my shoulder. "You mean . . . ?"

"Fate brought us together this time. Not I."

The thought was strangely moving. I looked up at the painting behind Arden's head: a depiction of nude women bathing in a hammam not unlike this one.

"Do you believe?" I asked, vaguely aware that I was interrogating him. "Not just in fate but . . . in God, I suppose. Any of them."

As he adjusted himself on the seating ledge, I battled the urge to look down at the lean lines of his body. The dark hair on his chest. The hard grooves of his hips.

"I am not sure," he said. "If I had been born here and only here, I think I would devote myself to Allah. The teachings are beautiful, and I often find myself swept away on their current. But I was not born only here. And what happens to us . . . it defies the teachings of the Qur'an."

I rubbed my neck with the soap. "In what sense?"

"Well, the fact we reincarnate, for a start. We do not lie in our graves awaiting our Day of Judgment. And there are the mechanics

Our Infinite Fates 203

of it all. For Muslims—and Christians too—the soul is breathed into the body by God at some point shortly after conception."

"Whereas we seem to die in one life and be born into another almost instantaneously?" I mused. "Our souls never seem to exist in a womb."

"Exactly." He once again stared up at the mosaicked vaults and domes of the ceiling, eyes blurred and unfocused. "I've been tracking our births and deaths over these last few centuries, and they are usually within moments of each other. Which would suggest, then, that a soul is born at first breath."

"What about the other major religions? Do we fit neatly inside any of them?"

A subtle shake of his head. "Elements of us, yes. But not us in our entirety. In Judaism, as in Islam and Christianity, the soul transcends to a kind of afterlife, which we obviously do not. For Hindus, souls are infinite. Their energy has existed since the dawn of time, and they're reincarnated from one life to another. Thus, all souls are bound to saṃsāra—the infinite cycle of birth, death, and rebirth."

"Like us," I said triumphantly.

"Like us, but not like us." There was something wistful to his expression. "Hindus also believe that souls are continually reincarnated in different physical forms according to the law of karma. At the time of death, the sum total of karma determines our status in the next life. Human or beast."

"We're always human." I reached into his basket and retrieved the mother-of-pearl comb, dragging it through my wavy hair.

"We are. And our standing in the next life appears entirely random, no matter what atrocities we commit against each other." His hand curled into a fist at the thought of it. "If karma had a bearing, we would surely be locusts by now. Buddhists believe in reincarnation, but not that there is an eternal, unchanging *soul*

204 * Laura Steven *

that transmigrates from one life to the next. It is more a flame of consciousness, heavily influenced by morality and karmic energy."

Dropping my comb-bearing hand into the water, I let all this sink in. "So, theologically speaking, we should not exist."

The idea was profoundly lonely, that our existence fell outside the beliefs of most of the world's population. It made me feel wrong, somehow. Shunned by the gods, broken in a way that could not be mended by worship or prayer.

Alone, but not alone. Because there was always Arden.

And together we were sacrilege.

As though to escape the weight of the moment, Arden submerged himself underwater, running his hands over his head and face, then breaking the surface once more.

All at once, I wanted to be held by him. I wanted to press our warm, clean, perfumed bodies together. I wanted to mourn together and hope together. I wanted to *be together,* in all the ways it was possible to be so. A clashing of mouths, a tangling of limbs, his hands on my body and mine on his. I wanted—oh, how I *wanted*—to feel our existential pain melt away beneath his touch.

Truth be told, I had wanted it for centuries. I had *burned* for it.

And centuries were a long time to spend burning.

This being has slaughtered you more times than you can count, I reminded myself fiercely. *You have slaughtered each other, and still you know not why.*

But my traitorous body would not listen to logic.

In this crooked universe, there was only me and Arden.

For the thousandth time, I longed to ask him why he did this to us over and over again, but I knew he would shut down. There would be no answers. Not today, and perhaps not ever. But it was comforting to know he too agonized over the *how.*

His hand started to rummage in the basket for something, and

Our Infinite Fates   205

with a snap I realized he needed his comb—which was still in my curled hand.

"Here," I said roughly. "Let me."

Without allowing myself the luxury of forethought, I slid along the seating ledge and began combing his short black hair. As the spokes glided over his scalp, he let out an almost imperceptible shudder, then swallowed so hard his throat bobbed. He moved toward me, only a few inches, the water shifting around his body. The heat of him pressed against me, even though we did not touch.

As I combed, a strange kind of urgency came over me, somewhere between panic and possessiveness.

Soon, he would belong to the sultan. Every inch of his body, his mind, his soul.

But I wanted him to be mine.

Blood rushed and pulsed through my body, and I was dizzy with it. Laying the comb on the tiles, I leaned over and cupped a hand around his neck.

His eyes fluttered shut, and he hung his head against my wrist. "Evelyn, I . . . I can't . . ."

"Why not?" I urged, unexpectedly fierce.

Breathlessly, his hand went to my side, his skin somehow both warmer and colder than the bathwater. Part of me expected a blade to my ribs, but it was only the hard-softness of his palm. "You know what I have to do."

I leaned in, until our lips were mere breaths apart. "So don't."

His grip on my ribs tightened, desperate and raw, and I let out the smallest of gasps—shocked by how deep and masculine the sound was. In his throat, a frantic pulse thudded against my palm.

As our lips finally touched, soft and hard and desperate, every inch of me shivered before igniting into flame, and his tongue flickered over mine and I moaned.

My hand went to his hip, the edge of my thumb nestling into the crease between thigh and inguen, and as the coarse breath slipped from his mouth, there was a gathering in my lower belly. A pulsing of desire, deep and pristine and singular. His lips went to my jaw, my throat, and I was almost dizzy with the need to feel him inside me.

There was only one thought on my mind, bright and sharp as an emerald:

I have never wanted anything more.

Then, behind us, a cleared throat.

Folded arms. Livid grimace. Around a thick waist, an embroidered towel finer than any other.

The sultan.

Wales

2022

The next day was agonising—in more ways than one.

When I told Arden the news about the emergency appointment, he allowed himself the smallest glint of relief, of hope, before switching straight back into detached mode.

His anger from the bookshop cooled and hardened. I got the sense his hostile introversion was driven by shame—at the way he'd had to threaten me all over again, the crassness of it so at odds with who he really was. Quills and inkwells, soft parchment and warm jumpers, vials of sugar water and twangy folk music, carefully pressed flower petals between tissue paper.

In any case, he barely looked at me as we repaired fences and trundled around the fields. A few times I tried to start conversation—asking questions about what he was doing with the crops, voicing some fears over the impending marrow harvest—but I was greeted with grunts and one-word answers.

Usually I was cuffed to the bed each night with a grimace and an apology, but the apology now dropped off entirely.

That night, as he was about to manacle me anew, I had the desperate urge to cup his jaw, to force him to look at me. Really, really look at me. But truth be told, I was livid.

There were so many small humiliations tucked inside my fate.

Death threats in front of a crowd, the cuff around my wrist as I slept, lying to the people I loved most in the world. It reminded me so acutely of those weeks and months spent in a rusted cage in the asylum hallway, shivering uncontrollably, arms strapped to my waist, dozens of pitying eyes observing me like a rare creature in a squalid city zoo.

And then there was the not remembering where it had started.

It was infuriating, knowing that our origin story was buried just beyond reach, and yet no matter how hard I dug at the earth, dirt crusted beneath my desperate fingernails, I could never quite grasp it. It was innately unfair, this power Arden had over me, a knowledge he chose time and time again not to share. Just to remind me who was in control. Who was winning.

Was that a fair accusation? Maybe not.

Did Arden ever wonder if I had forgotten because I just didn't care enough? It must have felt that way, sometimes, in the darkest moments.

Such a casual wound: *I remember, and they do not.*

I felt it every time my sister shrugged when I recounted a childhood story that meant so much to me, but of which she had no memory. I felt it every time I thought of my ancestors, who had likely also been reincarnated and yet did not remember me at all. I remembered them: my parents, my siblings, my kin. Not every detail, every story, but their texture, their feel.

Despite the utter exhaustion burning at my eyelids, I lay awake in the cottage bedroom for hours, stewing in silence. From the lack of screaming, I guessed Arden was doing the same, only his back was turned and he stared unmovingly at the wall.

Frustration cast a long shadow over me. I knew the Arden who'd changed his mind about killing me in Siberia had to be in there somewhere, but I had no idea how to reach him. After all, he'd had thirty-six years to rebuild his walls since then. The cut-

Our Infinite Fates

209

throat execution attempt in El Salvador had proved he'd done just that. Now his fortress was harder to breach than ever.

Yet maybe I would not have to breach it to survive.

After the altercation in the bookshop, I had sent Ceri the secret video. The camera showed only the dark swirled wood of the counter, but the audio was crisp enough to make out what was being said: a clear death threat. Cowering in the bathroom of Arden's cottage under the guise of a long shower, steam billowing around me, I typed out the accompanying message to Ceri:

> If you really want to help me, please take this video to the police—but not yet. The bone marrow harvest is set for Friday at 4.45 p.m. at a private practice called Verdant Park, and it should be wrapped up by 6 p.m. If they want to arrest Dylan, they should do it then. That way, if it goes wrong and he kills me before they can cuff him, at least I've saved my sister. Again, I am so sorry for everything. Bran x

I awoke in the middle of the night to the sound of crying. Not the ragged, raw screams of the nightmare, but something hollower, more devastating. It was soft, muffled with attempts to silence it, but there was no mistaking the hitch in Arden's breath, the sniffing of his nose, the uneven rise and fall of his shoulders.

Everything in me softened. The soul I loved was still in there. He was not as unfeeling as he pretended to be. The walls he had built around himself only kept the emotions gated inside—it didn't stop them from existing altogether.

"Arden," I whispered, but even that sounded too loud in the still of the night.

He quietened as best he could, but there was still a tremble to his outline, an unnatural lack of breathing.

210 ✳ **Laura Steven** ✳

"Arden, come here. Please."

Still no response. The air in the small bedroom was cool, taut, almost rippling with tension.

Frustration reared in my chest, but I tried to bridle it into something more productive. I didn't want to add any anger or heat to this conversation. I wanted to scale the walls of Arden's emotions, not build them higher with my bullishness.

I shuffled onto my side so that I faced him properly, ignoring the yank in my shoulder from where my wrist was cuffed. "Do you remember on the Western Front when——"

"I'll remember the Western Front until the end of time," he muttered, a subtle shudder to the words. "Sometimes I think I'd give anything to forget."

I closed my eyes briefly, picturing damp rats and crooked shell sculptures and rolling fields of poppies. "Back then you said, 'I love you, and I have loved you, and I will love you.' What happened to the future tense? What changed? Why have you closed yourself off to me?"

A stiff beat. Then: "You were right. Siberia hurt too much."

There it was. Something real at last. My arms yearned to hold him. To share this mutual pain.

"Please, come here." A gust of wind rattled the window. "I feel like I'll implode if I don't get to hold you."

"I can't," he said, but the words had more give than they usually did.

A tear slid down my cheek unbidden. I couldn't remember it forming, couldn't remember the point at which my body had decided to cry. "I miss you so much."

He rolled over onto his back, sniffing and facing the ceiling. "I'm right here."

"You're not, though, are you? Not really." One of his poems came back to me, forming a shape from smoke and shadow. "'My

Our Infinite Fates

211

heart is a haunted house surrounded by a moat of my own digging, kept empty of warmth so that I will not miss it come winter.' It's beautiful, Arden. All of it. But that part broke me. You don't have to do this to yourself. You are allowed to feel warmth."

"I can't," he whispered again.

"Arden, if you don't come to me right this second, I swear to god I will yank on this cuff until my wrist bleeds. I will gnaw my actual hand off. Do you really want to see me go full beaver on myself?"

Despite the raw emotion of the situation, Arden spluttered with shocked laughter. "*Full beaver?*"

"I said what I said."

The crude joke was what finally broke the standoff. He climbed into bed, shivering, his bare upper body flecked with goose pimples. Heart tugging in my chest, I rested my face on my cuffed arm and let my other hand go to his cheek. It was rough with stubble and wet with tears.

"Talk to me. Why all this?" I wiped a tear from his cheek, but it was immediately replaced by another. The sight of him so sad was like having my ribs cracked open one by one.

The inches between our two bodies felt like miles, and I longed to close the gap, but I knew I had to do this slowly, steadily. I couldn't scare him away just when he was finally lowering a drawbridge.

He pressed his eyes closed. "We got married, once. Do you remember?"

I almost said *no,* but then it came back to me, the memory gossamer-thin.

"There were waves, somewhere," I recalled. "And . . . and the scents of pine resin and sage. Woodsmoke."

His lips twisted into a grimace, loose hair falling into his face. "Something went wrong, and I had to kill you in front of all our loved ones. I have never felt so monstrous in all my days. I still see your throat opening like a bleeding mouth whenever I try to fall asleep. I am haunted, Evelyn. I am *haunted*."

"So why do you do it?" I asked, out of habit more than anything.

The drawbridge pulled up a little in response. "Please, don't ask. Please. Please, let's just . . . talk."

I nodded.

A fraught breath shook itself loose. "To you, I'm always changing—changing faces, bodies, strategies. But I'm always just *me*. And it breaks me to see the change on your face when you realise the truth . . . even when some part of you knows already. There's always the tipping point. The moment we can't come back from. When you *know,* and I know, and it has to happen. But it *ruins* me. The second your joyful face changes ruins me."

Hurt cleaved through me like a hot knife. I had never really thought about it from his point of view.

I wrapped a hand around the back of his neck. The feeling of his skin against mine sent a shiver down my back, my legs. "I don't think I've ever seen you cry before, other than in Siberia."

He scoffed, sniffed, wiped away another errant tear. "That seems unlikely."

"No, really. Not in the trenches, not in the asylum. You're far too good at guarding your heart. El Salvador absolutely terrified me. How you could just shut off centuries' worth of love and emotion and keep your distance. I could never do that."

"I did write some particularly angst-filled poetry in those years. But keeping my distance is not just to protect myself. It's to protect you too. That night in the trenches, when I told you I would lay my body over yours, war after war after war, life after life after life. This is me doing that. You deserve to live the fullest eighteen years you can in every incarnation without the complication of loving me. You deserve a quick and painless death, not

Our Infinite Fates

devastating poison in a frozen grave." A ragged breath. "If that means swallowing my emotions, so be it."

"And I'm asking you not to do that. Come back to me, Arden. Please. Come back to me."

At last, I closed the inches between our bodies, lying flush against his bare chest, nuzzling my face into his throat. Though his skin was cold, his body was warm, and having it pressed against me after nearly four decades apart felt like coming home. I wanted to lie there forever in his arms. I wanted to forget that we had ever stabbed or strangled or impaled each other on jutting coral.

I wanted to make pancakes with him on a Sunday morning, his folk music playing in the background, the window cracked open to let in the fresh scent of the moors.

I wanted us to be ordinary.

Was that so much to ask?

"I love you," he moaned, as though it was the most painful thing he had ever said, and it was. He pressed his forehead to mine, and pure, raw emotion surged through me. His breath was on my lips, his red-rimmed eyes searching mine in plea, or prayer, or something altogether more devastating. "And I will always be yours. But I gave up the right to call you mine a long time ago."

He brushed his lips over my tear-salted cheek, lingering for a few beautiful, wrenching seconds. My heart leaped against my ribs, pulse fluttering wildly, hope and longing curling through me.

But then he was gone, out of the bed, out of his own heart.

"Arden," I pleaded, barely able to see through my sobs. I had him. I *had* him. He was in my grasp, in the notches between my ribs. "Come back. Come *back*."

But he didn't. He laid his body once more on the hard, unforgiving floor, his bare back facing me, his racked shoulders finally stilled.

Mali Empire

1290

The Sahara shimmered with heat as our strongest camel drew water from the well. Grunting with exertion, it walked staunchly in the opposite direction while a neat snare of camel-hair ropes and leather buckets collected our lifeblood.

I looked around, stomach knotted with worry. My best friend, Lalla, usually coaxed and comforted the beasts as they worked, but she was nowhere to be seen in the baked vastness.

In fact, I had not seen her all morning.

After setting off at dawn to the call of horns and kettledrums, we had stopped to assemble a crop of tents in which to seek shade from the ferocious midday sun. Our thousand-strong caravan was traveling north from Timbuktu, hauling as much gold and ivory as we could carry. We would bring salt and cloth, metal and incense, pearls and garnets and writing paper back to the West.

We were only two days into the two-month journey and already it had been fraught with problems, despite our having doubled our numbers to protect ourselves from bandits. First there had been the sandstorm, then the nest of vicious scorpions. Then our runners had returned from the oasis at which we were supposed to resupply, reporting that the tribe was demanding a far

Our Infinite Fates   215

higher passage tax than on our last trip. We could not afford the chunk of profits it would devour, and so while the khabir had gone to negotiate, the rest of us were doing the best we could with a small well—thinking longingly of the date palms and fig trees at the oasis nearby. After such a prolific streak of bad luck, Lalla's grandfather, Yufayyur, was convinced our caravan was plagued by one of the supernatural demons rumored to haunt the desert.

As I worked at the ropes dangling in the well, Aderfi, one of Yufayyur's friends, nudged me with a teasing elbow. In our caravan, a child of one was a child of all, and Aderfi treated me like his own granddaughter—warm, always, but with an air of elder authority.

"Thiyya, you are far more useful when you are not being distracted by our Lalla." His tone was one of jest, not vexation. The rigors of the desert had not yet eroded his good spirits.

Lalla and I were always being chastised for messing around instead of working. A gifted scribe from just ten years old, she was supposed to be learning the ways of her father, mapping our routes and recording transactions. But I was the omnipresent parrot squawking at her shoulder, making fun of everyone and everything. We had been inseparable almost since birth—our friendship was gods-fated, our families believed, as we had been born within moments of each other.

"Do you know where she is?" I asked Aderfi, running the rough rope over my calloused palms. A bead of salted sweat slicked into the corner of my stinging eye.

"Last time I saw her, she was in her tent with Ridha," said Aderfi, leaning over the side of the well to adjust a bucket.

Ridha was Lalla's father—a studious man made all the more earnest by the recent death of Lalla's brother, who had fallen victim to the guinea worm. Some dark part of me was grateful that Lalla too was racked with grief. I'd spent years mourning my own mother: a raindrop falling through the cracks in my cupped palms, returning irrevocably to the scorched earth below. The necessary cycle, the fountain of life, but still so unbearably painful. I longed for her embrace with a thirst I could never slake.

I looked up from the well, and after scanning the company saw Ridha deep in conversation with another scribe. Abandoning my task as though water was of little importance, I set off in the direction of Lalla's tent, ignoring the calls of protest from Aderfi.

The distant dunes were warped with heat, the hot breeze carrying the scent of lovegrass flowers and desert thyme. As I ducked into Lalla's goat-hide tent, the cool of the shade was an instant balm. My skin felt tight and raw, as though the top layer had been peeled off and rubbed with salt.

Lalla sat cross-legged on a woven mat, loose leaves of paper and parchment sprawled out around her. Ridha had been teaching her how to navigate and record routes with traditional methods— dune shadows and desert winds, mountains and rocks and pebbles, the sun and the stars, ancient eroded gullies and the presence of mirages. But Lalla had an almost supernatural sense of direction, an internal compass the rest of the caravan had always marveled at, as though she were connected to the terrain in some fundamental way.

"Do you want to cause some trouble?" I asked playfully, wondering how we might trick Yufayyur this time.

She jolted as though I'd awoken her from a strange reverie, a transaction ledger falling from her lap. Her smooth cheeks were wet with tears.

I sat down beside her and nudged my shoulder against hers. Her skin was far cooler than mine. "Are you all right?"

"Fine." Her tone was terse and irritable. She was always prickly as a cactus whenever she was upset.

Rolling my eyes, I replied, "No, you are not."

Our Infinite Fates   217

"I am, Thiyya."

"You are the most stubborn person I have ever known," I said, with a half chuckle. "Like a mule. Remember that herd of ornery goats that blocked our path for days last year? You belong with them. Go on, give me your finest bleat." She did not even toss me a cursory smile, and the mirth in my stomach curdled. This was serious. "What is it? Is it your brother?"

"Not in the way you think."

She tucked her knees to her chest. Her body was curved and rounded where mine was sinewy and lithe; she filled out her djellaba in ways I never would. "I mourn my brother, yes, but . . ." She peered up at the roof of the tent. "What if I never live up to him, in my father's eyes?"

I made a *pssh* noise. "Not to speak ill of the dead, but you have ten times the talent of Maqrin."

"But no penis."

A bark of laughter escaped my lips before I could snatch it back. "True enough."

"I often wish I did," she whispered, as though confessing something deeply sinful. "Everything would be simpler."

Nodding sagely, I said, "I shall make you one, if you like. Perhaps with goat meat, wrapped in a vine leaf. Or you can borrow one from the next camel who dies."

She finally laughed, then—a glorious peal that spread warmth through the tent—and shoved me, playfully, so that I toppled over. "You are disgusting."

"But you love me for it."

Sitting back up, I noticed I had squashed some precious papers as I fell. I smoothed out the maps, running a soft finger over Lalla's distinctive swirling penmanship. I struggled to read any of it, in truth. It was as though the letters danced and rearranged themselves as I tried to parse them.

"What is your secret anyway?" I asked. "How can you read the land in a way none of your ancestors have been able to?"

Brushing away the last of her tears, she sighed. "You really want to know?"

"I do."

A long beat, then she said plainly, "Camel dung."

"Pardon?" I blinked, not sure I'd heard her correctly. Was she cursing at me in some new and inventive way?

Her lips twitched. "It always points in the direction of the next water source."

"That cannot be true."

She shrugged, a smile pulling at her lips. "I have not yet been wrong."

Camel dung.

She was no genius. Or perhaps she was, in her own way.

Suddenly, nothing had ever been so hilarious. I roared with laughter so loud my ribs ached, and soon Lalla was shrieking too. We rocked and rolled on the woven mat, clutching at each other the moment we caught our breath.

"Does your father know of this?" I asked, gasping from the hilarity.

"No." She chuckled, sitting up and dusting off her djellaba. "Let him think me magic. It is the only value I have, in his eyes."

Her features sank once more into sorrow. She rubbed at her collarbone, and I fought the pang of fear that she'd been bitten by something again. Last time it had gotten infected, and she had almost succumbed to the fever. I had never been so frightened in all my life.

Who would I be without her?

"Do you want a game of senterej?" I offered, gesturing at the velvet drawstring bag containing our favorite board game. "It might cheer you up."

Our Infinite Fates 219

"Are you sure? I always beat you so horribly."

It was true. Her intellect was a different breed from my own. I contributed to the caravan in broad strokes and raw enthusiasm, wild but inaccurate passion, while she agonized over the finest of details, every grain of sand as important as the next.

Stroking my chin like a sage old bearded man, I said, "I shall blindfold you. It might give me a fighting chance."

"As you wish." Lalla would rather have rolled around in a scorpions' nest than lose at senterej, so I knew winning even with her eyes closed would give her immense satisfaction.

We set up the game—green and gold pieces on a blue-and-red-striped board—and I tied a long silk scarf around her eyes so that only the tip of her nose protruded from the bottom. Then we moved our pieces around the board in the werera marshaling phase, and I read aloud the squares they had moved to so Lalla could visualize it in her mind's eye. After mere moments, Lalla had captured my feresenya, and we began taking turns.

"I heard on the winds that Badis has been sniffing around your skirts," I said, watching with dismay as Lalla captured my alfil.

"Sniffing around my skirts?" Lalla snorted. "Thiyya! He is not a feral dog!"

"Well, you know what I mean. He likes you." I swallowed down the jealousy bobbing in my throat. I did not want to share her with her brother's best friend. "Do you like him?"

"I suppose he is nice enough." She shrugged, as though she cared not either way. "But he is too sad without Maqrin. Like a crown with the garnet missing."

"I can think of one way you might make him happy."

Ever the childish one, I started making vulgar kissing noises. Lalla shrieked with laughter, tugging down her blindfold.

"Gods, Evelyn, will you stop—?"

Everything in me stilled, as though a great gust of wind through the dunes had suddenly died, every grain of sand dropping to earth at once.

"What did you just call me?" I whispered, a cold dread creeping up my rib cage.

Our eyes were fixed on each other with an intensity I could not parse.

Why was my heart thumping so hard?

"Nothing, I—"

My lungs tightened as I said, "We have met before."

I knew not where the realization came from, only that it answered a niggling question that had lurked on the tip of my tongue for years. I could not even say for certain what the question was, only that there was something critical that I did not know, something just beyond the horizon that threatened my very existence.

Lalla blinked, water filling her eyes once more. "What do you mean, 'before'?"

But I knew that she knew. She was just testing how much I remembered.

Dragon gates painted red and gold. Lotus leaves on rolling rivers. Candles flickering in stone churches. Forests so dense they obliterated the sky. Greek tragedies in wine-drunk amphitheaters.

"In other lives," I all but choked. "And you have hurt me. You have *killed* me before."

She dropped her head into her hands, shoulders trembling. "It is not how you think. I do not kill you because I want to. After Bianjing . . . the memory of what you did for me plagues me still."

Bianjing. It stood out as a kind of axis point, a place where things between the hunter and me had tilted. Northern Song was a blur of gray, but there was a general sense of sharpness, of rawness, in my final hours. I tried to pull at some of the half memories—the dragon gates, the lotus leaves—but they were dug in too firmly at the root to unearth.

Our Infinite Fates   221

Images of our various ends stained my mind's eye like mirages. A stone to the temple in Samarqand, a rope around my neck in Al-Andalus, a pillow over my face in deepest Iceland.

How could I reconcile those blunt and brutal deaths with Lalla? My Lalla.

The pain of the betrayal bent me double.

"In the past . . ." I started, voice watery, "you did not allow us to become close. You killed me cleanly." My words became furnished with something anger-hot. "You are a hunter."

Lalla shook her head wildly. "It is not for sport. I have to, Thiyya. Evelyn. I have to kill you, in every life. That is our true destiny. The true reason we were born within moments of each other. Gods-fated." Her moon-round face was wrinkled with sorrow. "I cannot tell you why, but you have to believe me. I have no choice."

I began shaking involuntarily, with a fear so visceral it made my head light and my blood cold. "So you intend to kill me again, then?"

"Not now," she replied hoarsely. "But before we are eighteen."

"How could you do this?" Hysteria mounted in me like a storm. "How could you let me get so close to you when you knew what you would eventually do to me?"

"How could I not?" Lalla wept even harder, and my Berber spirit protested—albeit meekly—at all the water we were both wasting. "All our parents ever talked about was how we were destined to be best friends. How our bond was thicker than blood and water both, for it was written in the stars. And the first few years . . . I did not remember that mutual death was our true fate until we were seven or eight years old. What was I supposed to do then? Murder a child, when I was a child myself? Stop talking to you entirely, leaving you to agonize for years over why I suddenly hated you?" A rollicking sob almost caved her chest inward. "Gods,

Thiyya, I love you. I love the bones of you. I cannot fathom how I will bring a blade to your throat after all that we have shared."

All the childlike innocence in me withered and died in an instant.

The things she had done, knowing that she would one day bleed me dry.

She had played endless board games and screamed as I left empty snakeskins in her bed. She had braided my hair and applied salve to sunburned shoulders, mourned my mother and listened to my worries about what it would be like to become a woman without her. She had shared with me her favorite poems and proverbs, and it had felt like she was baring her very soul. She had chased me through the midnight desert, pulling from a well of boundless energy that only tiny children can draw from.

Together we had stolen kola nuts from her grandfather's reserves, and acted out silly little plays to entertain our fellow traders, and laughed and run and danced and cried and lived, every moment of every day, with each other.

The cruelest fate the gods and stars had ever written: the person I loved most in the world was the person who would ultimately destroy me.

if people are songs
written in the major or the minor key,
then you, my dear, are major.

a climb, a crescendo, a thousand trumpets,
a clashing of cymbals, joy and awe,
rousing, reaching, always to the stars.

and I am but a dirge, a requiem, a lamentation,
a melancholic harp in D minor,
forever wondering why you chose me.

—AUTHOR UNKNOWN

Wales

2022

We made it to the day of the bone marrow harvest without major incident, without a reply from Ceri, without a visit from the police—and without a single scrap of emotion from Arden. It was as though that tearful, manacled night in his bed had never happened, as though I had never wiped the salt slicks from his cheeks, as though he had never said those words that unravelled me every single time: *I love you.*

I tried to break through the freshly constructed fortress, tried to coax that drawbridge low, but whatever had caused that raw outpouring was once again lost.

I will always be yours. But I gave up the right to call you mine a long time ago.

As much as it drove me wild, as much as it felt like grit scratching beneath my skin, I did understand. Because, in his eyes, with the day of the bone marrow harvest also came the day I was going to die.

The day he was going to *kill* me.

And so, really, how could he be soft, how could he let himself love, when he was about to execute me?

I woke that morning with a sense of unease low in my belly. There were so many ways the day could unfold, and I had no control over any of it. Was I going to die today? Or would my hastily

Our Infinite Fates

225

hatched plan with Ceri—who had left my message on the two blue ticks—somehow save my life?

Then, another fear beneath it all. A fear that felt primal, animal, carnal.

What would happen if I *did* survive?

A blurred storm of images broke over my mind's eye. Sheets of white hair, and black fingernails curling into grotesque helixes. A bone world raining ash. Pain larger than me, larger than anything. Arden, begging, pleading.

When he had convinced me to trust him in the trenches, I believed he was acting from a place of protection—or I had thought I did, which was all that mattered.

Was I a fool to want to live regardless?

Or should I be trusting Arden still?

After much internal debate, I decided not to tell my mum or Gracie about the private appointment. It saved them the worry. I would rather be able to visit the hospital later that night and tell my sister the good news: that my part was done. That I had done everything in my power to make sure she was going to be okay. That if everything else went to plan, she'd have a long life of chasing sexy nurses ahead of her.

I tried not to think about what else I might have to say: *Goodbye.*

My eighteenth birthday was tomorrow. I had been born a little before seven in the morning, which meant Arden had less than a day to end my life after the procedure. Surely, surely, he would not do it straight away. A needless cruelty. And yet I thought of the poisoned hip flask in starlit Russia. His words: *I knew my willpower would falter at the last minute.*

I didn't know which would be worse—having to say goodbye to my sister or not being able to say it at all.

Arden and I spent the morning working on the rain-slicked farm in silence, the sky dark as smudged charcoal, the air between us fraught. By the time we climbed into the car to drive to Newport, the tension was tighter than ever.

For a few moments, I watched the dramatic hills roll by, the tops of them obscured by grey fog. My stomach lurched at the thought that this might be my last ever sighting of them.

Number four on my dream list: complete the Three Peaks Challenge.

There was no reason, really, only that it seemed like the sort of thing thirtysomethings did to convince themselves they were not middle-aged, that their bodies were not yet failing them. And so this entry on the list was more about reaching that age in the first place; the sore legs and breathless views would be a happy bonus.

If this final gambit didn't work, and Arden overpowered me . . . would I be spawned somewhere wholly flat next? The salt flats of Bolivia? The Everglades of Florida? The outback of Australia?

How long would I have to wait to see Arden again?

And why did the thought of another seventeen years without them hurt so damn much?

Unable to quash the questions, I muttered, "Are we really going to spend our last day together like this? If you get your way, we won't get another chance to talk as the real *us* for nearly two decades. Is there absolutely nothing you want to say to me before then?"

Instead of answering, he stabbed the radio's On button. An obnoxious male voice started yammering through the speakers about how the cost-of-living crisis was a fallacy, and in the very next breath addressed the swelling strikes gripping the nation.

"Same shit, different century," I said, trying to lighten the mood. "Maybe we should revolt, like we did in Lyon."

A token puff of laughter. "Yeah."

Irritation prickled beneath my skin. "Arden, please. Talk to me. I'm not going to beg, because it'll be uncomfortable for everyone involved. But surely there's something between I-won't-let-myself-love-you and *this*. I deserve conversation, at least."

A distant roll of thunder rumbled through the sky. "It's not about what you do or don't deserve."

I folded my arms across the cream silk blouse I'd found at a vintage shop. I'd refurbished the stained buttons with a pink rose-print fabric. "Ah, yes, it's about you and your inner turmoil, which is so complex that a lesser being like me could never hope to understand it."

Arden clenched his jaw. "Don't."

His eyes were strained with tiredness. He hadn't screamed last night, nor had I heard him sob beneath the stars, and I got the distinct sense he'd kept himself awake so that I could get some sleep. Or so that I wouldn't catch him with his guard down again.

Keeping my voice level, I said, "After everything we've been through, you don't even have a comforting word to say as I drive to a clinic to have a giant needle shoved into my bone?"

His grip tightened on the steering wheel. "I'll be there with you the whole time."

"What a relief," I snarked. "Almost makes up for the fact you'll be murdering me a few hours later."

We drove the rest of the way in silence. The whole time I tried to guess what he might be thinking. Was he steeling himself? Or was he so exhausted from lack of sleep that he could not think at all?

The private hospital of Verdant Park was a low red-brick building separated from a residential street by a neatly pruned row of hedges. We parked in a small car park with spaces far too narrow for the Jeep, and strode toward the revolving doors in silence—me slightly ahead of Arden. Out of the corner of my eye, I caught him pinching the bridge of his nose, taking a beat to steady himself.

After checking in at reception, a short, mousy-haired nurse led us through to a private room with a wall-mounted TV and a painting of a waterfall hung above a single hospital bed. I sat uncertainly on the bed, while Arden eased into a high-backed blue armchair. The nurse ran through a pre-op consultation and had me answer some questions about my medical history and my anaesthesia allergy. Then she handed me a backless surgical gown, and I went into the en suite bathroom to change out of my regular clothes.

I took a moment to steady myself in the mirror. Staring at my reflection—so young; how did I still look so young?—I thought of Gracie, and of how good it would feel to tell her everything had gone well. I thought of the full life ahead of her and fought away the inescapable idea that I might not be around for it.

Dr. Schneider—my therapist's wife—breezed into the room almost as soon as the nurse had left. She was a broad-shouldered woman with natural-blond hair and a strong jaw. Her pale blue surgical scrubs were immaculately ironed, and her posture was rod-straight. She had the air of a military drill sergeant, but once she smiled—exposing a row of gently crooked teeth—her whole manner relaxed into something resembling sunniness.

"Branwen, hi!" she said, her German accent making it more like *Bran-ven*. "Welcome. How are you feeling?"

"I'm okay." I smiled, but it felt tight. "Nervous. Thank you so much for agreeing to do this."

"Not a problem." She picked up my chart from the foot of the bed. "My wife thinks very highly of you. Anything I can do to help a patient is my pleasure."

She flipped through the pages. Her fingernails were cut right back, and she wore no jewellery. With a small nod, she said, "Now,

Our Infinite Fates 229

we're going to be giving you some fairly robust pain relief—codeine, ibuprofen, and oral morphine—but they won't take all the discomfort away during the procedure itself. There's a reason we usually use general anaesthetic, okay?"

Fear flickered in my stomach, but I wouldn't let Arden see me nervous. He wasn't the only one with a proud streak. "Okay."

As it happened, he shifted in his chair and asked, "Are you sure you don't want to try local anaesthetic?" The question was directed at me, but his gaze was fixed squarely on the doctor. "You might not be allergic to that. And even if you do have a reaction . . ."

He trailed off, but I knew what he was going to say.

Even if I had a reaction, I was going to die soon anyway. As long as Gracie got the marrow, it didn't matter.

But I still had to be able to run if I had to.

Because the police might come.

They might arrest and charge Arden, given the dark threats he had levelled at me—and even if he was released on bail, those precious few hours should be enough for me to make it far, far away from Abergavenny. If I was in anaphylaxis, that would be slightly trickier.

"I'm sure," I said plainly, and something unreadable darted across his face.

Half an hour later, I lay on my front on a sterile operating table. A clean sheet had been laid over it for my comfort, but I still felt the cold metal pressing through the fabric and against my stomach and thighs.

Arden stood off to the side, dressed in a rumpled pair of scrubs, his dark hair tied back from his face with an elastic band. His presence had been a bone of contention—it was irregular for a patient's loved ones to be in during the surgery—but because I wasn't having any anaesthetic, he'd argued that his support would be needed. Eventually, they'd allowed him to come in, providing he changed into clean scrubs and washed his hands to within an inch of their lives.

I didn't really understand why he'd fought so hard to be in here with me. It wasn't like I was about to up and run from the operating table.

After sterilizing the back of my hip, Dr. Schneider said, "Now, we're about to insert a special needle into the marrow cavity of the hip bone, where stem cells and blood are aspirated. To obtain this lovely rich marrow, many small aspirations must be done, and we will also be harvesting lots of red blood cells. We'll give those back to you intravenously once you're in the recovery room. The whole thing will take around an hour, okay? Are you ready?"

No. The biopsy had been bad enough, all those months ago.

"Yes," I said, lacing my fingers together under my chin and gripping hard.

The needle piercing my skin wasn't so bad, but I couldn't fight the gasp once it burrowed into my bone. The pain was at once sharp and dull, like a shard of ice pressed against a nerve ending, the excruciating feeling of a toothache amplified tenfold.

When the needle began to move around, I thought I might vomit. It took all my effort to stay still, when every inch of my body wanted to tear itself away from the source of the pain. I let out an involuntary whimper, pressing my forehead into the back of my hand.

There was the squeak of footsteps on the immaculate floor, and then two palms on my forearms.

"Hey," said Arden softly. There was a slight click of joints as he sank to his haunches, so our faces were inches apart. "Hey. I'm here. Okay? I'm here."

Our Infinite Fates   231

The needle was pulled out and then reinserted, and I whimpered again.

"Fuck," I moaned, tears sliding down my face.

Arden wiped them away with a caressing thumb, the touch so tender it threatened to unravel me. "It's okay, love. It's okay. It'll be over soon, okay? Just look at me."

I lifted my head, vision starry. "It hurts."

He took my hands in his and pressed his forehead against mine. "I know. I know. I would do it for you if I could."

I sucked the air through my teeth. "Maybe you can."

"I already checked," he whispered. "I'm not a match."

"You already checked?"

"Of course," he said, his voice rough. "Months and months ago, before you went through all this. You have to know I would take all the pain for you if I had the chance."

I simultaneously wanted to smack him around the head and burrow my face into his chest. "You're infuriating."

"I know." His face was twisted with concern, with regret, with love, and it hurt just as much as the surgery.

Another pullback of the needle, another savage reinsertion. "Arghhhhhh."

"Tell me your small joys."

"What?"

He swallowed hard, tucking my loose hair behind my ear. "Back in the trenches"—he shot a panicked look at the medical professionals, but none of them reacted to the strange statement—"you told me that big joy and small joy are the same. What are your small joys, from this life?"

A bid to distract me, and a welcome one.

Because it almost sounded like he was letting me convince him to change his mind.

"Analysing Taylor Swift lyrics with Gracie. All of us decorating the Christmas tree, with peppermint hot chocolate, feeling sick from too many candy canes." The pain in my hip was so bad my vision blurred, the room canting around me. "The first frost on the Beacons each autumn. A new season of my favourite TV show dropping. Finding the perfect vintage piece in a thrift shop. Listening to friends argue in coffee shops because they both want to pay, both want to treat the other."

Arden's eyes shone. "I'm starting to see it more and more," he admitted, as though confessing to a mortal sin. "The small joy. A few weeks ago, I saw these two teenage girls sitting on a bench at a bus stop. Their legs were twined together, and one of them was painting Pride flags on the other's eyelids, and they were giggling so much that she couldn't keep her hands still. They both ended up covered in glitter and eyeshadow. And I thought, *Evelyn would love that*." A wistful smile. "You've rubbed off on me, these last thousand years."

"Keep talking." I gasped through fresh peals of pain.

"One of my favourite words is *confelicity*."

"Does it mean 'with Felicity' in Spanish?"

He mimed flicking my forehead. "I'm astounded you remember so much of a previous tongue."

"Fuck off. Or: Vete a la mierda. Gracias."

He stroked my sweat-slicked temple with his thumb. "*Confelicity*—an English word with Latin roots—means a kind of vicarious happiness. You've always been so good at that. When you see other people happy, it makes *you* happy. Doesn't matter who those people are, whether loved ones or perfect strangers. You just let their joy radiate through you, and it's miraculous. I've never mastered it, really. Except with you. When you're happy, I'm happy. And when you hurt, I hurt."

Tears spilled ever faster. I was so dizzy I could barely see him.

Our Infinite Fates 233

"It hurts so much." I didn't know whether I meant my hip or the other thing, the big thing, the awful thing.

"I know." As his thumb wiped away more of my tears, his lips brushed my forehead. "I'm here. Everything's going to be okay."

A beautiful, beautiful lie.

Wales

2022

After the procedure, I was wheeled through to a recovery room, where the painkillers kicked in relatively fast. Then I was hooked up to an IV through a cannula in my forearm, and my red blood cells were pumped back into me. A small radio sat on the windowsill, blaring out upbeat indie folk. I was light-headed and a little disorientated, and the fast-paced fiddle made me feel as though my veins were being plucked like strings. A nurse brought me water in a plastic cup and told me to buzz her if I needed anything. I was advised to rest there for an hour before the discharge nurse came to see me.

A curious mixture of emotions coursed through me. Relief that it was over. Dread at what would come next. A strange kind of elation—a likely by-product of the post-pain endorphins my body was merrily producing. Like I had fought a great foe and won.

And most potent of all: anticipation.

Were the police about to storm the building? Or had Ceri deleted my message in a spiteful instant?

And if they didn't come . . . how was I going to die?

When?

Arden sat on a chair beside me, staring out a window that looked onto the leafy suburban street.

"What was all that about?" I asked, once we were alone. "One

Our Infinite Fates 235

minute you're treating me like I'm nothing, the next you're wiping away my tears and kissing my forehead?"

I knew as I said it that it was going to provoke a reaction. He had never treated me like I was nothing, never in all our lives. But I had to shake those emotions loose somehow, had to elicit a reaction strong enough that he might still change his mind.

"Like you're nothing?" A puff of frustration as he dropped his head into his hands, and I felt the smallest pulse of satisfaction. "Fuck, you have no idea, do you?"

My teeth clenched so hard it made my jaw ache. "Enlighten me, then."

His words were muffled as he spoke into his palms. "Everything I do, everything I have ever done, is to protect you. Shielding you from my emotions is to protect you, because they're so fucking overwhelming that I can barely deal with them myself."

"That's why most people *do* share emotions. Because they're impossible to process alone. You'd think, after all these centuries, you'd have figured that out by—"

"I would do anything to protect you," he went on, as though I hadn't spoken. "And it will torture me forever to know that I can't protect you from *me*. I have to cuff you to a bed, have to threaten you in a bookshop like a fucking psychopath. I have to kill you in . . . god, in hours. Because if I don't—" He curled his hand into a fist but didn't finish the sentence. "God, if I'd just said no, back in Lundenburg. If I'd just . . . but then there wouldn't be us. And which is worse, really?"

My chest started to pound. Lundenburg—the London of a thousand years ago. That was where this had all begun?

When he didn't elaborate, I tried to gently coax. "Arden—"

"I have to go to the bathroom."

He stormed out of the recovery room in search of a toilet. He must have been severely rattled by his own outburst of emotion,

236 ⁕ **Laura Steven** ⁕

because he didn't even try to tell me to stay put. Then again, the chances of me running anywhere were fairly slim—my hip, though no longer subject to the sharp, scraping pain, felt both stiff and weak.

Still, that candle of hope burned in me. Maybe this time it would be different.

I had done what I had set out to do—I had saved Gracie. But I wanted more than that.

I wanted to save *myself*.

I wanted to stay in this life so badly that it ached.

I wanted to watch my sister heal and grow, to see who she would become without the shackles of illness. I wanted to go on shopping trips into the city with her and Mum, where we'd toast to good health over mimosas, and they'd despair of my bizarre thrifted clothes. I wanted to take home my rare and absurd finds and run them through my beloved red Singer, to feel the shudder and give beneath my palms, to feel that bolt of pure, uncomplicated joy when I held them up to the light and saw what I'd created. I wanted the shop on the high street, the lunches with Nia, the jam-and-butter croissants at the big oak table in the farmhouse. I wanted the Welsh wilds, I wanted a home of my own, I wanted to meet my twenty-year-old self and my thirty-year-old self; I wanted to see my body wrinkle and sag. I wanted to marry, to bear children, grand-children, the family around me so big and wild that I couldn't cup it in my palms even if I tried.

I wanted, I wanted, I *wanted*.

I wanted, more than anything, the impossible thing: Arden there with me.

If only want were enough.

I leaned my head back against the headrest, sick and woozy. My eyes fluttered closed for a moment and, as they did, I heard the distant wail of a siren.

Our Infinite Fates

237

A distant siren getting closer.

As the screech got louder and louder, blue and red lights appeared over the hedge separating the hospital from the road. Two police cars turned into the car park, driving right up to the front of the building, the officers quickly clambering out.

Everything in me soared.

Ceri had done it. He had really done it.

Maybe all that *want* would finally amount to something.

Nonetheless, an acute sense of foreboding came over me as I heard a commotion of voices in the corridor, and several booted feet marching down the hall toward the recovery room. I was dizzy, flooded with adrenaline, half expecting Arden to dart back in there from the toilet to slit my pale throat.

I had nothing with which to defend myself.

But though my blood roared, and my guts churned, he didn't come back.

Four police officers appeared in the doorway.

"Ms. Blythe, are you all right?" asked the first—a spindly man with a tall forehead and a spotted chin.

I nodded numbly. I was safe. I was safe, and now four cops were here.

How could he kill me now?

A female police officer said, "And where is Mr. Green?"

"He said he was going to the toilet." My own voice seemed very far away.

"Check them all," muttered the policewoman to the youngest two cops. "And make sure nobody gets in or out of the hospital."

Two sets of boots clomped out of the room, and the policewoman stepped toward me. She was tall, thin, and light-brown-skinned, with close-together eyes and sunken cheeks. Her black hair was pulled back in a severe bun, streaked grey at the temples.

"Mr. Hughes told us everything," said the policewoman. "About the assault in the stables, and about your reasons for doing it. I must confess, it's a tall tale. And yet the threats from Mr. Green sounded very real indeed."

A monitor to my right made several low-pitched beeps. "Am I going to be arrested?"

"Mr. Hughes has no interest in pressing charges against you," said the policewoman. "We'd simply like to ask you some questions."

"At the police station?" I asked.

The policewoman gestured to the IV of red blood cells and the myriad monitors and pill packets around me. "Given the circumstances, here is fine."

My mind swam.

Where was Arden?

The two cops who'd been sent to find him hadn't yet returned.

"Thank you for cooperating, Ms. Blythe," said the policewoman. "I'm DI Dehghani, and I just want you to describe what happened, in your own words."

I swallowed hard, meeting her ferocious gaze.

And then I told her everything.

The truth, the whole truth, and nothing but the truth. No matter how ludicrous it sounded.

"That's why I fought so hard to do this procedure early," I finished, biting my lip. "I was terrified Dylan would kill me and Gracie would be left without my marrow."

Where is he, where is he, where is he?

DI Dehghani looked thoroughly bewildered—and completely out of her depth. She looked over her shoulder as a nurse entered the room with a clipboard, then hastily exited again. "All right, well, we'll need you to come down to the station for a more official conversation, but I see no immediate need to do so, given the medical circumstances. Come in tomorrow, once you've had the chance to seek legal representation."

Our Infinite Fates

"Legal representation? But you said yourself, Ceri has no interest in pressing charges against me for the stable incident."

"Believe it or not," replied the mustachioed officer next to her, "the police can press charges without the victim's consent. And no matter what the circumstances, you still knocked someone out and tied them up in a stable with your own two hands. To that you have already confessed."

"Come to think of it," mused Dehghani, "I wonder if it might be best to have this Dr. Chiang present too. This all seems to have been rather distressing for you, and you seem very confused about what's going on. Psychiatric help may be required." She muttered this last part to the other officer, as though I couldn't hear her.

Some dormant animal in me bucked at the idea of institutionalised psychiatry—ice picks and starched white straitjackets, pain and fear and humiliation—but I nodded in agreement, almost but not quite numb.

I was weak and exhausted, but my mind was also rattling with all manner of escape plans. If they didn't need to speak to me in the station until tomorrow, that gave me a decent escape window.

And yet . . .

There was the clomp of boots in the corridor, and then the two police officers who'd been searching for Arden came back. One of them—a round, dark-skinned man with a solemn expression—made eye contact with the detective and gave a subtle jerk of the jaw.

I took the terse headshake to mean one thing.

Arden had escaped.

Wales

2022

When the police left the hospital to search for Arden in earnest, they gave clear instructions to call them if he tried to make contact. I agreed to go down to the station the next morning to have a more formal conversation, and they asked if I would like a police chaperone to stay with me in the meantime. It was for my own protection, with the suspect still at large, but I declined. It would be hard to flee South Wales with a cop at my side.

And running away was hardly the behaviour of an innocent teenage girl.

At around eight in the evening, Dehghani dropped Mum and me back at the farmhouse, which had already been searched for any trace of Arden. My blood fizzed with the acute sensation that he was going to jump out on us at any moment, and I briefly regretted my decision to turn down police protection, but I knew my only shot at survival was to get as far from here as possible before turning eighteen—which was in a little under eleven hours' time.

I don't know if I really believed that running away would work. It never had before; the tether had always led Arden to me, somehow. But when the only alternative was to lie in wait for Arden to find me . . . I had to try. There was nothing left to lose.

I didn't want to have to run for my life, but I wanted my life enough to run.

Our Infinite Fates

241

Once I was home, Mum flipped on the under-cabinet lighting in the kitchen, casting the room in an almost orphic glow. My eyes searched every shadow for Arden, but he wasn't lurking in any of them. Every inch of me crackled with fear, anticipation, and myriad other emotions that made no sense. It was like I had my finger jammed in a plug socket, electricity coursing up and down my veins.

It was dark outside, but the night was clear, the sky swirled with silver stars. The kind of night that made me want to lie on a picnic blanket on the grass and just look up. Think about the relentless passage of time, how vast my existence had felt, and yet how small compared to the universe.

"Do you want a cup of tea, love?" Mum asked.

She'd stopped sobbing at last—and stopped chastising me for arranging the procedure without her knowledge, without her there to comfort me. I'd told her a vastly simplified version of events, omitting the reincarnation backstory and just keeping to the death threats. First she had been almost catatonic with shock—*Dylan? Our Dylan?*—and had fallen silent for almost ten entire minutes before mustering any words at all. Then came the self-blame. She was horrified at herself for not spotting the warning signs—despite there not being any—and quite prolifically beating herself up for allowing a near-stranger so willingly into our lives.

I bit my bottom lip, not wanting to upset her even more. "Is it okay if I go and rest for a bit? I'm so tired."

"Of course." She could barely stand up, and slumped forward onto the kitchen island, elbows on the marble and palms on either side of her face. "I can't believe it. I just can't bloody believe it. Dylan? He was so . . . *Dylan*. And—god, I'm so sorry, Bran. I should've done background checks. I should never have let him get so close to you and Gracie." She ran her hands through her hair, shoulders trembling with shock. "I just always think the best of people—I can't help it—and I . . . If I'd lost you both . . ."

My heart curled in my chest like a wounded animal.

I always think the best of people.

Like mother, like daughter.

"Mum, it's okay." I crossed over to the counter and wrapped an arm round her shoulders. It was a strange feeling, to technically be her child, but in actual fact to be so much older than she could ever comprehend. "You didn't lose us. We're still here, okay?" I allowed myself a beat, to let the impossible reality of the statement sink in. "And I'm all right. Really, I am. The whole thing was like some weird dream."

"But he's still out there. He doesn't have a key to the house, but how on earth are we supposed to sleep tonight? What if he comes to finish the job? What if he bangs the front door down?" Her fingers gripped harder at her hair, pulling at the scalp. "God, I can't believe this is Dylan we're talking about. *Finish the job,* like he's some kind of . . . psychopath. It doesn't make *sense.* He's never shown a single sign of aggression in his life. He rescues bumblebees with broken wings. He carries a vial of sugar water, for god's sake."

"Yeah, well. Hitler was a vegetarian."

Mum let out a shocked bark of laughter. "I've never met anyone with a darker sense of humour than you. Except maybe Gracie."

A smile twisted my lips, but I hadn't really been joking. If there was one thing that living through history had taught me, it was that everyone had their own moral code, one that made perfect sense to them—no matter how monstrous.

Not that I believed Arden was monstrous.

"And to think you'd only just told me you were in love." Mum shook her head fiercely. "When did the abuse start, Bran? Before or after that conversation?"

Our Infinite Fates 243

She so clearly wanted the answer to be *after*. She didn't want to regret having missed the signs as I'd stood in the kitchen and told her, out of nowhere, I was dating her farmhand.

"After," I said firmly. "Only in the last few days."

"But that doesn't make any sense, either. I just . . . I can't wrap my head around it. That someone could change so suddenly, so severely. I'm not saying I don't believe you, Bran. Not for a minute. I'm just saying I'm shocked beyond belief." A fraught headshake. "What triggered it, do you think?"

"Remember that sheepdog we had when we were kids, and he had a tumour pressing on his brain? And it made him develop sudden rage syndrome?"

"God, yes. Percy. He was a lovely animal, until he wasn't."

I shrugged. "Humans are just animals too, aren't we?"

She stared at me, her eyes faded, red raw. "Are you seriously suggesting Dylan only turned murderous because of a brain tumour?"

"I dunno, Mum." All the fight was leaving me, all the propensity for twisted jokes and mad theories. I rubbed my face with exhaustion, still pumped with painkillers, still stiff and aching. "But I'm tired. Can I go to bed?"

Somewhere outside, a branch cracked, and we both jumped. She went to peer out the window but didn't seem to find anything too troubling. Still, my pulse pattered like rain on a roof.

She stood up straighter, suddenly decisive. "That's it. I'm sleeping in your room with you."

"Mum, no," I replied instantly, insistently. "Please. The police are going to be keeping an eye on the house anyway." It was a problem my mind was trying to untangle as I planned my own escape. "Stay awake all night if you have to, but I need some peace and privacy. And I trust the police to find him. I really do."

She sighed, letting loose an awful day, an awful month, an

244 ✳ Laura Steven ✳

awful year. "Oh, all right. I just feel like I'm doing a bad job, you know. As a mum."

"That's ridiculous. Why do you say that?"

Fiddling with the plain white gold wedding band she still wore, she mumbled, "Not picking up on the signs with Dylan. Not spotting Gracie's illness sooner. Letting your father go out drinking on Christmas Eve when he should've been home with his girls. I've dropped too many important balls."

"Mum, we caught Gracie's sickness early. You know that. Nobody could have predicted Dad's accident. And Dylan . . . I had no idea, either. When he first threatened me, I was as shocked as you were."

"I suppose, but . . ."

"You've been an amazing mum." The words choked in my throat as I tried to convince myself they were not a goodbye. "You always have, even when you were grieving Dad. I know how much it killed you to lose him, but you never let Gracie and me see how badly you were hurting." I couldn't help it; the tears spilled over, hot and fat, and it felt as though I might never stop. I sniffed fiercely. "I love you very much."

Mum threw her arms around me, and in the dim pools of light I saw the wetness on her cheeks too. "Oh, I love you too, Bran." She wiped away a tear on my cheek with her thumb, fixed her watery blue eyes on me. She gazed as though the secrets of the universe were buried in the depths of my pupils. "My heart beats for you both. You are the lights of my life. I hope you know that."

Swallowing the ragged lump in my throat, I said, "I do."

She gave me a final squeeze. "Now get some sleep. I'll check on you in a bit. And don't go thinking for a second I've forgotten it's your birthday tomorrow." Her eyes crinkled with warmth and affection. "We're going to make it special. I promise."

Our Infinite Fates * 245

"Coffee cake from Francine's Bakery?" I asked, trying to imbue my voice with genuine hope for a cake I would never eat.

Mum smiled. "Coffee cake from Francine's Bakery."

As I climbed the stairs, I wondered whether that was the last thing she'd ever say to me.

So much fresh devastation, over and over again. No matter how many people I loved and lost, it felt like a fishing hook through my heart every time.

Alone in my room, the adrenaline threatened to leave me all at once. The urge to sink to my knees and sob consumed me, as though gravity had suddenly become too overwhelming a force. I flicked on the light and tried not to crumple at the reminders of a life I loved so much.

Three stuffed animals: a penguin, a pig, and a hippo. From my mum, my dad, and my sister, each of them faded and matted by time and tears shed into their fur. A pink feather boa strung over the mirror on the vanity—a relic of Gracie and me dressing up as country music singers. Star-shaped glitter sunglasses and a jewellery box filled with friendship bracelets and lockets. School textbooks notched on the bookcase, Polaroids stuck to the walls, jigsaw puzzles and board games stacked on top of each other.

I was still a kid, and yet I wasn't.

The walls were covered in posters and vinyl covers—Taylor Swift and The Jam and ABBA, collected because they reminded me of the people closest to me. Taylor for Gracie, The Jam for my dad, ABBA for my mum. Little connections to them that might, if I was lucky, transcend time and death and fate. Maybe I would hear one of their songs in a future life and, for the smallest of moments, be back here with them.

Looking around, I saw my dad tucked into so many little corners

246 ✳ **Laura Steven** ✳

of the room. Photographs, old toys I couldn't bring myself to throw away, the Terry Pratchett books we'd read together. A gift wrapped inside my curse: even when I died, my memories of him would endure. He would endure. My immortality kept my loved ones immortal too. My grief built monuments in their honour, and I visited them from life to life. Until, inevitably, they faded. How many others had I loved and lost and eventually forgotten?

> *life gives us grief like mounds of wet clay,*
> *ripe and heavy beneath our reluctant hands,*
> *and with it we can do one of three things.*

At the thought of Arden's poem, sadness opened its maw and threatened to devour me whole.

Because even if I did survive the night, this birthday, this fate, it was still the end of something. Arden would no longer be in my life. He would no longer be the sun around which I orbited. He would be caught, eventually, and likely charged. The Dylan who had become a part of this family would be gone. There would be no more watching morning cartoons with him and Gracie, no more jam-and-butter croissants with him and my mum. No more Formula One and roast beef. No more trundling over the vast and wondrous land with him, my feet kicked up on the dashboard of a tractor. No more.

The ridiculous, ridiculous truth: I wanted to take Arden by the hand and run with him—forgetting that he was the very thing I was running from.

I slumped on the bed, the rusty springs in the mattress groaning under my weight. I ran my fingers over the bedspread—embroidered with little daisies and violets—and wondered if it might be the last time I ever touched it.

Don't be maudlin, I thought, but I couldn't help it. I'd always had

Our Infinite Fates

247

an unhealthy attachment to objects. They felt like touchstones of the lives I loved, and yet I could never take them with me.

My hands went, at last, to the old Singer sewing machine at the back of my wardrobe. The physical representation of what could have been. The vintage clothing store next to Beacon Books, the buying trips around the glorious world, or my own fashion line—eccentric, unexpected, with a cultish celebrity following. Maybe I'd just be a seamstress, tailoring and mending beloved garments, finding peace in the hum of the machine and the steady flow of fabric beneath my palms.

I left the wardrobe ajar, as though that would keep the doors to my dreams propped open too.

Shaking, I opened the bus timetable and saw that there was a bus to Cardiff leaving Abergavenny at 10:30 P.M.

And I was going to be on it.

My escape plan was hastily formed and wholly reliant on a lack of police presence out at the back of the farm. I suspected they would be watching the entrance to the country road that snaked up to the farmhouse, but they might not be vigilant enough—or have the manpower—to keep tabs on the overgrown farm track beyond the stables.

The stables. I wondered dimly how Ceri was doing and hoped we hadn't traumatised him too much. I owed him a thousand apologies, and a thousand thanks for doing what he'd done.

Switching the light off, I curled up under the covers and waited until Mum came up to check on me, as promised. The door clicked open, and I pressed my eyes shut, feigning sleep. I couldn't face another emotional conversation or I might not have the strength for what came next.

Once she'd padded back downstairs to sit vigil, I grabbed my backpack and a pair of shoes, and crept over to the window.

There was a ledge on the outside around the right size for my full body to crawl onto. Once I was out, I closed the window quietly behind me. The moonlight shone on the faces of my three stuffed animals, my bed still rumpled and unmade.

From the ledge it was a small jump down to the roof of the conservatory. I just had to hope Mum was in the kitchen, not the living room, or she'd see me on my final descent.

As I sat on the lip of the roof, I took a deep breath and then let myself drop. I was an old hand at such things, after several centuries of jewel thievery and general deviancy, and remembered to bend my knees to minimise the jarring impact. There was a soft crunching noise as I hit gravel, a keen pain in my bandaged hip, and I crouched in a ball for a few moments, praying Mum hadn't heard it and wouldn't flick the outside light on.

After a few moments, nothing.

So I ran.

Northern Song

1042

My secret sweetheart and I strolled down Imperial Boulevard, our hands brushing but never touching. We were two boys of seventeen, something sweet and heady blossoming between us like the pear trees that lined the banks of the Bian River. I was the son of the emperor's favorite concubine, and Sun Tao was a sword-swallower famous far beyond the entertainment quarter, and we were so delicious and so scandalous and so *right*.

"Do you want to be emperor some day?" asked Sun Tao, biting wetly into an overripe peach he had plucked from a tree.

"No. I do not have the stomach for it." I let my palm drift idly over the black fence running along the bank of the river, fighting the urge to lace my fingers through Sun Tao's. "I would rather set a snake loose in my chaofu than dole out a punishment."

Ahead of us was the Xuande Gate, painted a stark bloodred and adorned with golden tacks. Its walls were decorated with phoenixes and floating clouds; two glazed dragons bit down on each end of the rooftop ridge, tails arched into the dusky sky. The Imperial Corridors lined either side of the river, merchants hawking their wares from makeshift shops notched into the corridors. Bolts of silk spilled into the street, and I longed to examine each

250   ✳   **Laura Steven**   ✳

one in detail, to imagine the luxurious garments they could be stitched into.

Sun Tao finished his peach and tossed the pit into the river. It landed on a lotus and capsized the flower. "What have you against the punishments?"

"They are grotesque. If you have never seen a set of eyebrows sliced off with a sword, I do not wish the image upon you. Particularly when the victim does not deserve it. Last week a boy was executed for murdering his father—which is fair, perhaps—but his teacher was subjected to the same thousand cuts, simply for not imparting the right wisdom to his student. Tell me, is that just?"

Sun Tao shrugged, as though it were of little consequence to him. "It is the way things are done, and one must trust they are done for a reason."

My attraction to him waned a little. I had thought him more visionary, but perhaps the repeated thrusting of steel down his gullet had sawed away any sense of enlightenment in him.

"I cannot explain it," I said, looking away from him. A donkey clopped along the boulevard, pulling a wooden cart laden with millet. One of its eyes had become mangy, and flies pestered it. "When I witness suffering, it is as though I feel it in my own body."

"Empathy." Sun Tao *tsk*ed. "The human curse."

One from which you do not appear to suffer, I muttered inwardly.

Righteous fire filling my chest, I urged, "China is greater than this. We can light the sky with fireworks and print books in their thousands. We can send a ship to sea with magnetic compasses and trust it may find its way home. And still we butcher our people like animals. We offer them no way of proving their innocence, no trial, no counsel. It is barbarous and wrong.

"There is a girl in the palace keep right this moment," I went on. We crossed a balustraded stone bridge with a gilded pavilion crowning its center. Fishing boats bobbed cheerfully on the water. "She was caught last night scaling the walls, trying to break in for an audience with the emperor. A runty thing, by all accounts, and the guards confess she poses little real threat, but still they would subject her to forced suicide. Perhaps I should throw myself before the court and insist on receiving the punishment in her stead. My mother would soon demand the emperor have mercy. They might see the cruelty for what it is."

Sun Tao laughed and shook his head. "Or they might execute you without a second thought. But you always have been a martyr. A naive one at that."

More heat flared in my lungs. "Better to light a candle than to curse the darkness."

Then, without a backward glance at my sweetheart's muscled frame, I swept toward the palace with resolve steeling my ribs.

Upon my gusty arrival at the palace keep, the guarding officer—Wu Baihu, a round-bellied eunuch in a silken purple robe—furrowed his brow.

"Zhao Sheng," he acknowledged with a slight head bow. "I thought you were attending the Refined Music Society with your mother."

"I demand to see the prisoner," I said, puffing up my chest, tilting up my jaw, drawing myself to my full height. "The emperor has authorized it."

Wu Baihu stilled. "To what end?"

"Does it matter?"

"I suppose not," he said warily, as though sensing a trap just beyond his scope. "But I shall accompany you regardless." His hand went to the loop of brass keys at his waist.

I swallowed hard, my heart thudding. I had not expected to be accommodated so readily, and now the enormity of what I was about to do left me winded.

252 ✳ **Laura Steven** ✳

"Who is she?" I asked, in an attempt to orient myself in the moment. To remind myself of the *why*.

"A nong." A peasant. A nobody. "She has not said a word, nor uttered a name—even when threatened with the bamboo—but Jiang Wen recognized her. A pig farmer's daughter. She weaves mats and sells them at the market."

"Have her family paid the remittance yet?"

"They have not the coppers."

Another reason I loathed the Five Punishments. The rich bought their freedom, while the poor only watched in despair as their loved ones were tormented and executed. Life itself should not be a commodity.

We pushed into the keep, and I fought the urge to retch at the smell of unwashed bodies and stale waste buckets. It was dingy, with no natural light and a single reluctant lantern burning on the farthest stone wall. A far cry from the gilded splendor of the rest of the palace.

There was a row of cells separated by iron bars, but only two had occupants. In the first hunched an older man wearing only undergarments. His arms and face were covered in skin tags, and his back striped with angry welts. He rocked back and forth, gibbering in a foreign tongue. A Mongol prisoner.

Then there was the girl.

She did not cower in the corner of the cell, as many prisoners did. Nor did she press her face desperately to the bars, as though sheer force of will might cause them to bend around her. Instead, she lay flat on her back, one heel kicked over the other, her palms resting on her stomach and her fingers laced together. She might have been asleep, had her eyes not been fixed resolutely on the ceiling—where hung a thick brown rope, looped into a noose.

A wooden stool sat squarely beneath it.

An invitation.

Our Infinite Fates   253

We drew closer, but she did not cast us a single glance. She wore ragged duanhe made of coarse cloth, and her bare feet were dark with grime. Her lank black hair was shaggy around her shoulders.

I cleared my throat, and it echoed in the dim keep. "Excuse me. What is your name?"

Nothing. Not even the slightest twitch of a muscle.

This was not at all how I had pictured my act of self-sacrifice unfolding.

"My name is Zhao Sheng, and I am the emperor's son." At this, she snapped upright, as though poison had suddenly been released into her bloodstream. But still she said nothing, simply stared at me as though I were a ghost—or a monster. "If you tell me your name, I will take your punishment for you."

There was something to her tempestuous stare that made my stomach churn. An almost-familiarity, a primal attraction, an unnameable force I had never felt before in my life. There was a loathing there too, which I could not quite understand given that we were strangers.

I imagined how she must see me, in all my meretricious costumery. The red court robes, the brocade ribbons, the jade ornaments and bracelets, the butter-soft black leather shoes and socks of damask silk. Hatred erupted from her like volcanic ash, cloying and deathly.

"Why?" Her first word was a croak; the water jug in the corner of the cell had been left untouched. A stubborn ox of a girl.

Stoic, I met her unflinching gaze. "For it is wrong."

Wu Baihu stepped forward, his official purple robes grazing the cold stone floor. "What is the meaning of this, Zhao Sheng?"

My throat was dry, and I longed to grab the water jug from the mule-girl's cell. "I mean to protest the cruelty of the Five Punishments."

254 · ✳ **Laura Steven** ✳ ·

"Protest?" Wu Baihu's expression was somewhere between incredulous and indignant. "You will be dead, child."

"My mother will surely pay the forty-two guàn and remit the death penalty." I gulped back the fear licking up my chest. What if she didn't? "The bamboo strokes I will receive willingly." The rack of canes on the wall sent an involuntary shudder through me.

Wu Baihu's mouth widened, letting loose a bark of ill-humored laughter. "Have you gone mad?"

"Perhaps," I admitted. "Will you—the court—allow it?"

"I will not," the girl said sharply, standing suddenly and sending the wooden stool clattering onto its side.

My attention snapped from Wu Baihu back to her. "I beg your pardon?"

"I will do it." She picked up the stool with unshaking hands, setting it tidily beneath the noose once more. "I will kill myself. I do not want to live in his debt." She climbed onto the stool, one filthy foot after the other, and stared up at the length of fraying rope with a dark expression on her face.

Panic rose in me. "You will owe me nothing."

She tilted her jaw back down, glaring at me once more. "Why would you do this? Guilt? Shame?"

"Simply because it is right."

She shook her head, long, slow, disbelieving. "You do not remember."

"Remember what?" A shiver bolted up my spine.

"Any of it."

Her voice was barely a whisper, and yet there was a pulse of hatred, of heat, between us that I did not understand. She was a stranger to me. So why did my bones grind with recognition? Why did the chambers of my heart flutter beneath her furious gaze?

On the periphery of my mind, of my very consciousness, there was a kind of almost-comprehension, a veil not lifting but flut-

Our Infinite Fates

255

tering, and I knew something significant sat behind it. But what could it be? Had I met this girl before? I thought not, and yet . . .

I took a step toward her, gripping the bars so tightly my knuckles turned white. "You would sooner die than have me help you."

Her teeth ground together like a pestle and mortar. "I would."

I thought of calling her a fool, but then would I be so different from Sun Tao? We all made our choices. I could not begin to comprehend the complexities of this girl's life, the hardships that had driven her to scale the palace wall in the first place. She had wanted an audience with the emperor—at any cost. What had made her so desperate? I would likely never know or understand. The thought felt slick and slimy as an eel in my stomach.

Casting a final defiant glance in my direction, the girl began to loop the noose around her neck. Wu Baihu did not move to stop her.

"No!" My pulse hammered against my skull.

I had inadvertently driven her to the thing she had so boldly resisted until now.

The door to the keep banged suddenly open, and another guard half dragged a wrist-bound man along the floor. The new prisoner's head was lolling dangerously, as though he had recently sustained a blow to the temple.

At the sight of him, the girl yanked the noose over her head and leaped down from the stool in a frenzy. "Bàba!"

My blood ran cold. The father who could not afford the remittance.

The sound of her shrill voice jolted the man back to full consciousness, and he yanked the guard forward toward his daughter with a look of existential fear on his face. "My girl, my girl, I will not let them do this to you, I will— Arrrrgh!"

The guard had grabbed a bamboo cane from the rack and brought it down on the man's back.

"No!" begged the girl, her face suddenly childlike and terrified. She wrapped her hands around the bars, our fingers grazing with a curious reverberation. "Please! Leave him alone!"

Still the lashes fell.

I looked at her, and she looked at me, eyes strained and watery, and she nodded without nodding, pleaded without pleading, something rich and complex knotting between us, and I threw myself to the ground beneath the bamboo, and as the pain rained down on my back I knew, somehow, somewhere, I had felt such agonies before, had felt the skin and flesh on my back scream out, felt the furious stripes of pain all the way to the bone.

And I also knew that somehow, somewhere, this girl was to blame.

Wales

2022

I ran for the stables and the fields beyond, darting between the outbuildings and their shadows, slipping through the cracks of humanity like I had for a millennium, tears blurring my vision, my heart beating so painfully in my chest that I struggled to breathe.

I ran down the farm track, the way illuminated only by the moon and stars, the night air cold and ripe, the scent of manure, of wet grass and spring earth, and I thought I could be anywhere, anywhere in history.

I ran, half expecting Arden to jump out at any moment, but I had the curious sensation that he would not be able to catch me.

I ran faster than I ever had in this life, farther and more furiously than I had thought myself capable of. The weakness in my hip made my gait strange, but there was little pain, thanks to the adrenaline and the myriad drugs I'd been pumped with. There was just me, and my feet, and the earth beneath them.

I ran and ran, until I reached the country road that wound into Abergavenny. I ran perpendicular to it, on the field side of the hedge to avoid the blare of headlights and the curiosity my sprint would likely invite. I ran until the cowpats and hay bales became low pastel buildings and wonky grey cobbles. I ran all the way to the bus station, panting and heaving and almost bursting at the seams, and by the time I finally stopped, so too had my tears.

258   ✳ **Laura Steven** ✳

Pressing my back to the closest glass shelter, my lungs were screaming, my hip finally waking up to what I was forcing it to do, my stomach threatening to empty itself on to the pavement, and I almost buckled to the ground. Slowly, though, my breath came back to me. Slowly, the stars behind my eyes dimmed. Slowly, I registered what I'd done.

I'd almost done it. I'd almost escaped.

I looked around, but there were no suspicious figures lurking in the shadows. There were only a few others at the various stops—a student with a huge rucksack, an elderly couple sharing a flask of something steaming hot, a harried father with three kids who definitely did not want to be at the bus stop at—

Nine thirty.

It was only nine thirty.

How was that possible?

There was still an hour until the bus showed up. An hour in which I had to stay alive.

And yet wasn't it obvious that I would be here? Wouldn't he be watching this exit point like a hawk, waiting for me to run away like I had in the Azores?

I tried to think of somewhere to hide, somewhere he would not think to look, but my mind was scrubbed raw from the furious run, and nowhere came to me. All the cafes were closed. The bookshop. The florist's. There was only the pub down the street, the pub outside which my father had died, but that was no less obvious than here.

Where else could I go?

My heart sang out a single clear note, but at first I was afraid to hear it.

It would be excruciating, I told myself. Agonising.

And yet would it be less painful, once I'd grounded myself in

✳ Our Infinite Fates ✳ 259

my next life and remembered Gracie all over again? Would that really be less painful for not having said goodbye?

My hand went to the wishbone dangling against my clavicle.

After all this time, all these lives, could I really let grief defeat me?

The Evelyn I know . . . they love over and over and over again, even though it can only ever end in tragedy. Even though they've lost everyone they've ever loved, and they miss them in the next life, and the next, and the next. Never have they developed hard edges, like I have. Never have they tried to protect themselves from that pain. They love softly, and fiercely, and openly, and it's the bravest thing I know. The most human thing I know.

I had an hour to kill. The hospital was on the other side of town, and so I likely wouldn't make it if I walked. And besides, my hip was really starting to protest.

But there was a taxi rank on the next street over. I could take a black cab. I'd be there in a few minutes, spend half an hour with her before I had to leave again.

And then, as though her sisterly spider senses were tingling, as though my pain had transmitted down the shimmering strand of sibling connection science could never truly explain, my phone flashed in my hand with a new message.

batshit INSANE turn of events??

Dylan????? Dylan who made the grotesque pressed flower "art"???????

not enough question marks in the known universe

for real are you good?????

Everything in me twisted with sadness.

My heart made the decision long before my brain caught up.

My perfect bald sister was propped up in bed. The main lights were off for the night, and her face was illuminated by the lesbian vampire show.

"Hey," I said, my voice hoarser than I'd expected it to be. It was warm in the room, even with a window cracked open a tiny bit. It smelled of shepherd's pie and minted peas and of the polish she'd just applied to the maple body of her violin.

She looked up and frowned—almost imperceptibly, due to her lack of eyebrows.

"What are you doing here? Mum said you were resting." She hit pause on Netflix, lest she miss a single moment of paranormal lust. "You had to steal my thunder, didn't you?"

I laughed in the way only Gracie could make me laugh. "Your thunder will never be stolen. I'm fine, by the way. Thanks so much for asking."

She rolled her eyes, laying the tablet on the bedside table next to her violin and sheet music. "I repeat: What are you doing here?" She studied me. "You look weird."

I looked down at myself, half expecting to see filth from the farm track or even blood from my hip bandages, but there was nothing. "I just wanted to see you."

"Okaaay." She smacked her lips, visibly uncomfortable, then stabbed a thumb at the tablet. "Well, I'm watching my show, so . . ."

"The procedure went well," I replied hurriedly, for lack of anything better to say. Anything better than goodbye. "The bone marrow one. *Thanks so much for asking.*"

Another exaggerated eye-roll. She took a sip from a carton of caramel iced coffee I was fairly sure she was not supposed to be drinking. "All right, you're a top sister. Do you want a medal? Per-

Our Infinite Fates   261

haps a village fete thrown in your honour? I'll dress up as a clown and scare the children."

I crossed to her bedside and picked up the tablet. "Can I watch with you for a little while?"

She looked like I'd asked if I might take a shit into her bedpan. "I mean, there's no room on the bed."

I'd forgotten how much it felt like pulling teeth talking to her, sometimes. She was spiky and difficult and hilarious and wonderful. I'd never known anyone quite like her.

Dragging a chair so it was right next to the bed, I said, "I'll sit here. Just turn the screen toward me a little."

She conceded, and hit play. There was a dramatic confrontation between a vampire hunter and their mark, in which it was not quite clear whether they were about to murder each other or have passionate intercourse against the library wall.

Relatable.

Tears slid silently down my cheeks as we watched. A small, miraculous thing so many people took for granted. Watching television with their sister. Needling each other with loving barbs. On an impulse, I took her hand in mine and gave it a squeeze—she was freezing cold, and it filled me with creeping dread. When a loved one is sick, you fixate on every tiny detail, every fluctuation in temperature, ascribing sinister meaning to it. Praying, even if you don't pray, that it's nothing.

Gracie snatched her hand away. "What are you doing? Gross."

"I love you," I whispered.

She sighed, paused the show, and said, "Look, I'm really trying to just watch the hot vampires, and now you're making me feel like I'm at death's door. Is there something you're not telling me? Do I have the bubonic plague and you just haven't the heart to let me know?"

"No, I just—"

262   ✳ Laura Steven ✳

"*Love me.* I know. But you don't have to be so maudlin about it. Like, why are you weeping? Openly, brazenly weeping."

I shrugged, swiping the steady flow of tears with the back of my hand. "I don't know. Dylan threatening to kill me . . . I thought I was going to die. And I realised we didn't say it enough. That we love each other."

Something earnest passed over Gracie's moon-pale face, if only for a moment. "Some things are just a given. And do please try not to die before me. As previously stated, I do not wish to have my thunder stolen. You borrowed it for a while, and I'll let it slide, but if you could just stop being dramatic for literally fifteen seconds—"

I threw my arms round her, squeezing her frail frame, and some of the stubborn tension in her body eased for a moment. She sank into me with an almost imperceptible sigh, and I did understand what she meant.

Some things are just a given.

"Get off," she whispered, giving me a little shove.

We watched the show for another few minutes before she spoke again. "A few weeks ago, when you asked me what I wanted to do when I got out of here?"

"Yeah?"

"After I deface the grave, I was wondering . . . Can we go into London to see a show?" She seemed almost embarrassed by her rare moment of sincerity, of raw and earnest hope. "I think I might want to be on the stage. Maybe we could tie it into Fashion Week, for you."

I nodded, but the tears were too strong now, and I could only murmur, "I have to go," and then I was pulling away, suddenly overcome with emotion, knowing I couldn't stay there any longer without a full-blown meltdown, and how would I explain that? "I don't want Mum to go into my room and find me gone."

I'd left her a note, but I knew she'd lose her mind with worry.

Our Infinite Fates   263

That Dylan had made me write it under duress. That I was dead in a ditch somewhere. Guilt racked me, but I had little other choice.

Once I was in Cardiff, I'd just bide my time and come back for them once it was safe, I reasoned.

This was not a goodbye.

So why did it feel so dangerously like one?

Never. Such an agonising word. Such an unbearable full stop.

"I love you so much," I said again, every syllable stitched through with pain.

"Nobody listens to a word I say, do they?" she muttered, with a final over-the-top eye-roll. "Love you too, weirdo."

Bundling myself back into my coat, I left her room without looking back.

I walked down the ward corridor in a daze, the lights too bright, the emotions too big, my breathing too loud in my head, and I thought that hospitals heard more prayers than churches ever did.

On the bitterly cold street outside, breath plumed in front of my face.

A figure stood on the opposite side of the street, cloaked in shadow.

Arden.

Wales

2022

Love had been my downfall, as it always was. If I'd just left without saying goodbye to Gracie, if I'd stayed hidden away from this obvious place, I might have made it out of Abergavenny before Arden caught me.

I had the heart of a fool, and I never learned.

How many times would fate teach me the same lesson before I listened?

Arden crossed the empty street toward me. All at once, the urge to flee deserted me, as though the fire fuelling a hot-air balloon had been suddenly extinguished. It took every ounce of energy I had left not to fold to the tarmac.

I was never going to make it to Cardiff.

I should have wanted to kill him. I should have thrown my body at him, kicking and screaming, and snapped his fucking neck.

But I didn't. I burst into tears all over again.

At the sight of me, Arden's face softened. "Oh, my love."

Despite the fact it was all his fault, all of it, I fell into his arms.

"I hate you," I whispered, face pressed to his thumping chest, voice thick and desperate.

He kissed my forehead, feather-soft. "I know."

"Please don't kill me." My quiet sobs turned to full-blown hysteria, my whole body shaking and convulsing with the weight of

Our Infinite Fates   265

the sadness. "I'll never see Gracie again." His knitted jumper was wet through in seconds. "I can't do it. I can't do it. I'm not strong enough."

He cupped my chin with his hand and tugged my face gently up. His eyes burned like sapphires. "You're the strongest person I've ever known."

Sniffing, I shook my head ferociously. "I'm not."

He pressed his forehead to mine. "Sometimes I think the force of your love could mend the earth."

"I don't need it to mend the earth. I just need it to mend *this*." I curled a hand into a feeble fist and thumped it against the hollow of his shoulder, but there was no real weight behind it.

"I would give anything in the world for that to happen." His voice was almost too even, as though it cost him dearly to keep his emotions in check, but there was a rough undercurrent, a thickness to the words, that gave him away.

"It's overwhelming, loving like this," I said weakly, my chest aching and aching. "My heart feels like an open wound. I don't understand how everyone just . . . walks around with the knowledge that everyone they love will soon be dead. I look at my sister, my mum, and it's all I can see. Inevitable loss. I look at them and I think, *I love you so much, and we will one day lose each other forever, and I might die from the pain of it.* So I try to pull myself back, to detach, to keep a healthy distance, like you do, but I can't. I can't."

I sniffed back the tears threatening to surge afresh. "And part of me believes I'm tempting fate just saying this—if I show the universe how much I love my family, they'll be taken from me in spite. Maybe that's all love is, in the end. An endless tempting of fate."

I sounded mad, I knew I did, but it was flowing out of me, a millennium of love and loss. The constant games we play with ourselves to try to keep our loved ones safe. The thousand tiny bargains we make with the universe every single day.

266   ✳   **Laura Steven**   ✳

And yet, what Arden and I shared . . . it defied all of it. Time and grief and death and separation and renewal. This fundamental human experience, flouted. I had never truly lost Arden; we ran through each other's lives like stitches through a seam.

But at my outpouring, Arden looked genuinely bewildered.

"Am I alone?" I asked, breathless. "Does everyone feel like this, and they just don't talk about it? Or am I certifiably insane?"

"I honestly don't know," admitted Arden.

"I wish I could be like you."

He shook his head. "I'm so glad you're not like me."

I scoffed, pulling away and wiping my sodden face on my sleeve. "Easy for you to say."

He looked away, teeth gritted. "You think it's easy for me to watch you go through this?"

"I don't know. I don't fucking know, Arden." I planted my palms on his chest and pushed back, and this time it cost him some effort to steady his footing. "I've loved you for longer than most people can even fathom, but still I have no idea what goes through your head."

As ever, he was silent. Stoic. An oyster I'd been trying to shuck for a millennium.

Then he asked a question that felt like an arrow through my heart: "How do you want me to do it?"

How do you want to die?

It was like a physical blow.

I had begged and begged, and it hadn't mattered. Siberia had been a one-off.

I turned away from him, up to the silhouette of Sugar Loaf. A full moon hung above the peak, a pearlescent marble. A constant, no matter who or where I was.

"Just make it look like an accident," I muttered. "My mum can't think I was killed, or she'd never forgive herself for letting you into our lives."

✳ Our Infinite Fates ✳ 267

"There's a cliff edge overlooking the valley," he said, so unfeeling that it made me glad he was about to die too. "We could jump together. Everyone will think we fell."

Or that you pushed me.

I didn't bother voicing the concern. Given the events of the last few days, there was no way anyone would believe our simultaneous deaths were an accident.

A shudder rollicked through me. Falling was a better death than most, but still my mother would have to live with the image of our mangled bodies and shattered bones for the rest of her life.

How long would it take for Mountain Rescue to find us?

I could still run, I thought fleetingly, desperately. But it wouldn't be fast enough. He had almost a foot on me and a robust fitness from years of working outdoors.

And besides, where would I even go? Would it be worth living if I never returned to these people I loved? To Mum? To Gracie?

To Arden?

Then again, I had always found a way to live with the grief of the loves I had lost—to carry them inside me like candles that never blew out, until the slow tide of time eventually extinguished the memories.

"Let's go," said Arden, reaching out a hand.

I didn't take it.

Slowly, a plan came to me. Not a plan to survive, but a plan to find peace at last.

Squaring my shoulders, I replied, "I can make this easy, or I can make this difficult. I can come willingly. Or I can make you tackle me to the ground and risk attracting attention."

A bemused beat. "There's no one around."

I shrugged. "Maybe not out here. But I'm pretty sure I can outpace you the hundred yards it takes to get back inside the hospital."

A bluff, and he knew it. But he also knew that I ran on pure blind hope, and you could never underestimate just how far that took you.

He pinched the bridge of his nose. "Why are you like this?"

"I think it's fair to say, at this point, that you've had a decent hand in forging me."

He looked at me, through me, down to my very bones. Either the fight had gone out of him, as it had me, or his love for me was entirely overriding his good sense. "Fine. What are your terms?"

"I want to know why," I said, chin tilted upwards, meeting his impenetrable gaze. "Not here. Not now. But when we get up to that cliff, and we're looking down over the valley, and we're contemplating our lives and our deaths, I want to know why."

He ran a hand over his face. His perfect, infuriating face. "It will hurt you."

"At this point, it'll hurt me more not to know." A flipped mirror of what he'd said to me in Siberia.

He laughed bitterly. "I don't think that's possible."

"I don't care, Arden. If we're going to do this over and over again, if we're going to defy time and fate and death together—if we're going to keep falling for each other—then I need equal power. And right now, you hold it all."

Fear was etched into his very outline now. The kind of fear I so rarely saw on him. "This is not power, Evelyn."

"It'll be so much easier for you if we don't have to fight every time." My voice was filled with heat and longing and loathing and, impossibly, love. "This is just existentially exhausting. I know you feel it too. And if I understand why you do it . . . and if it's as good a reason as you say it is—"

"It is," he replied fiercely. "It's an unstoppable force, and our love is an immovable object."

And I trusted him more fully than I ever had.

Our Infinite Fates 269

Sheets of white hair, curling black nails. Bone world, falling ash. Pain, pleading.

This has gone on long enough.

The full picture had eluded me for centuries. It was time to lift the veil. I knew it, and Arden did too.

"Okay." I nodded. "Then I'll work with you. We can jump from cliffs together in every life, when the time comes. And it'll still hurt, but not like this."

A long, pulsing quiet. There was an almost-sentience to the silent air between us.

"I do hate that I've forced you into such sequacity."

"Go on, enlighten me. What does that mean?"

He sighed exaggeratedly. "Honestly, why does language sift through your brain like flour through a sieve? You retain only the words you absolutely need, and everything else——"

"Arden," I snapped.

Then, finally, defeatedly, his shoulders slumped.

"All right."

"All right?" I asked, disbelieving, my blood thundering in my ears.

I was about to have a thousand years of questions answered.

"I'll tell you," he whispered, and he looked younger than I'd ever seen him. Innocent and afraid and so unsure, a millennium of conviction crumbling to the earth. "I'll tell you everything."

Wales

2022

Pale silver moonlight washed the valley clean. The craggy hills, pocked with gorse and sheep. The dark, shadowed river, bracketed by blossoming trees, water gushing like low static on a distant radio.

The stars, indifferent.

My love, beside me.

Our deaths, imminent.

We sat on the cliff edge, legs dangling over, shoulders pressed together, having walked up the steep hill by torchlight. My eyes stung with tiredness and grief, and I sucked in deep lungfuls of the ripe country air, relishing the chill of it in my chest.

Neither of us spoke. Once we did, there was no going back.

Even though I'd chased these answers for ten hundred years, I was suddenly afraid to hear them. I knew nothing would be the same hereafter, and the thought was both a blessing and a curse. I was at the very outer edge of my limits—Gracie a hard boundary I would do anything not to cross—but I was so immortally afraid of losing Arden in the process of chasing the truth.

Arden had always promised this would hurt, and I was so tired of pain.

Yet what other choice did I have?

This moment was a crux, a seam, an axis.

Our Infinite Fates 271

I chose to postpone it for a little while longer. To just be here with Arden, our hearts beating, alive, if not for much longer. To lift the veil as slowly as I could.

"When did you first fall in love with me?" There was a tremble beneath my words—from the cold, and from something more visceral still.

He stared up at the waxed moon. "Sometimes I think it was seeded from the start. Decided by the very hand that wrote the universe. But as for when the thought first truly struck me . . . it was Northern Song. You laid down your body for me, for my father, even though I was then a stranger. I had lived a few by then and never before seen such selflessness. Such *goodness.*"

There was an old-fashioned cadence to his words, as though he was connecting himself to eras that had ended long ago.

I rested my head on his shoulder, a thoughtless intimacy. "In your less charitable moments, you call it martyrdom."

"It's hard, remembering things you don't." He wrapped an arm around me, then the length of his scarf, until we were cocooned. "The very foundations of us—the moments in which our love was forged—just don't exist to you."

Something I'd been grappling with lately. How profoundly sad it must be to carry our origins alone. "I get glimpses in really sharp focus, but they often vanish as soon as they arrive."

"How far back can you get?" he asked, and I got the sense he'd been wanting to ask me this for a long time but didn't feel he had the right—not when he'd neglected to answer so many of my own questions. "In those glimpses?"

"Northern Song, I suppose, but not all of it. Slivers. The hot welts from the bamboo." I shuddered. "And other stuff comes to me seemingly at random. Like the other morning, when I mentioned the coffee in the Ottoman Empire and you clammed up. Straight away I felt why you were embarrassed—"

"I wasn't embarrassed, Evelyn. I was inappropriately turned on."

We both laughed, enjoying the small moment of normal teenagedom.

"The clearest memories, where I can remember full scenes, not just snippets . . ." I searched the darkest recesses of my mind. "The asylum. That one stuck. Sometimes I think the memory lapses are a trauma response to all those hideous experiments. Other times I think it's just human, to forget huge swathes of your life. How many people can honestly say they remember their first few years of existence?"

"Do you have any sense of when you started to love me back?"

His voice sounded so young, so insecure, like a door had suddenly opened in the sky-high walls around his heart. This too felt like another question he had never dared to pose, but one that had needled him for centuries. He had asked *why,* back in the trenches. But not *when.* Not *how.*

I thought for a moment, unsure how to put such a complex thing into words. So I pressed my eyes shut once more and searched for the right image. It came.

"Whenever I try to pull at that thread, it leads me back to the desert. There were camels and tents, gold and salt, lakes and sand and date palms, and I felt something for you very deeply. Something that destroyed me, in the end."

Arden swallowed hard, resting his head against mine. "We were best friends. The closest we had ever been spawned together, and we were raised almost as siblings, so tightly knitted were our families. That was one of the worst." He winced at the memory. "To gradually remember, as the years unpeeled, that I would have to kill the person I cared about most in the world. I can't explain how . . . I was just a little girl. We were just kids. We played board games and pranked our elders. Our fate never felt so cruel to me as it did then."

Our Infinite Fates 273

Something else I had never considered from his perspective. How it must feel to gradually realise what you have to do—and just how early that happened. How young he sometimes was when he began the search for me. How it stole his childhood again and again and again.

He ran a hand through his tangled hair. "Are you sure you want to know the truth?"

"I'm sure," I said quickly, though now I was right up against the thing, the fear was almost enough to make me turn away. To make me hurl myself from the great height before I had to confront anything more terrible than I had already faced.

Several silent beats, our hearts pounding violently as one. He laced his fingers through mine, cold against my perpetually warm palm, and squeezed so hard I almost winced.

Finally, he spoke. Calm and measured and afraid. "Every time I've considered telling you, I've agonised over how to do it. Which words to choose. Which phrasing would take the most sting out of it. And I still don't know."

"I think I've imagined every possible explanation," I admitted. "I'm not sure you can surprise me. Hurt me, yes. But surprise me? No."

He ran a thumb over the veins on the back of my hand. "What have you imagined?"

"Well, there are the more human options, such as revenge. I did something awful to you, and the only way you can live with it is by punishing me again and again."

He shook his head, but there was a certain tension to it that made me think I wasn't entirely off base.

"Or there's the fact that you might just have kind of a thing for killing," I said. "Like, it gets you off."

He snorted. "Couldn't be further from the truth."

An owl hooted above us, wistful and melancholy.

"Then there's the more supernatural stuff," I went on. "All of it sounds absurd, but what happens to us is absurd, so I haven't ruled anything out. Ancient curses. Small gods. Malevolent witches." White hair, black nails. "What else? Oh, blood magic. You need my blood for something. But my most compelling theory is that we made a deal with the devil."

At this last suggestion, Arden stilled, and my bones knew something before my mind did.

My heart hitched in my throat, my whole existence on the brink of free fall.

"We didn't make a deal with the devil, Evelyn. You *are* the devil."

Lundenburg

1006

If I did not reap my first soul by the end of the night, the Mother would destroy me. She would nail me to a bed of seething coals. She would cackle gleefully as the flesh melted from my bones, crack the knuckles on her wretched hands as I begged for mercy that would not come. I would never die, for I was not mortal. The suffering would be agonizing and eternal.

And dawn was but an hour away.

Seek out the moments of life and death, the Mother had said. *Listen for the hopeless pleas, the desperate prayers. Look for love, and for the imminent loss of it. There you will find a soul for the claiming.*

Yet tonight Lundenburg was at peace, no matter how transient. The savage Viking raids of earlier months had, for now, been vanquished, and the spring warmth had dispelled any lingering spates of winter sickness. The neat rows of thatched houses were quiet as dormice in slumber, illuminated by a supernova's swirling smear across the night sky. The streets were ripe with the scent of tomato vines and freesia, hayricks and fresh-spread manure, the sour tang of warm bodies, the distant stench of a rat-infested tithe barn.

Not a desperate prayer to be heard.

To the passing eye, I resembled a normal human girl. I wore a simple blue dress and soft leather boots, dark hair falling to my waist in plaits. The devilish ash tone had faded from my skin as I'd entered the mortal realm, pink as a newborn babe.

But much as I longed to be, I was not a normal human girl. I never would be.

Panic beat in my temples like a pulse as I paced the dirt-packed streets lying in the shadows of Æthered's palace. I had come of age nearly a moon ago, and yet the new power that thrummed through me remained unspent. Whether through deep-rooted reluctance or genuine ineptitude, I had wandered the streets night after night and returned to the Underrealm empty-handed.

It was as though I was unlike the other devils in some fundamental way. They had a hunger for it, a marrow-deep thirst that only human souls could slake. They showed no morsel of mercy or regret as their victims burned on the coals to save their loved ones. I, on the other hand, possessed the single worst trait it was possible for a devil to possess: empathy. I felt human pain in my own flesh and sinews. Felt my heartbeat like theirs in a place there should have been no heart at all.

Almost as though I had a soul of my own.

I knew in my bones that I was not meant for this life. All I wanted was to tend to a garden, the way humans did. To dig up earth-rich carrots and prune pretty pink roses. Perhaps I could mend clothes—I'd always had an eye for fabrics—or eschew the expectations of young women and become an apprentice at the forge. I could join a makers' guild, or bale hay, or bake bread, or sow wheat, or anything, anything, anything but this.

Indigo rose on the horizon beyond the palace, and I knew my time was about to run out.

As I stooped defeatedly past a low stone church, an echoing sob—louder than it should have feasibly been—lifted out of a tiny window. The sound plucked at the strings in my chest. There was a desperate timbre to the cry, something visceral and resonant

Our Infinite Fates   277

that tugged at me, and all of a sudden the Mother's counsel made sense.

Look for love, and for the imminent loss of it.

All my crooked instincts told me this was the moment.

I had to act before I convinced myself otherwise.

Inside, the church was cooler than the night air, and I shivered as my eyes adjusted to the dim light. The space carried the scent of stewed lamb and buttered cabbage. Perhaps there had been a spring feast. In the corner, I picked out a lone sickle propped against the stone wall.

A young man—twenty at most—hunched in a pew with his head in his hands. Beside him, a candle sputtered at the wick, casting him in strange shadows. He had blond hair to his shoulders, a badly patched brown tunic, and all the sloping contours of a man weighed down by grief.

I walked softly up the aisle and slid into the pew behind him. The candle reeked of melting fat. He sobbed desperately, muttering a frantic litany of *please please please.* He had not heard me approach.

"Are you all right?" I asked, for lack of a better introduction.

He jerked in the pew, swiveling to face me, and I felt a prickle of shame at disturbing such a vulnerable moment.

Recovering as fast as he could, he sniffed and pressed the heel of one hand into his eye socket. "My sister is gravely sick. She has not long left."

He did not seem perturbed by the sudden appearance of a stranger in his midst.

In his palm was a dark bezoar stone, which he rolled rhythmically between his fingers. Tears slicked down his cheeks in glistening rivulets, soaking into the thin golden beard tufted at his jaw.

Foolish, I thought with a devil's distance. *It is all so foolish, to love and be loved, knowing it will always end like this,* and yet I yearned for it more than I yearned to breathe.

"I am sorry," I said, and I was.

"Beorma is but a child." His voice was low, hoarse, as though speaking hurt. "Our mother died birthing her. Now her sacrifice was for nothing."

"All sacrifices are, in the end," I replied. "But humans make them regardless."

"She was born in a caul," the man whispered. "It is supposed to bring good fortune. A lucky talisman. And now . . . It is not fair or right."

Silence rolled out between us, and there was only the distant scratch of an apple tree against the church wall. A framed painting near the altar depicted a reptilian winged figure with twisted features and long, cruel fingers. Below the imagery was a cautionary passage: *Discipline yourselves, keep alert. Like a roaring lion, your adversary the devil prowls around, looking for someone to devour.*

All of a sudden, the young man let out an almighty roar, a clap of thunder that vibrated through the bones, and then hurled the bezoar stone at the stoic wooden cross. The echoes of his yell reverberated long after it had rolled to a stop on the stone floor.

"I can save your sister," I blurted out, my voice not the clipped cold of the other devils but instead a painfully human fumble. Too much gravel in the throat, too much emotion in the words.

Breathing ragged, his pale brows knitted anguish and confusion together. "Are you a healer? You have not even asked what ails her."

"I have the power to cure disease, among other things, but only if enough is sacrificed in return."

An absurd statement, given what I had just said about the futility of martyrdom. But alas.

He shook his head and looked away. "If it is gold you seek, I have none. The tithes are already too steep."

"Not gold. Something far more valuable."

Our Infinite Fates

The air in the church stilled. "What might that be?"

"Your soul."

His gaze snapped back to me, and he studied my outline as though seeing me for the first time, the subtle glaze of wine in his misty stare, his teeth stained a bloody purple. "Beg your pardon?"

Something sharp hitched in my throat. "I can save your sister, but you must suffer immensely for it."

His eyes narrowed. "I am already suffering."

"Emotionally, perhaps. This is another thing entirely."

"I know not what you mean." His back had gone rod-straight, his expression sober as a priest's.

Now or never.

"If you agree to let me save your sister, you will be taken to the Underrealm. You will be nailed to burning coals for seven days and seven nights. Your pain will feed the Mother, and allow her to grow stronger. You will not die, nor will you enjoy the sweet release of passing out. You will feel every second of it. And then, for the rest of your mortal days, you will serve the Mother as I do. You will reap souls."

His expression was impossible to parse. "You expect me to believe this?"

I allowed a loaded beat to pass. "I think you have little other choice."

Please say yes. I am sorry, I am so sorry, but please say yes.

"Who are you?" he asked, face ashen, an awful hope burning in his eyes, and I wanted to die from the shame of it all.

How to answer? *The devil* would be the closest thing to the truth, and yet my lips would not form the shape of the word. I was born to the Mother; it had not been a choice. My terrible fate had been assigned to me seemingly at random.

This was all some cruel mistake. I was just a girl. A girl who wanted to please her Mother. A girl who wanted to let herself love, and be loved in return. A girl who wanted to live.

The most human things of all.

Grappling with the evil deed I was about to commit, I knew that this innocent person would suffer horribly in order for me to survive, but it would be temporary. If I did not reap his soul, my own pain would be eternal.

Still, an answer to his question did not readily appear, and so I decided to assign myself a name. A real, human name. One that felt right on my tongue, in the aching corners of my chest. One that was close enough to *devil* that I could argue to the Mother that it had been a simple slip of the tongue.

I swallowed hard, choking back the emotion of the moment. "Evelyn."

He nodded once—an unspoken agreement, a fate sealed, a promise that could never be unmade. A nod that would define a millennium.

"Arden."

in the last thousand years:
empires have risen and fallen
and I have loved you,
plagues have leaped from rat to daughter
and I have loved you,
humanity has conquered sea and sky
and I have loved you,
kings have been slain and forests razed and witches
  burned and gold struck and maps redrawn and
  fortunes traded and volcanoes erupted and moons
  landed and cathedrals sculpted and rivers dirtied
  and masterpieces painted and battlefields bloodied
and I love you,
and I have loved you,
and I will love you.

—AUTHOR UNKNOWN

Wales

2022

"I'm the devil," I choked out, everything I thought I knew about my existence splintering and shattering to the ground.

Not a victim of a cruel curse—the *maker* of the curse.

"I'm sorry," whispered Arden, and I could not look at him, this soul I had destroyed, this soul whose love for his sister I had turned into something monstrous, this soul I'd spent decades chastising for *not* caring enough about his family. "I'm so sorry."

"I reaped your soul?" Every word was a blight, a tumour, a sin, a whip-crack of self-loathing across my heart.

Propping his elbows on his knees, he clutched his temples and stared at the ground. "In exchange for my sister's survival. But it turns out I wasn't specific enough in my bargain. Her fever broke, only for her to die of choking the very next day."

No.

"Because of me?" Everything was reeling, spinning, my thoughts and feelings kaleidoscope fragments I couldn't quite grasp. "Surely I didn't willingly let her die."

"I don't think you did either. We both messed up the bargain. But I still hated you for it."

The knowledge was a pit in my heart, gaping and yawning in horror.

I was the *devil*.

Our Infinite Fates   283

I was everything evil in this world.

And I'd fucking *forgotten*. Like milk on a grocery list.

Yet as he'd described it, it had come back to me, every startling detail. As though it had always been there. Had my mind willingly buried it? Was it grotesque self-preservation? A refusal to look myself in the eye?

I lay flat on my back, the dizziness making it impossible to sit up for much longer. My hip twinged in pain, but it was distant, irrelevant. A mortal problem, and I was not mortal.

"Why didn't you tell me?"

"I did, the first few times, while I still hated you. But the last seven or eight hundred years . . . I couldn't bear the idea of telling you what you really were." Arden sniffed. "You're the furthest thing from a devil I can imagine. I didn't want you to have to carry the burden of everything you've done. The fate you've cursed us to."

I deserve to carry the burden, I wanted to scream at him. But he had only been trying to protect me.

"Were there others?" I asked, my throat both thick and dry. "Before you? Did I reap other souls?"

"I think I was your first."

A small solace, at least. I'd been such a terrible devil that my first mark was still hunting me down a thousand years later. If there was one thing in life it was good to be inept at, it was probably this.

I am not a monster. I am not a monster. I am not a monster.

I chanted it in my head in the hope it would feel true.

It was one thing to know your life—lives—defied some fundamental law of nature, but quite another to confirm the existence of something as arcane as *devils.* I supposed there was a *reason* the mythology of evil spirits and Faustian bargains transcended cultures and eras and faiths, a reason the idea had been sprinkled through the last thousand years like malignant confetti.

284   ✳ Laura Steven ✳

But it was a wholly ruinous thing, to grapple with the idea that you *were* one.

I tugged Arden's scarf up to my face, so his scent covered my mouth and nose, and breathed into it like a comfort blanket. Fresh air and clean linen, with underpinnings of hay and woodsmoke.

Words muffled, I asked, "What happened after Lundenburg?"

He looked away, down to where the river babbled indifferently below. "I spent seven days and seven nights on hot coals." A bitter laugh. "Hence the nightmares."

The horror in my chest billowed. The carnal screams every night, the way he clawed at his back in feral desperation, the existential terror in the alto yells. That unimaginable trauma was because of me.

I had subjected him to that—only to save myself.

No wonder I had spent a thousand years subconsciously atoning. Throwing my own body into the firing line again and again, a bone-deep need to right a historic wrong. A martyr, a lamb for sacrifice. A devil seeking redemption.

"And then you had to work for me," I finally managed. "For the Mother."

He nodded, now gazing up at the constellations sprayed across the night sky. "I was supposed to, but the moment I was back in Lundenburg, I realised my sister had died despite what I had sacrificed to save her. So I hunted you down and killed you instead. Partly out of hatred, but also because I thought it would free me from the futile bargain. But as soon as you took your final breath, I died too."

A stronger breeze picked up, rustling through the cluster of trees behind us. "So what about the next life? Why did you keep killing me if you knew it wouldn't free you?"

"At first I thought it had worked. I was a warrior in Bavaria, holding back the constant tide of raging Hungarians. I had quite the reputation on the battlefield as someone who could sustain many wounds without dying. As time went on and our eighteenth birthday approached, I did remember what had happened in our last life, but it had a sort of filmic quality. I thought that I could not possibly be actually recalling a previous existence. It felt more like a recurring dream. Even if it had been real, I could not have imagined the bargain would follow me into another life."

"But it did."

"The second I turned eighteen, I was wrenched back into the Underrealm and brought before the Mother. You were there too, but it wasn't . . ." He searched for the right words. "We weren't corporeal. I think our bodies were left behind in the mortal world, and our souls descended to the place they were forever tied to.

"Anyway, you had no memory of anything. No clue why you were there. It was horrible to watch—you were absolutely terrified by what was happening to you." He shook his head fiercely, a lock of dark hair falling free of its tie. "I've never understood that element of all this. The fact that all knowledge of who and what you were simply escaped you from one life to the next."

The magnitude of it all was impossible to process. It was so much bigger, and so much worse, than I had imagined. Not a trivial squabble with a forest witch, nor a petty grudge from long ago, but something deeper and darker, something that tied us to the very underbelly of the universe.

And I had just *forgotten*.

That's what I kept hitching on. The absurdity of my own bad memory.

"What happened when we were summoned back to the Underrealm?" I asked, determined to mine every last horrific detail from the shared earth between us.

"The Mother told us our souls had been marked as hers. And that now that we were of age and at our full power, it was time for us to begin reaping souls. Those we made bargains with would then be under our own command—and would also be required to start reaping, after their week on the coals was over. It would all ultimately sustain her. The suffering . . . it's her lifeblood. And she was growing stronger and stronger with every bargain made."

"It's a fucking pyramid scheme." I shot a withering look up at the sky. "How was my soul marked in the first place? Was I just born a devil?"

"That, I've never been able to figure out."

I thought of that fated trip back to the Underrealm in our second lives. "Why didn't we just refuse to reap?"

"We did, at first, but we were put on the hot coals until we obliged." A shudder shot through him, and he looked instantly embarrassed, clearing his throat and looking away. "You lasted a lot longer than I did. A martyr, even back then."

My toes curled inside my boots. "But I gave in, eventually."

"Don't hate yourself for it. The pain is impossible to describe."

Somewhere in the trees behind us, a twig snapped beneath the foot of a fox or a badger.

"What happened after we finally agreed to reap for the Mother?"

"We went back into the world—me to the battlefield and you to the monastery you'd lived in for years." His voice had taken on a soft, lilting cadence, like a storyteller by a campfire. "It would've been easy for me to find a desperate soul to bargain with, given where I was. So much death, and suffering, and loss. But instead I fled the battle and came to find you. Since we'd turned eighteen, my tether to you was a hundred times as powerful. Before, it had been a vague tug, but now it was a magnetic yank. I found you within days. You were utterly distraught, clawing at your back as though you still felt the flames licking up it. You were on the brink of reaping the almoner."

Guilt twisted through me. Arden had not been the one-off I'd

Our Infinite Fates   287

hoped. I had been prepared to do it again. "Why did you come and find me? Didn't you still hate me for what I'd done to you?"

"Because I wanted to tell you what I'd inadvertently discovered the first time I killed you. That if I killed you, we both died, and the clock would essentially reset. We would be born into new lives and have another eighteen years before we were torn back to the Underrealm. And we could keep doing that forever. We wouldn't have to reap anyone, nor would we ever go back to the hot coals, as long as we kept dying at the right time. No matter how much I resented you, it seemed a mutually beneficial solution."

Digging my nails into my palms, I whispered. "And I agreed?"

"You did. But then, when I came to find you in Northern Song . . ."

"I didn't remember."

"You didn't remember." He shook his head, as though the memory still confused and troubled him. "You didn't remember *anything,* in those early lives. Your memory seemed to be wiped entirely with every fresh incarnation. And yet, even without that tug of guilt, that need for redemption, you offered to take my punishment for me, my *father's* punishment. Even though you had no idea who I was. And god . . . I hated you for it. Because I hated you so much for the miserable existence you'd sentenced us to—I was beginning to understand, then, that I would never again be able to live or love the way others did—and you just *did not remember.* And in that moment, nothing could've felt worse than being in your debt. My pride wouldn't allow it."

Shadowy images drifted across my mind's eye—a wooden stool beneath a dangling rope. "You threatened to kill yourself. I remember that much."

As Arden puffed his breath out, it misted in the crisp night air. "Because it was becoming clear to me that I would not be able to kill us both. How could I have left that cell and got my hands on you? I was small and unarmed, and there were guards. My throwing stars had been taken from me upon my arrest. And because of your completely unfounded act of generosity and martyrdom, it was also clear that you were not likely to kill me. Even if I'd explained the situation to you, right there in front of the guard, I very much doubted you would have raised a blade to my throat. Your heart was too good, too pure. And I did not understand it one bit, given the way we began."

"So you thought if you killed yourself," I said slowly, "at least you would be saved from having to reap."

He nodded. "I wasn't sure whether my death would end your life too—suicide had not been the plan—but it was the only play I had left. And now, with a thousand years of hindsight, I know my attempt would not have been successful anyway. The only way we can die is by the other's hand."

What an almighty, devastating mess. A Greek tragedy with no end.

Unless.

Opening my mouth into the silence of the night, I said, with far more conviction than I felt, "I think we should let ourselves be called back to the Underrealm."

The valley practically trembled at the words. The distant gush of the river mirrored the roar of my own blood. Far above us, a falling star sailed across the dark canvas of the sky.

Arden turned to me as though I'd sprouted a thousand heads. "Why?"

I took a deep, steadying breath. "Because if your soul is marked to mine, and you are able to kill me, then . . ."

Understanding dawned in his eyes. "You should be able to kill the Mother. Because your soul is marked to hers."

"Exactly." A flurry of something bright and hopeful rose in my chest, like a snow globe turned upside down. "The flaw in the system, right? Maybe the very act of binding souls together makes them more vulnerable to each other. Maybe whatever dark magic tethers us—and protects us from all other types of death—also creates a kind of murderous back door."

The realisation was a potent one. And somewhere deep in my gut, I knew my theory was correct. No matter which life I'd been in, there had always been a push and pull to the universe; without light there was no shade. It was yin and yang. The karmic, cosmic balance of it all. The Mother could not be all-powerful. Nature didn't work that way.

For once, Arden wore his emotions all over his face as he processed the idea. A kind of inward darting to his gaze that made me think he was picking his way through each conflicting feeling, trying to find solid ground.

He turned to face me, resting on his shins, like an animal poised for attack. "What if destroying the Mother destroys us too?"

Softly as I could, I replied, "You've known of my martyring ways for a millennium. Surely you must know I would sacrifice myself a thousand times over to rid the world of this evil."

"But you're not just sacrificing yourself. You're sacrificing me. Us."

My eyes searched his. The light of the stars cast a silvery glow over his face, every beautiful line of it: the full lips, the thick brows, the kind eyes, the hard jaw and the high cheekbones, and the searing, burning Arden-ness of him. Flowers and ink.

"What other option do we have?" I asked, desperate now, because if there was another way, I would take it in a heartbeat.

"This," he said urgently, and he grasped my hands in his. I jolted at the touch, so warm and immediate, and something in my chest danced under the heat. "Now that you understand everything, we can just live out our eighteen years in various lives and mutually die when the time comes. There's no reason we can't keep doing this forever."

The thought was at once dark and alluring. It was like the urge to lie or steal or cheat—glittering and exciting, a sparkling imperial jewel ripe for the taking. It carried with it a thrill but also an undercurrent of shame.

"I don't think it's right," I whispered.

His posture was almost frantic now, coiled like a spring. "Why?"

Swallowing hard, I replied, "I think if we have the chance to destroy the Mother forever, we have to try. Think of all the other innocent souls we'll be freeing from this hell. No more hot coals, no more sentencing victims to the same fate. No more devils."

There was a long beat, and then, "Why do you have to be so good?" he asked, pained. "Why can't you be selfish, just this once?"

I smiled wryly. "Would you have loved me for so long if I wasn't selfless?"

His silence was answer enough.

"So what now?" I asked.

"I guess we wait to turn eighteen."

Wales

2022

It was around two in the morning when clouds began to swaddle the silver-coin moon. By normal standards, today was our birthday. We were legal adults. But the Mother clearly had a taste for pedantry—we wouldn't come into our powers for another five hours.

"What if the police send out a search before morning?" I shifted uncomfortably on the picnic blanket. The drugs had worn off, and I was becoming acutely aware of the pain in my hip, at once dull and sharp. Running into town had been a mistake. "If my mum notices me missing before dawn, there are going to be helicopters over these hills in no time."

Arden sighed and lay back on the blanket, resting his forearms above his head. "I suppose it doesn't matter, really. If we're caught and arrested—well, if *I'm* arrested—we'll be called back to the Underrealm from wherever we are. The plan doesn't change."

Try as I might to process what might happen in the next few hours, my brain couldn't scale the enormity of it, of what the Underrealm would look like, feel like, what it would *do* to us. Instead I fixated on logistical details.

"Do you have a weapon we can use against the Mother?"

A terse nod, then a pat of his lumberjack coat pocket. "The knife."

"Will that be brought with us?" I mused. "You said that last time our bodies stayed here, and only our souls descended. The odds of personal belongings also making it to the Underrealm seem slim."

He sighed. "I suppose you're right. But we've killed with our bare hands before. We can do it again."

I shuddered at a sudden memory from the vast Argentine pampas. Arden's throat, narrow and feminine, straining and bulging against my calloused palms. Self-loathing beat in my temples like a drum.

Devil, devil, you're a devil.

Back then, Arden had been a skinny seventeen-year-old girl. Killing the millennia-strong Mother, sustained by the power of eternal suffering, was an entirely different matter.

"What can you remember about the Mother?" I asked. "I mean, I know what she looks like. She was there in the trenches, wasn't she? But does she have much protection? Devil guards, or whatnot?"

"I truly don't know." Arden's eyes had fluttered closed, and I understood the feeling. Though tensions were running high and we were teetering on the edge of an uncertain fate, I was also just *tired.* From lack of sleep. From everything. "I haven't been to the Underrealm in a thousand years." A snort of laughter. "The ship in Batavia was a close call, mind you. But I would imagine she's gained a lot of strength in that time. And a lot of followers, willing or otherwise."

Willing or otherwise.

That might be our saving grace. Even if the Mother did have protectors, would they be truly loyal? Or would they be bound there against their wills, railing against the bonds of their bargains as Arden and I were? Might they take our side: rebel, revolt, overpower?

I lay back down next to Arden, only this time I lay in the crook of his chest. He stilled for a moment, tense, and then relaxed enough to wrap his arm around me. It felt deliciously, unbearably good. The first moment of peace in weeks, no matter how fleeting.

Our Infinite Fates   293

"How many other marked souls are out there, do you think?" I murmured. A star far above us blinked, white, then dark, then white again. "There must be so many now. Such is the nature of pyramid schemes. They grow and grow until the only people left to sell to are their own."

"I don't know that either. I've never been approached for another bargain, but then again, maybe the other reapers know I'm already marked."

A thought came to me, curious and bright. "Was it ever tempting to offer my mum a deal? For Gracie's life, I mean."

"No." The answer was quick and solid. "These bargains . . . they're slippery things. If we didn't get the phrasing exactly right, she could end up the same as me—without her loved one and without her freedom. Besides, can you imagine your mum spending a week on hot coals?"

The horror of the image twisted through me, swiftly followed by a rush of affection for the woman who would lay down her life for her daughters. "She's stronger than you think."

"I know," said Arden softly, the words floating up and vanishing in the towering night.

As we lay there in silence for a while, I had never felt as small or as infinite. We had lived for so long. We had been farmers and bakers and soldiers, jewellers and thieves, royals and rogues, sons and daughters, the shape of us changing with every life but not the heart of us. We had touched a thousand people, most of whom were now but bones in the earth. And yet, beneath the great canvas of the stars, we were nothing. A blip, a finger snap, a single note in the symphony of the universe. The realisation made me feel at once better and worse.

We were nothing, but we felt like everything.

The fifth item on my dream list: to grow old with the love of my life.

A wedding, a home, a child of our own, all the quiet rituals and shared stories of ordinary, long-lasting love.

I laid my arm over his stomach, over the soft fabric of his fleece-lined coat, and as he squeezed me tight, I wished I could press myself into his very being.

I love you, and I have loved you, and I will love you.

My heart beat with the agonising words. Arden was my family. A homeland I would defend with every fibre of my being.

I'd always believed him to be the villain, but he wasn't.

I was.

And he loved me still.

Tilting my chin up, I gazed into his face, every beautiful plane filling me with *want*. I lifted my hand from his waist to his jaw and ran my thumb along the hard ridge of it. His body stiffened beside me, a subtle tensing of his muscles and sinews.

I slid my hand backwards from his jaw, running my fingers through his soft dark hair and tugging myself ever so slightly up at the same time, my face inches from the hollow of his neck. Softly, so softly it took every ounce of restraint in my body, I brushed my lips against his throat.

His Adam's apple bobbed raggedly as he swallowed back the desire. "Evelyn, we can't . . ."

But he didn't move away. Didn't pull my hand away from the nape of his neck. Didn't release his firm grasp of my waist.

"Why not?" I whispered, the words brushing against his skin, and he shivered.

"I've killed you so many times." His voice was coarse, charged.

"I've killed you too." I kissed him once more on the throat, lingering a little longer this time, feeling his pulse quicken beneath my lips. "We had our reasons."

I lowered my hand from his neck to his hip, sliding my fingers under his thick coat to the strip of bare skin beneath. His stomach

Our Infinite Fates

was tight, muscled, warm beneath my touch. As I hooked my thumb into the waistband of his boxers and tugged, he let loose the softest groan and pressed his forehead against mine. The air between us was fraught with desire, underpinned by a devastating tenderness.

Our breath was hot and rough as he closed the gap between our lips, and we kissed for the first time since the Siberian wilderness.

It was at once a tentative graze and a desperate caress, my heart beating through my chest, the blood roaring in my ears. Every inch of me lit up, with familiarity and yearning and love, the deepest love there was, and even though our bodies were already pressed together I was overcome with the need to be closer to him, one with him.

The kiss grew from a whisper to a roar, our teeth clashing together. His tongue flicked tentatively over mine, first uncertain and then urgent, his hands finding the small of my back, the hollow of my waist, his touch at once hungry and restrained. I pressed myself so flush against him that every ridge jutted into me. One of my legs notched itself between his, and a peak rose against my thigh.

Something tightened deep below my belly, a tug, an ache—but one that felt wholly more pleasurable than the one in my hip.

I could have kissed him forever, but we might only have hours. Minutes.

Centuries of lust became a tidal undertow, threatening to pull me under. I ran my hand over his belt, thumb brushing against his tensed stomach, and I heard his breath snag as I paused over the buckle.

"Do you want to?" I whispered, pulling away the tiniest sliver.

He was hoarse as he murmured, "I've never wanted anything more."

A thousand years was a long time to spend wanting.

His hand cupped my jaw, and I felt him shaking. Every tremor found its echo deep in my chest.

I fumbled with the belt until it was undone, then slid open the top button of his jeans and rested my hand on the flat plane of his lower stomach.

"Can I?" I whispered.

"Yes." The single syllable was rough, raw, pleading, begging.

There was a gathering low in my belly as I explored him, thinking of the steaming hammam, of the tilting boat in the Arctic Circle, of all the moments I had spent trapped inside my own desire. He shivered, whether because of my touch—so intimate, so close—or the cold March night, I did not know.

Either way, it unleashed something in him.

Rolling me onto my back, he sat up, then hovered over me, pressing his chest against mine, drawing a line of kisses down my neck.

The ridges of his hips nudged against my inner thighs, and I felt the hardness of him against the place where warmth pooled.

As he tugged down the neckline of my jumper and kissed along my clavicle, I ran my hands down his back and pressed him even tighter against me, feeling the ache between my legs throb.

He pulled back, and for a moment my skin protested the absence of his heat, until he lifted the hem of my jumper and planted kisses on my ribs, my hips, then my waist, splaying his fingers over my bare skin, his breath hot against the very bottom of my stomach, and I thought I might unravel with want.

When he softly, so softly, tugged down my jeans, my underwear brushed against me and I shuddered, sighed, *yearned*. He lowered himself, one palm flat against the ground, the other cupping my chin, and his infinite eyes searched mine.

"Are you sure?" he asked, his voice trembling like he was about to collapse on top of me.

"I'm sure," I breathed.

He pressed a single sweet kiss against my forehead, and then, at long last, we were one.

Our Infinite Fates   297

We both gasped at once, enveloped in sharp pleasure, underpinned with a brief snap of pain. I no longer felt the cold of the night air, or heard the crunch of wildlife through the forest, or feared what was about to come to us.

There was only Arden, everywhere, filling everything, the soft ache of it, our hearts beating together, a floating sensation in my chest, my pulse throbbing in every inch of my body, blood rising to the surface of my skin. A whimper built in my throat, and I locked my fingers in his hair.

The years rolled back, then the centuries, and we were two girls on a fishing boat in Nauru, we were two boys in the devastating trenches and on the ashen streets of Pompeii. We were everything, we were everyone. We were love and want, pure and raw and perfect.

How could the soul fated to kill me be the one to make me feel so alive?

As he kissed my neck, my throat, the slope of my shoulders, his finger traced the shape of my mouth, the apple of my cheek, his touch at once cold and scorching and alight, like he was trying to memorise every inch of me, like he had been thirsty for a thousand years and could finally drink.

The other hand cupped the small of my back and gently arched me upwards, and despite the nagging in my hip I could not bite back the moan. It was hard and soft, pain and pleasure, our entire existence condensed and crystallised into a single diamond of a moment.

I loved Arden so much, and we were finally *together*. Finally whole.

I loved Arden so much I could have screamed it to the stars and the mountains and the sleeping gods.

The tug, the ache—it built and built until I was delirious with it.

His breath came harder, faster, and then, with a final shudder,

298 ✳ Laura Steven ✳

we sank into each other, a blissful surrender, a climax we had waited for since the dawn of time.

Arden hung his head, every inch of him trembling, and then he looked up at me through his eyelashes. They were flecked with tears, with grief, with *hope.*

"No matter what happens next," he whispered, the shuddering finally slowed to a breathless halt, "I love you, and I have loved you, and I will love you."

"I love you too," I whispered, hugging him to me like he was the last person in the world. "Always."

Afterwards, we lay there until the sky lightened to faded indigo, talking and kissing, just being. He pulled a notebook from his coat pocket—the one he'd hidden in his writing desk—and read me poetry about our lives.

Fifty minutes, then forty, then thirty.

We made love one more time, desperate, grief-filled. The last, perhaps.

Twenty, ten, five.

At two minutes to go, when dawn crept slowly to the horizon, the sky began to rumble.

It was low and distant, at first, a juddering growl.

And then the helicopters crested the mountains, beaming down their furious spotlights, the *tat-at-at-at* of propellers whipping the breeze.

They didn't make it to us.

All the breath was sucked from my lungs. An invisible lasso tightened round my middle, the acute sensation of being dragged backwards, downwards, away from myself in some fundamental way.

Arden grabbed my hand as he buckled at the waist.

With a final brush of his skin against mine, we were torn through the fabric of the mortal world.

The
Underrealm

The first thing I was aware of was the cold.

This was not hell as I'd always imagined. It was not unbearable heat and encircling orange flames. There were no screams of agony or maniacal cackles, no chaos or mutiny or loud, lawless violence.

Instead, there was a slow falling of ash from an imperceptible sky, rows of jagged white trees, and a dark, desolate ground that sprawled out like endless tundra. Everything was too stark, too smooth, the ground like black glass and the trees like pale marble. A silvery mist whorled in the canopy, but I got the sense that even if I could have seen through it, the sky would not really have been the sky at all. It would have been a sheet of purest black, or maybe white, no sun or moon or stars but instead a featureless canvas—something unnatural, something terrible, something that hurt the naked eye to behold.

My chest rose and fell in ragged peaks. I had seen this place before. It had lurked just beyond the periphery of my understanding, as though my body had always known it would come back here. I had caught glimpses when trying to flee the asylum—almost like the torture experiments had shaken it loose, had swept away the dust from the crypt to reveal what had always lain beneath.

Whatever a soul was, the Underrealm was seared onto mine like a brand.

300   ✳   Laura Steven   ✳

Clambering slowly to my feet, I took stock of my new form. In the vaguest of senses, my outline was ghostlike. Still the rough shape of Branwen Blythe, but altogether more ethereal, blurred around the edges, insubstantial in a way I found wholly unnerving. There was a lightness I had never felt before, as though gravity had lessened its pull.

All around was stark white and absolute black and deathly quiet.

And the most troubling thing of all was that it felt like coming *home*.

Long ago, I had lived here, come of age here.

Something in me sank with recognition—but not the fearful, disgusted kind. It was nostalgia. Almost . . . *peace*. Comfort. Belonging. I shook the feelings ferociously away, as though I could shrug off the complicated emotions like an old coat.

Beside me, Arden stirred.

This form too was an approximation of Dylan Green, but the more I stared, the more I picked out other features from various lives. The strong nose from Algeria, the atrophied leg from Vienna, the smooth, dark skin from the desert. These elements flickered in and out, a constant morphing waver, a hundred identities climbing to the surface. It struck me that none of them truly defined Arden, though. Something emanated from deep inside the soul, like a beacon, a lighthouse, the only true touchstone I had ever known. Flora and fauna and sepia-stained pages, sharp intelligence and stoic stubbornness, beautiful words and deep-rooted melancholy, so old and so young all at once.

Arden was neither girl nor boy, neither solid nor unwhole. "Are you all right?"

"Yes." The whisper felt like a lie on my tongue.

We were not clothed, but nor were we naked—it was more that our forms lacked the definition to pick out any intimate fea-

Our Infinite Fates

301

tures. We were a curious gray-silver, smudged like chalk sketches, and yet we were possibly the truest versions of ourselves we had ever been.

Arden patted the place where their coat pocket might have been. "No knife."

So it was to be my bare hands.

Unless . . .

I looked around at the hideous white trees. They were bare as skeletons, not a leaf or bloom to be seen. Could I snap a branch to use as a kind of sword? I approached the nearest tree, picking out a branch with a nicely pointed tip. But as I gripped it between my ghost hands and tried to snap it off, there was no give.

Was my spectral form incapable of physical feats? Was I unable to interact with this terrible landscape?

A memory came to me, rich and textured: my child-self clambering up the tallest tree I could find, trying to see how vast this world of mine was. The slick, cold surface beneath my palms, the slip of my foot on a narrow trunk. And then, when I reached the top, a soaring feeling of freedom, of joy, so potent that I'd *whooped*. I'd whooped, and it had echoed through this broken realm for a moment too long.

Nausea rose in me like mercury in a thermometer.

"Are you all right?" Arden asked again.

I nodded. "Just remembering an everything-the-light-touches-is-my-kingdom moment I had here as a child. Totally fine and normal."

"Do you remember much?"

No, but also *yes*.

Long stretches of not speaking to another soul, the songs and plays and solitary games I would make up to entertain myself. Notbodies pinned to seething coals, eyes bulging but no screams, wondering aimlessly whether I might save them. Running, running,

302 · ✳ Laura Steven ✳ ·

running, until my almost-lungs were fit to burst, until I was gasping on my hands and knees—just to make myself feel alive.

A loneliness so dark and absolute it felt like the bottom of a well, like a black hole that swallowed all else.

I shook away the memories. We could touch the landscape. That was all I needed to know.

I tried again to snap a branch; still nothing. Arden crossed over and made the same attempt, but there was not even the slightest creak of cracking bark.

In fact . . .

I took a step back and frowned. There was no bark at all. The branches were perfectly smooth, with an almost glossy, pearly sheen to them.

Like—

"Bones," murmured Arden in horror.

I fought the urge to retch. Ash continued to fall, a soft, muffling presence. White flakes clung to me, to the bridge of my nose and the tips of my eyelashes.

How could we snap *bones*?

But it was not impossible. I thought of how easy it was to snap a human finger and reasoned that we just had to find a branch slender enough.

I picked out a far narrower twig with an equally sharp end— more of a rapier than a cutlass, but it would do the job. Perhaps, because of its raw material, it would do the job better than a steel blade. There would be something immensely satisfying about plunging a bone into the Mother's throat.

You can't kill your own mother, whispered a low, hoarse voice in the back of my head, certainly not my own. *She raised you.*

She is not my mother, my consciousness snapped back. *My mother is in South Wales, searching every nook and cranny of the hills to find me. That is love. Not this.*

Our Infinite Fates

303

You still believe in love? asked the voice. *After all this time, your fate has not bled you dry of it? You still have not learned that love* cannot conquer all?

Love is the only thing worth believing in, I replied.

The voice said something else, but I tuned it out, pulling hard on the bone. The twig broke free with a crisp snap. I had no pockets in which to conceal the weapon, but it was easily hidden inside a clenched fist.

Would it be enough? Would she bleed? Or did the Mother have powers beyond our ken? Could she wield life and death like a bow and arrow? Was her form even material enough to destroy?

Back in the trenches, she'd seemed solid, three-dimensional, if not altogether human. But down here, Arden and I were something *other.* The Mother likely would be too.

What if the bone shard met nothing but air?

What then?

Arden swallowed and looked around. "How strong is your tether right now?"

I searched inside myself and almost instantly gripped the terrible thread that tied me to the Mother. It tugged at me like a magnet, guided me like a compass. There was no north or south or east or west in the Underrealm, but it pulled me somewhere beyond the trees.

"That way."

As we walked, disquiet swelled in my chest. Everything was too . . . stark. The light was too light and the dark was too dark, like the most dreadful chiaroscuro painting I'd ever seen. The bone trees glowed white as though lit from within, and the shadows moved around them with a hideous kind of orphic sentience.

The Underrealm felt like the death of everything.

And yet here, I had *lived.*

I couldn't reconcile those two things.

There was a low, distant chatter, though I couldn't ascertain where exactly it came from—because it was everywhere, in the stoic stretch of the sharp bone branches, in the flurries of ash that fell from above, in the light and in the shadows, pressing in from all angles. And while they were not the agonized screams I'd expected, they were somehow worse: frantic, disembodied, almost delirious.

I found it profoundly disturbing, not just because of the eerie sound, but because I also could not shake the feeling that these were the tortured voices of my ancestors. Their sweet faces came to me—my empress mother in Northern Song, my grandfather in the Berber caravan, my beloved sisters in Vardø—and it took everything in my power not to break down and weep.

They were so scared, and in so much pain, and I couldn't get to them.

Whether it was true or whether it was a cruel sound effect designed to weaken me, I did not know. But the impact was still awful and unrelenting, like standing beneath a waterfall and absorbing its full force.

As we passed several small white lakes, Arden shuddered viscerally. At first glance I thought they were frozen over, but as I looked closer I realized they too shone with an unnatural brightness, a searing ferocity.

Understanding—or perhaps memory—hit me like a physical blow.

The beds of coal, burning white-hot.

And yet still the air around them felt frigidly cold. Everything here was wrong, logic-defying, unsettling in a way that made me want to turn and run in the opposite direction.

But we had made the decision, and it could not be unmade.

Arden's entire outline was sharp, taut, as we passed coal bed upon coal bed, and I shuddered to imagine their helpless body

Our Infinite Fates

pinned to the white heat for an entire week. It had been so agonizing that the nightmares had followed for a millennium.

And I was responsible. I had caused that pain.

The farther we got into the forest of bone trees, the stronger the tether pulled, until I feared I wouldn't be able to stop walking even if I wanted to. In fact, it felt like all the energy in the Underrealm was being sucked toward the same polestar in a low, terrible orbit. I thought of reaped souls and the Mother sustained by suffering, and wondered if I was walking alongside that very pain. If I was just one more morsel on which she was about to feed—or if, after all this time, she might be happy to see me.

Right when I thought I was about to buckle beneath the intensity of the lure, we came to a glade in the skeletal trees. Ash rose and fell around the clearing in unassuming mounds, and the shadows writhed and groaned with darkness.

At the center of it all, there she was.

The Mother.

The
Underrealm

Fear sliced through me like a hot knife.

The Mother looked just the same as she had in the bloody trenches. White hair fell to the ground in sheets. She was tall and rake-thin, her cheeks sunken and hollow, her skin gray as the piles of ash around her. She wore black robes that reached up to her jaw, and the only flesh visible besides her face belonged to spidery hands. Her pointed nails were so long that they curled back on themselves in grotesque helixes, like fossils or snakes or something far worse.

Sitting atop a natural dais of raised ground, her throne too was made of bones. The shards had been unnaturally twisted around one another into the shape of roses, their stems woven together like braids. A curious substance swirled around her feet, a dark, metallic fog, as though the evil were seeping out of her in noxious whorls.

A dozen hooded figures swanned around her, spectral and almost floating as they sank to her feet in prayer.

Devils.

I understood this with a lurch in my chest, with unwavering clarity—because I had been one.

To the left-hand side of the dais, there was a white-hot bed of coals, burning silent and deadly. The glade echoed with that awful ritornello of suffering, and I had to fight the childish urge to clap my hands to my ears. I knew it wouldn't work anyway; the voices of my long-lost loved ones emanated from the deepest caverns of my own mind.

At the sight of us, the Mother grinned broadly, revealing a row of teeth so white they were almost silver.

"We meet again, at last." Her voice was cool, crisp, with a choral purity to it that sent shivers down my spine. "Quite the game of cat and mouse you've been playing."

Emotions pirouetted inside me: fear and loss and grief and yearning and . . . adoration, simple and childlike and terrible.

She was not just the Mother. She was *my* Mother.

She stared at me and only me. "Evelyn."

Maybe I imagined it, maybe I was just projecting, but there was a trace of tenderness beneath the name, the syllables fractured by some painfully human emotion. The name I had chosen for myself, and yet, on her lips, it sounded like the one I'd been born into. I could almost imagine her calling it out through the trees as she tried to find me in a game of hide-and-seek. Could almost imagine her cooing it as I fell asleep.

Did devils sleep?

I could not remember.

Arden looked from me to her, confused, *angry*. "Evelyn is not yours anymore."

A scathing bark. "Nor is she yours. You said it yourself." She threw her tone low in an approximation of Arden's voice. "'I will always be yours. But I gave up the right to call you mine a long time ago.'"

My wistful reverie shattered. "You were listening?"

The Mother shook her head, sheets of glossy hair shining in the unnatural glow of the glade. "No. I was *feeling*. I have felt everything you have felt for a thousand years."

Arden took a step toward the dais, not-body writhing with hatred. "Why do you have us wait to turn eighteen before we start reaping? Do you have some semblance of a conscience? An aversion to child labor?"

It figured that Arden would bypass the emotion and spring straight into the logistical questions. And I understood it, after so many lifetimes of trying to fathom the *how,* the *why.* We didn't know how long we had to find answers.

With an almighty clap of her hands, the Mother laughed rapturously, as though nobody had ever said anything quite so funny. "Good grief, no. Children are simply too messy. Emotional, gullible, sloppy in their execution. They create too many unwitting loopholes in their bargains. The sheer incompetence of them. Hardly worth the trouble."

"But *this* deal has a loophole," argued Arden. "It has always bothered me, the internal logic of it. Surely you had to know that someone would figure this out, sooner or later. That if we die before we turn eighteen, we never have to reap another soul."

A curious flicker across her skeletal face. "Souls aren't the only things that sustain me. Suffering does too. It flows to me along our tether, like blood through an artery. And my, have you two suffered so *deliciously.* I have dined upon it for centuries."

"So why come after us in the trenches?" I asked, voice nowhere near as steady or forceful as Arden's, and yet I did not think I was *afraid.* Not really. "Why did you decide *then* that this had gone on long enough?"

A shrug. "I grew greedy and impatient. Because you existed in one of the darkest moments the mortal world had ever known, and you were surrounded by souls for the reaping. More than at any other point in history. Enough to recruit me an entire army of my own. How many of your fellow soldiers would've sold their souls to end that war? How many would have sold their souls to revive their fallen? How many would've sold their souls to ease

Our Infinite Fates 309

their loved ones' suffering? It was fertile ground, and I wanted you to reap it."

I remembered the strange feeling I'd gotten when she'd appeared in those trenches—the foreign desire to run to her. It made a twisted sort of sense. She had been my mother, once, and I was but a child in a futile war, surrounded by pain so towering I could barely breathe. Little wonder I craved her comfort.

"And our wedding?" Arden snarled. "There was no misery that day. No souls on the brink of ruin. Just us, and joy."

"Precisely." The Mother gazed at them with utter indifference; whatever she felt for me did not extend to them. "I couldn't allow that. Not when there was such a glorious opportunity to turn the best day of your lives into the worst. That suffering was delectable. Like a heaping mound of dessert."

I shook my head, once again trying to banish the undercurrent of childlike love I felt for her. "Surely it still would've been better for you to have us reaping more souls than simply letting us suffer. You have a pyramid scheme to uphold."

I briefly wondered whether she'd understand the modern concept, but she bared her teeth in that sharp grin once more. "Suffering is in itself a pyramid scheme. Hurt people hurt people. One soul feels pain, so they inflict the same upon three more, in a bid to rid themselves of it. Those three pass it on to more still, and it spirals beyond all control. The human condition, so it seems."

"How did you come to be?" Arden asked, almost as soon as she'd finished talking. "You're the top of the pyramid, so you can't have made a bargain."

The Mother's eyes—black as coal—narrowed in appraisal. "My, you're quite the inquisitive little soul, aren't you?"

Arden's teeth ground together like pestle and mortar. "I have years of wondering behind me."

The Mother hooked a finger at one of the devils, who scurried over and began polishing the longest of their master's grim nails. "I have never understood my own origins well enough to explain them. Only a sense that I am suffering, manifest. I am the product of human pain, of millennia of hatred and bloodshed, loss and grief. I did not ask to exist, and yet I do. And whatever I am, I could not bear to be alone. So I soon taught myself how to find company, willing or otherwise."

Arden surveyed the barren landscape. "Still looks rather desolate to me."

The Mother's shoulders hitched almost imperceptibly, the slightest show of tension that anyone but her offspring might have missed. "The others are wandering the mortal realm, bringing me more souls, more suffering."

The devils exchanged the most curious of glances.

"You're lying," Arden said slowly, watching them, piecing it all together—a thousand years of theorizing finally bearing fruit. "Your numbers are dwindling. *That's* why you came after us in the trenches."

Arden peered at the devil polishing her nail, and my gaze followed. The devil was fading around the edges, even less corporeal than the two of us. Glitching, almost, like a printer running out of ink. There was something *wrong* with them. They didn't look or feel at all how I remembered. Arden seemed to come to the same realization, glaring back at the Mother.

"Something happens to the devils who reap. They're . . . crumbling." A frenetic calculation took place behind Arden's eyes. "Because the more broken souls they recruit, the more suffering flows toward them. And souls can only absorb so much suffering before it destroys them." Arden said this with the profound weight of a soul who had already borne too much pain, who had also begun to crumple beneath the weight of it. "They are not built like you. They are humans in devils' clothing. And so the suffering is too much to bear."

The Mother rearranged herself on the throne, and by now the tension had become full-fledged loathing.

Arden had struck a nerve.

"I trust you are ready to begin reaping for me," she said calmly—too calmly.

"No." I glared at her with the sun's own fury, and the Mother regarded me with a look I could not parse.

Emotions towered in my chest—shame and rejection, fear and desperation, and love, love, love. I longed to carve out everything I felt for her.

This woman—this being—had raised me as her own. Had we drawn hopscotch on the ground in trails of ash? Made dice out of carved femurs? Did she offer counsel on reaping, or was it woven into the very fabric of me?

"Where did I come from?" I whispered. "Did you give birth to me, like mortal women do? Do I have a father?"

She gave a twisted, self-satisfied smile. "Now, why would I tell you that when the pain of not knowing tastes so *good*?"

"You're evil." The words were like globules of spit landing at her feet, but I didn't even know if I truly meant them.

The Mother blinked in surprise. "Am I? Or am I simply doing what I must to survive? How am I so different from every other soul who enters willingly into a bargain with me? We are all primal creatures. We think of our own continuance above all else, irrespective of the cost."

Her tone was preening, and I wanted to rip it from her mouth.

Hatred trembled at the core of me like an avalanche hurtling down a slope.

"Why are you here, Evelyn?" the Mother murmured. The air between us shook like a rib cage. Another smug smile nicked at

312 ⁎ Laura Steven ⁎

the corners of her lips. "I think some small part of you *wanted* to see me again."

There was almost something searching in her gaze, some last wisp of kinship, a single drop of humanity in the vast ocean of her evil. As though she wanted to hear something tender—that I missed her, or loved her, or, at the very least, respected her.

It almost drew me in, the glint of it, like I was a child stooping to examine an old penny in a pond.

But now I knew what real motherhood was—jam and croissants and cups of tea, warm hugs by glowing fires. *You are the lights of my life.*

Resolve tightened my grip on the bone in my hand.

"Because I want to destroy you," I whispered, the faintest trace of a breath.

The quirk of an eyebrow. "Pardon?"

"BECAUSE I WANT TO DESTROY YOU!" I screamed.

And then I lunged toward the dais.

Instead of leaping to their master's defense, the devils parted like a sea—whether through some vague sense of self-preservation or because, in the deepest part of their indentured selves, they wanted to see the Mother taken down.

I launched myself into the air, and for a few moments it felt like I was floating. Below me, the Mother's expression was one of shock and hate.

She twisted out of the way, but it was not enough.

The bone shard plunged into the back of her neck.

There was no spurt of blood but rather a puff of pale gray mist emanating from the wound, the same immaterial fog that slicked around her ankles.

Wild arms grappled at me, then she weakened like a rag doll.

I wrenched the makeshift blade free of her neck and then plunged again, this time into the back of her shoulder.

Our Infinite Fates

313

Wrench, lift, bone into her heart.

Under the third blow, she crumpled next to the hot coals.

Breathing jaggedly, I stood back, this time leaving the blade inside her. I waited for myself to die too, the way Arden and I always did together, but nothing happened.

Yet she was folded around herself on the ground, small and sad and lifeless.

The servants stared at their fallen Mother. Arden stood silently behind me, not daring to move to my side.

I had done it.

I had destroyed the Mother.

My Mother.

And yet something was wrong.

I didn't know what I'd expected, but it had been more. Surely, at the defeat of the Mother, the Underrealm would crumble to dust, the other devils would slump to the ground, all their tethers severed at last. All the cruel tension would leave the world. We would be free—and we would be able to feel it.

Instead, everything teetered on a precipice.

After several taut beats, the Mother twitched, then breathed in a shallow, rasping breath. Horror licked at me like a white flame.

The devils leaped into action.

Three crouched at her side and turned her body over; almost-vacant eyes stared up at the falling ash. They plugged the wounds on her neck and shoulder with their hands, so the peculiar gray mist stopped flowing. They muttered low chants, like a litany.

Four more strode toward Arden.

Arden took a step back, face twisting with horror as the cloaked figures closed in and grabbed a limb each.

Despite Arden's writhing, the servants seemed unfathomably strong.

They dragged my love toward the bed of hot coals.

"No!" I screamed, but four more servants were at my own arms and legs, and I could not move. They had locked me in place so suddenly and absolutely that I was powerless.

They were so strong. Too strong. An ungodly power at their fingertips.

Arden's back was slammed against the hot coals, and coiling bonds appeared at the corners of the terrible bed. The servants secured them around Arden's wrists and ankles. The coals glowed a thousand times brighter than they had before, and an immense burst of heat burned at the peaks of my face, like the hottest Saharan wind I'd ever endured.

And Arden was pressed bare against the source.

The agony must have been world-ending.

And yet . . . Arden did not struggle, nor scream, nor call out. Somehow that was worse.

Instead, something black and vaporous began to seep out of Arden's body—and toward the Mother.

"What are you doing?" I yelled, wrenching futilely at the clawed hands gripping me.

No response.

The black mist swirled around the Mother. The servants removed their hands from their master's wounds, tearing free the bone shard from her chest.

And the blackness pressed into the wounds.

"What are you doing?" I repeated, a soprano cry.

Panic rose in my chest, the tortured voices in the shadows howled with me, and I didn't understand what was happening but I knew it was bad, that the Mother was taking something fundamental from Arden.

And it was healing her.

Held back by the iron grip of the devils, I could do nothing but watch.

Our Infinite Fates 315

Tears streaked down my face; hatred scorched through my veins.

I was no longer cold. I burned with a long, rich fury built up over a thousand years.

Yet I could not unleash it.

After several awful moments of leeching the black vapor, the Mother stirred.

Blinked.

Turned her cruel face toward me.

"Did you really think it would be that easy?" she growled, her voice no longer the honeyed trill of earlier but rather a low, gravelly rasp.

"What are you doing to Arden?" I hated the begging in my voice, but I couldn't help it. "Why is there no screaming?"

The Mother was regaining strength with every passing second. Now she sat up, propping one palm against the bone forest floor, though there was a strain, a discomfort to her actions. She no longer moved as fluidly as she had before. She clicked and jerked like a twitching spider.

As she replied, her eyes were alight with cruelty. "I find the suffering is more intense without a release valve. And the more intense the suffering . . . the greater its power."

The sheer horror of it was almost impossible to comprehend. That was what the black mist was—Arden's suffering. Not only could it sustain the Mother, but it could also *heal* her.

Why hadn't I anticipated it?

I had lost my chance. I had failed.

The Mother was alive.

And now we were trapped in the Underrealm.

The
Underrealm

The Mother ran her helix fingernails through her long sheets of white hair. The locks were stained charcoal gray in several places, and the hollows of her cheeks seemed more pronounced than before. The wounds I'd inflicted had closed, leaving behind blackish scars from the suffering that had healed them.

"I tried never to punish you as a child." Her words were cold, disaffected, but her eyes shone bright with hurt. "You were all I had. Letting you go *above* to reap was my mistake, because I soon grew addicted to your suffering. It was so raw, so potent, and it fueled me like nothing or nobody else. Perhaps *because* you were mine. An extension of me. And so when you suffer, it is more powerful than I ever could have imagined." A twist of her gnarled lips. "Since discovering that *quirk* of nature, I have not known what to do—let it keep flowing to me? Relish its power? Or come after you? Force you to do the real bidding, the real reaping?"

"Or you could've let me go," I snapped. "Cut me free of the tether, if you really loved me like a child."

Her mouth twisted bitterly. "But then I would have been alone once again. And that I could not bear."

As I yanked my hands and feet to no avail, I should have felt deathly afraid—and, in truth, I physically recoiled from the prospect of the coals.

But I was not scared.

Our Infinite Fates 317

Because my brain had kicked into gear, thinking through every possibility. And I realized the Mother didn't have all that many options.

If she put me on the coals next to Arden, for hours or days or weeks or months or years, that still did not serve her. She would take something from our suffering, yes, but Arden had struck upon something true—her devils were crumbling from that current of pain, and she needed *more.*

She had *always* needed more than simple suffering. Otherwise, she would only need to strap a few of her servants to the coal beds and flourish for an eternity. She needed fresh souls, ones that had not yet withered under the weight of suffering.

I thought of the way it all worked, the structure of it, both a pyramid and a self-fulfilling circle.

And I wondered.

Could it be that the stronger she got, the more suffering she needed to survive? The more souls she required to keep herself going? Did power need more power need more power?

"Put me on the coals, if you must." A final, desperate gambit. "But that's not what you really want, is it?"

Her eyes narrowed. "What do you know of what I want, child?"

"This is a stalemate." I was shaking from the fear and the frustration and the hate, from the vicarious agony of seeing Arden tortured, from the hope withering and dying and then rekindling in my chest. "There is no path forward for you. If you send us out into the world to reap, we'll simply kill each other and the cycle will repeat itself. We will be back here the next time we come of age, and we will be more prepared, and, sooner or later, we will succeed in destroying you."

The Mother shrugged, but it was labored now, pained, not the casual indifference of earlier. I thought, perhaps, that she was afraid. "I could simply leave you on hot coals for another thousand years."

318 ✴ **Laura Steven** ✴

"But I don't think that's enough for you, is it?" I retorted. "I think . . . I think that after this long, the suffering gained from the hot coals has lost its potency. It can heal wounds, yes, but it's not *enough,* in the deeper sense of the word. You're like an addict who always needs *more.* You need the pyramid to keep growing exponentially beneath you, or you will die. It's why you came after us in the trenches. You saw a rare opportunity."

Her hand was pressed to her black-filled chest. A reminder of her vulnerability, motivation for me to keep pushing her.

She did not deny it but said simply, "And yet you have said yourself you shall refuse to reap."

"Precisely," I said, tightening the reins on my breathing. "Stalemate."

"You appear to be advocating for your own demise, child."

"No," I replied, wishing I could pace, could release some of this coiled energy. "I ask simply that you make us another deal."

"Another deal?" snipped the Mother, my Mother, a trace of amusement on her face.

I squared my shoulders as best I could in the harsh grasp of the servants. "One that benefits us both, with clear parameters. One that grants us freedom from this tether once and for all. Because we are rapidly becoming more trouble than we're worth."

The Mother considered this for a moment. I glanced over at Arden's paralyzed body—eyes bulging and screaming where the mouth could not—and shuddered from head to toe.

This pain is all because of you, the chorus of shadow voices hissed at once, but I bridled the thought. Self-loathing would not serve us right now.

"There is something else that fuels me." The Mother was reverent, contemplative. "Something altogether harder to take by force. Something I have never quite mastered." She tapped her thin bottom lip with her black-tipped forefinger. "And yet, if you were willing donors . . . it might just work."

Something about the word *donors* made me shiver. "What is that?"

Her eyes lit up with greed. "Love."

Dread curled inside me, like a wounded animal trying to protect its exposed belly.

"The love you and your mark feel for each other . . . it has been enough to sustain the both of you for a millennium. It has transcended time, and death, and fate. I have good reason to believe it will fuel me too. It is rich and pure and potent—so much more so than suffering. A lifeblood." By now she was glittering with excitement. "And so my offer is this: I will sap the love from you both, drip by drip, until I am swimming in it. I will leech you dry. Then you both shall die."

I stared at her. "Why on earth would I agree to that?"

A meaningful pause. "Because in the next life, you will be free."

"Free," I repeated, not fully comprehending.

"There will be no obligation to reap once you come of age. You will turn eighteen without incident, and then nineteen, and then twenty, and you will never again be called to the Underrealm."

Oh.

Oh.

It was a horrible, horrible offer.

And yet.

We would be *free.* We would never have to reap. We could live to adulthood. No more killer and killed, no more hunter and hunted. Pure, simple life, with all its human flaws.

But the cost was each other.

My heart panged as I asked, "Would we remember any of it?"

The Mother grinned, broad and cruel. "You would not."

"And the love . . . it would be gone. Forever."

"It would."

I felt like collapsing to the ground. An impossible choice. There were no good paths, no ways to escape these hideous fates. But I supposed that was the nature of a deal with the devil—it was to be made in the absence of all other options. Nothing left to hope for but a miracle, no matter how tainted that miracle may be.

"I cannot make this decision alone," I said at last. "Free Arden."

"Very well." With a wave of her long, clawed hand, the Mother gestured for one of her servants to loose Arden from the shackles. Relief surged through me at the small victory.

Once the evil power holding Arden still and silent was removed, yells of anguish filled the world. They were raw, ragged, primal, and they ripped right through my heart. My love staggered over to me, body weak and tortured, and everything in me churned with loathing at the devil before us.

The devil who was, once again, about to win.

"Are you okay?" I whispered. An absurd question. The servants holding my wrists and ankles relinquished their grip, and I threw my arms around Arden.

Shaking uncontrollably, all Arden was capable of was a stiff nod.

Trying to keep the tremble from my voice, I pulled back and said, "We have another bargain to make."

As I explained everything the Mother had proposed, Arden sank to the ground. At last, I allowed myself to follow.

Pure, black horror swallowed Arden's irises whole. "We can't do that."

The fear was palpable in the words. It was all I could do not to break down. "What choice do we have?"

With a ferocious shake of the head, Arden urged, "Evelyn . . . We would be *gone,* in all meaningful ways. Everything we have. Everything we mean to each other. What even are we without us?"

It was a knife wound to the heart—because it was true.

It was the worst thing I could possibly imagine.

"I know." Cupping my hands around Arden's stoic face, I whispered, "You're my family. My homeland. My soulmate."

A twisted smile. "People throw that word around too easily. *Soulmate.*"

I pressed my face against Arden's chest, my breath coming in desperate rasps. Ash fell around us, and it was almost beautiful, if I forgot what it was.

A gentle finger tipped my chin up.

"We can't do this," Arden said softly. "I'll do anything but this."

"This is my only offer," the Mother said, cold as the Siberian wilderness, all trace of maternal instinct gone. Leeched out of her by my bone blade. "It is this or the eternal coals. Unless, of course, you have changed your mind about reaping for me . . ."

"We have not," I snapped, with more venom than I felt truly capable of. In reality, this whole conversation was tearing me apart, piece by eternal piece, and she knew it, and we all knew there was only one way it could end.

Arden said slowly, "What if . . ."

"No." I knew what the proposal would be: that we just do it. *We reap, and at least we'll be together.* "We can't subject anyone else to this twisted fate. We can't. You know me. You know I will lay my body and my life on the line before I hurt another living soul the way I hurt you." I swallowed sharply. "Remember what you said to me about heroes and villains? 'If a hero is someone who will give up love to save the world, then a villain is the reverse. Someone who will give up the world to save love.' I'm sorry, but I can't be a villain. I can't choose love over the world."

Another bitter chuckle, but it was filled with affection. "You never were a particularly good devil."

"I was fucking atrocious."

After a few terrible moments, resignation began to descend over Arden's face. "So we have to do this."

For some reason, hearing it from Arden's lips made it all the more awful. In a last-ditch suggestion I didn't truly mean, I said desperately, "There's always the coals."

Arden sighed. "What would be the point? Eternal suffering, and still we would not be together. We would be trapped in the cages of our own minds, with nothing but pain for company." A shudder rippled through Arden's almost-body, a visceral jerk. "It's even worse than I remembered. You think you'll die from it, but you never do."

"I'm sorry." The words choked out of my throat as I folded myself into Arden's arms.

A tender hand stroked my hair. Lips brushed my forehead. "Why are you sorry?"

"We made a mistake coming here. I should've let us jump from that cliff while we had the chance."

"You did what felt right."

I scoffed. "And I dragged you along with me."

"My unexplained murders have been dragging you along for centuries. It was time the scales tipped."

The Mother stepped forward, and I looked over at her hideous outline. My hatred for her was almost, almost as potent as my love for Arden. Almost.

"Is that a decision?"

We didn't have to answer. She knew she had won.

"Hold my hands," said Arden fiercely. "Stay with me as long as you can."

I kept my eyes fixed on the love of all my lives as the Mother

Our Infinite Fates

323

crossed closer to us, raising her hands and summoning whatever heinous powers would allow her to reap the immortal love from our not-quite-bodies.

For a moment, there was a charged silence, and nothing happened, and my heart skipped with the hope that maybe it wouldn't work. But then something loosened in my chest, a strange yank of an invisible rope, followed by a soft, warm flow into the ether.

The substance that poured from my chest was shimmering, ephemeral, the color of pearls and golden barley and every sunrise I had ever seen. It did not hurt, but it *did*. As I saw it pour from me, an immeasurable grief weighed down from above, from below, from everywhere.

I could not watch the love gush into the Mother, but I heard her moans of pleasure.

In that moment, I thought nothing in the world could be more painful than the impending goodbye.

"I can't lose you," I gasped, and I had never felt so irrevocably human.

Arden clutched me, and it was an altogether different yearning than it had been on the hilltop. It was almost feral with hurt. "I know. I know."

The loss was bigger than anything, a gaping cavern of grief, and I was teetering on the edge. Every fiber of me pleaded against it, but the force was too strong, and I was too human. Maybe if I'd been a better devil, I would have found a way around this. Or I would never have been here in the first place.

No. I wouldn't change my fragile, imperfect, human heart. Not for anything.

And hadn't I always known this? That to be human was to love and love and love, knowing it could only end in tragedy? Every babe in arms was born to this terrible fate, every parent and child, every spouse, every friend and lover and sibling, every uncle and aunt and great-great-grandfather, every found family, all of us bound to the perpetual cycle, all of it so awful and wonderful and inescapable.

To love was to live, and to live was to die.

In a thousand years I had never let this fundamental truth defeat me, and I would not let it bury me now. I would hold strong in the face of it, because what else could we do?

I grasped Arden's hands with existential desperation. "I have loved you so much."

Tears slid down Arden's beautiful cheeks, bright and shining as the moonlight on the glen. "I want you to know that wherever we are next, my heart will be with you." A shuddering sob. "It might not *know* it's with you, but hearts have their ways. Every atrium, every ventricle, every vein and artery will beat for you. Even if my mind has lost you. Because you are in the very fabric of me, all right? You are me, and I am you. And our love is stronger than anything."

"All the years I've prayed for an end to this," I whispered. "And now that ending is finally here, I'd do anything to live just one more life with you."

Our infinite fates were no longer infinite, and nothing could have hurt more.

The pearlescent current continued to cascade from us, gathering heat and speed, and with every fresh surge I felt both lighter and heavier.

"I love you," I repeated, because it was all I could say, the only thing that felt large enough, and yet still it would never be enough. "And I have loved you. And I will love you."

Arden's eyes were both the depth of the ocean and the height of the clouds. They were soaring wings and glimmering sapphires, they were my anchor and my sword and my ship and my whetstone, they were everything, everything, everything, and they would soon be gone.

Our Infinite Fates   325

A temple I'd worshipped at for a thousand years was slowly crumbling to the ground.

"Never let me go," Arden whispered, the grip on my hands tight and urgent.

I could speak no more.

As the love bled from me, so too did my life.

A slow, sleepy slipping away, oddly peaceful.

I thought then not just of Arden, but of everyone I had ever loved and lost. The father shot on the beach in Algeria, the mother mourned in the scorched desert, the sisters in paranoid Vardø. A ship's captain, an esteemed costumier, a mulish oligarch, an emperor's concubine.

I had tried to cup them in my palms for so long, and now the time had come to part my fingers.

To let go, at last, and let their memories seep back into the earth.

My farmer father, crushed to death. His parents, never able to recover.

My sweet mother, with her patchwork blanket of found family.

Gracie, her pristine strangeness.

Every precious raindrop, sliding forever away.

I let them fall, felt them patter into a clear mountain spring, felt them drift away on a stream, rainwater returning to its source.

Felt that stream become a river, gathering speed, a furious foam, the force of the love strong enough to drag a mere mortal away. A gush, a burst, tumbling over cliffs, swirling into pools.

A frantic, powerful hurtle toward the ocean.

And then, the screams.

Head drooping dangerously, I looked up from Arden's perfect hands.

The Mother was crouched to the ground, clutching at her chest.

"Stop! Stop!" she moaned, to whatever higher force she drew her dark powers from.

But the tide of love was too powerful to be stilled.

It kept flowing into her, rich and raw and bright, too strong for her withered soul to handle. It overtook her like a parasite, seeping into her every atom, bursting into glorious sunlight.

The anguish on her face melted into something else entirely.

Hope surged in my heart.

She was *dying*.

For real, this time. Somehow I knew this for certain.

But so was I. So was Arden.

Arden?

The name was familiar. It made me ache, yearn, but I couldn't say why.

Desperately I clutched at it, like trying to grab hold of a rock while sliding away on a river, but my fingers grasped on nothing.

The Mother let out a final agonized scream, then slumped to the ground, limp and still. All around her, the devils vanished in a puff of ashen smoke. The very walls of the Underrealm were crumbling, bone trees blurring into ash snow, the not-sky falling to the black earth.

With a final shuddering breath, the last of my love ebbed away, but the candle of hope in my chest still did not extinguish. It flickered, canted, dipped and then rose again, this thing that had kept me alive for so long, this thing that even death could not touch.

And the Underrealm faded to nothing.

even when we are but bones in the earth
my eternal heart will love you still,
for even when a star does perish
its light burns on for millennia

—AUTHOR UNKNOWN

Greece

986

I would love Calliope until the sun devoured the earth; that much I knew.

The air around the amphitheater was smudged with dust and haze, my fingers sticky from dates and nectarine juice, my blood slow and sleepy from the wine, and Calliope's laughing head on my shoulder was the most sweet and perfect thing in all the land. We had been to watch a new comedy about a peasant from Thessaly, and she was alight with it, with the feeling of tapping into the great current of human art.

"Have you any new ideas for your own play?" I asked as we stumbled home through the Athenian streets, for Calliope had been penning a tragedy for as long as I had known her. She would ink the story on any surface she could find—parchment and papyrus, shards of pottery and rags of fabric, even carving it into segments of peeled tree bark, her mind iridescent as the sky's bright ether.

And still she would not reveal the plot.

"Indeed." She smiled, her eyes as honey, desire poured upon her lovely face. Strolling down the arcaded street woven with vines, we passed our favorite marble fountain—admiring the curve of Aphrodite's sumptuous hips, the invitation of her outstretched palm—before entering the cool stone atrium of our communal

Our Infinite Fates   329

building. "I was thinking that perhaps my hero could, instead of falling for . . ."

Her eyes snapped wide and afraid, gripping my hand to the bone, and a kind of primal dread pooled in my lungs. "Daphne, I—"

Right as we crossed the threshold to our small abode, Calliope, my love, my light, collapsed suddenly and completely as a slain steed, a cruel froth foaming at her wine-red mouth, her limbs shuddering and smacking against the ground like a crazed puppet, her eyes devoured by their own bloodied whites.

"*Calliope!*" I screamed, ferocious, terror-stricken.

Still she seized.

I was known in my family for keeping a level head in grave circumstances, but the visceral panic bucking in my chest was impossible to bridle. I fell to my knees beside her, resting an ear on her soft chest, her whole body writhing, black hair fanned out behind her like a mourning wreath, and everything in me roared in agony as I felt the final beat of her heart against my cheek.

A cheek she had kissed not a moment earlier.

Finally, stillness.

Awful, terrible, impossible stillness.

A pain in my ribs so keen it folded me in two.

No. We were but nineteen years old. We had a whole life ahead of us.

How? Why?

No.

Disbelieving, I buried my face in her gentle stomach, pleading with whatever gods would listen to save her, save her, please, I would do anything, I would give anything.

But the glinting gold icon hung over the hearth was silent.

Unbreathing, I clawed at my face. It had happened so fast. How had it happened so fast? This could not be real. It was a nightmare from which I must surely, surely awake.

The cacophony of the nearby agora rang out in the soaring night. The sounds of laughter and barter, toasts raised and trades sealed, the meeting of old friends and the making of new, and it all seemed so impossibly distant, as though such joviality and mirth must surely exist on another plane of reality. For how could such happiness swell mere yards away when my love lay dead?

Did they not know? Could they not feel it, this seismic shift, this earth-shattering loss, this great before and after of my life?

Shhhhlick.

A sudden, almost imperceptible shift in the atmosphere, something dark and strange entering my immediate orbit.

A subhuman sound at the door we had not closed.

The raw dread in my lungs dropped a dozen degrees.

"That took rather longer than expected," drawled a cold, empty voice, its vowels echoing and cavernous. "The vial was tipped at the amphitheater. I have been following ever since."

My teary gaze snapped up.

There stood a tall, skeletal woman with skin so pink and new it was as though she had been born mere moments ago. Sheets of white-blond hair brushed the ground, and coal-black embers burned in her irises.

Breathing ragged, I stared at the stranger, deeply furious and deeply afraid.

"You poisoned her. Calliope." Each word was a puncture wound. "Why?"

She shrugged, the dark fabric of her gown shifting. "I saw the love you shared and knew it could be exploited."

It took a moment for the casual cruelty of the statement to land.

This woman had killed the love of my life for sport.

Our Infinite Fates 331

Everything in me screamed for me to throw myself at her, to wrestle her to the ground and smash her head against the marble slabs until her broken eyes burst in their sockets like overripe apricots. But there was something so unnerving about her, a body of still water, a sinister sea serpent coiled below its glassy surface. My limbs would not move.

"Get out," I snarled, low, animalistic. "Leave. Before I stab you in the chest."

"That would not achieve very much." She strode past the place where Calliope lay, her skirts gliding inhumanly along the floor, and took a seat in our best chair. My grandfather's heirloom, made of sweet chestnut and carved with friezes of leaves and flowers. "And besides, I believe you rather need me to make you a deal."

Understanding rolled through me like a clap of thunder.

It could not be. She could not be.

I had heard the stories, but . . .

"You are the devil," I whispered.

Her silence was charged as the sky before rain.

Hideous hope took seed in my chest, laying roots in the pooled dread, the whole thing monstrous and wrong.

"Then you have the power to save her," I croaked, suddenly shivering to the bone. "You can bring her back to life, for a price. And I will pay it. Anything."

She waved a dismissive hand, her elegant fingers not the cloven hooves one might expect, though her nails wound around themselves in hideous black helixes. "Necromancy is beyond my scope, child. I can heal the sick, and mend broken hearts, and make kings of the poor. I can smite and spite and ruin, just as I can empower and enrich and ensnare. I can wield Cupid's bow and take aim with his arrows. I can end wars and part tides, just as I can bring forth bountiful harvests and plentiful rain. Drought and famine and plague cower at my feet. But no, I cannot raise the dead, for their souls have already been reaped."

The grotesque hope in me withered. "Then there is nothing you can do for me."

"Is there not?" Her eyebrows quirked in amusement. "Perhaps you simply lack imagination."

"I know not what you mean." I turned away from her, back to Calliope, whose perfect heart was already growing cold. Whose soul had, if this devil could be believed, already been reaped. She was lost to me now, forever, and the pain of the realization left me breathless.

How could a mind so iridescent ever die?

How could such honeyed eyes ever cease to shine?

The devil's silken voice filled the room once more. "Do you believe in reincarnation, child?"

Something in me stilled, a deer sensing a nearby archer. "I do not."

"Perhaps it would be wise to start." She paused, the moment laden with significance.

Slowly her meaning dawned on me. "We can be together in our next life."

The devil grinned, wide and uncanny, her mouth a gaping maw. "You can be together in infinite lives."

My heart thumped anew. "You have the power to do that?"

"As previously established, my powers are almost entirely unfettered."

A stone lodged in my throat. I laced my fingers through Calliope's, tears slicking down my salt-crusted cheeks. My bones ached with the sudden loss of her, my lungs wrung out like dishrags, the disbelief settling into something entirely more devastating.

Our Infinite Fates   333

"What do you ask in return?" I muttered hoarsely, the words arid. "I know the devil does not bargain for nothing."

She leaned forward, a wolfish hunger in her stare. "You will spend seven days and seven nights upon burning coals, feeding me with your suffering. And then, for the rest of eternity, you will serve me, as too will your beloved."

"So we will be devils." That seemed less unbearable than being apart from Calliope, which I did recognize as an extraordinarily sapphic way to think.

"Indeed."

I studied this beastly devil like an ancient text, peering between the lines for hidden meaning, for traps and ruses disguised as opportunities. "Can devils even love at all?"

"A good question." She nodded appraisingly, and I loathed myself for the flicker of pride. "You are not one to be easily tricked. No, devils cannot love. But I will ensure enough of your human hearts remain that the time with your beloved is meaningful."

"So I shall die too." I thought of my mother, my brother, the life I had here, but it all paled next to the loss of Calliope. They would survive without me. I would not without my beloved. "Now. Tonight."

"Indeed," the devil repeated, every muscle and sinew in her body taut with anticipation.

"And then we will be born . . . elsewhere? As different people? You won't make us trees? Or locusts?"

"Another astute question—such a fierce mind, even in times of great sorrow. Yes, you will be spawned as human beings, in reasonably close proximity. If your love is as true as you believe it to be, you will find each other. There will be complications." A grinding bark of laughter. "Oh, the hardships you will face. Because the suffering will sustain me, you see? I feed not just on souls but on pain. Emotional, physical—it does not matter to me. Either you will turn eighteen and reap, and I will be fed, or you will suffer, and I will also be fed. The tether binding us together will be like an artery, pain flowing always toward me."

"What kind of hardships?" My voice was coarse with hatred, fists clenching and unclenching at my sides.

The devil tapped her bottom lip with a grotesque fingernail. "That depends upon how fiendishly inventive I can be. Perhaps in your next incarnation . . . yes. You will return to the Underrealm with me, and I will raise you as my own. I will make your love"—a scathing gesture toward Calliope—"a lowly mortal commoner, and have you reap them. And they will always remember that as your beginning, always bear that scar of resentment. A terrible foundation for a relationship." She gave a shudder of delight, as though the thought had just stroked her somewhere intimate.

"Will *I* remember this deal at all?"

She considered this. "No. There is too much comfort in the *why*. Nothing tortures the human mind quite like the unknown."

"But you promise that we will be together," I said fiercely, relinquishing myself to that monstrous hope. "In the next life."

"And the next. And the next. And the next. As too you will be devils."

So there it was. Live without Calliope, or live with her forever as a devil.

Even with the promise of a week on searing coals, it was barely a question.

I took in a last breath of dusty Athenian air.

"Then we have a deal."

Scotland

2054

It was León Cazares's first day as a barista-in-training, serving up an unholy quantity of pistachio-milk lattes to the patrons of Waterstones, Edinburgh.

Unfortunately, he was not particularly good at it.

He was *good* at clothes.

He'd spent his twenties studying fashion at the Istituto Europeo di Design in Barcelona, travelling the world with a backpack and an empty suitcase, hoarding the most curious and unusual vintage garments from far-flung lands, and interning under many of the fashion greats (and several overhyped frauds) before eventually launching his own luxury line. Casa Cazares had been slow to get off the ground and initially bemused critics, what with its eccentric collation of historical cuts and intricate beadwork, strange textiles and mishmashed styles, but León didn't especially care. Acclaim had never been his purpose, only joy.

Everything had changed, however, when a BAFTA-winning actress had worn Casa Cazares to the Met Gala.

Gracie Blythe was precisely as eccentric as her choice of raiment. The gala's theme had been "Troubled Sea," and rather than opting for the ethereal oceanic satins of her peers, she'd chosen a scarlet silk gown adorned with a startling array of buttons, coupled with a cropped damask waistcoat and a chunky gold cross necklace—a look closely inspired by a Golden Age pirate called Le Joli Rouge.

When she'd made best-dressed lists around the globe, Gracie had sent a personal thank-you note to León, which had made him cry quite profoundly, though he couldn't say for certain why.

He didn't know *why* watching her act on-screen was such a comfort to him, or *why* her voice spread warmth through his chest every single time he heard it, or *why* he often lost entire days to watching her press junkets. She had legions of similarly devout fans, of course—she was playful and hilarious, cruel-tongued and spiky, and she could make anything sound interesting. She bled charisma.

But it wasn't just charisma that drew him to her. Their connection felt strangely intimate, and not in the unbalanced parasocial way of her other obsessed fans. It was as though he missed her, on some level, even though they'd never met. The personal note had felt curiously like a full-circle moment.

León was no stranger to these peculiar existential *tugs*. Sometimes he'd visit a new city on a buying trip, only to be overcome by the sense that he'd been there before, and not just as a tourist—no, he had lived in the intimate seams of the place, had known them like his own heartbeat.

There was also the vague sense that he was searching for something—something ephemeral and elusive, as powerful as it was intangible. Perhaps that was the real reason he was drawn to foreign lands. Perhaps that was why he'd become so hell-bent on establishing Casa Cazares in every major capital in the world.

How could he ever find *it* if he stayed in one place for too long?

Upon arriving in Edinburgh several months ago—ostensibly to open a new boutique on Princes Street—there had been the profound *click* of the world slotting into place, like a magnet's north pole finally finding south.

Our Infinite Fates 337

"You're doing it wrong," said the blue-haired barista beside him. She was short and round, with as many piercings on her face as there were freckles. Her apron was covered in cake crumbs.

"Oh," said León cheerfully, brushing his dark curls out of his face, not too troubled by his failure.

In fact, he didn't really understand why he'd taken the job in the first place, other than some vague, inexplicable instinct. The shifts would distract from his now world-renowned fashion line, of course, and the people he worked with thought his little sabbatical was almost certainly a sign of complete psychological breakdown. His personal assistant and closest confidante, Madge, had been rather vocal about it.

But a little over a month ago, he'd come to the Waterstones café to grab a book of photography and a pumpkin spice latte— his taste in coffee had never been especially sophisticated—and within a moment of walking through the doors, he'd been overcome with a sense of *rightness*. The utterly illogical and entirely absurd suspicion that this was an important place to be, in that grand and nonsensical search of his.

And so he'd followed the instinct, just like he'd followed the peculiar urge to open a shop in Edinburgh instead of Lima. There was a fairly high chance Madge would assassinate him at any moment, but he didn't care much.

This mattered. Somehow, it mattered.

Hope flickered in his chest, bright and strong in the cupped hands of his ribs.

I still believe.

He did not know what the internal words pertained to, exactly, but he felt them so often, so viscerally, that they were a familiar comfort, a perpetual lighthouse beckoning him home, a mantra and a faith and a purpose.

Outside, the day was cloudy and autumnal. The castle on the

hill was circled in gold and bronze foliage, and shoppers bustled up and down the pavements in puffy coats and plaid scarves. A tram glided past, whipping up a sudden gust of wind and red-brown leaves. There was the distant sound of bagpipes bleating at tourists, as well as the clatter of cups and saucers, the soft turning of pages. Just as León's eyes were drifting back to the now-burnt pistachio milk in the brushed-steel jug, his gaze snagged on something.

Or, rather, *someone.*

A tall, broad-shouldered man of around León's age, with short ginger hair soft enough to run fingers through. He wore tortoise-shell glasses and a cream cable-knit sweater—dotted with several climate action pins—and carried with him a neat oxblood satchel, which he looped over the back of a seat by the window.

León dropped the milk jug to the floor with a metallic crash, heart bucking fiercely in his chest.

The redhead lowered himself into the chair and arranged his teapot on the table. The steam swirled up from the spout, illuminated by the pale grey light filtering through the window. Then he sank a ringless hand into the leather satchel and pulled out a fountain pen and a notebook.

A notebook.

And then, from the shopping bag on his lap, he withdrew another book. Black cover, gold lettering. *Ten Hundred Years of You.* Author unknown.

Everything in León soared.

He couldn't explain it, why the sight of this book was a thunderclap, why this entirely unknown person made him feel like melting into a puddle on the ground, made him feel like running out into the street and whooping for joy, made him feel like confetti cannons and streaming banners, like an orchestra reaching a crescendo.

Our Infinite Fates   339

Why it made him feel like a lifelong search had finally borne fruit.

His heart had always felt like fallow ground: barren, haunted by something that had once flourished there but had since wilted. And yet, at the sight of this perfect stranger, that fallow ground began to stir, ripen, as though new life were sprouting from ancient roots.

Ignoring the blasphemy streaming from his supervisor's mouth, León stepped out from behind the counter and walked, dazed, toward the stranger with the notebook.

As he approached, the stranger looked up, and their eyes met with an impossible lurch, and the whole world grew still and silent, the very axis of the earth tilting in some fundamental way.

An eternity sprawled out between them, acres and acres of emotion and hope and grief, a force so powerful it stole the breath from León's lungs, almost made him bend double at the waist, or burst into a lifetime of unshed tears, or something, *something*—

"Excuse me," he said, breathless. "Have we met before?"

Acknowledgments

Let's see if I can get through this without bawling, shall we?

First, to my incredible agent, Chloe Seager, who has changed my life immeasurably. You listened to all my wildest dreams, and instead of trying to make them realistic, instead of trying to make them smaller, you just made them come true. I owe you everything.

To Maddy Belton, for the excellent notes. I need you to read and fix everything I ever write, okay? To Hannah Ladds and Casey Dexter, for all your work on the screen side. And to Kelly Chin and Valentina Paulmichl, for all you do to support me.

To my publishing teams on both sides of the Atlantic. My editors, Eileen Rothschild at Wednesday Books and Carmen McCullough at Penguin, responded to this manuscript with such immediate energy and belief that I couldn't imagine a better home for Evelyn and Arden. My thanks also to the team at Wednesday: Sam Dauer, Hannah Dragone, Char Dreyer, Olga Grlic, Meghan Harrington, Brant Janeway, Eric Meyer, Devan Norman, Alexis Neuville, Soleil Paz, Melanie Sanders, and everyone else whose hands touched this book. And the wider team at Penguin: Josh Benn, Toni Budden, Beth Fennell, Alice Grigg, Andrea Kearney, Michelle Nathan, Harriet Venn, Becki Wells, Amy Wilkerson, and everyone who welcomed me with champagne a few weeks

342 ✳ Acknowledgments ✳

after we struck the deal—one of the best days of my life. And thanks to my incredible foreign publishers—thank you for taking this book global. Your collective passion and commitment blow my mind.

To my first readers, Kate Potter and Imi McDonnell. Your love of my work keeps me going. Thank you for the cheerleading, the critiques, and the confidence boosts (and the coffee).

To all the readers since—bloggers, booksellers, reviewers, and fans—who love this book as much as I do. It belongs to you now.

There are simply too many author friends to mention—I've been in this job for a decade, after all—but a special mention to V. E. Schwab and Sarah Maria Griffin. For the retreats, the great food, the deep chats, the celebrations, and the commiserations. And to Heather Askwith, my oldest writing friend—I'm so glad to have you in my life.

And hugest thanks to everyone who has (at the time of writing!) been generous enough to blurb this book: Bea Fitzgerald, Ayana Gray, Rachel Greenlaw, Lindsey Kelk, Kara A. Kennedy, M. K. Lobb, Rebecca Mix, V. E. Schwab, Emma Theriault, Diana Urban, and Amélie Wen Zhao.

Now it's time to get really weepy.

Like Evelyn, I love very deeply and spend most of my waking hours worrying about losing the people in my life. I'm also deeply neurotic, and some part of me believes that putting their names here, in writing, will somehow tempt fate into taking them from me.

Maybe that's all love is, in the end. An endless tempting of fate.

To my best friends in the world: Toria, Lucy, Nic, Lauren, and Hilary. To my dog, Obi, who cannot read but deserves to be thanked regardless. To my brother, Jack, and my sister-in-law, Lauren. To Mum and Dad. I don't have the words for what you all mean to me. Or maybe I do—they're just all in this story.

✳ Acknowledgments ✳ 343

To my gran, whom I lost not long before this book's release. I miss you.

To Louis, whom I love enough to find in any lifetime.

And to Blair, the light of my life.

About the Author

LAURA STEVEN is an award-winning author and shameless coffee addict from the northernmost town in England. She has published several books for young adults, and the forthcoming Silvercloak trilogy, written as L.K. Steven, will mark her adult debut. When she's not writing, you can find her trail running, reading chunky fantasy novels, baking cookies, playing old men at chess, or ignoring her husband and son to perfect her *Stardew Valley* farm. You can find her on Instagram (@laurasteven) and TikTok (@authorlaurasteven).